OUTSTANDING PRAISE
FOR CASEY SHERMAN

A ROSE FOR MARY:
THE HUNT FOR THE REAL BOSTON STRANGLER
(Later published as SEARCH FOR THE STRANGLER)

"A passionate, intimate look (at the Boston Strangler case) … Dramatic."
                                                    —*The Boston Herald*

"Rich in detail … compelling … chillingly realistic. Exhaustively researched, this is a must read for true crime aficionados."
                                                    —*Booklist*

"Substantial … Valuable."

                                                    —*Kirkus Reviews*

"Nobel Prize-winning writer and erstwhile law student Gabriel Garcia Marquez once wrote, "Justice limps along but gets there all the same." In the case of the Boston Strangler, justice took forty years to arrive. That it's here at all we can part thank Casey Sherman, whose fascinating *A Rose for Mary* recounts his ten year odyssey to find his aunt's true killer."
                                                    —*Northeastern University Magazine*

"The author makes a compelling argument for reopening the case".
                                                    —*The Improper Bostonian*

BLACK DRAGON

BLACK DRAGON

A Heath Rosary novel

Casey Sherman

From the Author of *Black Irish*

iUniverse, Inc.
New York Bloomington Shanghai

Black Dragon
A Heath Rosary novel

Copyright © 2008 by Casey Sherman

iUniverse books may be ordered through booksellers or by contacting:

iUniverse
1663 Liberty Drive
Bloomington, IN 47403
www.iuniverse.com
1-800-Authors (1-800-288-4677)

Because of the dynamic nature of the Internet, any Web addresses or links contained in this book may have changed since publication and may no longer be valid.

This is a work of fiction. All of the characters, names, incidents, organizations, and dialogue in this novel are either the products of the author's imagination or are used fictitiously.

ISBN: 978-0-595-50384-1 (pbk)
ISBN: 978-0-595-49836-9 (cloth)
ISBN: 978-0-595-61483-7 (ebk)

Printed in the United States of America

A child's life is like a piece of paper on which every person leaves a mark.

—Chinese Proverb

Fight a wolf with a flex stock

—Chinese Proverb

For Jim Mellon
The bravest cop I ever knew

Acknowledgements

Of course, a writer is only as good as the support that he or she has around them. I fortunately have been blessed with a bounty of family and friends who carry me over the finish line each time out. My wife Laura always receives and deserves the most credit for her love, patience and understanding, because it ain't easy being married to a writer. Hugs and kisses go out to my daughters Bella and Mia who prop me up when I'm feeling down, and who tell their teachers, "My daddy is a famous writer". Not quite sweethearts, but I'm working on it. I offer both love and gratitude to my mother, Diane Dodd and her husband Ken, each of whom read the manuscript and offered keen advice to make it better. A heartfelt thanks to my brother Todd, who continues to push me harder in my craft. Thanks again to Bob Stone who poured through the manuscript for mistakes and implausible situations. Kudos to Pete & Lixian Barry, who read the book with an Asian eye and offered several helpful suggestions along the way. I would also like to thank Cheryl, Carlie, Joey and the kind folks at Borders Express in Hanover for offering a great atmosphere for me to hawk my wares. You guys are the best!

I also thank the following people for their support and for helping me to find a greater audience; Howie Carr, Joyce Kulhawik, Jon Keller, Steve Burton, Liz Walker, Donna Greer, Rick Radzik, John Dennis & Gerry Callahan, Tom Finneran, Dan Rea, the gals from the *Inside Track,* Mark Schmidt from the Winslow House, the folks at the *Patriot Ledger,* The great people at Fryeburg Academy, Uncle Jim Sherman and the gang at Hot Diggity Dogs in Hyannis, Frank & Denise Judge, John & Colleen Somers, Toby & Herb Duane, Corly Quirk, Marc & Denise Lidsky, Jessi Miller, Debbie Kim, David Robichaud, Kasey Kaufman, Eileen Curran, Keith & Zoe Schofield, and of course, the bus stop gang on Congress Street.

I would also like to express my gratitude to the writers who have inspired me and who continuously raise the bar each time out; my friend William Martin, James Patterson (thanks for the advice) Ditto to Andy Gross. Tom Clancy, Vince Flynn, Jack Higgins, and Daniel Silva. You are the masters. Anyone interested in the film rights to *Black Dragon* or any one of my books can contact me directly at myspace.com/caseyshermanbooks.

CHAPTER 1

▼

BANGKOK, THAILAND

The two and a half minute commercial break felt like an eternity. After three grueling rounds of evening gowns, swimsuits, and final questions, the field of 81 women had been narrowed down to just three. 22-year-old Sophie Doucet shared polite smiles with the girls on each side of her. On the left was Miss South Africa, a six-foot bronze sculpture come to life. She wore her black hair tight to the scalp and her gown, made of gold silk only accentuated her Nubian beauty. On the right stood Miss Dominican Republic; not only was Renata Elizondo strikingly beautiful with her long silky brown hair and caramel skin, but she was also brilliant. Elizondo drew wild cheers from the crowd when the host announced that she would be attending Yale Medical School in the fall.

Sophie Doucet felt like a mangy sheepdog standing between two prized poodles. She was not supposed to be here. The so-called pageant experts did not even have her placing in the top twenty, yet here she was sharing center stage in the grand auditorium at the IMPACT Muang Thong Thani, Bangkok's largest exhibition center. A third place finish here would be more than the five-foot-ten inch red head could have dreamed of. Her porcelain skin and lush lips gave her a classic look, but Sophie felt like the invisible woman standing next to these two exotic creatures. The fact that she was representing France would also be a mark against her, she thought. Her native country was no longer considered among the world's great powers, but the bitter after taste of Colonialism still lingered here in the third world. Sophie flashed her sparkling green eyes toward the judges table. She could hear her mother's stern voice in her head. *Focus on the judges, but do not stare them down.* The panel was an odd collection of pseudo celebrities led by a Danish supermodel, a well known American chef, and Thailand's national treasure; Porntip Nakhirunkanok Simon who won the pageant herself in 1988.

The klieg lights which were hung over the stage flashed three times signaling the end to the commercial break. Doucet smiled graciously as the orchestra struck up the pageant's theme. A television camera fixed to a jib followed the show's host from the back of the large auditorium down to the stage. He rode on the back of a small elephant and waved a large white envelope high over his head. *This is ridiculous,* Sophie thought. The host was a self important American star of an entertainment news program she had never heard of. In the four days that he had been there, he had managed to hit on nearly every contestant including Sophie, but she simply smiled at him as her mother lied and said that she did not understand English.

Sophie's gaze went from the clown on the elephant to her mother sitting in the fourth row. Their eyes met and both wanted to cry, but for different reasons. This was her mother's dream and somewhere along the line it had become Sophie's also. After the show, they would celebrate with a nice bottle of Chateau Thieuley. Her mother would drink to the years of hard work and sacrifice putting her only daughter's life ahead of her own, while Sophie would be celebrating the prospect of life beyond her mother's control. Two Thai handlers held the small elephant as the pageant host slid down its rough side and onto the massive stage. The crowd roared with applause and then grew silent.

"Now ladies and gentlemen, the moment we've all been waiting for," The host announced through teeth whiter than Sophie's. "600 million people are watching this broadcast live in 180 countries around the world. All of us are asking the same question. Who will be the next Miss Universe? Will it be Miss South Africa Kenyatta Mugabi?"

The spotlight shined on the beautiful African.

"Will it be Miss France Sophie Doucet?"

Not a chance, Sophie thought.

"Or will the judges choose Miss Dominican Republic Miss Renata Elizondo? The envelope I have in my hand holds the answer."

The host paused for dramatic effect and then tore open the large white envelope. The sound of shredding paper echoed through the silent exhibition center.

Smile, hug the winner and walk off the stage, Sophie told herself.

"And the woman who will wear the crown of Miss Universe is … Miss France; Sophie Doucet!"

Sophie's mother shot out of her fourth row seat pumping her fists in the air. Five thousand spectators followed her cue. Miss South Africa approached first hugging her and wiping a tear off Sophie's cheek. Miss Dominican Republic came next with another hug and a whisper of congratulations in Sophie's ear.

Am I dreaming? She asked herself.

She looked stage right and saw the reigning Miss Universe walking toward her. Last year's winner handed her an overflowing bouquet of red roses and placed the diamond studded tiara on top of Sophie's head.

I'm not dreaming. I am the most beautiful woman in the world.

Mister Wong watched the coronation from the privacy of his luxury box in the upper level of the IMPACT Muang Thong Thani. He flipped open the cover of his Nokia cell phone and hit speed dial.

"Yes?" came the voice from the other end of the line.

"I must commend you on your taste sir," Mister Wong said. "The judges certainly agree. However, this turn of events will certainly make our plan more challenging."

"Are you saying that it cannot be done?"

"No sir. I have never let you down. I have taken the necessary precautions. The package will be delivered on time."

"Make it so."

The voice on the other end broke the connection and the line went dead. Mister Wong slipped the phone back into his breast pocket and counted down the minutes for the *real show* to begin.

After thanking the judges and blowing a kiss to the audience, Miss Universe was whisked off the stage and ushered down a long corridor into her own private dressing room. As she entered, Sophie was immediately intoxicated by the fragrant odor of white orchids that filled the large space. No longer was she sharing cramped quarters with the other 80 contestants. A bottle of Dom Perignon chilled in a silver bucket of ice on a table in the center of the room. Sophie walked past the champagne and collapsed on a large white sofa set against the dressing room wall. She closed her hazel eyes and could hear her mother ordering everyone outside.

"Sophie needs a moment to be alone. She will be down to the press conference in twenty minutes," Rebecca Doucet told a throng of people that included the pageant's owner, New York billionaire Donald Trump.

"Thank you mama," Sophie said in her native French.

"My child, enjoy these next few minutes as Sophie Doucet and then we'll both say au revior to the girl we once knew. As Miss Universe, your life is about change forever my darling."

"Oui maman," Sophie replied, her new title already weighing heavily on her shoulders.

Mae-Noi squeezed into the small tuk-tuk with two other girls from the red-light district on Patpong Road. The teenaged driver of the three wheeled taxi pulled out onto the busy street cutting off two oncoming cars. Horns blared but Mae-Noi and her companions did not flinch. It was the survival of the fittest out on the narrow streets of Bangkok.

"Take us to the IMPACT," she ordered the driver.

Mae-Noi was working today although she was not wearing her usual uniform. Instead of a brightly colored tube top and mini-skirt, the light skinned Thai wore a traditional orange silk wrap that was compliments of her mystery man. She had met him several days ago when he offered to buy her a plate of yam wun sen (noodle salad). It was curious foreplay, but Mae-Noi had granted much odder requests to be sure. Over lunch the neatly dressed gentleman explained that he was not looking for sex, instead he would pay her handsomely to perform another kind of service. Getting paid for something that did not require her to lie on her back in a sweat soaked room was something new to her. She gladly accepted the offer and recruited a dozen more working girls to perform this mission.

Mister Wong walked down the corridor toward Sophie Doucet's dressing room where two beefy Mongolian guards stood at attention by the door. Wong nodded to the men as one opened the door allowing him inside.

"Monsieur Nang, I made it perfectly clear that my daughter would like a few minutes alone," Rebecca Doucet announced in a shrill tone. Sophie was now sitting up on the couch with a glass of champagne in her hand.

"I understand completely Madame, however as director of security for IMPACT, I must tell you about a situation that we are currently dealing with," Wong replied with false sincerity. He had taken his current job and current identity four months prior when it was announced that Thailand would host the Miss Universe pageant. His employers had received sterling recommendations from the chief executive officers of companies that did not exist. Wong was not sure whether he could actually pull it off, but with enough money he found out that anything was possible.

The Miss Universe pageant would be Thailand's first major event since the tsunami that killed at least 5,300 people in resort areas along the coast. The country spent 265 million baht ($6.7 million) to host the pageant and hoped to turn that investment into an $80 million dollar windfall for the devastated nation.

"I regret to inform you that we've had a security breach in the media center," Wong told the Doucet women. "A group of protesters has gained access to the area and they have attacked one of the contestants."

Miss Universe dropped her champagne flute and shot off the couch. Wong saw fear in her beautiful green eyes. *Fear is good.*

"Monsieur Nang, Are they still upset over the temple?" Sophie asked.

Wong nodded. Two weeks prior to the pageant, organizers had sparked an outrage by photographing bikini clad contestants on a river cruise with the famed Wat Arun or "Temple of Dawn" in the background. Thailand's religious leaders claimed the photo violated the country's traditional values in the days leading up to an important Buddhist holiday. The argument was ironic considering Thailand's reputation as the sex capital of the world. Still, pageant officials told the government that any further video footage of Miss Universe hopefuls would be vetted by the pageant's Thai partners.

"We have moved your press conference from the media center to an exhibition room on a lower level," Wong explained. "Reporters have been notified and French television is making a cable run from the third floor to the basement. I have been told that they want to carry your news conference live back home in Paris. I will personally escort you when you are ready."

"I will not let some religious zealots ruin the greatest moment in my daughter's life," Madame Doucet shouted.

Embarrassed by her mother's outburst, Sophie attempted to soothe the director of security.

"I'm sure that you are doing all you can, Monsieur Nang. The girl who was attacked, is she going to be alright?"

"It appears so mademoiselle. She was pelted with a bushel of oranges that a protester managed to get inside."

"Visakha Bucha, Visakha Bucha," Mae-Noi screamed as she was dragged away from the media room. The diversion was now in play. "You have sinned against Buddha."

As a security guard held her tightly around her tiny waist, Mae-Noi reached for his fleshy cheeks and scratched him with her long red fingernails. The brightly colored fingernails should have given spectators a clue that what they were seeing was not real. The guard raised his hand and slapped her hard across the face. Both were playing their respective roles to perfection. It was the security guard who had opened the door for Mae-Noi and her companions in the underground parking garage. The prostitute had no doubt that the guard would be paid handsomely for his performance and for his wounds. The other girls had to fend for themselves against security guards who were not playing the game. Mae-Noi glanced at the twelve women who were giving the guards more than they could handle. The prostitutes pelted the guards with fruit as they were being chased around the conference large room. The girls seemed to relish their roles in this great charade, Mae-Noi thought.

"Are you ready Miss Doucet?" Wong asked concentrating solely on Sophie.

"I believe we are," Her mother replied.

Having the mother there would pose a problem, but it was Mister Wong's job to plan for all scenarios. He led the women out of the dressing room and into the corridor. Wong nodded at one burly guard who followed them into a service elevator.

"Again Miss Universe, on behalf of IMPACT and the government of Thailand, I offer my sincere apologies for this inconvenience," Wong said as they stepped into the lift.

"Oui, Monsieur Nang. It is not your fault and I do apologize on behalf of the pageant for any trouble we may have caused," Sophie replied.

Her mother simply rolled her eyes.

Mister Wong and the security guard positioned themselves directly behind the women.

Chivalry is not dead, even in Thailand, Sophie thought.

Wong nodded to the guard and both men sprung into action. The Mongolian grabbed the back of Sophie's neck with one hand while the other swung around and forced a wet kerchief over her nose and mouth. She breathed in the chloral hydrate and collapsed into his arms within seconds. Simultaneously, Mister Wong pulled the mother's hair back and came around with a long sharp knife. He ran it across the older woman's neck letting her warm blood cascade down the cold steel of the blade. Mister Wong smiled as he let her body drop to the floor. *I've wanted to do that all morning,* he thought.

The elevator door opened to the underground garage where a white van awaited them. The security guard grabbed Miss Universe, threw her over his shoulder and ran toward the back of the vehicle. Mister Wong tore off the name tag that read; *Phra Nang Director of Security* from his blue blazer. He dropped it on Rebecca Doucet's body and exited the elevator. The van would take them to a private airstrip where a Lear jet was fueled and waiting.

CHAPTER 2

▼

HONG KONG

Ju-Long Lew stood in the corner of his daughter's bedroom with arms folded. He watched closely as the artist applied the finishing touches to the large mural that covered all four walls of the room. The idea was conceived when Lew took his daughter on a private tour of the new Hong Kong Disneyland theme park. The 15-year-old was instantly captivated by Mickey Mouse and friends and especially by Sleeping Beauty's castle. Lew had made the common mistake of calling it Cinderella's castle, but his precocious daughter corrected him immediately. "You can tell it's Aurora's castle by the cones on top," she explained. The Magic Kingdom was now being recreated in the girl's sprawling bedroom. He watched the artist closely. The man felt the pressure, but tried not to show it. Lew did not intend to make the painter nervous, but like every project he oversaw; he wanted to make sure it was done to perfection. His Nextel phone was in vibrate mode and buzzed on his hip. He took the phone off its clip and brought it to his ear.

"Wei?" *Hello?*

"The driver is bringing Miss Bao around sir."

Lew did not respond. He placed the Nextel back on its clip and nodded to the artist.

"Are we finished?"

"One more brush stroke sir," the painter replied as his steady hand filled in the small purple flag on top of Sleeping Beauty's castle. He then stepped back from the mural and surveyed his work. Satisfied, the artist turned and gave a thumb's up to his employer.

"Feichang xiexie ni," Lew replied. *Thank you very much.*

The painter breathed a sigh of relief and smiled. Ju-Long Lew left the room and walked down the marble corridor toward the sound of his daughter's voice.

Bao Lew saw her father and shuffled awkwardly toward him, stepping with her right foot; then dragging the left behind it. He drew his teenaged daughter in and squeezed her tightly. She giggled as he kissed her soft cheek. It was a feeling of love on which the billionaire oil magnate could not put a price tag.

"Baba, Mama says you have a surprise for me," the girl said slowly, making sure every word came out just right.

"She is right my fang-hua *fragrant flower*. Close your eyes and follow me."

Lew took his daughter by the hand and walked her down the long hallway.

"No peeking," he ordered playfully.

She placed her delicate hands over her eyes and giggled.

The father turned the brass knob of her bedroom door and opened it.

"Open your eyes now, petal."

Bao Lew did as she was told and let out a loud scream. Her father laughed and clapped his hands as she limped toward the mural.

"Hao ji le," she said with delight. *It's wonderful.*

"All of your favorite characters are there," he pointed out. "You can spend hours trying to find them."

The girl shuffled back to her father and hugged him again. "Feichang xiexie, Baba." *Thank you, daddy.*

At that moment, Lew's wife Lixian came up behind him and whispered in his ear.

"You have made our daughter very happy, my husband."

The Lew mansion rested on a hill atop Victoria's Peak, Hong Kong's most exclusive neighborhood, and the multi-million dollar home offered some of the most spectacular views of Victoria Harbor and Kowloon. Ju-Long Lew slurped his pu-erh tea while sitting at the head of a long mahogany table in the formal dining room. Floor to ceiling windows blessed him an intoxicating view at the sparkling city below. The tea aided Lew's digestion and helped him think. He savored the rich, mahogany flavor of the well aged tea leaves while staring out at the city lights twinkling in the distance. This was his way of unwinding after a grueling day at the office. Lew was no longer wearing the armor of a corporate tycoon, he had replaced his $5000 business suit with a blue sweater and tan slacks. The casual clothes hung off his muscular body perfectly. Lew maintained a rigorous workout schedule and still had the body of a 20-year-old. Only flashes of gray hair gathered around his temple offered evidence of his true age. Lixian entered the room and rubbed his shoulders.

"Sorry to disturb you husband, but Bao would like you to put her to bed."

Lew smiled and set his teacup down on its saucer.

"I don't think sleep will come easy for her in a bedroom like that," he told his wife.

"Do you think we are spoiling her?" she responded with concern.

"How can we not?" he replied. "She is a special girl. Life can be cruel for a child with her problems. We made a promise to each other that Bao would never want for anything, remember?"

Lixian nodded and kissed her husband on the lips. He stood up from the table and walked off toward his daughter's room. When he arrived, he was surprised to find her already fast asleep. He kissed her forehead gently. She stirred but did not wake. Lew pulled her blanket up over her small shoulders and crept out of the room. He retreated to his study and locked the door behind him. Lixian knew her husband was not to be disturbed while he was working. Lew walked over to his flat screen computer which sat on a shimmering glass desk top. The financial markets were open now in Britain and America and he wanted to see if there was any movement in crude oil prices overseas. Oil was Ju-Long Lew's business. As founder of Lew Petroleum, he had made a fortune feeding China's growing appetite for fossil fuel. The country was making a rapid transition away from bicycles toward automobiles and by the year 2010, experts predicted that cars would eclipse bicycles by ninety percent. Projections also showed that China would surpass the U.S. in automobile production by 2030. This phenomenon had transformed Ju-Long Lew from successful businessman into one of the most powerful men in Asia. Lew Petroleum was China's only privately owned oil company; and with its $4.2 billion bid to take over a major oil producer in Kazakhstan, it had also become China's largest.

At 48-years-old, Ju-Long Lew was a man who could afford anything, yet he thirsted for possessions that were beyond his reach. He placed the knuckle of his index finger into his mouth and bit down hard. Lew closed one window of his computer and opened another. He typed in his access code and stood up from his desk. Against the wall of his study stood a one ton statue of the Buddha carved from green jade, that had cost him a small fortune. Due to the hardness of the stone, the statue took three years to carve by hand. Jade is associated with mystical powers including the ability to keep away malign influences. Lew smiled at the thought.

As impressive as the statue was, it was nothing compared to the treasures that lay behind it. He watched as the massive jade Buddha slid on rollers across the oak floor barely making a sound. Hidden behind the statue was an elevator door.

Lew walked forward and placed his right eye up to the retinal scan. The elevator door opened and the oil magnate walked inside.

Sophie Doucet looked around the room with blurred vision. She had just woken up only to find herself back in the nightmare. The walls around her were made of stainless steel and there were no windows in the room. The only light came from a soft bulb fixed to the ceiling. Sophie did not know if it was day or night. The only thing she did know was that he would be coming for her again.

The elevator descended to the lower level of the mansion, a level that even Lew's wife Lixian was unaware of. The elevator door opened to a private gallery that was Lew's sanctuary. Hung on the wall facing the elevator was Claude Monet's *Marine,* an oil on canvas depicting an orange cliff side that overlooked a breathtaking lavender seascape. The works of Matisse, Dali and Picasso also filled the room. He had acquired the masterpieces following a visit to The Museu Chacara do Ceu in Rio de Janiero a year before. Through careful planning by the talented Mister Wong, the artworks were stolen from the museum six months later. Wong pulled off the heist amid the celebrations of Carnivale as he and a hand picked team of thieves walked into the crowded museum in midmorning; overtook the lone armed guard and disabled the security cameras. They pulled the four paintings off the wall, walked out the front entrance and disappeared into a thick crowd of samba revelers. The paintings were worth $50 million. Lew's gallery was filled with other stolen works including Picasso's *Nature morte a'la Charlotte.* Mister Wong had plundered that oil on canvas from the conservation labs of the Pompidou Center in Paris in 2004. The collection brought the owner tremendous happiness, but it was the newest acquisition that gave Ju-Long his greatest joy.

Sophie Doucet curled up in bed and tried to replay the past few days in her mind. Her memory was clouded by whatever drugs they had administered to her; however she did recall winning the Miss Universe Pageant and being led into an elevator with her mother. *Mama, what did they do with you?* Sophie shuddered at the thought. She remembered nothing more, other than waking up in this cell-like room. *That was what? Five, six days ago?* She had lost the concept of time. The only thing she could keep track of were the assaults committed against her body. At first, she had tried to fight off her mysterious attacker, but his strength had easily overwhelmed her. Now she was giving her body to him freely in hopes that he would one day let her go.

Her captor walked through his private gallery and entered a smaller room; its floor covered by oversized satin pillows of various colors. Lew sat down on a soft cushion; folded his legs and reached for the bamboo tube and porcelain bowl that lay on a small table in the center of the room. He placed four pods of black tar opium on a small sheet of tin-foil that covered the bottom of the bowl. He placed a cigarette lighter down on the tin-foil and slowly ignited the pods. Lew placed his mouth over the opening of the bamboo tube and inhaled deeply. He closed his eyes as the vapors invaded his lungs. It took but a few seconds for the powerful drug to take hold of Lew's body and mind. The room began to spin and he collapsed on the pillows, his thoughts invaded by vivid hallucinations. He moaned as the dark illusions took over body and soul. Lew watched the smoke stream out of his nostrils, he was no longer a man, he was transforming into something else. He looked down at his hands and saw razor sharp talons. He felt rough scales rolling up his spine. He had the dead eyes of a reptile and he breathed fire. In Ju-Long Lew's drug filled dream, he had become a dragon. In Chinese culture, the dragon is a sign of change and the transformation from loving father to frightening monster was now taking place. He awoke moments later, but the opium maintained firm control over his conscious thoughts. Lew smiled as he pulled himself up off the pillows and reached into his pocket for the pick me up he needed. He took out a small vial of cocaine, brought it up to his left nostril and snorted quickly. The rush of the white powder was immediate; his mind had gone from zero to sixty in just a matter of seconds. His heart began to pound and his eyes were fully alert. The dragon was hungry now. Lew stripped naked and walked across the room toward the back wall, which was adorned with three ceramic masks popular in Chinese opera. The first mask was that of an opera character called Guan Yu. The mask was painted red and black, the colors which signified devotion and integrity. The second mask was painted green and represented Zheng Wun, an opera character known for his justice and chivalry. Lew bypassed the first two masks and pulled the third one off the wall. The fierce eyes of Tu Xingsun stared back at him. The mask was painted yellow, the color of cruelty. Lew placed it over his face and went to call on his prey.

Sophie could hear the footsteps shuffling down the hall. Her body stiffened as he entered the room. Like each time before, her rapist was wearing some kind of mask, but this one was like nothing she had ever seen. He looked up toward a small camera fixed high on a wall in the corner of the room. Their every moment together was being videotaped.

"Do not fear my flower," he whispered in French from behind the mask.

The words startled Sophie. She had never heard his voice before. She never even knew what he sounded like. He did not speak. He did not grunt. He had remained completely silent, even while raping her.

"Please ... let me go. I will do anything you ask," she trembled.

"You have nothing to worry about, I can assure you petal. You will be leaving this room tonight," he replied in a soothing voice. "Now, turn over onto your stomach like a good girl."

Sophie did as she was told. She felt his cold hands grip her buttocks and the pain that followed. As she was being ravaged, Sophie buried her face in the pillow and forced her mind to leave her body.

I am not here. I am back in Paris, sitting with friends at the Café du Theatre on Rue Yvonne. The coffee is black, but the conversation is quite colorful. I'm telling my friends how much I'm looking forward to going to school once my modeling career is over. They laugh at me. How can a beautiful girl want for anything? They ask. I describe in detail my daily beauty regimen and they recoil in horror. No one should have to go through that, they tell me. Soon we are all laughing again. Will I ever get back there?

The dragon finished after several minutes. He gave her two powerful thrusts and collapsed on her back. Sophie lifted her head from the pillow and looked back at the masked man now lying on top of her.

"Will you please let me go now?" she cried.

"You are free my flower," he responded.

Ju-Long Lew then grabbed Sophie's red hair tightly around her scalp and pulled. He closed his eyes as another wave of pleasure washed over him. Seconds later, he could hear the snapping of the hyoid bone in her neck. Miss Universe made a gurgling sound and her body went limp.

CHAPTER 3

▼

SOUTH BOSTON, MASSACHUSETTS

Six Months Later

Heath Rosary poured himself a glass of Samuel Adams *Winter Fest* and examined his DVD collection. He had been forced to watch the latest Bridget Jones movie the previous night, now it was his turn to choose. *Will it be White Heat with Cagney? Or The Maltese Falcon with Bogie?* He debated. Perusing Rosary's DVD collection was like opening the vault at Turner Classic Movies, he did not own a film that was made after 1980. Rosary pulled out the disk for *White Heat*.

"Made it Ma, top of the world," Rosary muttered to himself.

"Not a James Cagney movie," his girlfriend groaned as she climbed the stairs from the bedroom to the living room.

"Not *a* James Cagney movie," he corrected her. "*White Heat* is *the* James Cagney movie."

Rosary glanced over at Grace Chen and began having second thoughts about movie night. She was fresh from the shower and her skin smelled of lavender. Her dark hair was pulled back and she wore an extra large white cotton t-shirt that read; *You Elect 'Em—We Protect 'Em.* It was a souvenir from Rosary's days in the United States Secret Service. He walked over and hugged Grace tightly around her small waist. Rosary closed his eyes and breathed in her scent.

"You're beautiful," he told her. "You know that?"

"You tell me that every day," she replied sheepishly.

Their lips locked in a slow, wet kiss.

She ran her delicate hands down his chest and could feel the muscles rippling under his red Polo shirt.

"How about a glass of wine first?" she whispered in his ear.

"What would you like?" he asked, his face still buried in her neck.

Grace pulled away. "I'll pour the wine," she told him. "You just relax on the couch and think romantic thoughts."

Rosary downed his glass of *Sam Adams,* retreated to his leather couch and watched as Grace disappeared into the galley kitchen. *She is beautiful,* he thought. In fact, they both were. Heath Rosary was six-feet tall and had the body of a professional athlete, which he once was. Friends of Grace always told her that he was a dead ringer for Denzel Washington, but she believed her man was even more handsome than the Oscar winning actor. Together they made an exotic couple; Grace Chen was a classic Asian beauty with alluring brown eyes and silky black hair that she grew down to her shoulders. They were constantly targeted by photographers at the countless number of benefits and galas she dragged him to. Grace's photograph was always popping up in the society columns, especially the Inside Track in the Boston *Herald.* She worked as a television producer for WBZ-News, but what made her truly a darling of the gossip columns was the fact that she was the only daughter of billionaire Tommy Chen, founder of a Fortune 500 pharmaceutical company located north of Boston.

She reached for two glasses and pulled a bottle of Castell Del Remei from an iron wine rack that hung over the sink. Grace enjoyed the subtle sweetness of the Spanish Merlot. As she popped the cork, she noticed a large manila envelope lying on the blue granite countertop next to the stainless steel refrigerator. It was made out to Heath and the return address was from a major publishing house out of New York. The envelope had been sitting on the counter for weeks and it still had not been opened. She poured two glasses of wine, tucked the envelope under her arm and returned to the living room. Grace handed Rosary his glass and sat down beside him on the brown leather couch.

"What do you have there?" he asked.

"You know exactly what I have here," she replied slapping him playfully on the knee. "You haven't even opened it. Aren't you the least bit curious?"

Rosary took a sip of wine and shrugged. "I already know what's inside and the dollar amount."

"You've already told me how much they're willing to pay," Grace replied. "Very few people get offered a six figure advance to write a book."

Rosary got up off the couch and walked toward the French doors leading out to the deck. "First of all, I hate it when agents in the FBI or CIA quit and write a tell-all book criticizing the government. It smells dirty to me." He drained the glass of Merlot. "Even if I did write a book, do you think I could tell the truth?"

Grace did not respond, she knew he was talking about the Sistani case. It was the case that forced Heath Rosary to resign from the United States Secret Service in 1996, when he had been in charge of the security detail assigned to protect Jennifer Bosworth, the only daughter of then President Evan Hamilton Bosworth. Jennifer, a 22-year-old senior at Harvard University, was America's sweetheart and the blond haired, blue eyed beauty graced covers of magazines around the world. Only Rosary and a handful of agents knew what a handful Jennifer Bosworth really was.

His patience and skills were put to the test one evening when the First Daughter evaded her assigned agent inside a cavernous Boston nightclub. After several nerve wracking hours, Rosary and his team trailed her to an apartment building near Fenway Park. The young woman was inside with a college student named Ahmet Sistani. Sistani, a Syrian national was enrolled at the Mass College of Art, but chemistry was his true passion. He supplied drugs to dozens of fellow students in the Fenway area.

The cache of heroin, cocaine and marijuana were on display when Rosary and a fellow agent entered the apartment. It was too late to hide the drugs, so a jittery and strung out Sistani reached for his gun instead. There was no way that he was going to prison. He had seen a few TV documentaries about inmates and the often cruel things they did to one another. Sistani knew he could not survive that. For him, there was only one way out. He sprinted toward the agents firing his weapon as he ran. Rosary was hit in the leg and badly wounded, but instinct immediately took over. He returned fire, killing the college student/drug pusher with a single shot to the head. Fellow agent Nikki Tavano; Rosary's colleague and closest friend, found the president's daughter in a back room spread out on a bed in a heroin induced slumber. News that the First Daughter was a drug addict never came to light, instead government agents manipulated the crime scene to make it appear that Jennifer Bosworth had been kidnapped by a Syrian terrorist. Rosary was first told of the story while lying in a hospital bed recovering from his leg wound. The bullet had come within an inch of his femoral artery. Upon his release from the hospital, his first order of business was to hand in his badge and service revolver. But it did not end there, the case also brought him a wave of unwanted publicity as *People* magazine and *Newsweek* both ran cover stories about him. *People* called Rosary "America's last line of defense." That's when America's new hero turned his back on it all and became a private investigator.

"Maybe you don't have to write about the Sistani case," Grace suggested. "The publisher appears much more interested in what happened on Cape Cod anyway."

Rosary laughed. "What would I call the book, *Dead to Rights*? That's exactly where Michael Logan had me in that bell tower."

"Heath, if it wasn't for you a lot more people would have gotten hurt."

Rosary knew she was right. Back in May, he made national headlines again, this time for foiling an attempt on the British prime minister's life at the Kennedy Compound in Hyannisport. He nearly lost his own life in the attempt. After the details of the incident came to light, interview requests came pouring in from every major newspaper and talk show in the nation, and even some overseas. He declined them all, and that decision had made him even more attractive to New York's top book editors.

"I don't know if I want to go down that path again Grace," Rosary told her. "You know, the man you call the *bravest* on the planet still has nightmares about that day. Now you want me to relive it all over again?"

He needed some air. He opened the French doors and stepped out onto the deck. Night was falling now and Boston Harbor was partially illuminated by the glow of a Hunter's Moon. It was an unusually balmy November evening with the temperature hovering just below 60 degrees. Rosary rested his strong arms on the wooden railing and watched as the passenger ferry from nearby Logan Airport pulled into Rowe's Wharf. He heard the French doors open, but did not look back. Moments later he felt the familiar touch of his woman as she hugged him from behind. Grace stood on her tiptoes and whispered into his ear.

"Make love to me right here, right now."

Heath Rosary followed his orders.

CHAPTER 4

▼

Rosary pulled his 1986 silver Jaguar XJ6 sedan into an empty space on Boylston Street. He stepped out the vehicle, walked around and opened the passenger door. Grace climbed out and brought her arms around his neck.

"Thanks for last night," she said smiling. She then kissed him fully on the lips.

"I'll think about the book baby, I really will," he promised.

"I want you to do whatever makes you happy," she replied.

Grace kissed him once more and the couple parted ways. She walked into a Starbuck's Coffee Shop; he walked into the Dunkin' Donuts next door. He felt that he had already made plenty of sacrifices in their relationship, watching *Bridget Jones* was one of them. But he was not about to give up his large regular Hazelnut coffee for any woman. Rosary stood in line for several more minutes before placing his order. By now, Grace was probably enjoying her Grande Latte Cappuccino while strolling toward her condo on nearby Marlborough Street. It was now 8:30 a.m. and both had important meetings later that morning. Grace was sitting down with members of the art department at WBZ-News to discuss the station's latest change to the anchor set, while Rosary was going to see one of his most important clients, and one of the few clients that he actually liked.

He purchased his coffee and blueberry muffin and headed back to his car. The Jaguar was the only luxury item he had purchased after getting drafted by the New England Patriots in 1987. The car was now more than twenty years old, but because he seldom drove it, it still looked new. Rosary's other vehicle; the one he used on the job was a blue Toyota Camry. It was perfect for conducting surveillance because no one looked twice at a blue Camry. Rosary drove up Boylston Street past the Public Garden and the Boston Common. The warm weather of the previous day had now been replaced by an arctic cold front. "Maybe I should've taken the Camry," he muttered to himself. The only problem with the Jaguar was that its heater had a mind of its own. It only worked when it wanted to. Today it didn't want to. Rosary stopped at a traffic light and watched the throngs of people pour out of the MBTA station at Park Street. Workers wrapped themselves up against the blustery wind and went about their business with barely an acknowledgement to the person walking beside them. It was the beginning of November and summer was a fading memory. Christmas was still nearly two months away and the holiday spirit had yet to take hold. To make the collective mood even worse, the Patriots had suffered a rare overtime loss to the dreaded New York Jets the day before.

Rosary continued on to Washington Street, where he took a left and began hunting for a parking space. This section of Washington Street had changed greatly from the time Rosary was a kid. He could remember walking through the red light district known as the Combat Zone with his Uncle James, bypassing the peep shows, prostitutes and pimps. "Stare at the ground," his uncle would order as they pushed their way by the street trash toward the Publex Theater, a 70's style grindhouse that showed three kung-fu movies each day. Rosary remembered how excited he got when he saw a rare Bruce Lee treasure on the marquee. The Publex Theater was a parking lot now. Most of the seedy strip joints were gone too. He missed it all. Sure, The Combat Zone was a scab on the city, but it did add to its character. He spotted a parking space directly in front of the Liberty Tree building and pulled in. Rosary could not believe his luck. *Two great parking spaces in one day? Looks like today's gonna be a good day.*

He grabbed his briefcase and exited the vehicle. Rosary set the car alarm by remote control and walked toward the sidewalk. The Jaguar was equipped with a top of the line alarm system that emitted an ear piercing whine if anyone so much as brushed past it. It would certainly give any car thief second thoughts. Rosary entered the building and spotted his client seated on a wooden bench by the elevator. Herb Duane smiled as he stood up and offered his hand.

"You look good Herb," Rosary commented. The 73-year-old Duane was still recovering from open heart surgery six months before. He wore a tan suit and green tie under his brown trench coat.

"You look great too Heath."

Rosary had hung up the suit and tie years ago after resigning from the Secret Service. His current uniform was a gray turtle neck and black slacks which he wore under a black leather coat. His relationship with Herb Duane dated back over ten years. Duane was the owner of Duane Corporation, the oldest demolition company in Boston. The family business had been around since 1918 and was best known for tearing down the city's West End neighborhood to make way for new development in the 1950's. That project sparked outrage from many of the thousands of West End residents forced out of the neighborhood, but that was nothing compared to the heat Herb Duane felt after aiding the Boston Fire Department in the rescue of three crew members trapped after a devastating condominium blaze on Beacon Hill in 1996. Duane, a structural engineer was asked to find the safest way for the rescuers to get in and out of the burned building without getting them trapped inside. Like many condominiums on Beacon Hill, this four story condo complex had once been a private home. Duane poured over the building's blue prints and found an existing air shaft that had once been used as a dumb waiter. The shaft was small, but apparently undamaged by the flames. The rescue mission took several hours as firefighters inched their way up the narrow shaft one at a time. They eventually made it up to the fourth floor where their comrades lay trapped under burned out beams of wood. The rescuers freed their fellow firefighters and all made it out of the building alive. Many credited Duane for the dramatic rescue. The story should have ended there, but something did not sit right with Herb Duane. All of the condo residents had been accounted for, so why had the firefighters gone back inside the building? The question gnawed at Duane and he did a little investigating of his own. He found out that firefighters from that particular station house had acquired a certain nickname from members of Boston's business community. They were known as *Ali Baba and the Forty Thieves*. Once Duane heard that some fire victims were missing money and jewelry, he alerted the media. "Of course they went back in to rip the place off," he told one reporter. "Why do you think those fire jackets come with so many pockets?" The comment drew anger from the department and that is when the death threats began.

Duane hired Rosary, who was able to trace the threats back to three firefighters from that notorious station. Heath alerted a detective friend in the Boston Police department, who then attained a search warrant for their apartments. The detective discovered some of the jewelry missing from the condo fire. The other valuables had already been fenced. Charges were brought against the fire fighters and Herb Duane received a written apology from city fire officials. Duane was still considered Public Enemy #1 by the rank and file. He knew that if his own business ever caught fire, it was as good as gone. Duane kept Rosary on a retainer and called on him to perform different services from time to time.

"So where do we stand Heath?" Duane asked while rubbing the gray whiskers of his neatly trimmed beard.

"I don't think you have anything to worry about," he replied pointing to his briefcase. "All the evidence you need is right here."

The two men got into the elevator and Duane hit the button for the 2nd floor. They arrived moments later and both men followed signs for the office of Judge Robert Stone in Suite 205. They entered the office and found an attractive young secretary working behind the desk. The small sitting area was empty.

"Mister Duane?" asked the twenty-something brunette with large breasts.

"Yes," he responded. "I have a meeting with Judge Stone."

He motioned to Rosary. "This is Heath Rosary, head of security for Duane Corporation."

Rosary eyed him curiously. He had never heard that title before.

"Mister Rosary is acting as my corporate investigator in this matter," Duane informed the secretary.

"Well the judge is waiting for you in his office. The other party is there also."

The buxom young woman stepped away from her desk and escorted the men down the hall. The secretary led the way and Duane sized up her round backside with a hungry stare. Rosary caught the old man's gaze and scolded him like a child.

"I'd say she's young enough to be your daughter," he whispered. "But she's really young enough to be your grand-daughter."

Duane chuckled as the secretary pointed toward the door and walked away. The men were all business again.

"This guy could recognize me Herb. I'll wait here by the door," Rosary told him. "Once you get his pants down, call for me. I'll come in and we'll turn his world upside down."

Duane stepped inside the palatial office and spotted Spider Mulgravey seated on a brown leather sofa next to his lawyer. Mulgravey was wearing a neck brace as he rolled the tip of a long wooden cane back and forth in the palms of his large hands. His long blond hair was pulled back in a pony tail for the occasion. Tattoos of cobwebs covered both elbows and he wore a black t-shirt covered by a leather vest, which bore emblems of the Salem Warlocks motorcycle gang. In a stark contrast, his young attorney wore a white oxford, blue blazer and a yellow paisley bow-tie. Lawyer and client made quite an odd couple. Judge Stone sat behind his desk and steered the meeting.

"As both parties are aware, I've been asked to mediate this Workman's Compensation case for the Commonwealth of Massachusetts. I will hear both sides this morning and will rule at a later date. Mister Lowenthal, you may proceed."

The young attorney kept his notes in his hands as he got up off the sofa.

"Your honor, this case is filed under chapter 152, section 66 of the Massachusetts Workman's Compensation Law. As you are now aware, my client Steven Mulgravey slipped and injured himself while in the employ of Duane Corporation. The accident happened on October 2nd while Mister Mulgravey was performing his duties as head mechanic at a Duane owned garage at 117 Pleasant Street in Dorchester. My client slipped on an oil puddle that had not been properly cleaned up by his employer. It is our position that Mister Duane is negligent in this matter and that my client deserves full weekly compensation with benefits until he is healthy enough to work again."

Judge Stone folded his hands and rested them under his dimpled chin. "Mister Lowenthal, do you have pictures of this oil spill or any other proof that this accident occurred?"

The young lawyer pointed an accusing finger at Herb Duane. "No, the employer cleaned up the spill immediately after it happened. But that was too late for my client, judge. I do have a medical report that shows my client suffered injuries to his neck and back. Just look at him." Lowenthal turned his finger toward Mulgravey. "He's in tremendous pain. And through great pain he was barely able to make it here to this hearing today."

The judge nodded and turned his attention toward Duane.

"Are you represented by counsel here this morning, Mister Duane?"

Duane shook his head no. "I do not believe counsel will be necessary." He then walked over to the door and opened it. "Judge, may I introduce my corporation's head of security Heath Rosary."

Rosary walked in holding his briefcase. His gaze went from the judge to Spider Mulgravey, who was still seated on the sofa. The mechanic had a look of bewilderment on his puffy, unshaven face. *Remember Me?* Rosary wanted to say.

Heath nodded to the man and smiled. He set the briefcase down and popped the latches. Rosary retrieved a small manila envelope and placed it on the judge's desk.

"Your Honor, the photographs in that envelope are clear evidence that Steven Mulgravey has committed Workman's Compensation fraud against Duane Corporation."

Rosary continued on as the judge studied the pictures. "On October 3rd, the day after the alleged accident, I placed the plaintiff under surveillance. The first photo you see is that of Mister Mulgravey carrying two large barrels of trash in the driveway of his Lynn home. Each photo is dated electronically by the camera."

Judge Stone looked over at the plaintiff who was now staring down at the floor.

"The next picture shows Mister Mulgravey riding his motorcycle also on October 3rd. There are thirty-six more pictures taken during the weeks after the alleged accident that show Mister Mulgravey in perfect health. You will find no neck brace or cane present in any of them. Here is my favorite," Rosary said as he took another photo from his briefcase. "This was taken at Gold's Gym in Braintree. It shows the plaintiff pressing three hundred pounds on the weight bench. As you can see by the date, that picture was taken just yesterday." Rosary turned toward Mulgravey. "Remember that Spider? I even offered to spot you, but you said no."

Mulgravey met Rosary's stare. *You're dead,* he mouthed.

"Do you have anything to add here?" the judge asked the young attorney.

The lawyer turned to his client who shook his head.

"No sir," the once bold attorney replied, folding like a beach chair.

The judge waved the manila envelope toward the mechanic and his lawyer.

"I am ruling on behalf of the defendant in this case. However, Mister Mulgravey, I will also hand over these pictures to the Suffolk County district attorney's office. That office will determine whether there is enough evidence to pursue fraud charges against you. This case is dismissed."

"Did you see the look on Spider's face?" Duane asked Rosary in the lobby. "It was priceless!"

Rosary laughed. "He's certainly not the brightest bulb out there. When are you gonna learn to hire smarter, more honest people?" he asked his old friend.

"You find me an Ivy leaguer willing to run a Brokk machine," Duane added. "What about you? When are you going to accept my invitation to join the Ancients and Honorables? It's a great place to network."

The Ancients are the third oldest chartered military organization in the world with its headquarters in historic Faneuil Hall. Its membership consisted of many of Boston's biggest movers and shakers.

"Is it true you guys have the real Declaration of Independence in there?" Rosary asked with a smile.

"No, that's the Free Masons, and that's only in the movies. We didn't dig up Geronimo either, that was the Yalies from Skull and Bones. The Ancients are known mostly for our battle cry."

"Which is?"

"Open bar." Duane chuckled.

Mulgravey exited the men's room on the 2nd floor after snorting a vial of cocaine in one of the stalls. He walked down the hall toward a large window and waited for the high to kick in. He looked down with wild eyes onto Washington Street and spotted Rosary getting into his Jaguar. Mulgravey took out a pen and pad of paper he had brought with him to the hearing. He wrote down Rosary's license plate number as the car pulled out slowly onto the street. The beefy biker then pulled a sleek black cell phone from a pocket of his leather vest and punched in a number.

"Registry of Motor Vehicles," announced the woman on the other end of the line.

"Suzy baby, it's Spider. I have a license plate number that I need you to run for me."

CHAPTER 5

▼

Rosary hit the gym for a quick workout before heading off to his next appointment, a meeting he had been dreading for days. Feeling relaxed and re-energized, he pulled the Jaguar up to the curb in front of 84 Beacon Street, hopped out and handed his keys to the valet. A crowd of tourists were gathered outside posing for pictures in front of the Bulfinch Pub, the cellar bar that gained international fame as the model for the classic television comedy *Cheers*. The street outside looked as it did on the show, but that's where the similarities ended. Tourists were in for a rude awakening once they descended the steps into the pub. Most visitors were surprised to discover the real *Cheers* looked nothing like the television version. *Oh well, at least they can buy a t-shirt,* Rosary thought. Over the bar stood a five story Georgian revival townhouse known as the Hampshire House. The turn of the century mansion was now home to one of the city's most elegant restaurants. Rosary walked into the grand entryway and tried to bypass the maître d' who stopped him by clearing his throat.

"Are you here for lunch, sir?" the impeccably dressed host asked over the classical music playing softly in the background.

Rosary stared at the neatly attired Boston Brahmin with a pencil thin mustache. *Bet you don't even know what you're listening to,* he thought. Heath correctly identified Bach's Brandenburg Concerto Number five in D. Rosary had an ear for classical music nurtured by his uncle James Rosary who once had a friend who worked as head janitor at Symphony Hall on Huntington Avenue. The janitor would sneak in Heath and his younger sister Carla to see the Boston Pops and Boston Symphony Orchestra when they were kids.

"I'm here to meet Tim Reilly," Rosary replied.

"Ah yes, Mister Reilly is dining in the library."

The host turned and opened a small closet door and pulled out a Brooks Brothers blazer.

"You'll be needing one of these, sir. I believe this one will fit nicely."

Ah, here's why I avoid places like this, Rosary thought.

He said nothing as he took off his black leather coat and handed it to the maitre d'.

He put his arms through the sleeves of the sport coat and spun around.

"Do I fit in now?" he asked the host.

The man noticed the bulge coming from the small of Rosary's back and his eyes went wide.

"Don't worry, I'm a private investigator and licensed to carry a firearm at all times."

"Well this is most un-regular sir."

"I'll give you that Jeeves," Rosary responded with a laugh. "There's nothing regular about me coming to a place like this for lunch. I'm more of a burger and beer man myself."

The desk phone rang before the host could respond. The man nodded his head and then placed a hand over the receiver and addressed Rosary.

"What did you say your name was?" he asked.

"I didn't."

Rosary was now fed up with the hoity-toity attitude.

"My name is Heathcliff Rosary."

"Mister Reilly will see you now. The library is up the staircase to your left."

Rosary nodded and walked down the corridor toward the Italian marble staircase. He took the steps two at a time and reached the second floor where a security man was waiting for him.

"Would you turn around sir?" the large man asked foregoing any pleasantries.

Rosary had seen his type before. The bodyguard had the frame of a bodybuilder and looked a bit uncomfortable stuffed into his gray suit. With his blond crew-cut he was probably former military, Rosary guessed. He had seen a number of guys like this get washed out of the Secret Service program. *All action, no intellect,* Rosary thought.

"I am carrying a fire arm," he told the bodyguard. "I'm a private investigator and it goes with the job."

"I'm sorry sir, you'll have to relinquish your weapon to me," the security man said sternly.

"I'm sorry too," Rosary replied. "It looks like Mister Reilly will be dining alone."

"Nonsense," the booming voice came from the library. "C'mon in Heath, we've got plenty of catching up to do."

Rosary smiled at the bodyguard as he walked into the oak paneled library where he found Tim Reilly seated in a wheelchair staring out the tall Palladian windows overlooking Beacon Street and the Public Garden.

"I love being back in Boston with all its history," Reilly said in a leisurely Southern drawl. "We don't have scenery like this down in Tallahassee."

The man turned his wheelchair toward his guest.

"Look at you," Reilly observed. "You still look like you could play cornerback for the B.C. Eagles."

Rosary laughed. He knew Reilly was a die-hard fan of Florida State, his alma-mater.

"I remember the day Boston College whupped up on my Seminoles. You ran an interception back for a touch down as I recall."

Rosary remembered the play as if it happened yesterday. The win over Florida State propelled Boston College to its first ever national championship game. The Eagles won that one too, again thanks to an interception and touch down by Heath Rosary.

"I licked my wounds and told all my friends to put their money on B.C. in the championship game, even the guys who'd gone to Michigan," Reilly said. "We really cleaned up after you beat the Wolverines for the title. Tough break with the Pats though, I had you pegged for a five time all-pro. So did most of the scouts if I recall."

Rosary's mind wandered briefly back to the summer of 1987. He had been drafted by the Patriots in the second round and had won the starting cornerback job in training camp. He had a stellar preseason with three interceptions, one of which he ran back for a touchdown against the defending Super Bowl champion, New York Giants. The following week, the Patriots took on the New York Jets in the final preseason game. The starting players only saw limited action, but that limited action was enough to end Rosary's career. He remembered tackling Jets receiver Al Toon after a short route during the first quarter. Toon had a reputation for surrendering his whole body for positive yardage and once he was hit by Rosary, the receiver fought vigorously for a few extra feet. During this gridiron battle, Rosary got his cleat stuck in a patch of unforgiving astro-turf and as Toon twisted forward, so did Rosary; only his foot remained planted in the ground. The highly touted rookie cornerback blew out his knee and never played again.

Now, he only had an old Jaguar and a knee full of torn cartilage to remind him of his playing days.

Fortunately, Rosary had taken out a hefty insurance policy just in case of an injury like that one. He used the money to go back to Boston College and got his law degree. Upon graduation, Rosary was recruited by some of the area's top law firms, but instead of sailing off into a boardroom or courtroom, he applied for and was accepted into the U.S. Secret Service training program. Rosary was a physical being and he needed a job where he could use his mind and his body. That's what brought him here to the Hampshire House.

Tim Reilly wheeled away from the Palladian window and motioned Rosary to their table. It was the only table in the room.

"Cozy," Rosary observed.

"I figured we needed a bit of privacy," Reilly replied as he shoehorned his large girth between the wheel chair and the small table. "But right now, the only thing I can think about is lunch."

The two men briefly studied their menus as the waitress entered the room. Rosary ordered a wood-grilled Black Angus sirloin steak, but passed on the smothered onions. His companion ordered Maine lobster sautéed with farfalle, scallions and black olives. "Another Scotch and water," Reilly said pointing to his empty glass.

"Oh, and a Valrona Chocolate Torte for dessert," he added.

Rosary stared across the table at the heart attack in waiting seated in front of him. Tim Reilly had a round body, pudgy face and droopy eyes that made him look as if he was always half asleep. He had lost the use of his legs in a car accident while serving as a Florida state senator thirty years before. Still, Reilly could've taken better care of himself, even in his current state. Over the years, some rivals had underestimated him because of his appearance and they paid the price for it. What Tim Reilly lacked in will power, he made up for in his no-holds barred approach to the game of politics. He was now one of the most powerful insiders in Washington, willing to twist any arm and stab any back to get what he wanted. Those who had been foolish enough to cross Reilly had paid for it with their careers. The former state legislator amassed his power after working tirelessly to secure the state of Florida for Evan Bosworth during his run for President. Bosworth thanked Reilly by selecting him as White House Chief of Staff. Reilly served the President in that capacity for Bosworth's two terms in the Oval Office.

"How is the President doing these days?" Rosary asked between bites of steak.

"The Virginia farm keeps him busy," Reilly replied. "He's also compiling his memoirs. I understand you're doing a bit of writing too?"

"I knew that's what this little luncheon was about," Rosary replied shaking his head. "Look Tim, I'm not gonna try to play poker with you and deny that I've been offered a book deal. But it's really none of your business." *I've decided against writing the book, but why tell you?* He thought.

Reilly sat back in his chair and drained his glass of Scotch. He set the glass on the table, leaned forward and whispered.

"That's where you're wrong Heathcliff. It is very much my business. You see, Jennifer Bosworth is about to make a run for her father's old seat in the U.S. Senate, and a tell-all book written by you could cause her big problems."

"So her father has sent you here to dissuade me from telling the truth?" Rosary shot back. He could feel the vein in his neck bulging. "I know you've got influence, but you can't hurt me."

"What's the truth?" asked Reilly. "The world believes she was kidnapped by a terrorist and that you saved her. Now you're gonna come out more than ten years after the fact with some bullshit story about a drug overdose? Who would believe you?"

Rosary tried to control his temper. "We both know what happened back in 1996. I took a bullet in the leg for that girl, but hey, that's part of the job. What bothers me is that I've had to live with a lie."

Reilly laughed. "We all have to live with lies." His expression turned serious as he leaned forward. "You write a book and I'll fucking break you," he whispered. "I'll paint you as just another angry nigger waving his middle finger at the world."

Rosary was taken aback, but tried to play it cool. "Nigger, Tim? I thought you were a Democrat? You just lost *my* black vote."

"Do you really know who you're fucking with boy?" Reilly hissed.

Rosary was tempted to lean across the table and slap the smile off the man's pudgy face. Both men grew silent as the waitress came around to clear off the table. Rosary had to think quickly. He really didn't want to stop Jennifer Bosworth from running for office. The incident happened a lifetime ago, and he knew deep down that she was a good kid. If Jennifer was clean and sober now, then more power to her. But he could not sit there and allow this Washington blowfish threaten him like this. He decided on a plan and waited for the waitress to leave the room.

"I've been offered $100,000 for my story," he informed Reilly. "If you can match that number, I'll walk away."

Reilly's fleshy face formed a perverted smile. A hundred grand was a drop in the bucket. He had won again. "I knew that we could come to an agreement

Heath. It was nice doing business with you," he said before biting into his chocolate torte.

"Call my office tomorrow," Rosary told him. "I'll give you an account number where you can wire the money." He wiped his mouth with the linen napkin, got up and walked over to Reilly's side of the table. "You know something Tim, I really do wish that you could get out of that wheelchair and stand up."

Reilly gazed up scornfully. "Why is that?"

Rosary smiled. "So that I could have the pleasure of sitting you back down."

The bodyguard saw that his boss was growing angry and felt that he had to do something. "That's enough pal," he said moving forward. Rosary felt a tight grip on the shoulder of his borrowed sport coat. He reached back and grabbed the bodyguard's thumb and twisted it up behind the man's back.

"Chill out Robo-cop, I think we're all through here," Rosary told him.

Defenseless, the bodyguard looked down at his boss for an idea of what to do.

"Rosary's right. It's all over. Let him go on his way," Reilly ordered.

Heath released the man's thumb and strolled casually out of the library.

He walked down the staircase and spotted the maitre d' standing at attention in the entryway. Rosary took off the blazer and exchanged it for his leather coat.

"Was everything satisfactory?" asked the host.

"It couldn't have gone better," Rosary replied.

CHAPTER 6

▼

The soothing melody of John Coltrane's *A Love Supreme* filled the car as Rosary drove down Blue Hill Avenue into Roxbury. He had been raised in this neighborhood made up predominantly of low-income and dirt poor African Americans, and while every other Boston neighborhood had lost much of its flavor through gentrification, the Roxbury that Rosary remembered growing up had survived unscathed. The hood was still plagued by crime, drugs and despair. Rosary watched the blighted landscape pass as the Jaguar rolled along. He saw one boarded up building after another. It was a part of the city that had been forgotten by the politicians. Shootings here didn't even warrant ink space in the local papers anymore. Violence here was at an all-time high, and because the victims were black, nobody gave a shit. He remembered that scene in *The Godfather*, where a mob boss was discussing the sale of herion in *colored* neighborhoods. "They're animals anyway," Don Zaluchi said. "So let them lose their souls." It may have been a fictional quote, but art imitated life on this side of Boston. The only thriving businesses along this stretch of road were liquor stores and bail bondsmen. One beacon of hope however, could be found inside the Phyllis Wheatley Charter School. It was named after the young black poet from Providence, Rhode Island who had offered General George Washington encouragement during the darkest days of the Revolutionary War. She wrote; *Proceed, great chief, with virtue on thy side/Thy every action let the goddess guide.* General Washington, a slave owner was so taken by Wheatley's poem that he wrote the free black woman back in his own hand and offered to meet with her if she were to ever visit his military headquarters in Cambridge.

Wheatley's poem now hung on a large banner over the entrance of the school.

Rosary spotted his sister's black Volkswagon Jetta as he pulled into the parking lot. The back window was covered by stickers with slogans like *Think globally, act locally* and *Treat yourself, mentor a student.* Carla Rosary was living proof that there was good in the world. Heath walked up to the front door and rang the buzzer. As a result of the high crime rate in the area, the Wheatley School was locked at all times. Rosary identified himself over the intercom and was buzzed inside. The one story brick building housed four classrooms and a small computer lab. Rosary walked down a hallway and into the lab where he found his sister sitting with a young girl at a computer terminal.

"Hey big brother," she waved. Carla was still dressed in her green scrubs.

The 26-year-old medical student was finishing up her residency at Beth Israel Hospital, yet she still found time to volunteer a few days a week at the Wheatley School. Carla knew her brother could be uncomfortable around kids, so she made the introduction. "Heathcliff, this is Danielle," she announced, motioning to the 13-year-old girl seated beside her. The girl wore a white blouse, blue skirt and black shoes. Uniforms were mandatory at the charter school. Danielle did have a head full of beaded braids which allowed her to express a little individuality. "Today, we're learning about climates," Carla said with excitement in her voice. Danielle did not share the enthusiasm. Heath chuckled as the teenager rolled her eyes. Danielle Robinson was smart though, in fact all the students had been hand picked out of public schools because of their high test scores. Wheatley officials took great pride in the fact that all of their graduates had gone on to college. Many former students, like Carla often came back to help. Yet the school struggled to keep its doors open. Like most charter schools, it was dependent upon private donations and contributions were way down from years passed.

"The famous Heath Rosary," announced Gloria Mendes.

He turned and saw the school's head mistress standing in the door frame.

"To what do we owe this pleasure?" she asked tilting her wire rimmed glasses down on the bridge of her nose. Mendes was an attractive woman in her mid-fifties born to a black mother and Hispanic father. She had a curvaceous figure, long curly black hair and her skin was a shade darker than the average Hispanic woman. Mendes had grown up poor in the nearby Bromley-Heath housing project. Her father was a local jazz musician, who was also self-educated and well read. There had always been an abundance of books scattered around their cramped tenement apartment. Mendes fondly remembered leafing through one her father's paperbacks, a collection of poems that included Allen Ginsberg's *Howl.* She was six-years-old when she read it the first time, twelve when she could finally understand it. *I saw the best minds of my generation destroyed by madness, starving hysterical naked, dragging themselves through the Negro streets at dawn look-ing for an angry fix …*

Howl was pretty heady stuff for a preteen. Through reading, Gloria Mendes discovered that a whole new world existed beyond the borders of Roxbury, and she was going to see it all. After receiving a doctorate in education from Smith College, Mendes traveled the globe before settling in Paris, where she ran an exclusive boarding school catering to the sons and daughters of the rich and famous. She had achieved happiness and success, yet something was calling her back home. It was time to give back. Mendes was a product of public education and had recognized its failings early on. She left Paris relinquishing money and stability in order to make a difference in her old neighborhood. She founded the Wheatley School in 1987 and chose Carla Rosary as one her first pupils.

Heath followed Mendes out to the hallway where he could see evidence of the school's financial trouble first hand. Yellow paint chipped away from the walls that were bare. "What happened to all the banners?" Rosary asked. "These walls used to be covered with artwork."

"We've had to cut the art program," Mendes sighed. "We barely have enough paper and material for class assignments."

Rosary shook his head. "That's why I'm here, Gloria."

He followed the head mistress into her office where he discussed his newly found wealth. Mendes sat back in her swivel chair and tried to comprehend the offer.

"One hundred thousand dollars is certainly a lot of money. Are you sure you want to do this Heath?"

"I want to make sure the doors to this school stay open. Lives are changed here Gloria, my sister is a shining example of that. Once the money is in my account, my lawyer will draw up the papers."

Mendes got up and wrapped her arms around him.

"You are a Godsend, Heath Rosary."

"No, Gloria. You are."

CHAPTER 7

▼

Rosary crossed Andrew Square into South Boston and replayed the long day in his mind. "Did I just give away a hundred grand?" he asked aloud. "C'mon man, it was money you never had," he tried to assure himself.

The gift to the Wheatley School did make him feel good though. It was a small price to pay compared to the sacrifices made by people like Gloria Mendes. *Still, a hundred thousand would have been nice. Shut up you selfish prick.* Rosary shook his head and laughed over the sound of Coltrane's horn. He felt the angel and devil on both shoulders fighting for attention. "I'll never be the rich man Grace's father wants for her," he said resigning himself to the fact.

He drove the Jaguar up Telegraph Hill and around Thomas Park to his condo, which stood opposite South Boston High School. Grace was having dinner with her father at his estate in Gloucester and Heath didn't want to be alone. He parked the Jag in his one car garage (the Camry he left out on the street) and made his way down the hill toward his favorite tavern, the Sligo. A Shepherd's Pie and a twenty ounce Sam Adams would certainly hit the spot. Plus, the Celtics were playing the Lakers at the Garden. Kevin Garnett versus Kobe Bryant, the rivalry was finally living up to the days of Bird and Magic again.

It was a Monday evening and the street was relatively quiet. Rosary continued his walk and suddenly heard shuffling on the pavement behind him. The foot steps grew louder as he descended Telegraph Hill. He moved passed a parked van and glanced quickly into its side mirror. He could see two rough looking men about ten yards back and they were gaining ground quickly. Both wore wool caps that they had just pulled down over their faces. *Hired muscle,* Rosary thought. He reacted immediately, darting behind the parked van as the two men gave chase.

He pulled out his 9mm Glock and held it tightly in his right hand. He heard the heavy breathing of one attacker as the man came around the van. Rosary lunged forward with his knee toward the man's crotch. The attacker's legs buckled as Rosary spun him around and slammed him up against the side of the van. Heath's left forearm was now under the man's chin; in his right hand was the semiautomatic, which was now pressed against the thug's temple. Rosary heard another set of foot steps and spun the attacker around once more. The man let out a loud scream as the heavy chain came crashing down on his back. The first attacker fell to the ground as the second backed up, the long steel chain still in his hand. Rosary now had his gun trained on the second man who continued back pedaling as he dropped the thick iron chain to the ground.

"I'll give you a five second head start," Rosary growled at him.

The second attacker turned on his heel and ran as fast as his legs could take him.

"There goes your ride," Heath told the first man who was still lying on the ground writhing in pain.

Rosary grabbed the thug by the collar of his jean jacket and hoisted him up from the pavement. He pulled off the man's wool cap and tossed it on the ground. Under the light of the street lamp, Rosary could see the thug's pimply, pale face. He had to be no older that eighteen.

"Clearly this ain't no mug and run," Heath told him. "Who sent you?"

The teen smiled. "Fuck you, nigger."

Rosary responded by ramming the butt of his gun across the thug's wide nose.

"Now that's the second time I've been called nigger today," he barked. "Wanna try for a third?"

The young punk shook his head as the blood poured down his chin.

"You here under orders from a cockroach named Spider Mulgravey?"

The teenager kept his head down and nodded yes.

With his right hand, Rosary kept his gun aimed at the thug's chest, with his left hand he retrieved his cell phone from his jacket and dialed 911. What was supposed to be a quiet night turned into a long one. When police finally arrived, the young thug told them he would not talk without his lawyer being present, but Rosary was questioned at length. *No, this wasn't a random attack. Yes, the kid said he'd been sent by a member of the Salem Warlocks to rough me up.* Rosary never made it to the neighborhood tavern, instead he returned to his condo where he devoured a carton of left over Chinese and collapsed on the couch.

He had been asked by police to attend the young thug's arraignment on assault and battery charges the following morning, but Rosary had other plans.

He dressed in a black Nike sweat suit, jumped into the Jaguar and headed for Gold's Gym in Braintree. His cell phone rang; he flipped it open and stared at the small digital screen. It was Grace.

"Hey baby."

"I'm so proud of you," she exclaimed. "Carla called last night and told me what you did. I should have known that you had a plan in mind."

"Well, the plan just kind of came to me during lunch," he admitted. "I wasn't sure how you'd feel about it. A hundred thousand dollars is a lot of money."

"C'mon Heathcliff, you know me better than that. You can't put a price tag on a clear conscience. You know I don't care about the money. I never have."

He knew that Grace was telling the truth. She could have had a cushy job in her father's company, but instead had turned her back on the family business in exchange for the excitement and meager pay working behind the scenes in television news. She did have a multi-million dollar trust fund however.

"Looks like you'll have to be my sugar momma for a little while longer," he said with a laugh.

"You'll have to earn it in bed," she giggled.

"It's a little early for dirty talk, don't you think?"

"Just wait until you see me tonight," she purred.

A wide smile came over Rosary's face.

"How was dinner with your father?" he asked. "Did he bring over another Harvard grad to tempt you with?"

"He stopped doing that a long time ago," she replied. "He knows how much I love you."

"Yes, and it must be killing him."

There was a moment of awkward silence between them. Rosary was right, her father did not approve of their relationship. Tommy Chen held a doctorate from Harvard Medical School and was considered one of the smartest men in America, yet he was still blinded by ignorance. He could not get past the color of Rosary's skin.

"How was your evening?" Grace asked changing the subject.

Rosary told her about his run in with the young thugs. He did not want to hide anything from her. She knew how dangerous his job could be.

"So what are you going to do?" she asked with concern in her voice.

"I'm gonna end it for good."

"Be careful, darling."

"Always, love."

Rosary pulled his Jaguar into the parking lot of Gold's Gym and just as he suspected, Spider Mulgravey's blue Chevy Suburban was parked out front. The SUV was parked in a space reserved for the club member of the month. Rosary noticed the sign and laughed. He wished he had brought his camera. *I'm sure the judge would love to see that,* he thought. Rosary signed in at the front desk and walked down a flight of stairs to the weight room. Fortunately, the gym was not crowded. He strolled by a couple of women climbing to the beat of Beyonce's latest hit on their Stairmasters. It was early morning and Spider Mulgravey was alone in the free weight area. The biker loved the gym, but hated the music. He was laying on the weight bench with his eyes closed, lost in AC-DC's *Back in Black* which blared from his I-Pod. A red bandana was wrapped around his head and the sleeves of his sweatshirt were cut off exposing his thick arms. He was between bench press sets, a weight bar with three hundred pounds of iron plates rested on a rack above him. Rosary walked up behind the bench and used both hands to lift the bar up off the rack. Mulgravey felt the bench shake and he opened his eyes. He watched in horror as the bar came crashing down on top of his wide chest. Mulgravey screamed out in pain. He felt as if he'd been hit across the chest with a baseball bat. Rosary kept the heavy bar pressed against Spider's chest, moving it up slightly toward his neck.

"You sent a couple of kids by my place last night?"

Mulgravey had the wind knocked out of him and could not respond. It did not matter; Rosary already knew the answer to his own question.

"You too much of a coward to face me yourself?"

"I don't know what you're talking about," Spider said finally as he gasped for air.

Rosary was buying none of it. "If I so much as smell you or one of your *interns* around me or my place again, I'll come down on you hard Spider."

Mulgravey heeded the warning with a shake of his head and Rosary hoisted the bar off the biker's chest and returned it to the rack. Mulgravey began to cough as he felt the air rush back into his lungs. He placed both hands up to his neck and tried to catch his breath. He turned and watched Rosary walk breezily out of the free weight area. Heath was in the parking lot heading toward his car when Mulgravey burst out of the front door.

"Come back here, you mother fucker," he shouted across the parking lot.

Rosary turned and watched as the hefty biker charged toward him like a wild animal. Mulgravey outweighed him by at least sixty pounds and if the larger man tackled him to the ground, there could be trouble. Heath would not let that happen. He planted both legs in a horse stance, tightened his fists and waited. Mulgravey ran at him at full speed, and like a matador, Rosary side stepped the raging bull. The biker turned around and Heath kicked him with tremendous force in the right knee cap. Both men heard a loud pop and Spider fell to the ground, his kneecap shattered. Mulgravey clutched his injured leg as tears formed at the corners of his eyes. He had never felt that kind of intense pain before.

"Good thing you bought that cane," Rosary told him adding salt to the wound.

He knelt down over the injured man and whispered. "It's over Spider. We're even now. Let it go. Don't make me hurt you permanently."

Spider Mulgravey bit his lip and closed his eyes. He knew that he had been beaten.

Rosary reached in the front pocket of his track suit and retrieved his cell phone. He dialed 911.

"There's been an accident at Gold's Gym in Braintree," he told the dispatcher. "Guy slipped on the ice and popped out his knee."

Rosary left the injured man lying in the parking lot, got back into his Jaguar, and drove away.

CHAPTER 8

▼

HONG KONG

Mister Wong rubbed cold cream over the swollen knuckles of his scarred hands. He had just finished working out on a wooden dummy, which was set up on the balcony of his spacious flat in the Lan Kwai Fong district of Hong Kong. *Pain is good,* he told himself. The wooden dummy was used in Kung-Fu (Gong-fu) much like the heavy bag was used in boxing, to build punching strength, only this piece of equipment came with wooden arms and legs protruding from a center beam. It was designed to help a martial artist develop timing and coordination. It also allowed the user to deflect and redirect an opponent's attack. The method had originated centuries ago at the Shoalin Temple, where according to legend; monks who completed their training were required to pass through a dark tunnel filled with 108 wooden dummies. Each dummy performed a specific technique which the monks had to overcome. There were 108 combat techniques that could be used on the wooden dummy. Mister Wong had just tried them all.

He poured himself a cup of tea, sat down at his desk and logged onto his computer.

He typed in the web address for Interpol and waited for the site to appear. The words *International Criminal Police Organization (ICPO)* flashed across the screen and a listing of offenses appeared in small type on the left hand side of the home page. Wong scrolled his computer mouse past *terrorism* and *genocide* and clicked on the *wanted* icon. The homepage was replaced by a list of Interpol's most wanted fugitives. The fugitives were categorized by alphabetical order and Wong scrolled down until he found the name he had used as an alias during his last job; *Phra Nang.* Wong right clicked on his mouse and his photograph immediately appeared. It was the picture taken for his employment identification card at the IMPACT Muang Thong Thani. He was now wanted for the offenses of kidnapping and murder. The internet posting would have given an ordinary criminal pause, but Mister Wong was no ordinary criminal, and he had little fear of getting caught. Thanks to a skilled plastic surgeon, his face looked nothing like the one staring back at him from the computer screen. The doctor had cut a semilunar crease in Wong's eyelids, widening them and giving him a more occidental look. He also underwent craniofacial surgery; the surgeon shaved his cheek bones down while adding BOTOX to the jaw line. The results were more than satisfactory. With just a few changes to Wong's facial structure, he looked like a new man. He rubbed his smooth chin as he remembered lying on the operating table in great pain. Wong would not allow the surgeon to administer anesthesia. He endured the operation while squeezing the black handle of his Beretta which he held to his side. Once the procedure was finished, the doctor gave him the okay sign. Wong returned the gesture by lifting his right arm and squeezing the trigger. The surgeon took a bullet in the head and collapsed in the makeshift operating room. *No Witnesses.*

Still staring at the computer screen, Wong tried to remember what his original face had looked like. He had gone through several transformations over the past 15 years. The only evidence investigators had in the kidnapping case of Miss Universe was the photo of a stranger. Wong's accomplices, two security guards and a Thai hooker were murdered by hired guns soon after his Lear jet was wheels up leaving Bangkok. He left nothing behind, not even fingerprints. Wong had burned his own off in a Chinese prison decades before.

He took a long sip of green tea and sat back on his comfortable leather swivel chair. Techno music and laughter from Club 97 were now pumping through large bay windows in the living room from the street below. Wong enjoyed living in the heart of Hong Kong's nightclub scene, the loud noise kept him sane. He feared silence above all other things. The fear was born years ago on a mountainside in Southwest China's Sichuan Province. Wong had been one of just a hundred inmates housed in the clay walled barracks of Chuanxi Prison, built in 1953 to jail China's most feared criminals. The prison stood 1,400 meters in elevation near the top of a cone shaped mountain and inmates there were forced to live in brutal conditions, where it snowed non-stop in the winter months and rained during the rest of the year. Prisoners were dying at the rate of two a week, but the government always had more hardened criminals waiting to replace them. So isolated was the prison, inmates and those ordered to guard them had to be flown in by helicopter; there were no roads leading down the rugged mountain. The Chuanxi Prison was China's own version of Alcatraz. Officials believed there was no way to escape. Mister Wong would prove them wrong.

Wong, then known by another name, was seventeen-years-old when he was first thrown in jail. He had grown up in a ghetto built in the shadow of Beijing's Forbidden City. He was the oldest of five children and served as a surrogate father to his siblings; his own father had died of tuberculosis when Wong was ten. Disease was a constant companion in the ghetto. They lived in a two room shack surrounded by several others along a narrow hutong, which was a maze of alleys built in ancient China. The acrid smoke of burning trash hung low over the hutong and the smell of despair was impossible to overcome.

At an early age, Wong knew that he was different from the other boys in his impoverished neighborhood. Physically, he was superior to the other children and feared by most, but still boys whispered behind Wong's back. "Tong-Xing (*Homo*)," they called him. Homosexuality was forbidden in China during this time, but Wong never hid his preference for men. As a teenager, he began frequenting the Nam Li Shi Lu subway station, a known cruising area, where he sought out older men willing to pay for sex. Soon, he was able to bring enough money home to help feed is three sisters and younger brother. He never told them how he earned his money and they never asked.

During one of his visits to the subway station, he was propositioned by a government official who offered to take Wong to a nearby hotel. His surveillance skills were non-existant at the time, and he did not know the bureaucrat's chief rival within the Zhenzhi Ju *Politburo* had followed them to the hotel. Wong was caught in bed with the official and sent off to jail. His family was never told what had happened to him. He simply disappeared. Frightened at first, Wong soon realized that conditions at the Zhe Jiang Provincial prison were actually better than those he had left behind in the hutong. At least in jail, Wong received two servings of rice per day instead of one. He did fear for his brother and sisters back home though, and that wasn't his only concern. Prison was not like his old neighborhood, where the taunts were whispered behind his back. Here, they were shouted and spat at him by his fellow inmates. *Pingzi* they would call him, referring to the bizarre practice of inserting a glass bottle in one's anus. Wong brushed off the taunts and retreated within himself until one inmate made the mistake of touching him without his consent. In front of several other prisoners, the older man grabbed Wong by the arm and asked the teen if he could give a better blow job than a woman. Wong responded by reaching for the man's neck and crushing his windpipe with his thumbs. He kept squeezing until he saw the older man's eyes roll up toward the back of his head. Wong threw his tormenter's body to the floor and stared down the dozen other inmates whom had all been cheering the dead man on. Those prisoners immediately backed off and cut a wide berth for

Wong as he walked back to his cell. After killing the inmate, Wong figured that he too would be put to death. Through prayer, the teenager quietly prepared himself for a trip to the gallows. Instead, prison officials handed down a more brutal punishment. They banished him to the isolation of Chuanxi Prison.

Wong arrived at Chuanxi in mid-January; the weather was even colder than he had expected. In fact, it was one of the coldest months on record. He stepped off the helicopter during a snow squall wearing shackles on both his ankles and his wrists. Sheets of ice whipped up in the air by the helicopter's rotor blades slapped his bare face. Wong's hands were tied in the back and he had no defense against the stinging snow. He and two other prisoners were ushered off the landing pad, pushed across a barren courtyard and into the main building of the prison. While he was getting processed, a prison official told him that he no longer had a name, only a prison number. The name he had been born with no longer existed. He was declared dead on all public records in China. The teen wondered why he had not simply been shot and his family charged for the cost of the bullet. Inmate #261 was issued a blue uniform with a white shoulder stripe and led into a clay walled cave that served as a prison barracks. There was no door to the cave, it was just an open hole that allowed the snow to blow in and pile up inside. Along the wall of the cave sat five starving men in uniforms identical to Wong's. The teen eyed his cellmates curiously and waited for the taunts to begin. The men did not even bother to look up at their new roommate. Their brown eyes were blank; they were curled up inside their own living hell. Inmate #261 sat down and took his place next to the others. The prison guard quickly shouted out the rules of the barracks and walked over and kicked him in the chest for good measure. Wong fell to his side screaming in pain. Satisfied, the guard turned on his heel and walked out.

"Chi," a voice whispered to him. *Eat.*

Wong opened his eyes as the man sitting next to him leaned over; opened his dirty hand and offered three rolled up tea leaves. Despite the burn in his chest, Wong sat up and grabbed the man's hand.

"Xiexie ni," he whispered back. *Thank you.*

The prisoner who had shown the generosity was serving a drug trafficking sentence and had arrived a month before. His name was Hao Lew and he quickly got Wong up to speed on the politics of the prison.

"We pick leaves from the green tea trees. They are abundant here on this nameless mountain," Hao Lew told him as he pointed out the open window of their barracks. "Snow, rain, it makes no difference to the guards. We are forced to pick every day."

Wong was confused. "Is that all the prisoners are here to do? Pick tea leaves?"

"Oh no," his new friend whispered. "The picking is used only to keep us busy. Medical experiments are the true reason we are here."

"What kind of experiments?"

"The worst kind," Hao Lew replied. "Only a week ago, I was ordered to hand out soaked cabbage leaves to ten other prisoners," he took a deep breath before continuing with the story. "After giving out the cabbage leaves, I was very hungry and asked the guard if I could eat one too. He laughed and told me to look around, and what I saw still gives me nightmares. It was a scene from Hell; the prisoners were screaming and vomiting black blood. Blood was also leaking out of their eyes and their buttocks, I had never seen so much blood before. It took the prisoners several minutes to die."

"What did you do then?" Wong asked.

"I said a silent prayer for the prisoners and returned to my barracks. Their bodies were tossed on a pile of logs in the middle of the courtyard and burned in front of the other prisoners. We were told the men had tried to escape, but I know differently. I can still hear their screams in my sleep," Lew replied wiping a tear from his eye.

"What do you think the cabbage leaves were laced with?"

"I'm no expert, but I did overhear a guard whisper something about tests needed for the military so I assume it was a biological agent of some sort."

Lew had also heard rumors that prisoners were being injected with huoluan (cholera), tianhua (smallpox), and even meidu (syphillis). The story made perfect sense to Wong, the inmates had all been declared dead after all.

Several weeks had passed and Wong got closer to his new friend. The closeness turned to intimacy and Wong found himself in love for the first time in his young life. The relationship did not seem to bother the other prisoners who shared the barracks. They did not voice their objections to the nightly panting and grunting in the darkness. In the daylight hours, the prisoners picked their leaves in silence. The monotony of the exercise caused many inmates to volunteer for a trip to the medical ward. For them, a dreadful disease was the easy way out. Wong and Hao Lew had no intention of following in their foot steps. When they weren't exploring each other's bodies during the night, the young lovers were using the darkness to hatch their escape plan. The first plan of attack was to overcome the barracks guard they called, Pockmarked Chan. A bad case of acne had left the guard with a textured map of peaks and valleys covering his weathered face.

Overpowering the guard would be Wong's job. There was no way that the rail thin, effeminate Hao Lew could match the guard's strength. The escape would take place at night; Hao Lew would complain of stomach pains and call for help. Wong would be waiting in the darkness to attack Pockmarked Chan and kill him if he had to. He actually relished the thought. The guard had been exceptionally brutal to him. The prisoners would then have to make their way across a brightly lit courtyard to the row of green tea trees. This would pose the greatest challenge. Three armed guards patrolled the courtyard through the night. Wong and Lew would make their escape during a snow storm in order to cut down on the guards' visibility. If they made it past the guards, they would climb the tallest tea tree; hoist themselves over an eleven foot wall and into freedom. It wasn't the perfect plan, but it was *a plan,* and it was the only hope the two men had.

The strategy changed however one brutally cold afternoon as the prisoners were taking a five minute break from their leaf picking duties. Wong, Lew and two others were huddled around a small fire trying to warm their numb hands. Wong saw Pockmarked Chan exit the medical hut and begin walking in their direction. Chan pointed at Hao Lew.

"The doctor needs to see you," he barked.

Lew gazed over at his lover. *They've come for me.*

Hao Lew closed his eyes and whispered a prayer. Chan smiled at the prisoner's reaction. "I love you," Lew told Wong. He then turned quickly from the fire and ran in the opposite direction toward the tea trees. Chan took his rifle off his shoulder and gave chase. Wong watched the spectacle and knew that he had to do something. Before he could react, the guard raised his AK-47 and opened fire. Hao Lew was cut down before he could reach the tree line. Chan waited for the prisoner to get up and when he didn't, the guard shot him three more times for good measure. Pockmarked Chan lowered his weapon, turned and started walking back to the fire. He would have to find another subject for the doctors to work with. Wong saw his lover lying motionless in the snow and fireworks began shooting off in his mind. He turned back to the fire. His rage was immediate and all consuming. Without thinking, Wong threw his hands into the flames. The pain was excruciating and the smell of his own burning flesh turned his stomach. Wong felt the guard's warm breath on the back of his neck. He spun around and thrust his burning fingers into the eyes of Pockmarked Chan. The guard screamed, as Wong ripped the man's eyeballs out of their sockets. Chan dropped to the ground in agony, his rifle fell next to him in the snow. Wong looked down at the guard and saw a pair of black, bloody holes where his eyes had just been. He picked up the guard's rifle and sprayed the courtyard with bullets. The other prison guards ducked for cover. Wong sprinted toward the tea trees and could hear the bullets as they flew past him. The pain in his burning hands was enough to make anyone pass out, but Wong's body was in shock and he was feeding only on adrenaline now. He climbed the tallest tree and paid no attention to the gun shots exploding the branches around him. He reached the top of the tree and catapulted himself over the prison wall.

Wong landed hard on the snow covered ground below. He could hear the sound of alarms going off and the distant shouts of prison guards scrambling to figure out what had happened. It would not be long before they too were outside the prison walls. Wong got to his feet and limped toward a boulder lined path just east of the prison. He placed the rifle strap over his shoulder as the snow began to fall again. He took it as a good sign. The fresh powder would cover his tracks. Wong felt another pang of anxiety when he heard the sound of the MD-369 helicopter rotor blades coming from the prison launch pad. The Chinese employed the MD-369 because it was the only helicopter certified to fly in snow. They would be searching for him by air as well. Wong had no idea where he was going, he and Hao Lew had never gotten that far in the planning. He just knew that he had to continue moving down the slope of the mountain. After about twenty minutes, he stopped to catch his breath and to pack snow on his scorched finger tips. He could no longer hear the sounds of the guard patrol; they had been called back to quell an uprising ignited by Wong's actions inside the prison. However, the buzz of the search helicopter was getting closer. Wong looked for cover and spotted a rock cave a few meters away. It may as well have been a few miles away, for Wong could walk no more. His feet were frozen and the pain in his hands overwhelming. However, somehow he found the strength to move forward. He limped his way into the cave where he finally collapsed in a dark corner, away from the wind and the snow.

Wong lost consciousness, but awoke just minutes later to a loud purring sound coming from somewhere in the darkness. He craned his neck to the right and found himself staring straight into the bright yellow eyes of a Manchurian tiger that lay down at the far end of the cavern. At first, he thought it was a hallucination brought on by intense pain and trauma. He shook his head in hopes of making the bad dream go away. It did not go away. The purring of the beast only got louder. He now realized he was not in a cave, but a tiger's den. The curious creature got up slowly, its nostrils flaring at the smell of Wong's burned fingertips. By the movement of its shadow, Wong was able to determine the animal was quite large. In fact, the tiger measured nearly ten feet long and weighed six hundred pounds. It had been more than twelve hours since the animal had eaten last. The beast was hungry and therefore less cunning and cautious than it normally would have been. Escape was now impossible, Wong thought. The mouth of the cave was several feet away. The tiger would pounce on him the second he got to his feet. *After all that I have had to endure, I will not die in valor, but in the belly of a beast.* Suddenly, he remembered the rifle. It was lying beside him on the floor of the cave. He slowly reached for it with open hands. Using only his palms, he managed to bring the weapon into his lap. He bit down hard on his lower lip as he placed a burned finger on the trigger. The pain was mind numbing. The tiger moved closer with its head down; its hypnotic eyes now fixed on the small creature that had crossed its threshold. The beast was now ten yards away, when it suddenly lurched forward. Wong squeezed his injured finger and pulled the trigger. Man and beast both let out a loud roar as the bullet struck the tiger above the left eye. He was hoping to stop the animal, but the shot did much more than that. The bullet ripped off a large piece of the tiger's skull. The huge creature came crashing down on Wong, smothering him with its orange fur. He was now somewhere under the tiger's front legs, close enough to hear its heart, which was not beating. Wong rolled out from under the animal and finally caught his breath. He looked down at the dead cat with bewilderment in his eyes. *Why am I not dead?* He asked himself. Wong was too tired to answer his own question. He curled up to the warm carcass and fell asleep.

He slept for nearly twenty hours. When he finally awoke, he was cold, hungry and half-crazed. He stumbled out of the cave and into the sunlight. There were no patrols and no helicopters. Only the rugged terrain of this unforgiving mountain stood between him and his freedom. Wong pressed on, mentally fighting the pain of his burned hands and quenching his thirst with fallen snow. As he continued down the mountain, there were many times that he wanted to give up, that he wanted to die. But he owed it to the memory of Hao Lew to survive. Three days after his journey had begun; he finally reached the base of the mountain and marched on to the nearest village, which was another four kilometers away. He reached the small town of Dawu, which bordered the Tibetan plateau and could walk no further. He was in dire need of food and medical attention and would have to gamble on the kindness of the villagers. To his relief, these people followed the peaceful teachings of their Tibetan cousins and were staunchly anti-government. The villagers took him in and nursed him back to health, providing him with a cot and around the clock care. He did not know what ingredients were mixed in the potions he was being given, but the results were miraculous. His health returned within just a few weeks. The medicine man of Dawu warned him however, that the damage to his hands was irreversible. He had lost his sense of touch, but he knew it was a small price to pay for his freedom and his life. They called him, Hu *Tiger* after hearing about his exploits in the mountain cave. What he did not know was that his legend had traveled beyond the borders of the tiny village. Hao Lew's brother, a wealthy Hong Kong businessman, had paid off several prison officials for information concerning the whereabouts of his beloved sibling. The trail led to the Chuanxi Prison and the incredible story about the jailbreak. Ju-Long Lew wanted to meet the man who avenged his brother's death.

Lew sent a team of paid agents to the area in hopes of finding this man. Evidence pointed to the village of Dawu. Using discretion, the businessman traveled to the tiny town and came face to face with the man known as Tiger. The meeting was quite emotional and Lew could sense that the relationship between his brother and Tiger was more than just *friendly*. This realization did not bother Lew; for he had his own complications with the opposite sex. Lew also realized Tiger was a man of action with innate skills that could become quite useful.

"I was able to find you with relative ease," Lew told him. "It will not be long before the soldiers come here to kill you and these kind villagers for granting you shelter. That is why I want you to leave this place right now."

"Where would I go?" asked Tiger.

"I want you to come and work for me," Lew replied, as both men sipped from a bowl of rice wine. "I hear the villagers call you Tiger. You do not look like a beast to me; you have just been locked in a cage for far too long. Work for me and I will make you rich. When you don't have to count every grain of rice in your bowl, you are much less of an animal and much more of a man. You can keep the name Tiger, but I would like to call you something else."

"What is that?" the teen asked curiously.

"From now on, you will be known as Mister Wong."

The pager went off bringing Mister Wong back to the here and now. He looked down at the device's small digital screen, which displayed the message; *package needs pick up*. Wong just shook his head. He got up and walked into his bedroom where a fleet of hand made Italian suits hung in the closet. It was taxing work, being on call twenty-four hours a day, but the money he earned certainly made up for it. After getting dressed, Wong took the elevator down to the garage, hopped into his black Mercedes-Benz and headed toward Victoria's Peak.

Once he arrived, Wong showed his identification to the armed security guard at the top of the drive way. The guard pressed a button opening the thick iron gate and Wong continued down a straight away lined with exotic plants and trees. He parked his luxury sedan in the circular driveway and walked up to the front entrance of the Lew mansion. Like most Chinese homes, a shiny set of Pa Kua mirrors hung over the front door. The octagonal mirrors were decorated with the marks of the eight trigrams. The mirrors were used to scare evil spirits away by reflecting their own faces. Mister Wong smiled at the irony.

He rang the door bell and waited patiently with arms folded in the front archway.

The guard stationed inside the foyer, recognized the visitor from a security camera positioned over the door. The guard summoned the mistress of the home and seconds later, a smiling Bao Lew opened the double door.

"Hello, little lady," Wong said with a smile. "I'm here to see your father."

"He's in the study," the young girl announced slowly. "I was just about to play for him."

"Do you mind if I listen as well?"

She paused a moment before answering. "I don't mind. But please don't try to make me laugh Mister Wong," she giggled. Bao had finally become accustomed to Mister Wong's new face. She had been told that her father's confidante had been seriously hurt in an auto crash.

"I'll do my best," he replied.

The girl led him by the hand into the mansion and down the long marble corridor toward her father's office. Wong was habitually a brisk walker, but he had learned to move slowly around Bao.

Wait until she drags her left foot forward before taking another step, he told himself.

"Wait right there," she ordered. "I have to get my instrument."

Bao came shuffling back moments later carrying her erhu *Chinese violin.*

They entered the office and saw a smiling Ju-Long Lew seated behind his large desk.

"You're just in time for the concert," He told his subordinate. "Bao has been practicing quite hard."

The girl bent down at the waist in a curtsy and began to play. She had been practicing a nine note scale for nearly a year. Wong studied Bao's face as her expressions volleyed back and forth between concentration and frustration.

He gazed over at his boss who was completely captivated by his daughter. The sentiment warmed Wong's heart. Because of Bao's mental challenges, most Chinese that Wong knew would have had her committed to a state hospital if she was their daughter, but not Ju-Long Lew, he catered to every one of her needs and reveled in her tiniest accomplishments. It was a stark contrast to the way his boss could treat others. *How could a man filled with so much hate still find love in his heart?* Wong asked himself. Watching Lew with his daughter reminded Wong of those eerie news reels that showed Adolph Hitler smiling as he played with his German Shepherds at his Eagle's Nest retreat in the Bavarian mountains.

After completing the nine note scale with great difficulty, Bao curtsied again and limped over to hug her father. He squeezed his daughter tightly and kissed her gently on the forehead.

"I think you are ready for the school concert," he told her.

"Thank you, Baba."

Lew patted his daughter on the head and waved her out of the office. She giggled and retreated down the hall.

"She's a gem," Wong told his boss.

"She is my most valuable possession," Lew confided with great joy.

The men shared a brief moment of silence before getting to the business at hand.

"I take it the package is no longer useful to you?" Wong asked him.

"I need you to dispose of it and find me a suitable replacement as quickly as possible."

"Would you want the same model?"

Lew nodded his head and got up from his desk. "I will leave you to your work."

The oil magnate walked out of the office and closed the door behind him.

Mister Wong stood alone and weighed his options. Since murdering Miss Universe, Sophie Doucet, his boss had raped and tortured two more women. Scarlet haired beauties were hard to come by in China. Wong would have to think about finding a suitable replacement later, right now he had another task to perform. He sat down at his boss's computer and typed in the access code. Seconds later, the jade Buddha slid across the floor. Wong walked over to the retinal scan and placed his right eye over the laser beam. He was the only other man allowed into Ju-Long Lew's private gallery. The elevator took him down into the bowels of the mansion. The door opened and the smell of sex and murder filled the air. Wong made his way to the sterile compartment that served as the rape chamber. He found the cherry haired woman lying on the bed, her lifeless eyes wide with horror. A chunk of flesh was missing from the victim's blood soaked neck and several more bite marks covered her pale body. *Poor girl,* he thought.

Wong had divorced himself from the reality of his own involvement in her murder. She was an exchange student from London and Wong had first spotted her at a nightclub in his neighborhood. She had not been blessed with the heart stopping beauty of Sophie Doucet, but few people were. She was attractive enough though, and she possessed most of the physical attributes his employer was looking for. Wong did his homework and found out the young woman was an art major from Cambridge University participating in the semester abroad program. He trailed her for several days before making his approach inside the Pageone bookstore on Canton Road. She was browsing in the arts section when Wong walked by and purposely tripped over her backpack, which had been lying in the aisle. She apologized and he accepted. A conversation about Renior followed and she was immediately struck by his grasp of the English language and his knowledge of her life's passion. Mister Wong knew a great deal about art, not because he liked it all that much, but because his boss did. They continued their chat over a cup of tea at an outdoor café. She had been an easy mark, too easy. Wong slipped a potent tablet in her cup and minutes later she was passed out in the backseat of his Mercedes.

Wong stripped down to his underwear and dragged the body into a nearby bathroom. He placed the girl in the bathtub, grabbed a butcher knife and went to work. Two hours later, the attractive woman's remains were stuffed into four large garbage bags. Satisfied with the job, Wong cleaned himself up and walked over to a small computer set up in his master's opium den. He retrieved a small floppy disk off the table and slid it into the computer's hard drive. The horrific images of the woman's murder flashed across the screen moments later. Wong stared at the computer and noticed that Ju-Long Lew had not worn a mask this time; instead he wore what appeared to be a set of razor sharp false teeth. The video rolled and Wong watched as Lew chased the exchange student around the small room for several moments. He could have taken hold of his victim at any time, but Ju-Long Lew was clearly enjoying the game. The woman kept the satin sheet around her naked body as she attempted to elude him in the enclosed area. Lew caught her in the middle of the king sized bed and pulled her down on top of him. Holding both of her arms tightly in his hands; Lew impaled her with his rigid penis and penetrated her neck with his pointed fangs. He bit right down to her collar bone and ripped a chunk of flesh from her neck. A river of blood began to flow down her pale back and onto the white satin sheet. Lew spat the meat across the room and looked up at the video camera fixed on the wall. His crazed brown eyes were filled with lust and showed no remorse. *He's gone insane*, Wong thought to himself.

He downloaded the file and attached it to an email that he was about to send out. He typed in the secure address and added a short note. *Your Excellency, please accept this gift from your most trusted friend in China. As you will see; he takes great pleasure in his work.* Wong pressed *send* and then went back for the garbage bags.

CHAPTER 9

▼

ROXBURY, MASSACHUSETTS

The two men stood in the center of the octagonal ring pawing one another with their black fingerless gloves, neither man appeared willing to commit to the battle. Outside the ring, Heath Rosary stood next to his uncle, who monitored the action with a stop watch in the palm of his hand.

"What do you think of these two?" Heath whispered.

"They're not ready for prime time," James Rosary replied without hesitation. "They watch it on Pay-Per-View and think it looks easy," he added. "Reality is a slap in the face when they come here."

Heath nodded to his uncle and gazed around the gym. The *Jeet Kune Do* studio had doubled in size since James Rosary began training cage fighters more than a year ago.

"Ramon, don't box him. Sweep the leg and get him on the ground," James Rosary shouted at one of his fighters. "Jake, use your jab to set up the right hook," he told the other. The men ignored the advice and continued their dance in the middle of the ring.

"Time," James yelled in disgust as he hit the stop watch. He opened the chain-link fence door of the octagon and stepped inside. He shook his head at the two weary fighters as beads of sweat rolled off their muscular bodies. The men hung their heads down low, like a pair of dogs that just pissed on the carpet. James Rosary could have chewed them out, but what would his fighters gain from that? He was a teacher after all.

"Gentlemen, you cannot wait for your opponent to attack, before countering the technique," Rosary told them. "You must try to intercept the attack before it is launched. *Jeet Kune Do* is an offensive martial art, not a defensive one. There are plenty of fighters looking for time inside the octagon. If you both are not willing to engage one another, I will be forced to give your ring time to someone else."

The reluctant warriors nodded and left the ring without protest. They knew better than to disrespect James Rosary in his own dojo. Rosary was a living legend in the martial arts world. He was one of the only certified masters of *Jeet Kune Do* on the east coast and unlike the others; Rosary had studied the system under its founder Bruce Lee. The two had met as college students at the University of Washington in the early 1960's, years before Lee skyrocketed to superstardom on the big screen. Rosary was a star tailback for the Huskies and the big man on campus. A teammate had told him about a small Chinese man who wowed audiences in the school's cafeteria with his super human feats of strength. Rosary was cynical of the claims and wanted to see for himself. On this particular day, Lee was demonstrating his one-inch punch technique in front of a large gathering of fellow students. Lee stood exactly one inch away from his assistant, and with a jerk of the wrist, sent the man flying backward.

The demonstration drew loud cheers from the crowd, but James Rosary was less than convinced. *It had to be some kind of parlor trick,* he thought. Bruce Lee saw that he had a skeptic in the audience and asked Rosary if he would like a personal demonstration. Rosary accepted the challenge and walked into the center of the circle. Again, Lee positioned himself exactly one inch away from Rosary's chest. James towered over the five-foot-seven inch Chinese man.

"Give it your best shot Superman," Rosary laughed.

The kung-fu master jerked his wrist once more and James Rosary was airborne. He had been knocked even farther back than Lee's assistant. Rosary laid flat on his back in the middle of the cafeteria and waited for his breath to come back. A smiling Lee walked over and offered him a hand. It was the beginning of a beautiful friendship. James Rosary became one of Lee's original non-Chinese students and helped the master devise his fighting system. *Jeet Kune Do* (the way of the intercepting fist) was the first hybrid martial art. Bruce Lee had taken the most effective techniques from all the fighting styles and pooled them into one system. He simply discarded the techniques that did not work. James Rosary was carrying on his master's legacy and now everyone wanted to train with the man who had been trained by *the man.*

"Do you think Bruce would have appreciated all this?" Heath asked his uncle.

"Bruce Lee created this," James replied, referring to the mixed martial artists who were training around them. "He used to tell me that the true measure of a martial artist could only be taken in combat. That's why he never used a belt system. I've seen plenty of black belts get their asses kicked when they had more than just a shiny trophy on the line."

James Rosary looked over and smiled at his nephew. "You were one of the best students I ever had. I bet you could have had quite a career in the UFC."

"They don't let you take your gun into the ring in those Ultimate Fighting shows. I don't like those rules," Heath replied.

Uncle James grabbed two large red hand pads and put them on.

"C'mon son, show this old man what you got," he taunted Heath.

The younger Rosary took off his leather coat and put his fists up. He attacked the pads with a lightening fast punch combination; two straight hands followed by a left hook. The demonstration turned the heads of a few hardened warriors who were training nearby.

"That's my boy," Uncle James yelled out for all to hear.

Heath fired off another combination that ended with a spinning back fist to the center of the pad.

"Think Spider Mulgravey has learned his lesson?" James asked, talking much softer now.

"How the hell did you know about that?"

Heath already knew the answer. His uncle had friends in high places over at Boston Police headquarters.

"I'm waiting for your answer," James replied.

"Well, he's laid up with a blown out kneecap, so I don't think he's in any condition to come after me right now."

"What about three months from now?" James asked.

"I can't predict the future, but I can try to be ready for it."

Heath punched the hand pad extra hard to emphasize his point.

"It was a nice thing you did for the Wheatley School," James said changing the subject.

"Good news travels fast," Heath replied with annoyance in his voice. "Has Carla alerted the Boston *Globe* and the *Herald* yet?"

"You speak nice about your sister," James scolded him. "She's just proud of you. Gloria Mendes is too."

Uncle James raised his hand pad as Heath lunged a front kick into the stuffing.

The two men had always had their heart to heart talks while working up a sweat in the dojo.

"Now why don't you pay Gloria a visit?" Heath asked his uncle. "She's a good looking lady; you're somewhat of a good looking man yourself."

James brought the pad around and slapped Heath playfully on the side of his head.

"Somewhat good looking?"

The fact was, James Rosary looked like an older, more distinguished version of his nephew. The 55-year-old kept in perfect physical condition. The only differences between James and Heath were a few wrinkle lines and a mustache.

"You better hope you look like me when you're my age," James boasted. "Don't worry about my love life. When are you going to smarten up and marry that wonderful lady of yours?"

James had been kidding his nephew about it for years.

"That's kind of why I came here today," Heath replied in a serious voice.

"Don't bullshit me boy."

"I'm not Uncle James. I'm taking her up to a little B&B in ski country this weekend. I'm gonna pop the question up there."

Tears welled up in James Rosary's brown eyes. He was the dictionary definition of tough, but could dissolve into a puddle around his kids. That's exactly what Heath and Carla were, they were *his kids*. After graduating college, James Rosary signed up for officer's training school and three combat tours in Vietnam. He survived that horror and returned to Roxbury in the early 1970's where he found another war being fought in the old neighborhood. It was a war on drugs and like most inner city neighborhoods, Roxbury was losing badly. Rosary took custody of his young nephew and niece after their heroin addicted mother ran away with some man she had met at a bar. He raised them as his own, with the belief that his sister would never come back. He had never adopted the children, but he was their parent all the same. Uncle James was mommy and daddy all rolled into one.

"I was hoping this day would come," He said wrapping his nephew tightly in his powerful arms. "Look at me. I'm crying like a damn baby."

"It's alright, Uncle James. I have a feeling Grace's father will be crying to, but for different reasons."

CHAPTER 10

▼

BOSTON

Jessi Miller sat with her back straight and arms folded at the anchor desk. She wore a hunter green blazer that matched her eyes perfectly. She had just thrown it over to the meteorologist when her producer informed her of breaking news.

"The President has just announced that he's sending his father to China as Special Envoy for the six-nation talks with North Korea," Grace Chen told her in her earpiece. "The summit is set for the third week of November and will also include South Korea, Japan and Russia. After weather, I want you to ad-lib a reader on the summit before you toss to sports."

Miller gave the okay sign and jotted down a few notes while the weather man was describing the seven day forecast, which proved almost never to be right. The meteorologist finished his report at the chroma-key wall and the studio camera zoomed in on the anchor woman for a single shot.

"Cue Jessi," the control room director ordered.

Miller thanked the weatherman with a smile and then turned serious. She ad-libbed the breaking story as it had been told to her by Grace. Miller also pointed out that the President's father was no stranger to China, having served as American ambassador there himself in the mid-seventies. She promised the audience more information on this breaking story coming up on the network news. Miller then turned to her sports anchor for a preview of the upcoming Patriots showdown with the Dallas Cowboys. The sports guy made a few unscripted wise cracks and pitched to a reporter live at Gillette Stadium in Foxboro. The camera was off Miller and she looked down at her watch. *Just a few more minutes,* she told herself.

"Just a few more minutes," Grace whispered into her earpiece.

Miller smiled. Not only was Grace Chen the best television producer she had ever worked with, she was also her best friend. The two had been inseparable since rooming together during their freshman year at Boston University. Grace was the urbane sophisticate. Miller was the wide-eyed farm girl from Fort Kent, Maine, having grown up working the potato fields of Aroostooc County along the Canadian border. Picking potatoes in early fall in the hot Maine sun had strengthened her arms and stained her hands a permanent shade of green. She never really noticed it until she came to Boston and classmates began looking at her funny. Thank God for Grace, who was able to hide the blemishes with a few layers of makeup. Beauty tips were not the only advice Grace offered; she had also opened Jessi's eyes to a whole new world of art, music and fashion that did not exist at the northern tip of Maine. Miller was a single child and Grace had two older brothers. To call theirs, a friendship was an understatement; Jessi Miller and Grace Chen were sisters. They grew even closer the day they both graduated from Boston University with degrees in Journalism. She remembered sitting next to Grace in their matching black caps and red gowns at Boston University's Nickerson Field, where they shared an umbrella and tried to stay dry in the driving rain. When she was called to the podium to receive her diploma, Jessi walked on stage; shook the university President's hand and received her degree. She then looked out over the rain swept crowd hoping to see her parents standing and clapping. They should have been there; they had started out on the long drive from Fort Kent to Boston well before dawn. Jessi was on a full academic scholarship and her parents could not afford to spend the night at a pricey Boston hotel. She did not see her parents in the crowd, or at the cocktail reception that followed. Jessi was concerned, but what she did not know was that her parents, Carl and Connie Miller, had been killed hours earlier in a head-on collision with a drunken trucker on his way back to Quebec City. B.U. officials had been informed of the crash and an information officer was on his way to deliver the news. The man entered the reception tent and asked a colleague to point out Jessi Miller. Grace was close by chatting with a classmate and her head spun around. She asked the information officer what he wanted to see her friend about and he reluctantly told her. Fighting back tears, Grace took down the all the details on the crash and urged the man back to his office. She took a moment to compose herself and then waded through the lively crowd in search of her best friend. Grace took Jessi by the hand and led her away from the party. The rain had stopped and the sun was shining now. She found a quiet place under a shaded tree and broke the news.

Grace had been there for her then, and she was there for her now. The friends had separated briefly after college when Grace had parlayed an internship into a full time position at WBZ News and Jessi went back to Northern Maine, where small television stations hired on air talent right out of college. The pay was horrible, but at least Jessi was accustomed to the harsh weather. Her friend Grace meanwhile, climbed through the ranks of the television newsroom and landed the job as producer for the six o'clock news. It was one of the most coveted positions in the newsroom, and Grace wielded enough influence with her employers to convince them to take a chance on her friend from Northern Maine. In just a few short years, Jessi Miller would become the most popular television personality in Boston, and the first solo female anchor in the station's 60-year history. Her salary topped seven hundred thousand dollars and she lived in a luxury condominium in the heart of the city. Her agent had just told her that she was even beginning to turn heads at the network level. Jessi Miller had fame; she had fortune but the one thing she was missing was true love. Not true love in the romantic sense. She had plenty of admirers, though she felt most men were insecure about her beauty and high profile career. What she was missing now was the love of family. Grace filled that void somewhat, but she had her own life with Heath and Jessi did not want to spoil that. She needed someone that she could care about more than she cared for herself. Her daydream was broken by the voice of her producer in her earpiece.

"Adlib your goodbye and remember to tease more about that breaking story on the CBS Evening News," Grace reminded her.

Jessi thanked the viewers for watching as music began to play under her words. She shuffled her scripts while the studio camera took a sweeping shot of the anchor set.

"That's a keeper," Grace told her.

Jessi took out her earpiece and marched out of the studio to the applause of her co-workers. They knew this would be her last show for the next few months.

She met Grace in the hallway and wrapped her arms around her in a tight squeeze.

"Now, the girls have a little something planned for you upstairs in the cafeteria," Grace informed her.

Jessi arched an eyebrow and looked at her friend. "What have you been up to?"

"What?" Grace replied throwing up her arms in mock protest. "You don't think I'd let my best friend fly off to China without a little baby shower do you?"

The friends hugged again as Grace led her to the staircase and up to the café.

With pink and yellow streamers hanging from the ceiling, the lunchroom had been transformed into a nursery for the occasion. The café was packed with colleagues from the television station and some old friends from college. A bouquet of balloons was wrapped around a wicker chair in the middle of the room. Jessi barely noticed it however; she was mesmerized by a large poster sized photo of her new daughter resting on the menu board. She wanted to cry. A banner that read; *Welcome Sasha* hung over the poster. The picture was the only one sent by the Chinese government three months before, when Jessi was finally granted permission to adopt the child. Little Sasha was just six months old in the picture and her rosy cheeks reminded Jessi of her favorite Russian grandmother, the woman she had named the baby for.

Once she had been matched with the child, Jessi had put together a care package and sent it off to the orphanage never thinking it would actually get there. But the poster was proof that it did. In the photograph, the baby wore the yellow jumper from the *GAP* and had ten ribbons in her hair. Jessi had mailed a package of ribbons, but could not imagine that the baby would be wearing all of them at once. The woman who ran the adoption agency said it was a sign that the orphanage wanted to please the new mother as much as possible. Jessi smiled at the poster and then turned to Grace.

"You've thought of everything," she told her best friend.

"Don't get weepy on me. Just sit down and open the presents," Grace replied wiping away her own tears.

A mountain of gifts awaited Jessi as she took her seat in the center of the room. She looked to the right and noticed a buffet table set up in the corner. The affair had been catered by a small Chinese joint located near the station. Grace walked over to the table and picked up an egg roll with her delicate fingers.

"Here's to your last dish of American-Chinese food," she told her friend while others laughed. "You won't be seeing this stuff when you get to China."

It had been a joke between the two friends. Grace had warned her that traditional Chinese cuisine was far more exotic than the Americanized version. Grace walked over to the presents and handed one to Jessi.

"Open it, open it," her female colleagues screamed.

Jessi studied the package briefly. It was a light weight tube of some kind covered in bright pink wrapping paper. She opened a small card attached to the present and read it aloud.

"It says, "you've certainly given us plenty of shit over the years. It's payback time." It's signed; the boys in the newsroom."

Jessi tore open the wrapping paper and burst into laughter. Her male colleagues had given her a Diaper Genie. A dizzying number of presents followed. Each little outfit was met with an emotional sigh from the gathered guests. In return, Jessi handed out hugs to her friends and told them what the day meant to her.

"Tomorrow, I'm getting on that plane to pick up my little girl," she said choking back tears. "I'll be bringing along a little piece of each of you with me."

After the guests had gone, it was just the two of them in the cafeteria. Grace was helping Jessi organize the bounty of baby gifts she had just received.

"Grace I want to ask you something," Jessi said while folding a tiny Irish knit sweater given to her by her news director.

"Sure babe, ask me anything," Grace replied nonchalantly.

Jessi reached over and held her friend's hand in her own.

"I want you to be the Godmother to my child."

A feeling of warmth washed over both of them. "You know that I would be honored," Grace told her.

"It's more than an honor, Grace. It's a commitment. I need to know that if anything ever happens to me, you'll take care of little Sasha."

Grace tried to laugh it off. "What could happen to you?"

"After the death of my parents, at least I had you to lean on." Jessi was crying now.

"Who will Sasha have? She's already been through so much in her little life already."

Grace understood the seriousness of the request.

"Jessi, if anything were to ever happened to you, I promise that I will watch over little Sasha and care for her as if she was my own."

"Thank you," Jessi replied as the two embraced and wept together.

CHAPTER 11

▼

HONG KONG

Ju-Long Lew bit down hard on his knuckle as he stared at the large jade Buddha positioned against the wall of his study. His front tooth pierced the skin of his finger and he tasted a droplet of warm blood on his tongue. The door was locked and he was alone. Beads of sweat covered his forehead as he fought off the painful urge to chase the dragon. Like a silk worm devouring a Mulberry leaf, his appetite was insatiable. The opium was now taking control of his body and his mind. He was also fighting the urge to do *other* things. Lew's addiction to the drug had been overcome only by his growing thirst to kill.

He had become a God in his protest against God. Instead of accepting the hand he had been dealt, he lashed out at the world around him. He was one of the world's richest men, and yet he could not have a manly relationship with his own wife. Her obstetrician had seen to that. Lixian had suffered severe perineal trauma to her vagina during the birth of their daughter. Despite Lixian's pushing, the baby's head could not get past her pelvic bone and Lixian's doctor, a red-haired, green-eyed American from Victoria Hospital had ignored pleas from a nurse to perform a caesarian section while they still had time. With the use of forceps, the doctor managed to pull the baby out, but the harm had already been done. The baby had suffered brain damage from a lack of oxygen during delivery, and the damage to Lixian was also irreversible. Because of the injury, the doctor informed her that she could no longer bear children. The physical pain Lixian felt, also made sexual intercourse impossible. The injury had turned the once frisky Asian beauty completely frigid toward her husband. Lew did not blame his wife; instead he blamed the doctor who should have known better. He would make her and anyone that looked like her pay for the injuries to his daughter, his wife and his pride. He remembered the power he felt when he strangled the doctor in a fit of rage inside her own office. He also remembered the strange feeling of arousal he got as he squeezed the life slowly out of her hazel eyes. Fortunately for him, he had the talented Mister Wong standing by to clean up the mess. Her murder file was still among the thousands of unsolved crimes collecting dust at the Hong Kong Police Department.

The murder of the doctor also fed his growing attraction and disdain for Caucasian women. Mister Wong had supplied him with look-alikes and had outdone himself in the kidnapping of Miss Universe. Her picture stood out among dozens of photos of contestants sent to Lew's office in a pageant brochure. Thai officials had offered front row seats to the pageant to several of Asia's top businessmen. Lew thought of going himself until he saw the small photo of Sophie Doucet staring at him from the pamphlet. That is when another plan began to form in his mind.

It had been several days since Mister Wong had desposed of the last victim. He promised that he would find a suitable replacement. *What was taking so long?*

Lew was getting restless; he felt the dragon growing inside of him. He was evolving without the use of the powerful hallucinogen. Now, when he sat at the head of the table during Lew Petroleum board meetings, he could only think about ripping off the heads of his subordinates as they talked about the latest profit margins and offered suggestions on how *he* could better run *his* company. *How dare these insolent little gnats tell me how to do things? I started with a small petrol station that serviced Hong Kong cabbies and grew it into the oil giant it is today.*

He had never killed a man before, at least not with his own hands. Mister Wong had been called upon to perform that duty on more than a few occasions. *What would it feel like?* Ju-Long Lew was now determined to find out. His twisted fantasies were pushing the real problems from his mind. The $3 billion Kazakhstan pipeline agreement had raised some angry eyebrows in Beijing. The government countered that pact with a mega deal of its own. China and Iran signed an agreement worth $100 billion soon after. The agreement would allow China's state oil company to participate in exploration, drilling and pipeline projects in Iran's Yad Avaran oil field. Lew had been working on his own Iranian oil deal for months, only to see it taken out from under him. It was just another sign that China was trying to relegate Lew Petroleum to the sidelines in the global oil game. He was already paying the Chinese government ten percent of his total earnings. It was a deal that was struck when Hong Kong reverted back to Chinese rule in 1997. If the communists had not agreed to the proposal, Lew would have taken his growing oil empire to Taiwan. What could stop them from seizing control of his company? The answer was nothing. That is why Lew paid handsome fees to spies within the Politburo and the military. If they were coming after him, at least he would have a head start.

There was even a provision in the 1997 charter that said the state could take control of Lew Petroleum if the company and its owner failed to meet certain standards of society and business. A team of international lawyers urged him not to take the deal, but Lew was a nationalist at heart and wanted to help the Republic of China take its rightful place among the world's super powers. It was now more than ten years later and Lew wished he had taken their advice. It was the one mistake he had made in a career of shrewd business maneuvers. He felt the weight of the world on his shoulders and his only relief could be found behind the jade Buddha.

BEIJING

Pu-Yan puffed on a Marlboro as he leafed through the Central Committee profile of his new objective. He had been reading for three hours and had only stopped periodically to flick fallen cigarette ashes off the pages. The pudgy, bespectacled bureaucrat had just been given a golden opportunity, one which he did not know whether he truly deserved. He gazed out his small office window at the vast public square below. A large group of tourists were gathered outside Chairman Mao's Memorial Hall for the changing of the guard ceremony. Dozens of multi-colored dragon kites chased one another across the smog filled sky. It was almost impossible to believe what had happened there in Tiananmen Square back in 1989. The bloody crackdown of students had been witnessed by a shocked and horrified world. Pu-Yan had been a college student himself then. He remembered cheering on the pro-democracy students in his own thoughts. Those thoughts were never articulated out loud, especially to his father, a powerful member of the Politburo.

Now behind his back, rivals were comparing Pu-Yan to the disgraced dissidents of Tiananmen Square. It was all because of the debacle called, the Mongolian Sour Milk Super Girl contest. Pu-Yan created the television show during his days as a rising star within the Ministry of Communications. The program was supposed to highlight China's most talented and beautiful women in a singing contest modeled after the western hit, *American Idol*. The Central Committee was not looking for a new singing star; what it was really trying to do was curb the alarming trend of young Chinese men marrying outside the country. A growing number were finding wives in Thailand, Korea and even Vietnam. Panic had set in among the xenophobic communist hierarchy. There were enough available women here in China, they believed; and the television show would be a showcase for that. The Mongolian Sour Milk Super Girl contest was a smash hit. More than 400 million Chinese tuned in every week; that was more than the populations of the United States and Mexico combined. As executive producer, Pu-Yan set out to imitate *American Idol* in every facet of the program, even how the number of contestants was narrowed down each week, and how a winner was eventually chosen. He thought nothing of it at the time, but Pu-Yan had given the Chinese people something they had never had before: the right to choose. Millions of viewers called in each week to vote for their favorite singer. In an otherwise meaningless television show, the seeds of democracy were being sewn.

If he were not the son of a high ranking Politburo official, Pu-Yan would have been exiled to some Godforsaken outpost in the Gobi desert, or thrown in prison for promoting Western thought. Instead, he had been given another chance, this time in the Ministry of Business Affairs. He wanted to make his father and the Politburo proud, and he knew the Central Committee responded favorably to only two things: power and money. Pu-Yan's plan would secure his government both. He stubbed out his cigarette and continued reading the personal file on Ju-Long Lew.

LYON, FRANCE

Henri Bouchard never carried an umbrella when he walked in the rain. He did not wear a hat either. He loved the feeling of raindrops beeding down on his bald scalp. The rain cleared his head and also helped clear the streets and wash away the garbage. Bouchard was walking through one of the most beautiful neighborhoods in France, but today it looked like a war zone. The metal shells of two burned out Peugeots sat smoldering along the side of the cobblestone street. Bouchard did his best to dodge the broken glass, which seemed to be everywhere. It had been another night of violence in Lyon and every other major city in France. Muslim youths were rioting in the streets to protest the deaths of two teenagers who were killed by an electrical transformer while fleeing police. A spokesperson for the Paris police department insisted the officers were not chasing the teens when they were electrocuted. The truth did not seem to matter now. Paris was burning again and the wild fire of religious fanaticism had spread across the country side. Young Muslims were now shouting *Jihad* as they hurled Molotov cocktails at police. The hatred felt by the disenfranchised youth had been incubated inside radical mosques that spread like locusts across Europe. Bouchard wondered when the bottle throwers would begin *Takfir*, the likely next step in their war to restore the *Caliphate*. *Takfir* was an extremist ideal that gave Muslim men carte-blanche to murder other Muslims who stood in the way of imposing *Sharia* law to the *Chosen* ones. *The world had truly gone crazy,* Bouchard thought to himself.

Bouchard had been desperate to get out for a walk and away from his colleagues at Interpol. Their jokes were now getting under the young detective's skin. His American and British counterparts were taking bets on how long it would take France to surrender this time. "How do you hold off the French police?" the American jokingly asked the Brit. "Don't throw Molotov cocktails, throw soap and toothpaste instead." The two men got a big laugh out of that one. They looked over at Bouchard and shrugged their shoulders as if to say, "Lighten up, it's only a joke."

The Frenchman was not in the mood for a confrontation. Tensions between him and his colleagues were already high thanks to their respective nation's stances on the war in Iraq. He did not want to add fuel to the fire.

That's a bad choice of words, he thought.

The rain was coming down hard now, so Bouchard ducked into the traboule of La Croix Rousse. The traboule was one of many ancient passageways in the area known as Europe's largest Renaissance quarter. Their original purpose was to provide shelter for silk weavers as they moved their materials from one place to the next. It was now Lyon's biggest tourist attraction. Bouchard had hung more than a dozen posters with Sophie Doucet's picture in the busy thoroughfare. The banner along the top of the posters read, *Missing* and her description was written out in six languages underneath. The posters were plastered on store fronts and electrical poles in an effort to keep the case fresh in people's minds. It had been six months since the kidnapping of Sophie Doucet and that seemed like a lifetime ago in today's twenty-four hour news cycle. Bouchard stared at the poster with hard blue eyes. His fingers scratched at the dark whiskers of his goatee.

"Where are you Sophie?" he whispered knowing the poster would not answer him back. The likelihood that she was still alive was slim, considering what her killer had done to her mother. Rebecca Doucet's throat had been cut across the Adam's apple and the crime scene was a bloody mess when investigators first arrived. It looked like the sloppy work of someone who was in a hurry. Would the kidnapper show so little patience with Sophie? There was another picture on the poster, a smaller one. It was that of Phra Nang, head of security at the IMPACT arena. There was strong evidence to suggest that Phra Nang was not even his real name. A check of his background led Bouchard through a labyrinth of forged documents, phony companies and dead ends. How the kidnapper managed to get hired was still a mystery to Bouchard. He voiced his anger several times to law enforcement officials in Thailand and now they were no longer cooperating with the investigation.

"I'll find you Kayser Soze," he whispered again at the poster. Bouchard had stopped calling the kidnapper by his alias; instead he renamed the man after the mysterious main character of his favorite movie *The Usual Suspects*.

"Do you even exist?" he asked, before immediately corrected himself. "Of course you do, and I will find you. What have you done with my Sophie?"

This was not just another criminal case for detective Henri Bouchard. He was not only searching for France's most famous woman, he was also searching for his childhood love.

CHAPTER 12

▼

BOSTON

Jessi Miller ground her perfect white teeth as she pulled the heavy cart carrying her suitcases toward the United Airlines terminal at Logan Airport. She brought with her four pieces of luggage; three for the baby and one for her. She wore a blue nylon track suit and had her red hair pulled back in a ponytail under a black Nike baseball cap. She wore the cap despite a warning from the adoption agency not to wear clothing with recognizable American labels. The Chinese were said to be outraged over the war in Iraq and the adoptive families were urged not to provoke any anti-American sentiments during their trip.

Jessi thought the warning was ridiculous and it certainly was the last thing on her mind right now as she ran toward the United Airlines check in counter. She was running late, *again*. She could never keep time and it was a habit that gave Grace fits in the minutes leading up to the nightly newscasts. Grace proved to be a life saver this morning though. Jessi had planned to take a cab to the airport, but her best friend had sent her a chauffeur driven limousine instead. The driver was holding a sign that read; *Congrats Mom! Love, Grace & Heath* when he rang the doorbell. The gesture made Jessi cry. In fact, she had been doing a lot of crying lately. *Gotta be the nerves. Get yourself together girl,* she thought to herself.

She had spent the morning going over her check list, and going over it once more. She had her passport and traveler's checks in a zipper locked belt tied tightly around her waist. The money belt was covered by her nylon jacket. Unlike the clothing warning, Jessi did take the warning about pick-pockets very seriously. She checked the baby's suitcases and then re-checked them. The luggage was packed with baby food, sanitary wipes, diapers and infant's Tylenol. Jessi also packed two jars of skin cream to deal with that mysterious Mongolian spot she had read so much about. She was surprised to discover that most Chinese babies were born with a large bluish spot on their buttocks. The Chinese called it, a *Mongolian spot*. It was not a birth mark per se, but a skin abnormality that would disappear over time. As for Sasha's clothes, Jessi made sure that her baby would be the best dressed child in China. One suitcase was filled with adorable little outfits from *Laura Ashley* and *Lord & Taylor*.

The focus on her luggage had taken Jessi's attention away from the clock. She was startled by the chauffeur's ring of the doorbell. She looked at the security monitor next to the front door and saw the driver in his black uniform waiting in the lobby.

"Fuck," she screamed as she turned her attention to the antique grandfather clock in the foyer of her condo. Jessi was running twenty minutes behind schedule. There would be no time for the glamorous anchor woman to put her face on. Instead, she put on a pair of Ray Ban sunglasses, grabbed her luggage and hit the door. Only the chauffeur's heart felt sign gave her a moment of pause to realize exactly how special this morning was. As the driver placed the suitcases in the trunk of his limo, Jessi looked back toward her building. *When I come back, I'll be a mommy.*

Jessi found her adoptive group at Logan airport and placed her bags alongside theirs. All the suitcases were marked with the bright yellow flags of the *Hands across the World* adoption agency. Jessi felt a little uncomfortable; after all, she was the only single woman traveling with twelve couples. Most were from the Boston area and had recognized her from television. One other couple had joined the group from Louisville, Kentucky. They were easy to point out because they were wearing blue University of Kentucky sweatshirts. They had also not heeded the warning about American clothing. Mitch and Gertie Anderson also brought along their two boys; Jeffrey age 13 and Mitch Jr. age 9.

"It's gonna be an experience of a lifetime for them," Mitch and Gertie beamed in unison to anyone within earshot.

The boys were already raising hell, making fart noises with their armpits as they climbed all over the plastic chairs near the check in counter. The kids were no doubt looking forward to spreading their adolescent terror to a foreign country. They reminded Jessi of the farm boys she grew up with back in Fort Kent, Maine.

It's going to be a long trip, she thought.

She just didn't realize how long. They took a jet from Boston to Chicago's O'Hare airport and transferred to a larger plane for the non-stop flight to Beijing, China.

Jessi hated to fly. After covering the September 11ᵗʰ attacks and seeing the raw unedited footage of the tragedy and its aftermath, she vowed never to fly again. It was an unrealistic vow, especially for one in her profession. But that all changed after she watched a PBS special on Chinese adoption. She had not planned on watching the program; Jessi was just flipping around the television channels one night when it caught her eye. The program not only captured her attention, it changed her life.

All her time and money over the next year was committed to adopting a baby. She filled out countless forms and suffered the embarrassment of having to explain to the Chinese government her arrest for using a fake ID while in college. After finally getting the approvals of both the Chinese and American governments and forking over $26,000, the moment was almost here. Minutes after take off from Chicago, the passengers settled in for the marathon flight ahead. Some selected a movie to watch, others pulled out a book to read. Jessi did neither. She stared at her baby's photo and prayed.

Please God, help me be a good mother to this child.

*   *   *   *

Back on the ground and a few thousand miles away, Heath Rosary was asking for help of his own. He was behind the wheel of Grace's black BMW driving toward the White Mountains of New Hampshire. He looked over at Grace, who was curled up in the passenger seat with her nose stuck in the latest Dara Joy romance novel. Heath could not make out the title, but he could see a long haired, bare chested man on the cover.

"Lemme guess, he's a dastardly pirate pursuing a forbidden romance with an admiral's daughter," he teased with a smile.

"Shut up, you dork," Grace laughingly replied without looking up from her book.

Heath was doing his best to keep up with the small talk. It helped disguise the panic he felt inside. He was going to ask her to marry him, and he was terrified by her likely reply.

She'll say yes won't she? Then what? I know I can be a good husband, but what about a good father? I didn't exactly have a set of model parents.

The voice inside Heath's head was replaced by the familiar stern voice of his uncle. He knew what James would say if he heard those questions.

I raised you and you turned out pretty damned good. You'll be a good father to your children Heathcliff, just like I was to you. Still, Rosary had never gotten over his fear of abandonment. He had never met his own father and was just eight-years-old when his mother left. He still had the journal he kept during the first months she was gone. It was filled with promises of how he'd be a better boy once she returned. *I don't know why I still have that musty notebook.* Deep down however, he did know. The journal was the only memory he had of his mother. There were no mementos of their life together, no pictures taken around the Christmas tree; he hadn't even seen a Christmas tree until he moved in with his uncle. Heath and his younger sister were born into a tough life. His mother would take off for days at a time, leaving Heath to care for Carla in their messy cockroach infested apartment. Looking back on it, Rosary realized that his abandonment was a blessing in disguise, yet it still haunted him. During the brief periods when she wasn't stoned, his mother would hug him and show him the kindness that he had yearned for. *Christ, I should be a guest on Dr. Phil,* he thought trying to shake the pain away.

He needed to focus his attention on something else for awhile, so he flipped through several CDs that were tucked away in pockets tied to the overhead visor.

Her taste in music is about as good as her taste in authors. Let's see, there's Sinead O'Connor, Tracy Chapman and Joni Mitchell.

It wasn't exactly what Heath called, driving music. His eyes lit up though, when we found a Santana CD. *It's not the new crap either,* Heath thought. He opened the case to Abraxas and slid the CD into the player. The sounds of *Oye Como Va* soon filled the car. Grace responded to his music selection with a curl of her lip. She clearly would have chosen Sinead O'Connor.

God she's beautiful, even when she's being a pain in the ass.

She could tell what he was thinking.

"I'd be in a better mood, if you'd just tell me where we're going," she baited him.

Heath held the steering wheel with his left hand and pulled a brochure from his jacket with his right.

"Here you go," he said handing it over to Grace, whose brown eyes lit up immediately. She sat up straight in the passenger seat and read the brochure aloud.

"The Nestlenook Farm resort in scenic Jackson, New Hampshire."

Grace gazed at a color picture of the Victorian Gingerbread inn emblazoned on the cover of the brochure.

"Oh Honey, it's beautiful. It says here the rooms have hand carved canopy beds, stone fireplaces and Jacuzzis!"

She leaned over and nibbled on his ear.

"I can't wait to take you for a swim."
"Neither can I baby," he responded. "Neither can I."
He placed his hand on her knee and the anxiety was gone.

CHAPTER 13

▼

The snow began to fall as Rosary drove the black BMW through the red covered bridge into Jackson, New Hampshire. The wintry scene was a Currier & Ives print come to life. They continued down a winding country road and took a right at the sign for the Nestlenook resort. The pavement gave way to a dirt road which led to the inn. Heath slowed the car down and drove cautiously down the path. The couple pulled into the resort and passed a large barn on the right.

"That's where they keep the horses," Heath pointed out. "According to the brochure, we can take a sleigh ride through white and drifted snow."

Further ahead, they saw a family ice skating on a frozen pond in front of the inn.

"This is like a fairy tale," Grace told Heath. "Can anything top this?"

I certainly hope so, Heath thought to himself.

He parked the sleek black sedan in the small parking lot and they both stepped out of the car to stretch their legs. The two and a half hour drive from Boston was tough on Rosary's knees. He brought his knees up to his chest and stretched the pain away. He then leaned over and pulled two sets of skis from the rack fastened to the roof of the car. Grace was a champion skier and had spent most of her life on the slopes, while Heath had picked up the sport relatively late in life. Skiing had been frowned upon in his last two professions. He remembered what his former coach used to say during his brief stint with the Patriots. "A Mountain is like a beautiful stripper. You can look, but you can't touch." His supervisor at the Secret Service had also warned him to stay off the slopes. An agent on crutches was as useless as tits on a bull, Rosary was told. He took the skis off the car, but fumbled when he tried to carry them both under his arms.

"You look like you could use some help with your pole," Grace teased with a grin. She fooled most people with her demure shell. Only Heath knew the shell opened up to a devil inside.

"Did I make you blush, Mister Rosary?"

"You can't make a black man blush," he countered.

"We'll just see about that."

They strolled through the quaint lobby and passed the succulent aroma of baked apples coming from the inn's rustic kitchen. Roast Pork was the special of the evening. Heath could hear his stomach growl as they climbed a majestic staircase to their second floor suite. A bellboy followed with their bags. Rosary tipped the man a twenty and watched as he disappeared back down the stairs. He turned the key to their suite and breathed a sigh of relief when he saw that the manager had followed through on his request. A pile of rose petals met them at the door and continued in a trail to the bed. They were still in the entryway when Grace turned and kissed him on the lips. He felt her tongue roll around his own.

"Close the door," she whispered breathlessly.

He followed the order without breaking the embrace. Once the door was closed, Grace attacked his clothes, pulling off his red ski jacket and tearing open his tan flannel shirt. She licked her way down his firm chest and began nibbling on his nipples. She knew this drove him wild and she got an immediate response. Grace grew moist, as she felt him growing harder against her thigh. He picked her up in his powerful arms and carried her toward the canopy bed. Heath laid her down on top of the soft comforter and began peeling off her clothes, first her jeans; then her white turtleneck. Soon they were both naked and wrapped in each other's arms. Grace continued to kiss him hungrily, as she rolled Heath onto his back and straddled his hips. She lowered herself onto his throbbing organ, while he massaged and kissed her small breasts. Their bodies were now moving rhythmically as one. Grace's loud moaning only excited him more. He could feel a powerful orgasm building up inside of him, as his thrusts came harder and faster. Grace was overcome by the sheer raw energy of their lovemaking. Her moans were amplified to the point where she was screaming out his name.

"Heath, oh my God. I'm cumming," she shouted, wrapping her legs around his.

Her words brought him immediately to climax.

They squeezed one another tightly and collapsed in each other's arms. They stayed that way for several minutes, both too exhausted to move. Heath continued to kiss her until they drifted off to sleep. They made love twice more that evening, exploring each other's bodies slowly, curiously, as if it were the first time.

Heath kneeled by the fire place stoking the Vermont logs with an iron poker. He gazed at the flames and then over to the bed where Grace was still asleep. Their lives were about to change forever, assuming she accepted his proposal. They had been dating for years while watching their friends sail off into the uncharted waters of marriage. Those friends called Heath and Grace, *Kurt* and *Goldie*, after the together forever, but never wed Hollywood stars. Those friends were unaware of the obstacles that had been put up to prevent them from taking the next step. One obstacle was their busy careers, but the biggest hurdle was clearly Grace's father. There was still no thaw in that cold war; he remained adamantly opposed to their relationship. Tommy Chen was her only surviving parent; her mother had died of breast cancer when she was a teenager. Chen was rich, powerful and somewhat distant to his only daughter. She spent her life fighting to gain his approval. He wanted her to marry a fellow Chinese, and when she told him she was involved with a black man; their delicate relationship fractured even more. Grace was caught between the two men she loved. She refused to stop seeing Heath, but did not flaunt the relationship in front of her father. Marriage would change all that. The five carat diamond engagement ring felt like a boulder in Rosary's pocket. Their relationship was nearly perfect, why would he want to take a chance to ruin it? He watched the reflection of the flames dancing off Grace's naked body and knew the answer.

I want to spend the rest of my life with this woman; that's why.

C H A P T E R 14

▼

HONG KONG

Tang Lung Wei checked his Rolex watch and tapped his shoe against the cobblestone entryway to the Lew Mansion. He then checked his reflection in the clear window of the front door. His hair was slicked back and his mustache neatly trimmed. He wore an aqua blue blazer and white cotton slacks. A white silk shirt opened at the collar and a pair of designer sunglasses completed the look. The young executive had a date with a delectable exotic dancer planned after this brief business meeting. He continued to tap his loafer against the cobblestone. He was getting angry. Wei was not a man who liked to be kept waiting. He served as Vice President of Lew Petroleum and knew that it was only a matter of time before he would take control of the entire company. Educated at Stanford University and only thirty-two-years old, Tang Lung Wei was brilliant, young and hungry. Unlike his boss, whom he felt no longer had the eye of the tiger when it came to business.

He already has his billions, of course he's no longer hungry to make more; but what about me? Wei thought, growing more agitated by the second. Suddenly, the front double door was opened and an armed guard ushered him inside. Wei walked on the marble floor and took in the opulence around him. He hated coming here to his boss's home. It wasn't really a home at all, it was a fortress fit for a king. Wei thought about his own home, which was modest in comparison. *I too will have a castle like this,* he vowed.

Bao Lew heard someone entering the mansion and shuffled down the hallway hoping to see Mister Wong. The girl's smiling face turned to a frown when she saw the man from her father's company. *No fun, just Baba's work,* she thought. Still, she acted like quite the lady and offered the man her hand.

Oh great, now I've got to kow-tow to the retard daughter, Wei thought to himself. He flashed an insincere smile and kissed the girl's hand. The timing was perfect; her father watched the gesture as he walked down the hall.

"My dear friend, this is a pleasant surprise," Lew said with open arms.

The men hugged briefly and Wei reached into his coat pocket for his cigarettes.

Lew had his back to his vice president, when the man lit the Marlboro red and puffed vigorously.

"What do you think you are doing?" Lew shouted as he spun around.

Wei shrugged nervously; he didn't know what was wrong.

Lew grabbed the cigarette from the man's lips; threw it to the ground and stamped it with his foot.

"There is no smoking in this house," he scolded his subordinate. "Bao has difficulty breathing as it is."

Wei offered his apology and both men walked toward Lew's office. Bao giggled and the young executive shot her a scowl when her father wasn't looking. The men entered the private den and closed the door. Wei stared at the large jade Buddha sitting against the wall. He envied the lavishness, and his hate for his boss grew deeper.

"So what is the meaning of this visit on a Saturday?" Lew asked, as he sat in the leather chair behind his glass top desk.

"I wish this was a more pleasurable visit," Wei told him. "I have come here today in hopes of persuading you to become more involved in the day to day operations of the company. We have missed two recent business opportunities because you were not available to approve the deals. The board is very concerned. The members do not know that I am here however. I have used discretion. I wanted to discuss this with you quietly, man to man."

Man to man? How dare you treat me with such a lack of respect, Lew thought to himself. He swallowed his anger and nodded at his subordinate, but did not reply.

Wei continued to bait him. "I must admit that I have found you distant in recent meetings. Is there something wrong with your health, sir?" *I certainly hope so.*

"There is nothing wrong with my health," Lew chuckled. "I was merely giving you a test. I wanted to see if you could handle this company on your own. I am grooming you to become my successor. I am getting old, and my company needs someone like you to take it into a new direction."

Wei was taken aback by the news. Maybe his boss wasn't so stupid after all.

"You have humbled me, sir," Wei said bowing to his superior.

I doubt that, Lew thought as he punched a key on his computer, stood up and hugged his vice president. Lew pointed to the wall as the large jade Buddha slid across the floor.

"Your success is well deserved," Lew told him. "Now that you will be taking over the business, I would like to show you some of the treasures that you too will now be able to afford."

The statue gave way to an elevator door. It was like something from a *James Bond* movie, Wei thought. His boss walked over and placed his eye up to the retinal scan, which opened the door. Both stepped inside and the elevator began moving down.

Moments later, the door opened.

"What is this place?" Wei asked his boss as he looked around the small art gallery.

"This is where I keep all my favorite paintings," Lew responded with pride.

Wei was something of an art buff himself. He walked over to Picasso's *Nature morte a'la Charlotte* and examined it closely.

"This is a remarkable reproduction," he told his boss. "The artist really has an eye for Picasso."

"That's because it is a Picasso," Lew replied with a laugh. He was clearly having fun now.

"But this painting was stolen in Paris a few years ago, wasn't it? I read about it in a magazine."

"Yes it was stolen and brought here," Lew beamed.

Wei looked at his boss curiously. *There is more to this man than meets the eye.*

"I'll explain later," Lew continued. "I want to show you something else."

He led the younger man down a corridor into a smaller room. Wei saw the opera masks lining the wall. There was also a Chinese broad sword hanging from two red silk ropes in the middle of the room.

"This is my private sanctuary," Lew told him.

Wei's eyes went from the wall to the floor, where he saw a pile of pillows crowded around a small table. On the table sat a bamboo tube and porcelain bowl. It made sense to him now. *So this is what is making him act so odd.* Wei was momentarily lost in thought and did not hear the subtle noises coming from behind him. He turned around and saw that his boss had one of the masks in his hand.

"Put this on please," Lew asked.

Wei thought it was a curious request, but did as he was told. He placed it over his face and found it difficult to breathe under the ceramic shell.

"You are wearing the mask of Guan Yu," Lew informed him. "Do you know much about the Chinese opera?"

Wei shook his head no.

"Oh what a pity," Lew sighed. "I've found that your generation is so ignorant to our culture and history."

Lew walked over and pulled the broad sword down from the silk ropes. The blade glistened in the darkened room. He gazed down at the sword and continued. "Guan Yu was a great general during the period of the three kingdoms. He was known for his faithfulness to his emperor Lui Bei. That's what your mask signifies; the red and black colors symbolize devotion and courage."

Wei realized where the conversation was headed. "I hope that I have demonstrated the same loyalty toward you."

Lew nodded, but did not answer the question. "Guan Yu is a great man in Chinese history, but scholars have now begun to criticize him for being arrogant and vain. Do you know what happened to Guan Yu?"

"No, I do not," Wei replied, his forehead growing moist under the mask.

"Let me show you," Lew said with a smile.

The dragon lifted the sword high above his head and swung it toward the man's neck. Tang Lung Wei had no time to scream, his body collapsed on the pillows and his detached head rolled like a bowling ball across the floor.

CHAPTER 15

▼

BEIJING

As the 747 jumbo jet made its final descent toward Beijing International Airport, Jessi Miller sat up in her passenger seat and tried to get her bearings. She had gotten only three hours of sleep during the eighteen hour flight from Chicago. The United Airlines jet flew with the sunlight as it crossed the time zones, and it was hard to tell if it was night or day. The lowlight of the flight came when the pilot informed the passengers they were flying over Siberia. The announcement drew *oohs* and *ahhs* from just about everyone except Jessi; she was nervous. *It would suck to crash, but it would really suck to crash out here in the middle of nowhere,* she thought at the time. The highlight had come when young Mitch Anderson Jr., tripped and did a face plant after running up and down the aisle screaming at the top of his tiny lungs. Jessi could not hide her smile over that one. *Sasha won't grow up to behave like that.*

She rubbed her eyes and checked her watch. Fortunately, she remembered to set her watch ahead thirteen hours. She held Sasha's picture again and closed her eyes as the jet lowered its landing gear and touched down on the runway. This was always the worst part of a flight for Jessi. She felt every bump and skid rattle through her bones.

The plane finally came to a stop and most passengers including Jessi, ignored the flight attendant's order to stay in their seats. They all had been on this plane far too long and they wanted out. Jessi grabbed her carry-on bag and stood in line to depart the plane. The adoptive parents all shared smiles with each other. *The adventure is about to begin.*

Jessi stepped out of the plane and the first thing she noticed was the stench. It attacked her nostrils the moment she stepped from the plane to the archway. Beijing had a foul odor that made it difficult to breathe. It was not a smell of rotten eggs; instead, it was an odor one would experience standing too close to a bonfire. She coughed uncontrollably and reached into her purse for a handkerchief.

"Are you okay, darling?" Gertie Anderson asked.

"Yes, I'll be alright," Jessi wheezed. "I just need to catch my breath."

"I read about the pollution here, but this smells awful," Gertie commented.

"That's why we're here to bring our babies home," Jessi replied.

Her statement gave her an instant shot of strength. She hoisted the carry-on bag over her shoulder and followed the other passengers toward customs. She and the other Americans had truly entered a different world. The Chinese were all wearing surgical masks to protect themselves from the Avian flu, SARS, or whatever the outbreak of the day happened to be. Jessi also noticed a strong military presence, as young Chinese soldiers with their brown uniforms and Kalashnikov rifles eyed every foreigner curiously, even suspiciously. Jessi knew these boys wouldn't hesitate to blow someone's head off. *I'd like to see Al Qaeda try tangling with these guys,* she thought.

The adoptive group stayed together to make sure every one of them cleared customs. The feeling of camaraderie was growing on her, as the husbands corralled the group's luggage and began carrying it through the airport. Jessi even had a pleasant conversation with young Mitch Anderson Jr. She showed him a picture of her baby and he smiled and said she was beautiful. *Maybe he's not such a little shit after all.* They walked in a group through the terminal and were met by two female representatives from *Hands across the World.* The women went by the American names, Claudia and Rita, and both appeared to be in their mid 20's. Rita was dressed like your average college student with blue jeans and a backpack pulled over her tan corduroy jacket. Claudia on the other hand, wore pin striped slacks under a long white fur coat. She wore heavy makeup, while it appeared that Rita went without. Both would act as social workers and tour guides during the group's two week journey through China. As they exited the airport terminal, the twelve families were divided up and ushered onto two separate buses.

"It looks like we have one extra person," Rita said in broken English. "Don't worry," she told Jessi. "Thirteen is not an unlucky number here in China."

Jessi placed her luggage on the second bus and both vehicles exited the airport. She stared out at the city from her window seat. It was now three o'clock in the afternoon. She remembered the pilot saying it was sunny and forty degrees when they landed, but it was hard to tell what the weather was now. Beijing was covered by a blanket of thick smog. Gertie Anderson was right; pollution was a

major problem here. Like many developing countries, China had very little con-
trols in place to monitor emissions, so factories burned coal around the clock.
Dust whipped up by sand storms from the nearby Gobi desert only added to the
pollution. Jessi pulled the collar of her blue turtleneck over her nose and inhaled
deeply. Soon the smell of fabric softener replaced the musty odor of China's capital city.

As they continued toward the hotel, Jessi was surprised by the number of cars
out on the roads; she figured that everyone in China rode bicycles. If there was a
speed limit posted, no one seemed to pay attention to it. Horns blared as motor-
ists, including the man driving Jessi's bus, drove with abandon toward their desti-
nations. *It's not as if Boston drivers are any better*, she reminded herself.

The buses pulled into the circular car port outside the Jianguo Hotel, and Jessi
could only think about checking into her room and getting a good night sleep.
The Americans stepped off the buses and were escorted through revolving brass
doors into the lobby. The dreary scenery outside was replaced by lavish color
inside. Exotic plants lined the lobby and a brightly lit crystal chandelier
demanded attention as it hung above the plush leather sitting area. The Jianguo
catered primarily to diplomats visiting Embassy Row, which was one block east
of the hotel.

Jessi walked across the smoke filled lobby toward the registration counter. She
was surprised to see that the anti-smoking nazis had yet to crack the Pacific Rim.

God could I go for a cigarette right now, she thought. Her smoking days had
ended a lifetime ago while she was still in college. Grace could not stand her best
friend's habit and forced her to run with her every morning. Jessi at first could
not run a city block without getting seriously winded. A few months and many
painful mornings later, she realized it was time to quit. Now, she was a long distance runner who made good time during the Boston Marathon every spring. *Just
one more thing that I owe Grace for,* she thought. *Who am I kidding? Grace should
be doing this, not me. She's got it all together. I'm the one who always needs to be
taken care of. I don't know the first thing about motherhood.*

Jessi took out a stick of Wrigley's spearmint gum and chewed it vigorously as
she tried to push the negative thoughts from her mind. *It's too late now girl, you're
here in China.*

"Your passport, I need your passport Ms. Miller."

Jessi did not respond. She was still in a momentary trance.

"I need your passport, please," Rita said again, this time tugging on her arm.

"Oh I'm so sorry," she blushed.

"Please, don't be sorry," Rita replied. "You have been on such a long trip, and you must be so tired. I need your passport, so I can get your room key. Claudia and I will take care of everything."

Jessi thanked the guide and pulled her passport out from the zipper locked belt tied around her waist. She handed it to Rita, who then handed it to a male clerk. The young man smiled sheepishly at Jessi and gave her back her passport along with a room key.

"He thinks you are very pretty," Rita laughed.

At another counter, the Chinese guides helped the families exchange their American dollars for Chinese Yuan. The families were also given a small index card that explained the exchange rate.

"This card will help if you dine at a restaurant or shop at a state run department store. Those places come with fixed prices," Rita told the group. "But the outdoor markets are much different. You are not expected to pay the list price for anything sold on the street. The venders expect you to barter with them for a price you can both feel comfortable with."

The Americans looked at each other with uneasy eyes. Jessi was the first to speak up.

"I'm sorry Rita, but we have so much back in America. I would feel guilty if I cheated a poor store owner out of a few dollars here."

"No, you don't understand," Rita laughed. "Haggling is an ancient tradition here in China. The shop keepers expect it and welcome it. The Chinese have been doing it for thousands of years."

"It's an ancient art back in America too, especially at Filene's Basement," Jessi replied with a grin. The other families smiled too. Rita was a little confused, but thought it best to laugh anyway.

CHAPTER 16

▼

Jessi entered her hotel room and was relieved to see her luggage waiting by the bed. She also noticed a small crib set up by the window. She walked over and lifted one of the heavy suitcases onto the queen sized bed. She opened it and worked her fingers through several infant outfits until she found what she was looking for. She pulled the soft pink teddy bear out of the suitcase and held it to her chest. The bear was identical to the one she had sent her baby in a recent care package. Jessi would bring the bear when she would meet her daughter. The head of the adoption agency believed most babies recognized their stuffed animals, and it would help ease the transition. If that did not work, Jessi had another plan in place to break the ice; *Cheerios*. She held onto the bear and reached for the baby's picture.

"Are you looking at your bear right now, like I'm looking at mine?" she asked aloud.

"I can't wait to meet you little Sasha."

It was hard to imagine that her baby was now just a few hundred miles away.

She looked around her small but tidy hotel room.

"This will be our first little home together."

Jessi spent the next few minutes unpacking and then headed straight for the shower. She brought with her a small traveling kit packed with shampoo, tooth-paste and a tooth brush. She reminded herself to place a face cloth over the water spout in the bathroom sink. Jessi had been told to brush her teeth with bottled water only. The quality of water pumping through the hotel pipes could spell disaster to a foreigner's stomach if he or she wasn't used to it. Jessi peeled off her turtleneck and jeans and let them fall to the floor. She then stepped naked into the shower and turned the knob all the way over. Soon her dirty pores and aching muscles were soothed by the hot water. She applied a healthy dose of *White Rain* shampoo to her scalp and began scrubbing eight thousand miles of travel out of her hair. She stayed in the shower for nearly a half hour as steam filled the small bathroom. It wasn't exactly a Jacuzzi at the Ritz, but it was the next best thing. Relaxed and composed, Jessi wanted nothing more than to crawl right into bed, but she felt an obligation to attend a group dinner at a nearby restaurant.

She put on a fresh pair of panties and bra and unpacked one of her favorite dresses. It was the red one she'd worn to the Emmy Awards earlier that year, when she took home an award for her expose on the new faces of the Boston mob.

She had profiled a Latin gang that now controlled neighborhoods once ruled by the Italian mafia and Irish gangsters. She was quite proud of it at the time. Few television anchors ventured outside the studio these days, and even fewer produced their own stories. Jessi's work ethic garnered the respect of her colleagues, and that was very important to her. She wasn't just another hot chick who could read a Teleprompter. This trip however, was a signal that she was putting her career on the backburner for something she felt was much more important. If that meant no more awards, then so be it.

Feeling refreshed, and looking beautiful, Jessi joined the other adoptive parents in the lobby of the hotel.

"You look like you're headed to Cinderella's Ball," Gertie Anderson told her.

"I can't help it. I'm just so excited to be here," Jessi replied. "I wanted to look nice for my first night in China."

Jessi now felt a little overdressed, especially standing next to Gertie. The woman had changed out of her old University of Kentucky sweatshirt into a new University of Kentucky sweatshirt identical to those worn by her husband and boys. She wore a baseball cap over her peroxide bleached hair and sweatpants. Gertie Anderson was short and plump, the outfit was clearly for comfort and not exercise.

Rita and Claudia entered the lobby together and walked over to the group.

"Tonight, you'll be treated to a real authentic Chinese feast at one of Beijing's finest restaurants," Rita told them.

"The *Ren Ren* specializes in *dim sum* and is just a short walk from here," Claudia added.

"Can we use chopsticks?" young Mitchell Anderson asked raising his hand.

"Of course you can," Claudia laughed. "But remember to use them quietly. There is an ancient Chinese saying that goes; "If you rattle your chopsticks against the bowl, you and your descendants will always be poor.""

The boy clearly did not understand the proverb. "We're not poor, we're rich," young Mitchell said loud enough for everyone in the lobby to hear. "My daddy owns two car dealerships."

His parents both let out an awkward laugh as they fell in line in back of the other group members, who were already headed to the revolving door. Outside the hotel, the dreary day time scenery was now replaced by a carnival of neon lights. The capital city was suddenly bustling with excitement. Jessi took out her small camcorder and began rolling. Her news director had asked her to document her journey for the viewers back in Boston. She politely declined the request, but privately thought it was a great idea for her daughter. Sasha would have the entire trip, her *adoption story*, on videotape to see when she was older. They walked by a Mongolian Firepit, where a small crowd of men cooked thinly sliced mutton over an open flame. Smoke filled the air and the aroma was mouthwatering.

"This is Beijing," she said into the microphone. "There is so much to see here Sasha. I can't wait until we can come back here together my darling."

They also passed a narrow store front where a small elderly woman waved and shouted at them in Chinese.

"What does she want?" Jessi asked Rita.

"She's something of a fortune teller," Rita answered. "The small sign in front of her on the table says; *Shouxiang Xue-Xianglian Fa*. That means she reads palms and faces. You'll see many fortune tellers on the streets of China's bigger cities."

The group passed the old woman as Jessi kept rolling with her video camera.

She peered through the view finder and caught the fortune teller staring directly into the camera lens. Her face was lined with deep wrinkles and she had her gray hair pulled back in a bun. She could have been 50-years-old, she could have been 90. Jessi had no way of knowing for sure. The woman continued to wave her over. Jessi felt a sudden urge to walk toward her, but then she noticed the group was walking nearly a block ahead of her now. She waved back at the fortune teller and trotted ahead to catch up with the families.

The Americans arrived at the restaurant a few moments later and were ushered inside by their guides. The walls of the restaurant were covered by silk tapestries and the place reminded Jessi of some restaurants she had dined in back in Boston's Chinatown. That is where the similarities ended. They took their places around a large round table, which was set up in front of a 500 gallon fish tank filled with some of the most bizarre sea creatures Jessi had ever seen. She spotted a large squid circling the tank. The sea creature looked like something out of a Godzilla movie.

"There's nothing like this back at the New England Aquarium," she told Rita.

"This is not an aquarium," Rita corrected her with a smile. "If you see something you like in there, the chef will take it out of the tank and cook it for you."

Grace was right, this stuff is nothing like American Chinese food, Jessi thought.

Several exotic dishes were brought out during the course of the meal as the *dim sum* wheel spun around the table. Jessi passed on the seafood dishes, but sampled the *Peking Duck* which had been wrapped in a pancake and smothered with scallions and a bean sauce. The conversation between the adoptive parents was a bit stunted at first, but soon began to flow with the help of rice wine and beer. Some asked Jessi what it was like to be on television, only to turn the conversation back to their own jobs, which was fine with her. She didn't like talking shop anyway. Soon the couples paired off to chat amongst themselves and that left Jessi alone with the Andersons from Kentucky. She dreaded this at first, but quickly realized how much more she had in common with them than with anyone else at the table.

"I was raised on a farm too," Gertie said with pride. "My daddy grew tobacco. I used to spend my summers picking that stuff. I saw so much of it that it actually snuffed out any urge I may have had to smoke cigarettes."

Jessi laughed and showed off her hands.

"The lighting in here isn't very good but trust me; my hands are green from all the potatoes I've picked in Maine."

"Green like the Grinch?" young Mitchell asked with great curiosity.

"A little lighter than the Grinch," Jessi laughed. "And I promise that I won't steal your presents on Christmas Eve."

Everyone got a good laugh out of that one.

After dinner, the group members made their way back to the hotel. The Mongolian Firepit had closed for the night, but Jessi was surprised to see that the fortune teller's shop was still open. The tiny woman sat in a folding chair in front of a tall crate which she used for a table. More than a dozen bamboo bird cages hung from the ceiling above her. All the cages appeared to be empty.

"Rita," Jessi yelled as she caught up to the guide. "I'd like to have my fortune told if it's not too much of an inconvenience."

"It's no problem at all," she replied.

Gertie Anderson overheard the request. "That sounds great," she said. "It'll be perfect for that movie you're making for your baby. Maybe the fortune teller can see if little Sasha will be governor of Massachusetts one day."

"I've covered state politics," Jessi replied with a grin. "It's a snake pit. I'd never wish that on my daughter."

The mother of two from Kentucky felt a tug on her arm. She didn't need to look down to see who it was.

"Can we go too?" young Mitchell asked. He turned his attention to Jessi. "There was a fortune teller at the county fair last summer, but Momma wouldn't let me go see her."

"Alright," Gertie replied with a roll of her eyes.

The boy let out a loud cheer as they all walked up to the narrow store front, where the fortune teller pointed to a small sign that was written in English.

"50 Yuan," Gertie read aloud. "That seems like a lot of money."

"No, eight Yuan is equal to about one American dollar," Rita corrected her.

Jessi reached into her purse and handed over the small bills. She then handed her camera to Gertie.

"Can you video tape this for me?"

After giving Gertie a brief explanation on how to work the camera, Jessi sat down on a small stool opposite the fortune teller.

The old woman pulled Jessi's hands into her own. She was surprised by the woman's strength. The fortune teller turned Jessi's hands over and began running her bony fingers along the palms. Soon her hands ran up Jessi's finger joints and then back down to her wrists. The woman looked into her eyes, but said nothing.

Her powerful hands began trembling as she squeezed Jessi's wrists.

"Is there something wrong?" Jessi asked, feeling a bit unnerved by the demonstration.

The fortune teller nodded her head. "You must go," she responded in broken English. "Something bad happen here. Leave China and not come back."

The elderly woman waved her arms, stood from her chair and retreated back into the store. Jessi looked nervously to Rita, who then followed the woman into the shop. The guide and the fortune teller began talking softly, but their conversation quickly dissolved into a shouting match filled with rapid fire words and wild hand gestures. Jessi had no idea what they were talking about, but knew it wasn't good.

"Please go away," the old woman screamed at Jessi. "You die. Very bad, very bad."

While Rita tried to calm the fortune teller down, Jessi was now completely spooked, and stumbled her way back into the street. Gertie Anderson was still rolling tape on the video camera.

"Are you okay, Darlin'?" she asked her new friend.

Jessi did not respond. The fortune teller's cries were growing louder now. "You die, you die!"

Jessi turned on her heel and started running up the street.

"Wait!" Gertie hollered.

"Where's she going Momma?" young Mitchell asked.

"I dunno."

Jessi did not know either. She just knew that she had to get away from that fortune teller. She kept running; running like it was a marathon. She could still hear the old woman's cries in the distance. What had the fortune teller seen? Jessi broke a heel on her pump as she turned the corner toward her hotel and disappeared into the darkness.

CHAPTER 17

▼

Mister Wong awoke in a cold sweat. The tiger was coming after him again. This time, he had no gun to defend himself. He could smell the foul odor of the beast's breath as it drew closer. He'd been having the same nightmare on and off since his escape from prison several years earlier. In each dream, Wong would wake up just seconds before the tiger was about to exact its bloody revenge. The nightmare was always followed by a phantom pain that surged through the dead nerves in his fingertips. He ran to the bathroom and turned the faucet to cold. Wong then let the icy water pour over his aching hands. The water was little relief, but it did provide him a few precious minutes to clear his head. The pain was psychological after all, wasn't it? He returned to bed, but the last thing he wanted was sleep. The tiger was still hungry. Television bored him, so he got dressed, collected his billfold and headed down to the hotel lobby for a late evening cocktail.

As he rode the elevator to the lobby, his thoughts altered from the tiger to the dragon. Wong realized that his boss was quickly losing his mind. The beheading of his top executive was proof of that. He had always tried to rationalize Lew's attacks on the female victims. In Lew's mind, women were dispensable. But to murder a male colleague? To Wong, that meant no one was safe, *not even him.* He had stashed away enough money to disappear, but then Ju-Long Lew had enough money to find him. He had already done it once before. Wong realized the key to his own survival was to continue supplying beautiful women and price-less works of art for his demanding boss.

*   *   *   *

Jessi was alone at the hotel bar nursing a gin and tonic while going over the evening's events in her mind. Why did she run away like that? Gertie and Rita must think she is crazy. *Maybe I am a little crazy,* she thought. Still, the fortune teller had spooked her. *You die, very bad, very bad.* Jessi could not get those words out of her head. Out of the corner of her eye, she caught the bartender smiling at her. It was the same young man who handed her the hotel key earlier that day. *He thinks you are very pretty.* Jessi raised her glass and smiled back at him. The young man blushed and disappeared back into the kitchen.

Mister Wong crossed the lobby of the Jianguo and opened a set of double doors leading to the hotel bar. He noticed her right away and could barely believe his eyes. She was Caucasian, had red hair and was breathtakingly beautiful. In fact, she looked amazingly like Sophie Doucet. *The Gods are smiling upon me,* he thought. Wong concealed his excitement as he sat three stools down and pulled a pack of Marlboros from his breast pocket. He was not a smoker, but he had found that cigarettes were a great way to initiate a conversation. Jessi noticed the pack and felt her mouth water. One cigarette wouldn't hurt, would it? It would certainly help her clear her head. She still had to figure out how she was going to face Rita and Gertie in the morning.

"Excuse me," she said, getting the well dressed man's attention. "Do you speak English?"

"Yes, fluently in fact," Wong replied with a smile.

"Can I have one of those?" she said pointing to the pack.

Wong slid the Marlboros and his lighter down the bar.

"My pleasure," he responded.

The gentlemanly thing would have been to light the woman's cigarette for her. But Wong was uneasy around any kind of flame. Jessi lit the cigarette and inhaled deeply. She held the smoke in her lungs and felt the buzz immediately. She blew a stream of smoke toward the ceiling and sighed.

"Thanks, you're a real life saver," she told him.

Actually Madame, I'm anything but, he wanted to say.

"What brings you to Beijing?" he asked.

"I'm here to adopt a baby," she replied with a smile. "Here's to my last drink, and my last cigarette. In two days, I'll be a mother."

Wong nodded his head and smiled.

"Do you work here in Beijing?" she asked.

"No, I am here on business." This was the truth.

"May I ask what business you're in?"

"Antiques mostly," He replied. "I work for a man who has a keen eye for rare and beautiful things." This was also the truth.

Wong had traveled to Beijing to meet with a former British soldier who claimed to have stolen some priceless works from the Baghdad museum during the fall of Iraq. The soldier said he had in his possession, painted polychrome ceramics dating back to the 6th millennium B.C. The ancient plates would have made a fine addition to his boss's gallery, but now they would have to wait.

"That sounds very interesting," Jessi told him. "Does your work ever bring you to America? I'm from Boston."

"Well my dear, we have much in common. I was educated across the Charles River at Harvard University," he lied.

Wong had traveled to Boston once, to tour the Isabella Stewart Gardner Museum. The museum, designed in the style of a 15th century Venetian palace, was the site of the richest art theft in U.S. history. In 1990, two men disguised as Boston police officers overpowered two security guards and forced their way into the museum. The plan was genius in its simplicity. The thieves got away with $300 million dollars worth of paintings by Degas, Manet and Rembrandt. There were rumors that the art work was currently housed in a warehouse, too hot even for sale on the black market. Wong had inquired about purchasing *Storm on the Sea of Galilee,* Rembrandt's only seascape, but talks went no where.

"I graduated from Boston University," Jessi told him. "I know it's not exactly Harvard, but we do kick your butts in the Beanpot every year."

She was referring to an annual college hockey tournament between B.U., Harvard, Northeastern University, and Boston College. Wong had no idea what she was talking about. He just smiled and nodded his head.

Wong noticed her glass was almost empty. "Can I buy you a drink?" he asked.

"I promised myself that I'd have just one," she replied. "We're traveling to the Great Wall tomorrow. You must be so proud of the incredible history you have here. Paul Revere's house is considered ancient back where I live."

"Yes, yes," he chuckled. "The wall is quite a marvel. But the Chinese have not always been proud of it. In fact it's quite the opposite. For many years, Chairman Mao considered the wall a horrifying example of imperial excess and China's great shame. Thousands if not millions of young men were taken from their villages and forced to work on the wall. Most men died of malnutrition and exhaustion and never saw their families again."

"The workers bodies were not brought back home for burial?" Jessi asked.

"No. They were not even buried. The bodies were simply thrown into the wall and used as filler. Some say that you can still hear their cries on each step you climb there."

They both looked down for a moment and said nothing.

"You know, I'll have that second drink after all."

Wong alerted the bartender, who was keeping a close eye on the ongoing flirtation between the two. A pang of jealousy shot through the young man's body. He had been immediately drawn to the American woman in the lobby earlier that day. She reminded him of the movie star, Julia Roberts, but with shorter hair. The bartender owned a bootleg copy of *Pretty Woman,* which he watched at least once a week, much to the annoyance of his roommate. Now, here was another guy trying to put the moves on her. Wong snapped his fingers and barked out something in Chinese. The bartender felt like slapping the man across the face, but instead he grabbed a shaker and reached down for a bottle of Blue Curacao.

"I've ordered you something a bit more exotic," Wong told Jessi. "I hope you do not mind. Here in China, we make the best Polynesian drinks this side of Tahiti."

The bartender returned with two Blue Hawaiians. Wong handed her a glass and lifted his own.

"As you say in America: Cheers."

Jessi toasted her new friend in return and then took a sip. It was a little too fruity for her taste, but still drinkable. Wong on the other hand hated the flavor. He had chosen the drink not for its content, but its color. Jessi excused herself to the ladies room and Wong made his subtle move. He pulled out a small pill from his pants pocket and slipped it into her cocktail. He watched closely as the rohypnol tablet dissolved quickly into the liquid. Rohypnol was a notorious date rape drug known to cause confusion, sleepiness and blurred vision, and the drug was banned in many countries including China. Under heavy criticism, the makers of the drug created new pills that once dissolved, would turn any liquid blue. The color change was designed to give any would-be rape victim fair notice. The warning system did not work however in cocktails that were colored blue to begin with. Wong sipped his Blue Hawaiian and waited for her to return.

CHAPTER 18

▼

JACKSON, NEW HAMPSHIRE

"Did I wear you out today," Grace asked Heath as they shared a loveseat in front of the roaring fire inside their hotel room.

"You've been wearing me out all weekend," he replied with a grin.

"That's not what I meant," she countered with a playful punch to his arm. "Is it always about sex with you?"

Heath just smiled and took a pull from his bottle of *Tuckerman's Pale Ale*, a locally brewed beer that had the same texture, but less bite than a *Samuel Adams*. He wouldn't tell Grace, but sex was the last thing on his mind right now. His legs were killing him. Grace had worn him out today, not in bed but on the ski slopes. They had made eight runs at Wildcat Mountain and capped the day with a trip down a black diamond trail. Grace conquered the moguls with ease, but Rosary spent more time on his ass than on his skis. The heat coming off the burning logs felt good now though. They were both out of their ski suits, but still in their long johns. Rosary ran his hand down Grace's thigh. That felt good too. *Maybe I could suck it up for another roll in the hay.* He knew that he had to conserve his energy though. Tonight was going to be the big night. He had it all planned out. They would enjoy a nice dinner at the Stonehurst Inn in North Conway, and after that, it was back to the Nestlenook for a romantic sleigh ride where he would finally pop the question. The sleigh driver was told to have a bottle of champagne ready to go when Grace said yes. *She will say yes, won't she?* He asked himself.

She found his hand on her thigh and wrapped her fingers in his. Grace then leaned over and kissed him on the cheek.

"I love this weekend, and I love you."

Her words melted his heart. He wanted to ask her to marry him right now, but thought better of it. *I can't do it in my long johns. I want it to be perfect.*

The serenity inside their room was broken by the ring of Grace's cell phone.

"Don't answer it baby. It's probably work. They've gotta learn to handle breaking news without you."

Grace let go of his hand and climbed slowly off the loveseat.

"Sorry honey," she told him. "It could be Jessi. I told her to call me when she got settled in China. It's been two days now. I wonder if she's picked up little Sasha yet?"

Grace ran over to her ski jacket and pulled the small cell phone out from the side pocket. She flipped it open, but didn't recognize the phone number of the incoming call. She pressed *send* and placed the receiver to her ear.

"Hello?"

"My name is Betty Hu. Is this Grace Chen?"

"It is."

"I am the director of the *Hands across the World* adoption agency. Jessi Miller left instructions that I should call this number if there was a problem."

Grace swallowed hard. "What's wrong? What's happened?"

Betty Hu was also panicked, but tried to remain calm. "I don't know how to say this, so I'm just going to say it. I'm afraid she has gone missing."

"Missing?" Grace screamed into the phone. "Missing from where?"

Her shouts got Heath's attention. He jumped off the loveseat and walked swiftly toward her. Grace did not appear to notice. All her energy was now focused on this phone call.

"Miss Miller has gone missing from her hotel in Beijing," Hu told her. "She did not take part in the group's tour of Great Wall the morning after her arrival. Today, the families are picking up the babies and she is no where to be found."

"What? How long has she been missing?"

"For a little more than 24 hours now. My guides telephoned her room repeatedly and even got hotel security to check on her. Ms. Miller's suitcases are in the room, but she is gone."

Grace's head was swimming. She could barely comprehend what this woman was telling her.

"You've waited all this time to call me?" Grace asked in an accusatory tone. She was clearly angry now.

"Miss Chen, many times our adoptive parents do not take part in group activities. My guides did not think much of it until yesterday afternoon. All parents were supposed to meet in the lobby to go over their documents needed for their adoptions, but Ms. Miller never showed."

For a brief moment, Grace had forgotten there was even a baby involved.

"Where is Sasha? Where is Jessi's baby now?"

"The child was placed back on a bus and driven back to the orphanage," Betty told her.

Grace felt like she was going to throw up. "Miss. Hu, I'm in New Hampshire right now. I'm going to get in my car and drive back to Boston. I will see you in three hours."

She grabbed a pen and wrote down the address of the adoption agency. Grace ended the phone call and looked over at Heath.

"What's going on?" he asked her.

"It's Jessi. She's disappeared."

*   *   *   *

Rosary packed up their things as quickly as he could. He took the diamond engagement ring out of his jacket pocket and placed it on the bottom of his suitcase. The proposal would have to wait. He carried their luggage down to the BMW and they both got in. Grace had barely uttered a word since the phone call. She was completely numb.

"Honey, I want you to tell me exactly what that woman told you. I'm a private investigator, remember? I might be able to help."

Grace went over the phone call with him and then went over the phone call with him again.

"So who is looking for Jessi right now?"

"I don't know," Grace replied. "I was so upset that I forgot to ask."

Heath reached for her hand as they drove down Route 16 and away from the White Mountains. The weekend of their dreams had just turned into a nightmare. They made the rest of the drive south in silence. A few hours later, the mountains were replaced by skyscrapers and they found themselves back in Boston. It was almost eight o'clock at night when Rosary took the Atlantic Avenue exit out of the Tip O'Neil Tunnel and headed toward Chinatown. He parked the BMW in a space on Ping On alley and then got out and walked around the car to open the door for Grace. Her silence worried him and he felt nervous for her. He on the other hand had to stay focused in order to get some real answers.

They entered the small building and climbed three flights of stairs to Betty Hu's office. It appeared that everyone else in the building had gone home for the night. The door to *Hands across the World* was open and the lights were on. The adoption agency headquarters was much smaller than Rosary had imagined. He saw three desks set up in two small rooms. Hundreds of pictures lined the walls all showing smiling couples with their adorable Chinese babies. A large map of China was pasted to the rear wall. It was decorated with red thumb tacks signaling the various orphanages with which the agency worked. Two young Asian women were typing on computers while Betty Hu worked the phone. She was an attractive middle aged Chinese woman with short hair and she wore a blue power suit that was more suitable for a boardroom than an adoption agency. Rosary could tell that she was all business. She saw Grace and Heath enter and placed her hand over the phone receiver.

"I'll be right with you," she whispered.

She continued her telephone conversation for several more minutes. She was apparently speaking to someone in China. Rosary was completely lost, but Grace understood every word. Betty Hu finally hung up the phone and walked over to Grace.

"What did the police have to say?" Grace asked her.

Betty began replying in Chinese, but Grace cut her off.

"Please speak English; my boyfriend would like to hear this too."

"I just spoke with the officer assigned to the case. He is trying to interview the hotel personnel and the other adoptive parents. That has been somewhat difficult because the families have just received their babies. It sounds quite hectic over there."

"Surely someone must know something," Grace said.

"I've spoken at length with my guides. They are both very good girls. One of them told me that Ms. Miller was involved with some kind of incident with a fortune teller on the evening they arrived."

"A fortune teller?" asked Rosary. He grabbed a notepad and a pen off a desk. "Please explain."

"Fortune tellers are popular in China," Betty told them. "They are taken very seriously. Ms. Miller got her palm read and the teller saw something she did not like."

"Which was?" asked Grace.

Betty Hu examined their faces before continuing. Were these rational people?

Hu believed they were. "The teller apparently told Ms. Miller that she would die if she didn't leave China right away."

"What the hell are you talking about?" Grace asked dumbfounded.

Rosary grabbed her arm gently. "Relax, honey. Let her tell us what we need to know."

The agency director nodded her head at Heath. "Thank you, mister?"

"Rosary. My name is Heath Rosary. I'm Grace's boyfriend, but I'm also a private investigator."

"Yes, I thought I recognized you." Betty Hu looked at him more closely. "Weren't you the one involved in the shooting at the Kennedy compound last spring?"

"That's another story for another time," he replied. "Let's get back to the fortune teller."

Hu nodded her head. "Of course, I apologize. The old woman was clearly crazy, but she gave Ms. Miller quite a scare. Your friend ran away from the shop and that's the last time anyone in my group has seen her."

"Where's the old woman now?" Rosary asked as he continued scribbling notes on a yellow writing pad.

"That's the curious thing," Hu replied rubbing her chin. "No one has been able to find her."

CHAPTER 19

▼

Heath and Grace arrived back at his condo well past midnight after placing several more phone calls from Betty Hu's office. The agency director notified the American Embassy in Beijing and was told that an attaché was already working with local police there. Grace called her father, who maintained several important contacts on the Chinese mainland. He promised her that he would begin pulling in favors immediately. Rosary reached out to his former colleague and best friend, Nikki Tavano. She had once worked under Rosary in the U.S. Secret Service in Boston. Tavano had risen quickly up the bureaucratic ladder and she now called Washington, D.C. home. Rosary could not reach her, but did find out that she was already in Beijing working as special agent in charge of the security detail assigned to the president's father, a former president himself, and now special envoy to the six-party talks with North Korea. *Nikki's already in China. That's a good sign,* he told himself.

BEIJING

Nikki Tavano sipped from a can of warm Diet Coke and pulled a small mirror out of her coat pocket. *It's official; I look like hell,* she thought to herself. She had dark circles under her beautiful brown eyes and counted at least three new gray hairs sprouting from her scalp. She sat at a small wooden desk inside her quarters at the American Embassy at 3 Xiushui Beijie, Jianguomenwai. She had been in Beijing for three weeks now, but still could not get used to the smell. *Why does a city so rich in history and beauty insist on choking itself to death?* She wondered. The air purifiers installed inside the embassy helped relieve the odor a little bit. Tavano glanced outside her small window, which overlooked the main entrance.

The embassy was surrounded by eight foot walls topped with barbed wire. U.S. marines stood guard inside the perimeter, while Chinese soldiers marched back and forth outside the embassy. It was clear the Chinese would shoot to kill if one of its citizens attempted to jump the wall into the American embassy to declare political asylum. She wondered whether any of those soldiers had been tempted to scale the wall themselves.

Tavano had just come from a three hour logistical meeting with her Chinese counterpart, and felt like she'd just gone 15 rounds with Marvelous Marvin Hagler.

The Chinese were insisting that the former President stay at the newly renovated Beijing Grand Hotel, but as head of the Secret Service advance team, Tavano told the Chinese that this was out of the question for several reasons. First, the Presidential Suite of the Beijing Grand Hotel was on the 15th floor. If there was a fire, the suite was six floors higher than the maximum height that a hook and ladder could reach. She also informed the Chinese that the official entourage would not only take over the 15th floor of the hotel, but also the floor directly above and below. This could be cause for concern for the other delegations that were to attend the summit. What she didn't tell the Chinese was that their plan had received a big thumbs down from the guys in the TSD (Technical Security Division). This elite group was in charge of the former President's communications. Matt Grove, an engineering whiz from MIT and senior officer of the TSD informed Tavano that the Chinese had top of the line audio equipment and state of the art microwave receivers that could be used to bug the hotel suite. The Chinese had done it before during a visit from President Ronald Reagan. The TSD had found a bug hidden in the nightstand of the President's bedroom. Tavano wanted to avoid any embarrassment on both sides and told her counterpart that it would be best for all if the former President stayed here at the American Embassy, a place he had once called home. The Chinese reluctantly agreed.

Now that the accommodations crisis was apparently settled, Tavano turned her attention back to the cast of characters involved in the upcoming round of six-way talks. She had the Chinese to deal with, and the North Koreans, who caused her great concern as did the Russians. Tavano had already worked with the Japanese and South Koreans and had found both security teams to be quite helpful. They were all here to make history and to avoid a nuclear showdown. *Talk about pressure,* she thought to herself. She plucked a gray hair from her head and stared at it briefly. Was it time to step away after this summit was over? Her pal Rosary seemed quite content in his new life. She shook her head and cleared away the cobwebs. *Who am I kidding?* She relished this kind of pressure. *Nothing can go wrong,* Tavano thought to herself. *Not on my watch.*

WASHINGTON, D.C.

Steve Trevane listened to Imus on his I-Pod as he jogged along the Capital Crescent Trail by the Fletcher Boat House. The building was boarded up and the row boats and canoes had been taken in for the winter. Dawn was breaking and a blanket of fog rolled in off the Potomac. The landmark told him that he had already run eight-point-two miles. He did not need the visual clue however, he could feel it. Trevane's legs were burning and his sneakers were soaked with sweat. He was pushing 40 now and no longer had the stamina he had once showed as captain of the Yale cross country team. *I no longer have the stamina or the hair,* he laughed to himself. A dark wool cap covered his bald head protecting it from the cold. He jogged in place and checked his watch. It was just after 6 a.m. He looked across the bike trail toward a small parking area at the top of a set of wooden steps along the tow path. A pair of headlights blinked twice in the fog. Trevane looked to his right and then to his left to make sure he was alone before jogging up the steps toward the headlights.

"You're late," Buzz Baxter grumbled, as Trevane got into the passenger seat of the tan Mercedes Benz S-class sedan.

"It's called *exercise,* Buzz. You should try it sometime," Trevane replied as he unzipped the top of his blue nylon jacket.

"I wish I could, but I don't have time."

Buzz Baxter was a busy man. He was a busy *and* important man. He served as assistant to the Vice President, but his power stretched beyond that job and far across the capital city. Baxter was something of an enigma, even among Washington insiders. He was one of those cocktail party guests who spent the whole evening locked in the den brokering deals with the other Beltway power players. Buzz Baxter was a good friend to have on your side, but a bad man to cross.

"I need you to do me a favor," Baxter told his young protégé.

Trevane was not in position to say no, whatever the request. He owed his entire career to the steely eyed operator sitting next to him. Both Baxter and Trevane had grown up in the scenic seaside community of Camden, Maine. Their families were friends, and although Baxter was twenty years older than Trevane, he kept a close eye on the young man who followed in his footsteps. Like Baxter, Steve Trevane attended Phillips Andover Academy, a prestigious prep school in Massachusetts and after graduation; he headed south to New Haven, Connecticut and Yale. Buzz Baxter was a Yale alumnus and had taught political science there when Trevane was a student. Baxter was happy to see how the younger man had molded himself into the older man's image. The kid was hungry and scrupulous, just like him.

Baxter took Trevane under his wing and then to the nation's capital, where he guided the young man through the head scratching maze that was Washington politics. Trevane had recently moved from a civilian desk job at the Pentagon to the State Department, where he now served as Director of Special Projects in the Bureau of East Asian and Pacific Affairs. It was a move that had been orchestrated by Baxter with today's conversation in mind.

"What do you need me to do?" Trevane asked his mentor.

"I want you to be my eyes and ears in China," Baxter replied in a gravelly voice.

The older man lit an unfiltered Camel and savored the taste. Baxter still put away two packs a day despite having suffered three heart attacks. His last wife had even given him an ultimatum; "The cigarettes or me," she said. He chose the smokes. Even his doctor had given up on him. Baxter knew that he was on borrowed time, but he was determined to stick around until *his* man won the Oval Office. Trevane's eyes began to water as the smoke rose inside the luxury car. He reached for the button to lower the window, but it would not budge. He looked over to Baxter, who had his finger on the control.

"You can kill yourself with those things, but not me. Wind down the window Buzz."

"Don't be such a pussy. I don't want anyone to pickup what I'm about to tell you."

Baxter was ever fearful of the CIA, NSA and every other alphabet soup intelligence service in Washington. He paused for a moment as he ran his fingers through the bristly blond hairs of his crew cut. He hadn't changed his hair style since he was a kid. That is how Raymond Baxter had gotten the nickname, Buzz.

"I assume that you're talking about the summit," Trevane said, breaking the silence.

Baxter nodded his head yes. "The President has drawn a hard line with the North Koreans with all that Axis of Evil shit. He's only got a year left in office and I'm afraid he's gonna leave Vice President Beresford with a big fucking mess on his hands."

Trevane listened, but said nothing.

Baxter kept talking. "Once the Vice President wins the presidency, and he will, Beresford wants to take a softer approach with North Korea. He feels that he has to." He took another long drag from his cigarette before continuing. "We are seriously overstretched militarily right now. We've got 120 thousand troops in Iraq and only 17 thousand in Afghanistan, where the Taliban has crawled out from under its rock to gain control of key areas again."

"What about the reserves?" Trevane asked.

"We're getting tapped out there too," Baxter responded with a shake of his head. "The army has already begun its 4th rotation of troops and all 15 of the National Guard's most readily deployable troops have already been mobilized. We're stretched too thin my young friend."

"So you're saying that it's not exactly the best time to provoke the North Koreans."

"I always knew you were a bright kid," Baxter smiled. "There are one million soldiers in the North Korean army. The wacko in charge over there is only a danger to himself and his people. We don't think he's really a serious nuclear threat. We're expecting bigger problems from Iran. Those are the pricks we need to keep a close eye on."

"I'm not so sure about that," Trevane replied. "After all, the North has tested a nuclear weapon."

"That was more fizzle than fission," Baxter countered. "The explosion had a seismic magnitude of four-point-two. That's much smaller than tests conducted by both Pakistan and India." Baxter sucked down on his cigarette once more. "Still, we don't want to piss this guy off any further. Christ, the President called him a "pygmy who behaved like a spoiled brat at the dinner table." Can you believe that shit?"

Trevane laughed. "I think the President hit the nail right on the head with that one."

"You have a lot to learn my young friend," Baxter said shaking his head. "This guy has a huge chip on his shoulder already. I mean, he wears elevator shoes and combs his hair in a giant bouffant to give him a few more inches. The President shouldn't have poked at that sore. Remember what Kaiser Wilhelm once said."

"I feel like I'm back at Yale," Trevane replied. "Please go on professor."

"Don't be such a wise ass," Baxter chuckled. "Wilhelm was pissed that the French never gave him a parade through Paris. He said, "The Monarchs of Europe have paid no attention to what I have to say." Soon after that, the Kaiser led the world into the Great War."

Trevane nodded, but said nothing. He let Baxter's words sink in.

He felt his mentor's hand on his shoulder. "This summit is merely a high stakes game of poker," Baxter told him. "We know that he's bluffing. He just needs a little money. We'll offer the wacko a ton of cash to halt the program and he'll walk away." Baxter started laughing. "Of course, he'll come back in a couple of years demanding more money and we'll give it to him. That's how the game works. Hell, we even overlook the criminal cabal he's got going over there."

"I assume you're talking about Bureau 39?"

"Damn straight I am," Baxter answered as he rolled his lit cigarette between his fingers.

Both men had a good idea about what really went on in the six story building, guarded by uniformed soldiers in the center of Pyongyang. Bureau 39 oversaw government owned businesses like textile factories, but according to the U.S. State Department, it also oversaw opium and heroin production and the manufacture of counterfeit cigarettes that netted the party leadership more than $ 1 billion per year.

"You afraid that one day you'll be duped into buying phony smokes?" Trevane asked facetiously.

"Hey, I'd smoke rolled up horse shit if it meant keeping us out of another un-winnable war."

"Where do I come in?" Trevane asked.

"I want you to be my fireman."

Trevane looked at him curiously.

"I mean that I want you to put out any fires that may arise over there. The wacko isn't the easiest guy to deal with, but he's important to us. You know the President's father. That Bible thumping bastard has spent the past twelve years building those fucking Habitats for Humanity. He's been out of the game too long. The Vice President and I believe that it was a huge mistake to send him. He'll want to address human rights abuses, but that is not on the agenda there. He likes to stay on his moral high horse so if you see him getting on, shoot him an elbow and knock him on his ass. But do it with subtlety."

CHAPTER 20

▼

SOUTH BOSTON

Heath and Grace felt they could not rely solely on the help of friends. The only way to find Jessi now was to go to China themselves. Betty Hu agreed. She told the couple they could join another adoptive group traveling to Beijing in two days. "I could tell the Chinese government that you both are writing a book on adoption practices over there," Betty had told them. "The government is not proud of its program, but it's an unfortunate reality that they are willing to share. Books have been written before. The government has grown to expect such interest. Grace's reputation as a journalist is already well established. Your trip shouldn't raise much suspicion."

Rosary did not want to wait two full days, but he knew the agency director was right. He hated the fact that he was going into a cold scene. He couldn't call it a crime scene because he didn't want to scare Grace and at this point, there was no evidence that a crime had been committed. *Maybe she fell and hit her head. Maybe she's lying in a Beijing hospital with amnesia.* It wasn't a pleasant thought, but it sure sounded better than the alternative. Traveling with the adoptive group would also provide him with good cover. If he went as an investigator, Betty told him he'd run into more problems than he realized. The Chinese police did not like anyone poking around in their backyard. *Hell, the Boston police don't like it either,* he told himself.

Heath lay in bed trying to make sense of the whole thing. Grace finally dozed off after crying herself to sleep. He tried to comfort her but she was inconsolable. He stared at the ceiling, his mind racing. He knew that the first twenty four hours were the most crucial in a missing persons' case. *How are Chinese police handling it? Do they get many cases like this in Beijing? Or do people over there vanish and become forgotten? No one wants to ask too many questions do they?*

The next morning, Rosary rattled around his condo looking for things to do. He caught up on his bills thanks to a sizable check from Herb Duane. He paid his mortgage, his car payment and that left him with enough money to cover the emergency trip to China. Grace had told him that she would pay for everything, but he declined. He would pay his own way. After all, he loved Jessi too. He wanted to call Grace and see how she was doing. She had left early in the morning while Heath was still asleep. There was a brief note from Grace saying that she wanted to be alone for awhile. She left it next to the coffee maker where she knew he'd see it. He wanted to respect her wishes, but he just had to hear her voice. He reached over for the phone when suddenly, it rang.

"Hello?"

"Heathcliff, it's Sammy,"

Grace's brother, shit. "What's up bro?"

"Grace told me what happened. I think it's horrible."

"Well, we don't know what happened," Rosary replied. "That's why we're going over there."

"That's why I'm calling. The old man wants to see you."

The old man was Tommy Chen. The two had done a masterful job avoiding each other over the past ten years.

"Why does your father want to see me?" he asked. "Sammy, you know where I stand with the old man."

"Yah, I know. I know. But you're taking his little girl to China and I think he wants to give you some advice. Just hear him out okay?"

Rosary despised the old man, but liked his son and loved his daughter. Was it time to repair old wounds?

"He's booked reservations at Lock-Ober. I told him that you didn't wear ties anymore, but he insisted."

Lock-Ober was a stuffy, yet historic Boston eatery that was about as comfortable for Rosary as the Hampshire House had been.

"C'mon Heathcliff. It's not that bad. I hear Orson Welles used to slurp oysters there."

Rosary laughed. "Tempting, but no thanks. If your father wants to talk, tell him to meet me at the Sligo at eight. I'll be the black guy sitting in the corner."

"Tommy Chen, having a pint in Southie? That should be interesting. You're really gonna make me tell him that?"

"Absolutely," Rosary replied.

"You owe me one pal," Sammy told him. "You're buying me a thick steak at Abe & Louie's got it?"

"That's fair."

"Seriously, I hope you find Jessi safe," Sammy told him. "She means the world to Grace. She means the world to us too."

Rosary checked his watch. It was now quarter to eight. He grabbed his black leather coat, gray scarf and hit the door. He walked cautiously down the front steps outside his condo. The temperature had dipped into the teens and the steps were icy. Rosary put his hands in his pockets as he carefully navigated his way down Telegraph Hill. He had his scarf wrapped around his face, but kept a watchful eye on his surroundings. Spider Mulgravey was still laid up with a shattered kneecap, but his leather clad associates could be out there somewhere, Rosary knew. He had his 9mm semiautomatic with him just in case. His weapon gave him comfort, and for good reason. Rosary's skills with a sidearm were legendary within the Secret Service. He had posted the top score for five years straight at the Secret Service training center in Beltsville, Maryland. His nickname there was *Hulk Hogan,* not for his size, but for his shooting skill, which was deadly accurate. Rosary reigned supreme at a shooting range called Hogan's Alley. It was the most difficult of the judgmental courses at the Beltsville facility. Hogan's Alley was a fake city street designed by a top movie studio where targets would pop up suddenly. Agents had a split second to determine whether the targets were good guys or bad guys. It was like a video game only, this one used real bullets.

Rosary did not notice any thugs lurking in the shadows, but he did see couches, chairs and even an old television set out on the street. It wasn't garbage day, it was a snow day. The items were left in shoveled out spots to secure a parking space for the shoveler when he or she came home from work. Street squatting was a tradition in all Boston neighborhoods, but the folks in Southie had raised it to an art form. Friends from his old Roxbury neighborhood still questioned why he lived here. Some called him a *Sell-Out,* because after all, South Boston did not exactly roll out the red carpet for African Americans. That was the perception anyway. But this was not the Southie of thirty years ago, when racial tensions between blacks and Irish Catholics spilled over to violent confrontations during the infamous busing crisis. The neighborhood had changed dramatically over the years. The tight knit Irish community was eroding with every million dollar condo sale. Southie was the trendy place to live now. Rosary had been ahead of the curve. He had chosen the neighborhood not for its chic potential, but for its waterfront location. Rosary loved the feel of the salty air on his face as he jogged along Carson Beach and around Castle Island. He even loved the Irish pubs, which were quickly getting replaced by mood lit bistros. His favorite tavern was still in operation though. Rosary reached the base of Telegraph Hill and found the Sligo. He walked down a set of stone steps, pulled open the thick wooden door and stepped back in time.

The Sligo was an old school Irish pub, dark yet inviting. It had been operating for more than a hundred years and had been owned by the same family for the last fifty. The tavern had a tall tin ceiling and a long oaken bar that offered a taste from the old country. A fiddle player plucked away at his instrument in the corner. Rosary had a good ear for music, but didn't recognize the tune. He nodded to a couple of neighborhood fellows at the bar and took a seat in one of the pub's wooden booths. Business was slow on this night and the bartender also doubled as the pub's only waiter.

"What'll it be tonight, Heath?" Sully asked with a gap toothed smile.

"How's the Shepherd's Pie tonight?" he replied without looking at the menu.

"It's the best in fucking Boston, like it is every night."

"Then I'll have a dish," Rosary laughed. "And I'll have a Sam Adams too."

"I dunno why I even ask," Sully said shaking his head. "You order the same thing every week."

"Hey Sully, I'm expecting some company. No one from the usual crowd. He's Chinese and he'll be wearing gold cufflinks as big as your car."

"I'll keep my eye out for him."

Rosary leaned back on the wooden bench and waited for his beer. He hoped that it would calm his nerves. He had stared down some pretty scary dudes in his time, but there was something about Tommy Chen that threw him off his game. Maybe it was Rosary's subconscious yearning for the man's approval. He was glad this meeting would take place on his own turf; the Sligo was like a second home to him. There was even a photo of him from his football days hanging behind the bar. The picture was hung next to an autographed photo of Patriots star Tom Brady. *Not bad company,* he thought. The bartender brought over the beer just as the front door of the pub opened wide. Tommy Chen walked in with two well dressed men at his side. It was a dramatic entrance to say the least. *He thinks he's the Emperor of China,* Rosary said to himself.

Tommy Chen was not the Emperor of China, but his peers did consider him royalty in the world of exploratory medicine. He had founded a global pharmaceutical empire that created and marketed vaccines and medicines to treat just about every ailment you could think of. His most popular drug, Cal-max was an alendronate sodium tablet designed to reverse bone loss in osteoporosis patients. The success of that drug had made Tommy Chen a billionaire several times over. Stock in Chen Pharmaceuticals was now selling at $34 per share on the New York Stock Exchange. Chen himself owned millions of shares and 54% of the company. Rosary did not like the old man, but respected what he had accomplished. Tommy Chen had emigrated from China with his wife and three small children after graduating Shanghai's prestigious Chiao Tung University in 1969. He attended Harvard Medical School where he graduated at the top of his class. After performing his residency at Massachusetts General Hospital, he was courted by the nation's best hospitals. Chen, however felt that he could help more people working in a laboratory than in an operating room, and with a $20,000 loan, he founded Chen Pharmaceuticals in 1975. From those humble beginnings, Tommy Chen was now near the top of the annual Forbes Magazine list of the world's richest people.

"Over here," Rosary said, waving his hand at the man who could be his future father in-law.

The diminutive Chen nodded back and then motioned his two men to wait for him outside. Tommy Chen stood only five-foot-three inches tall and his long black camel hair coat made him look even shorter than he really was. He wore a pair of eyeglasses that were too big for his face and had a long strip of unruly black hair combed sideways over his balding head. Still, the 65-year old tycoon exuded confidence and elegance as he walked toward Rosary's booth. Heath did not get up to shake his hand.

"Have a seat," Rosary offered showing little enthusiasm.

Chen smiled and sat down across from him.

"Hey Sully, how about a beer for my guest," Rosary barked at the bartender.

"Please, no. I'll just have a glass of water," Chen said softly.

"Suit yourself," Rosary shrugged. "Just a water for my friend here," he shouted to Sully. "And where's that Shepherd's Pie?"

The bartender responded by flipping him the bird.

Rosary was trying to act as if this meeting was no big deal, but the nonchalant attitude was bordering on belligerence. *Get a grip on yourself,* he thought.

"It's been a long time," the old man said.

"Yah, it has Tommy. Do you remember the last time we saw each other?"

Rosary was picking at an old scab now.

"It was a long time ago," Chen responded.

"Well, let me refresh your memory," Rosary said, taking a pull from his bottle of beer. "I believe that the last time I saw you, you were writing me a check for $50,000 to stay away from your daughter."

Tommy Chen bowed his head in shame.

"I should thank you for never telling Grace about that," Chen replied. "I am not proud of that moment."

The testy conversation was broken up by the bartender who ran over to the booth.

"You'd better go outside," Sully told the two of them.

"What's the problem?" Rosary asked.

"It's your friend here," Sully replied nodding toward Chen. "His security guys are moving some lawn chairs out of an empty space so they can park his limo."

"Oh shit," Rosary replied as he sprinted from the booth toward the door.

CHAPTER 21

▼

"I wouldn't do that if I were you," Rosary shouted to Chen's private bodyguard as the man carried a small wooden table to the side walk.

"We need to park the car," the other bodyguard shouted back. "Someone left all this crap out in the street."

"You don't get it do you?" Rosary said shaking his head. "Someone shoveled out that parking space. They put the table there so no one else would park in their spot. That table is like a flagpole."

"What the hell does that mean?"

"That means that you'll be lucky if no one sets fire to the limo before Tommy leaves," he informed the man. "Folks around here are serious about their spaces. Trust me, why don't you and your buddy just get back in the vehicle and circle the block a few times. It'll save you a heap of trouble."

The bodyguards did not answer, but they did return to the limo. Rosary waited until the driver pulled out of the space before heading back inside the pub. *One crisis averted; another waiting*, he thought. He went back inside and found Chen and a dish of Shepherd's Pie waiting for him in the booth.

"Is everything alright?" Chen asked.

Rosary rolled his eyes. "Your bodyguards should have done some location prep work. What I mean is, they should know that it's impossible to find a parking space in this neighborhood, especially after a snow storm."

"Is that what you did during your time in the Secret Service?"

Rosary nodded his head as he dug his fork through the mashed potato crust and into the hamburger and gravy center of the pie. "It's part of the POP, protection of the principal," he said after taking a bite. "It's rule one in the training guide. Always know your surroundings."

Chen leaned over the table and spoke in a whisper. "I know you think that I did not approve of you because you're black. That is somewhat true and as I said, I am ashamed of those feelings. But your job also played a role in my thoughts. You had a dangerous job then, and from what I've read in the newspapers you have a dangerous job now."

"Listen here Tommy," Heath said raising his voice. He was clearly angry now. "Before you try cutting me another check, I want you to know that I'm never going to leave your daughter."

Chen sat back in the wooden booth and smiled. Rosary was confused by the grin.

"I do not want you to leave my daughter. Grace loves you more than she loves me. I realize this now. I also realize my own shortcomings where my daughter is concerned. I have always been too stern with her, too demanding. It's how I was raised. In China, a child counts on a mother for nurturing and love. A child counts on a father for structure and discipline. Grace was much closer to her mother than she is to me."

Rosary nodded. Despite Tommy Chen's accomplishments, Grace had always seen her mother as the true heroine of her life. Lilly Chen had arrived in the United States knowing very little English with three small children in tow. She raised the children virtually on her own while her husband was building his career. Grace had always had a special bond with her mother, and when Lilly Chen succumbed to breast cancer when her daughter was seventeen, the divide between Grace and her father grew wider. She couldn't understand why he was working so hard to heal others while her mother was dying. It took Grace several years to realize that her anger toward him was unfounded, but by this time the damage was done. Added to all this was her relationship with Heath. Her father had almost disowned her, but his appearance here tonight meant that he too was willing to change.

"Grace has always acted with her heart, and that's what makes her so special," Tommy continued. "This journey to China could be very dangerous. I am glad that you will be by her side to protect her. I come here tonight to ask for your forgiveness."

Chen reached his hand across the table. It was the ultimate peace offering after all these years. Rosary took the old man's hand and shook it gently. He could see the tears forming in the corners of Tommy Chen's eyes.

"I came to ask your forgiveness, and I also came to offer some help. As I said, China can be a dangerous place. You will not be able to find Jessi on your own. I have elicited the aid of my nephews. They both work in Beijing and have many contacts across the country. They could be a great help to you."

"How can I contact them?" Rosary asked.

"They will find you. You cannot travel with a firearm, but I suppose you'll need a gun?"

Rosary had thought about this, but had not come up with a solution. *Can't exactly point my finger at someone and say, Bang you're dead.*

"You carry a 9mm semiautomatic, isn't that right?" Chen asked.

He knows more about me than I thought.

Rosary nodded his head.

"My nephews will supply you with a weapon. Please be careful Mister Rosary, the Chinese could get very rough with you if they find you with a firearm. Even my influence would not be enough to save you."

Chen took a sip of his water and shook Rosary's hand once more before getting up from the table.

"Is there anything else I can do for you?"

Rosary thought of the engagement ring still sitting in the bottom of his suitcase.

"Yes Tommy, there is one more thing that I'd like to discuss with you."

HONG KONG

Jessi held her daughter next to her naked breast and felt the softness of her baby's skin on her own. Sasha had her eyes closed and her warm cheek pressed against her mother's chest. The baby cooed in her sleep. "Sasha, my sweet baby, Mommy is so happy to see you." Jessi closed her eyes and hummed a Russian lullaby that had been sung to her when she was a baby. The serenity was shaken when Sasha's cooing turned to crying. Jessi tried to console the child, but the cries only got louder. She felt the baby being pulled from her arms. Jessi screamed and tried to hold on, but couldn't. She saw the baby floating away from her. Sasha's arms were still outstretched for her mother. The baby's cries soon faded into silence.

"Sasha!," Jessi yelled out in her sleep. She opened her eyes and looked around the room. She saw two of everything, but recognized nothing. It was not her hotel room; this she knew. There were no windows and there was no baby crib in the corner. She tried to rub her eyes, but had trouble lifting her arms. Jessi felt like she was moving under water. Her mind was clouded and her throat was severely dry.

"Where am I?" she asked herself.

Was it a hospital? She spread her hand across the white satin sheets of her bed and stared at the bare stainless steel walls around her. If it was a hospital, it was like none she had ever seen. Again, she shook her head trying to clear away the cobwebs. She had not felt this groggy since coming out of anesthesia after getting her gall bladder removed when she was a teenager. *I must be in the hospital, but what happened to me?*

"Nurse," she moaned.

Jessi got no response.

"Nurse," she called out again, this time more loudly.

Again, there was no answer. Jessi tried to stay awake but her eyes grew heavy. Seconds later, she was asleep.

She woke up three hours later, this time feeling more alert. She sat up in bed ready to call out for the nurse once more. Suddenly, she heard a horrifying noise coming from another room. It sounded like the cries of a wounded animal. The guttural screams made the hair stand up on the back of her neck. The noise was getting louder now, closer. Jessi used all of her strength to swing her legs over to one side of the bed. She stood up on weak knees; the floor was cold under her bare feet. She looked down and realized that she was still wearing the red dress she had put on back at the hotel. She remembered having a drink with that nice Chinese businessman, but nothing after that. She pinched herself to see if she was still locked in a dream. The pain was real.

Ju-Long Lew stumbled out of his opium den and down the long dimly lit corridor toward his prey. He could hear his own heavy breathing under the yellow opera mask. The hallucinations were more intense than ever before. The dragon was crawling down a passage way of flames, its powerful tail sliding back and forth over hot coals. A sacrifice had been made and the dragon was about to take its offering.

He had been waiting for this moment all day, since he saw the present Mister Wong had delivered. She was stunning, almost as beautiful as Miss Universe. But would she please him like Sophie Doucet had? The dragon would soon find out.

Jessi watched in horror as the man entered the room. He was completely naked save for the unusual mask he wore over his face. His body was glistening with sweat and his stiff erection told Jessi what he was coming for.

"Stay the fuck away from me," she screamed with clenched fists. She felt a rush of adrenalin and the grogginess was wearing off. "Where the hell am I?"

The masked man tilted his head, but said nothing. He let out a low growl as he moved closer toward her. Jessi was frightened, but did not show it. She had spent her youth wrestling away from overzealous boys back in Fort Kent. She knew how to fight back. The masked man reached out with both hands and grabbed her shoulders firmly. He tried to throw her to the bed, but Jessi responded with a powerful knee to his groin. The dragon felt a sharp pain as his legs buckled. He reached down to comfort his aching testicles and was struck again, this time on the side of his head. The force of the blow sent the yellow mask flying off his face and across the small room. The dragon was amazed by the strength of this beautiful woman. She came at his face again and he reached up to block the blow. His hands were held high leaving his crotch exposed once again. Jessi kicked him once more in the balls and dug her fingernails into the man's eyes. She had taken several self defense courses over the years and the training was coming back to her all at once. Jessi Miller was fighting for her life and she was fighting for her baby. Her attacker winced in pain as blood trickled down from the deep scratches on his face. She pushed the wounded man onto the bed and ran down the hall. Jessi had no idea where she was or where she was going. She just knew that she had to get away from him. She followed the corridor to another room, this one was brightly lit.

What is this place? She asked herself. It resembled one of the exhibit rooms at the Museum of Fine Arts back in Boston. Artworks accentuated by small overhead lights, hung on bleached white walls and artifacts propped up on pedestals shined brightly under glass. She felt like she was trapped in some perverted version of *Alice in Wonderland.* The sounds of heavy footsteps and moaning were growing louder from down the hall. Jessi had to think quickly. She scanned the room for something she could use to fend off the wild man. She pulled what looked to be some kind of golden chalice covered with jewels off the wall. She gripped the stem of the golden cup in her hands as if it was a small baseball bat. Jessi had played varsity softball in high school and was known for her mean swing. The footsteps were getting closer now. Jessi stood by the entryway and waited. As the attacker turned the corner, she swung the chalice with all of her might. The bejeweled weapon came crashing down on the man's skull with a deafening thud dropping him to the floor. Jessi raised the ancient artifact high over her head and swung it down once more with even greater force.

"You son of a bitch!," she screamed.

There was another loud thump as the chalice connected with the back of his Lew's skull. He lay on the ground with eyes closed as a river of blood poured out from the gaping wound on his head. Jessi thought she had killed him, but did not want to wait around to find out. She took the chalice and continued running until she came upon an elevator. *Is this the only way out? God I hope there's no one on the other side of this door when it opens.*

Her heart pounded as she gripped the chalice again and waited for the elevator to reach her floor. She stepped back as the door opened wide. The elevator was empty. Jessi stepped in and searched the wall for any buttons. She pressed the *down* arrow and the elevator began to move. The elevator ride took several seconds and those seconds felt like an eternity to Jessi Miller.

"C'mon, c'mon," she screamed impatiently. Where the elevator was taking her she had no clue. What she did know was that she was gaining ground between herself and her attacker. The elevator stopped and the door opened to darkness. Jessi stepped out of the lift and ran her hand along the wall as she slowly moved forward. She could see nothing, but she could hear the sound of rats scurrying around her. Jessi's fear was compounded by frustration and she began to weep in the darkness.

"God please get me out of here," she begged. "Please get me to my baby."

Suddenly, the wall ended and Jessi moved her hand to what felt like the coldness of a door. She searched frantically for some kind of knob and seconds later she found it. She turned the handle and pushed open the heavy door with her shoulder. She took in her surroundings and realized that her prayers had been answered. With the chalice in one hand, she stepped out into the bright sunlight.

CHAPTER 22

▼

BOSTON

Heath and Grace sat in silence in the backseat of the taxi cab as the driver fiddled with the radio.

"You can't keep shutting me out baby," Heath said while wrapping his arm around her. "You gotta tell me what you're feeling."

"We have to find her Heath," Grace replied, staring out the window at the freezing rain. "I should have gone there with her. I should never have let her go all alone."

"You can't blame yourself," he said, kissing her on the cheek. "You offered to go, but Jessi chose to travel alone. We'll find her honey."

Grace turned her head toward his. "Promise?" she asked.

"I promise," he replied.

Grace rested her head on his shoulder. She was comforted by his words. It was Rosary's turn to stare out the window now. *That's a promise that you may not be able to keep,* he told himself.

The taxi driver pulled up to Terminal E at Logan airport and got out to retrieve their luggage from the trunk. Rosary paid the fare and tipped the driver $10 for the quick ride. He then grabbed the bags and they entered the airport. They walked down the concourse toward the United Airlines gate and spotted Betty Hu talking to a group of what appeared to be adoptive parents. Hu saw them coming and quickly introduced them to the others.

"Ah, here is the couple I was telling you about," Betty said with a smile. "This is Grace Chen and Heath Rosary. Grace is a producer at Channel 4 and she's researching a book about Chinese adoption. Please make them feel welcome."

The couple offered smiles and handshakes to their traveling companions before getting pulled away from the crowd by Betty Hu.

"So I see that you've already given them our cover story," Rosary told her.

"Yes," Betty replied. "These families will all be under great stress over the next few weeks and I ask that you conduct your inquiries as quietly as possible."

Heath and Grace were both taken back by the apparent coldness of her words. "Anything new from your guides?" Heath asked her.

"They've done another check of the hospitals around Beijing. No one has been admitted fitting the description of Ms. Miller."

Heath and Grace began to walk away when the agency director tugged on their arms.

"I know that I appear to be this big strong business woman," she said, her voice showing the first signs of cracking. "I've placed more than two thousand Chinese babies with new families and this is the first time that something like this has ever happened. I could not live with myself knowing that I placed that sweet woman in harm's way."

Grace reached up and rubbed the older woman's shoulder. "It's not your fault," she told her. "I've seen many pictures of the babies that you've brought over here. You're doing God's work here."

Betty Hu fought to compose herself.

"We will find Jessi," Grace promised. "We will bring her and her baby home."

*   *   *   *

Heath and Grace placed their carry-on luggage in the overhead cargo hold and took their seats for the marathon flight to China. This United Airlines flight was non-stop and the video screens at their seats told them that the estimated flight time would be 22 hours. Grace buckled her seat belt and rubbed Heath's arm.

"Thanks for the window seat," she said with a smile. "And thanks for coming honey."

"I always told you that I'd follow you to the ends of the earth," he replied with a laugh.

Grace reached for a set of headphones and began scanning through the movie menu. She selected the latest flick starring Reese Witherspoon and settled into her seat. Heath saw this and smiled. *She's relaxed. That's good. Anything to keep her from thinking about Jessi.* That was Rosary's job. He pulled out a pen and a small notepad from the pocket of his coat and went to work. He was looking for any common denominators in this growing mystery. He wrote down the thoughts as they came into his head. *She was last seen getting scared shitless by the fortune teller. The fortune teller can't be found. Is the fortune teller the key? Hospitals-nothing yet, but still best case scenario.* It was difficult for him to think of her laid up with a bad injury in some Chinese infirmary. It was even more difficult for him to think about the alternative. Before the trip, Rosary had reached out to an old friend in the FBI who fed him some eye opening statistics about the white slavery trade. The feds estimated that 250,000 women and children were victims of human trafficking and most of it was happening in Asia. *Beautiful white woman could fetch high price,* he wrote in his notebook. Rosary had to think positive about this real possibility. *If she has been kidnapped, then there's a good chance that she's still alive. But where is she?*

That was the question he had no answer for and it was gnawing at him like no case he had ever investigated. This wasn't just a job; Grace and Jessi were like sisters. This was family.

LYON, FRANCE

Henri Bouchard returned to his desk on the third floor inside Interpol Headquarters. He was dressed casually in a pair of jeans and a gray wool sweater. It was supposed to be his day off, but he felt that he had to come in and catch up on the work that he had missed. He placed his coffee cup on a stack of mail piled high on his desk and fired up his computer. He noticed a few condolence cards in the pile under his cup. The cards were printed in soft tones with sympathetic words. The top card was colored light blue with a drawing of a white Lilly on the cover. Bouchard was a bit surprised by the outpouring of support from his colleagues. He had not actually ingratiated himself with his co-workers since transferring to Interpol from the Central Directorate Judicial Police (DCPJ) to lead the Doucet case. He kept mostly to himself, consumed by the search for his childhood sweetheart.

His relationship with Sophie Doucet had blossomed while they were both still in their teens. They had lived in the same apartment building in Paris and were both the only children of overbearing single parents. This bond formed the building blocks of a friendship, and that friendship soon evolved into love. They would hold hands on the front stoop of their apartment building and sneak kisses under the stairwell inside. Soon after, they were learning the art of making love during the precious hours that their parents were not home.

Sophie was not a classic beauty back then. She was tall and awkward with long red hair that she had no idea what to do with. Sophie would put her hair up in a pony tail and that was fine with her. It was not fine with her mother however, whom had big plans for her only daughter. Rebecca Doucet was a former model herself, a survivor of the drug fueled Paris catwalks of the 1970's. Why she had wanted her daughter to follow in her footsteps was a mystery to Bouchard. As he and Sophie got closer, so did their parents. Rebecca Bouchard was drawn to his father, a charismatic college professor who was tenured at the Sorbonne. The former model had fallen head over heals for the intellectual. The feeling was not mutual however. Sophie's mother realized this when she caught him in bed with one of his students. To make matters even worse, he had asked her to join them. The next morning, Rebecca Doucet and her daughter moved out of the building and relocated to the other side of the city. She ordered Sophie to stay away from Henri, but the girl refused, at least in the beginning. The young lovers would take the metro and meet at a small café in the center of Paris. The courtship continued for a couple of months until Sophie told Henri that her mother was sending her to modeling school and that all of her free time would be spent on her new career. Henri tried to protest, but with a kiss on the lips she was gone. He blamed his father for the breakup and his hatred for the man grew. The two remained distant until recently.

Henri leafed through the stack of condolence cards and smiled. He appreciated the gesture, but knew that his father would not have. Bouchard had been away from work for the past week. He had not been vacationing on some sunny beach along the Riviera; instead he had been in a dingy state run hospital watching his father die. For three days, he sat by the old man's bedside holding his hand. His father was too weak to protest the sign of affection. Sentiment was not part of Luc Bouchard's makeup; the man was an existentialist after all. He had modeled his life after the lead character in Albert Camus' *L'Etranger*. Like the character, Meursault, Luc Bouchard felt that human life was rendered meaningless by the mere fact of death. It was an absurdist view that Bouchard had taught to generations of college students. *Oh, if his students could have seen him in the hospital. They probably would have agreed with the old man,* Henri thought to himself. In his mind's eye, he could see his father's cancer riddled body lying under the white cotton bed sheet. The once intimidating college professor looked like a weak child in that pathetic state. After the old man's death, the son ordered that his body be cremated. Henri Bouchard then took the ashes and sprinkled them into the Seine River. If there was a heaven, and once Luc Bouchard was convinced that he was actually in it, he might even appreciate his son's gesture. Besides bedding young students, walking along the Seine had been Luc Bouchard's favorite activity.

Henri checked his email and got up to go to the bathroom. The route took him past the American and British desks, where he noticed both of his colleagues hunched over their computers staring at the same picture on their screens. Bouchard got a lump in his throat when he saw the photo.

"Why are the both of you staring at Sophie Doucet's photograph?" he asked them.

"You're wrong Bouchard. Look closer," the American told him.

Bouchard leaned down over the American's shoulder and could not believe his eyes.

"My God," he said. "She looks just like her."

"This one's a television reporter back in the States. She went to China to adopt a baby and has disappeared," the American said.

"Can you send that file over to my desk?" Bouchard asked excitedly.

"Consider it done," the American responded tapping a computer key.

Suddenly, Bouchard felt his bathroom break could wait and he began walking back to his desk.

"Hey Henri," the American called out.

Bouchard turned around.

"Sorry to hear about your father. I really am."

Bouchard nodded to the American and then returned to his desk. He sat back down in front of his computer terminal and opened the file for the missing American journalist. He stared at her picture again for several moments. The resemblance to Sophie Doucet was uncanny. Both women had brilliant red hair, although the Miller woman's hair was cut a bit shorter. Both women had the same high cheek bones and both had sparkling hazel eyes. The woman's file stated that she had gone missing four days ago in Beijing. Unlike Doucet's kidnapping, there were apparently no other victims and no witnesses with this one. Still, the resemblance couldn't be ignored. *Could this be more than just a coincidence?* Bouchard cross referenced their body type in the Interpol computer data base. He typed in the words; *Caucasian, red hair, hazel eyes* and *missing.* He pressed the *Enter* button and let the computer go to work. In a few moments, four photographs flashed across the screen. The first picture was that of the missing American, Jessi Miller. The second photo showed Sophie Doucet wearing the Miss Universe crown. The woman in the third picture was a young Cambridge University student named Amelda Fern. She had gone missing while attending a student exchange program in Hong Kong. The fourth photo showed a young red headed woman in a flight attendant's uniform. The small caption under the picture stated that Quantas Airlines flight attendant Nicole Jackson had disappeared during an overnight stay in the Chinese city of Guangzhou. All the women had gone missing in the past year. Bouchard could have kicked himself for not trying this sooner. He picked up his phone and dialed the extension for the Interpol travel office. A receptionist quickly answered.

"This is Special Agent Henri Bouchard from the Missing Persons Division," he told her. "I need you to get me on the first flight to Beijing."

CHAPTER 23

▼

BEIJING

Pu-Yan put both hands in the pockets of his brown winter coat and kept walking the perimeter of Tiananmen Square. The temperature was in the low thirties and the wind was howling, but he didn't mind. Tiananmen was the largest public square in the world and the walk gave the pudgy bureaucrat his much needed daily exercise. The walk also allowed him time to think. The case of Ju-Long Lew had become far more complex since the vice president of Lew Petroleum had gone missing. *Could Lew have been connected?* He asked himself. Right now, there was still no evidence to suggest the man had been murdered. The oil executive had simply disappeared. A police search of the man's home did find a cache of drugs and cash, which led investigators to believe that Tang Lung Wei may have been the victim of a drug deal gone bad. But from what Pu-Yan knew about the man, this would have been way out of character for Tang Lung Wei. He was a bit of a dandy especially when it came to women, but Wei had no criminal background, at least not on record. Pu-Yan was no policeman, he was a television producer turned bureaucrat after all. But something in his gut told him that Lew was connected somehow to the disappearance of his second in command. *Did Wei try for a power grab within Lew Petroleum?* If so, the company's board of directors was not talking and had little incentive to talk in the future. With Wei's disappearance, board members were in line to get bumped up within the corporate hierarchy now. Pu-Yan also did not trust the initial findings of the Hong Kong police. He believed that many of the officers were already in Ju-Long Lew's back pocket.

On the other hand, it could be exactly what it appeared to be. *Maybe I just want too much for Lew to be guilty of some crime. It would certainly make it easier to wrest control of his company away from him.* Pu-Yan wrestled with these thoughts as he continued his walk around the square. Tiananmen had changed so much since the bloody protests of 1989. He passed the massive granite Monument of Revolutionary Heroes and stood where the Goddess of Democracy had been erected during the historic student sit-in. Pu-Yan remembered how the Goddess stared in defiance at the large portrait of Mao hanging over the entrance to his mausoleum. He remembered the sea of young protesters wearing white head bands with their fists raised in the air. What became a sweeping national movement, had actually begun as a small but vocal request by Beijing college students for better food and better conditions in their dormitories. A few weeks later, the crowd swelled to 1.2 million as throngs of young Chinese blocked soldiers wearing green uniforms from entering the square from the Avenue of Eternal Peace. Pu-Yan recalled what his father had told fellow members of the Municipal Party Committee at the time. "If we don't put Beijing under martial law," he said. "We'll all end up under house arrest."

That's when the crackdown came for the entire world to see. The tanks rolled in and young soldiers were ordered to open fire on their brothers and sisters. *What a disgrace,* Pu-Yan thought. He looked across the crowded square and focused his eyes on the customers coming and going from a Starbucks Coffee house located next to the train station. He couldn't help but smile. *Who really won the standoff between the pro-democracy students and the government?* The answer to that question was becoming more clear every day. Pu-Yan had always been a silent admirer of free market economics and felt a twinge of guilt for going after an independent businessman like Ju-Long Lew. But he had to think of himself now. Lew's downfall would secure his own political survival. The odds were stacked against him though; Lew had purchased protection from the police, the military and now China's oldest political ally.

HONG KONG

"Baba's been hurt," Bao Lew said frantically, while tugging on the sleeve of Mister Wong's black leather jacket. He patted the girl's head as he walked swiftly across the marble floor toward the master bedroom inside the Lew Mansion. His mind had been racing since receiving the phone call from his boss's wife thirty minutes earlier. Wong reached the master bedroom and knocked softly on the dark mahogany door. An unfamiliar voice summoned Wong inside. Before entering, he leaned down and kissed Bao's tear stained cheek.

"You're father will be alright," he promised.

Bao smiled through her tears and limped back down the corridor. Wong entered the spacious master bedroom and saw the team of doctors surrounding the large brass bed in the center of the room. Lew's wife Lixian was seated on one of two white leather sofas positioned near a bay window overlooking Victoria Harbor. Lixian's eyes were puffy and it appeared that she too had been crying. A tall thin white man wearing a white coat approached Wong as he closed the bedroom door.

"Your friend has suffered a severe concussion," the doctor with a British accent told him. "He has also received thirty stitches to his skull. I have advised him to rest, but he says that he wants to talk with you. For his sake, please make your conversation brief."

Wong nodded his head as the doctor motioned his assistants to leave the room. The medical team stepped away from the bed allowing Wong to see his boss for the first time. Ju-Long Lew was lying in the middle of the large bed with his head propped up on three satin pillows. The man's face was almost completely wrapped in gauze. Two more bandages covered his eyes.

"Are we alone?" Ju-Long Lew asked softly. His once powerful voice was now reed thin.

"Your wife is sitting on the couch," Wong informed him.

"Please leave us," Lew ordered Lixian. This time his voice was more forceful.

The woman got up without a word, nodded to Mister Wong and walked quickly out of the bedroom.

Lew waited for the door to close before speaking.

"That woman has been crying at my bedside for an eternity," he said.

"She cares about you, that's all."

Lew shrugged his shoulders. "It is not as bad as it looks," he said through a mask of bandages.

Wong walked over to the bed and whispered in his boss's right ear. "What happened?"

"I told Lixian that I fainted and fell down the stairs and cracked my head open on a marble step."

"What *really* happened?"

Ju-Long Lew was growing angry now. His fists were balled up at his sides and his shoulders began to shake. He took a moment to calm himself down.

"That bitch did this to me," he said through clenched teeth. "She struck me over the head with my own chalice."

Play with fire and you eventually get burned, Wong thought to himself.

"Where is she now?" Wong asked, not sure if he wanted to know the answer.

"She's gone," Lew replied. "I woke up on the floor of my gallery in a pool of my own blood. I could not walk, so I crawled over to the elevator. I entered the main house and crawled to the foot of the staircase before calling out to my wife."

"Why do you have bandages covering your eyes?" Wong asked.

"The bitch scratched me with her claws," Lew moaned. "The doctor says that I have a torn cornea in my left eye. He shot my eyeball with some kind of dye and it should heal in a couple of days. It feels like I've got a shard of glass in my eye right now."

Wong knew pain and felt great sympathy for his boss, but he still had questions that needed to be answered. "How did you explain the scratches? It's not the kind of injury one usually gets by falling down the stairs."

"Do you take me for a fool?" Lew asked angrily. "I pulled a crystal glass off my desk and shattered it on the stairwell. I still do not know how I was able to think that clearly in the condition I was in."

"The brain and the body are capable of great things, especially during a time of great desperation," Wong replied. "What would you like me to do now?"

His boss did not hesitate. "I want you to find and kill that bitch. I also want you to bring my chalice back to me. I will leave you to your duty. I must concentrate on healing. The summit begins in four days. I must be ready."

CHAPTER 24

▼

Wong walked into his boss's private den and locked the door behind him. He stretched a pair of rubber gloves over his hands and reached down for a blood soaked towel that was balled up on the floor. He carried the towel with him over to the glass top desk where he quickly typed in a random series of twelve numbers and letters on the computer key pad and then hit *Enter.* The massive jade Buddha slid silently on its rollers revealing the hidden elevator. He placed his right eye to the retinal scan and the elevator door opened wide. Wong stepped inside and noticed droplets of blood on the floor of the lift. There was also a blood stained fingerprint on the arrow button pointing *up.* He would have to clean this mess later. Wong pressed the button pointing down and waited for the door to close. Moments later it opened again to Lew's private gallery. He dropped the towel to the floor and followed the blood trail to the center of the room. With the massive blood loss, he was amazed that his boss had actually made it to the elevator and upstairs. He looked to the bare white wall where the Ardagh Chalice once hung. It had been one of the prizes of Ju Long Lew's private collection.

The chalice had been discovered in 1868 by two men digging for potatoes at a ring fort at Reerasta, Ardagh in County Limerick. The bejeweled goblet dated back to the 8th century and had long been considered a crown jewel of Ireland's National Museum until Mister Wong stole it for his master three years ago.

Wong continued through the art gallery toward the corridor leading to the rape chamber. He entered the small room and saw the satin sheets bunched up on the bed. He also noticed the ceramic opera mask shattered into pieces on the floor.

Wong smiled. He admired the American woman for fighting back the way she did. Maybe the experience would prompt his boss to find another, less strenuous hobby.

He left the rape chamber, walked through the gallery and back to the elevator. He entered and pressed the *down* arrow. Jessi Miller had left the sanctum like the other victims had, down the elevator and through a long tunnel at the base of Victoria Peak. The major difference was that the American was still breathing, while the others had been cut up and stuffed into garbage bags. Wong stepped out of the elevator and into the dark passageway. He clicked on his penlight and tried to retrace her steps. He could hear the sound of squeaking rats all around him, but he did not flinch. Mister Wong had seen much worse in his lifetime. He reached the end of the tunnel and opened the door which led to a narrow alley-way. He followed the alleyway while his intense eyes darted from the ground to the tall buildings around him. *Did she leave any clues?* The answer he soon found out was no. The alley opened up to a busy street crammed with small shops and restaurants. She was gone, lost in the sea of people that called this cramped city home. Wong felt angry and frustrated. He was angry at his boss for allowing her to getaway as she did. He was frustrated because he knew that he'd have to spend all his waking moments tracking her down. Moments later however, one phone call would change all that.

*   *   *   *

Heath Rosary entered the concourse of Beijing International Airport, and like Jessi Miller before him, he was not prepared for the smell.

"God damn, pass the gas mask," he muttered to Grace.

"Sorry, honey. I should've warned you about the odor," Grace told him. "It's the pollution. And you make fun of me for being so eco-friendly."

The adoptive parents lined up as a group and made sure each person made it through customs before making a mad dash for the luggage area. In the Beijing International Airport, everyone moved fast. The women walked behind, while the men ran ahead.

"You should probably go with them," Grace nudged Heath.

Rosary responded by pulling the lid of his BC baseball cap over his forehead and bolting through the terminal showing signs of the speed he once had while chasing after wide receivers during football days.

Heath heard a voice behind him.

"Hey wait up!" the man called out.

Rosary slowed down just enough for the guy to catch up.

"BC grad?" the man asked, pointing to his own maroon and gold baseball cap. "Frank Capolino, class of 89."

"Rosary," Heath introduced himself. "Class of 86."

"Are you the same Rosary who played cornerback for the Eagles?" the man asked excitedly.

Rosary nodded with a smile and kept jogging.

"I was a freshman when you were a senior," the guy gushed. "I still get chills when I think about that touch down you ran back to win the Fiesta Bowl."

"That was a long time ago," Rosary replied as they reached the luggage conveyor belt.

"Still feels like yesterday to me," the man said extending his hand. "I'm in sales."

Rosary shook the man's hand. "I'm in *trouble* if I don't find our bags."

"I know what you mean," Capolino laughed as both men watched suitcase after suitcase roll by them on the conveyer belt.

The salesman grabbed three large suitcases off the rack and called over to Rosary.

"You brought brown leather bags right?"

Rosary nodded.

"I think they're coming now," Capolino told him. "Oh well, I'll see you on the bus."

Rosary waved as the man disappeared through the throng of people walking briskly through the terminal. Heath found his own luggage and followed signs written in English toward the entrance of the airport.

"What took you so long superstar?" Grace kidded him.

Rosary shrugged and looked out to the parking lot where some group members were already getting on the bus.

"I've just spoken briefly with Rita," Grace told him. "She wants to get the families settled in at the hotel and then she'll meet us in our room."

"Does it look like she's got new information?" he asked.

"I'm not sure," Grace responded. "But I hope so."

The couple joined the adoptive parents on the mini-bus, while Rita stood by the driver. She struggled with a small microphone for a few seconds before getting it to switch on.

"Sorry about that," she told the group with a nervous laugh. "My name is Rita and I will be your guide for your next two weeks in China. Are you excited to meet your babies?"

"Yes!" the parents cheered in unison.

"Good. Let me tell you a little bit about our city," Rita continued. "There have been several capital cities here in China, but Beijing was the last imperial capital and has remained so since 1949. Beijing is home to 15 million people and 50 thousand babies are born here each year."

The statistic drew a loud sigh from the adoptive parents seated on the bus.

"Beijing is built around the Forbidden City. The Mongols called it "The Great Within". That is because it was the Emperor's residence and the focal point for the entire kingdom. There are close to 10 thousand rooms in the Forbidden City, but I doubt we'll be able to see them all during our visit," Rita giggled. "The Forbidden City is surrounded by walls 33 feet high and it covers almost four miles. The key to making it through China is comfortable shoes. This is a very big country and we will be doing a lot of walking here."

Rita continued her little speech, but Rosary was blocking her out now. He stared out the bus window as the vast city flashed by. *How do you find one person in a city of 15 million?*

It was late afternoon and already dark when the group arrived at the Jianguo Hotel. As the Americans stepped off the buses, they were surrounded by peddlers pushing scarves, hats and other trinkets in their faces. Rita urged the group to smile and keep walking toward the entrance of the hotel. Peddlers, young and old, male and female were everywhere in Beijing. Rosary entered the lobby of the hotel and his antenna went up. As he and Grace waited in line at the registration desk, Heath silently studied the room committing every face to memory. It was a skill he had developed in the Secret Service. Agents were trained to identify certain gestures that could be deemed a threat. An intense glare could be just as noticeable as a sudden hand movement. Rosary wasn't hoping to catch someone staring menacingly at the group of Americans; he was hoping to catch someone consciously looking away. From the hotel manager to the bellhop, Rosary eyed all the workers with suspicion. If Jessi had been kidnapped from the Jianguo, someone must have seen something. He was beginning to feel strongly that Jessi had been the victim of foul play and not some random accident. He did not share these feelings with Grace however. He scanned the lobby, but did not find any fliers posted with Jessi's picture on them. He didn't really expect to since it would not be the best publicity for the hotel. Rosary could picture the brochure in his mind. *Come to China … and disappear!*

The neatly attired hotel staff offered smiles and courtesies to the Americans without giving off the faintest hint that a guest may have been abducted from the hotel. Jessi had disappeared and it was like she never existed. Rosary studied the faces around him, but he was also on the lookout for any clues that may have been left behind. He treated the hotel as if it was a crime scene. The only problem was that the crime scene was now four days old. Grace picked up the hotel key and Rosary escorted her to their room on the 7th floor.

"Unpack your things, but don't leave the room," he ordered her.

"Where are you going?" she asked.

"I want to take a walk around the hotel and check all the possible exits. It's hard to believe that Jessi could have been taken from the hotel without anyone seeing her."

Rosary regretted those words as soon as he uttered them.

"Do you really think she was kidnapped?" Grace asked with alarm in her voice.

"As an investigator, I start with the worst case scenario and work backward. I really don't know what to think right now."

He walked over and wrapped her in his strong arms. They shared a soft kiss before she broke the embrace. "Go do your job. I'll wait here for Rita's phone call."

Heath hugged her again and walked toward the door before spinning around.

Grace read his mind. "I know, I won't open the door for anyone unless it's Rita or you," she promised.

Rosary closed the door behind him and walked down the corridor. He made sure there was no one lurking around on the floor before pressing the elevator button. He hated to leave Grace alone, but the only way to help her was for him to do his job. The elevator door opened and he squeezed inside. He rode to the lobby with five other people. He was a head taller than all of them. Rosary was startled when one Chinese man lit a cigarette in the cramped quarters. Instinct told him to protest, but he remembered that he was a guest in *their* country.

Once he arrived at the lobby, he spent the next thirty minutes wandering around. He found emergency exits on far sides of the hotel near the stairwells. He did not notice any sign of a struggle in either location, but he did see surveillance cameras attached to the walls. Rosary found two more exits when he stumbled into the laundry room and the kitchen of the hotel. He apologized profusely in English and told workers that he had taken a wrong turn. He had no idea whether they understood him or not. Satisfied with this initial fact finding mission, Rosary returned to his room and found Grace and Rita in the middle of a conversation. Both were speaking in Chinese.

"No habla Espanol," He said waving his hands at the women.

"That means he doesn't understand Chinese," Grace told Rita.

"Any luck on your end?" Grace asked Heath.

"Not really. The bad news is that the hotel has at least five exits. The good news is that surveillance cameras were covering the exits I found."

Rosary turned to Rita who was sitting Indian style on the floor. "Have you asked the police about any surveillance tapes?"

Rita shook her head no. It was not in the nature of the Chinese to press police about anything, much less a possible criminal investigation.

"Here is what I know," Rita said in broken English. "Hotel staff all questioned by police. No one saw nothing. Miss Miller's luggage was taken to police headquarters and they told Ms. Hu that they would keep bags for 90 days."

"I'd say we're off to a great start," Heath said sarcastically.

"Rita does have news about the fortune teller," Grace announced.

Rosary's eyes lit up. Any nugget would be a 100% improvement over what they had now, which was nothing.

"Funny thing about fortune teller," Rita said as she took off her eyeglasses and cleaned them with her shirt sleeve. "Fortune teller did not even own shop. Owner was away visiting an uncle and does not know how old woman got in his store."

"The mystery continues," Heath sighed.

"Owner says it's not first time lady use his shop," Rita explained. "He thinks he know where she lives."

Heath looked at Grace and smiled. "This could be our first real clue," he told her.

CHAPTER 25

▼

The cab driver dropped them off on a busy street corner in front of a massive bill-board. The three of them stepped out of the vehicle and onto the curb. Both Heath and Grace looked confused.

"Are you sure this is the right place," Rosary asked as he looked around. "This doesn't look like much of a neighborhood to me."

They were still in the heart of Beijing's business district and were surrounded on three sides by skyscrapers so tall they nearly blocked out the sun. In front of them stood a wall of billboards nearly a city block long, each featured an NBA star's picture accompanied by a Nike swoosh. The biggest billboard on the block belonged to Houston Rockets center and Chinese national treasure, Yao Ming. The melody to *It's a small world* played in Rosary's head.

"It's not neighborhood like you have back in your country," Rita explained. "The entrance is right through that chain link fence."

She pointed to a hole in the metal fence. It looked as if it were made by some-one using a set of wire cutters and was wide enough for only one person to get through at a time.

"I should not tell you this, but government does not help poor of Beijing. It just hides them behind advertisements like this," Rita said with sadness in her voice.

The guide led the way through the narrow hole in the fence as Heath and Grace followed close behind. They had stepped out of the 21st century and into a place that had long been forgotten. The Americans could not believe their eyes. They held their noses while wading through piles of trash that were shin deep. The group of small children darted in and out of alleyways chasing a small chicken that clucked wildly as it tried to stay one step ahead. Heath and Grace looked over at one another and immediately fished surgical masks out of their coat pockets. Rita did the same.

"This is the Dashilan district of Beijing," Rita said, as she placed the mask over her face. "Most who live here are Turkic peoples from the west of China. Some are here to work construction job, others have been here for generations."

They continued walking single file down the narrow lane. Smoke permeated the air as old women boiled cabbage outside on small hot plates. Four teenaged girls wearing dingy tube tops and short skirts stood provocatively outside their small huts waving Rosary inside. The girls were on their way to the *other* side of town, but couldn't turn their backs on a prospective client. "Yindao, yindao," they called out.

"What are they saying?" Heath asked Grace.

"Vagina," she answered matter of fact.

"I'll never tell anyone that I grew up in the 'hood again," He whispered. "I've never seen a ghetto as bad as this."

Grace nodded her head, but said nothing. The scene made her so angry that she wanted to cry. *How could a government allow anyone to live like this?* She asked herself.

Rita avoided eye contact with the teenaged girls and approached one of the elderly women instead. The woman was small and frail and when she opened her mouth, one could see she was missing several teeth. Rita and the old woman had a rapid fire conversation in Chinese that even Grace did not understand. The elderly woman pointed to a shack that was six doors down from her own. Rita bowed her head to the woman and continued on. Grace and Heath followed. Grace was walking a few steps ahead when she suddenly let out a scream and looked down at the pant leg of her jeans. Rosary ran forward and pulled her out of the way.

"What happened?" he yelled.

"He … spit on me," she replied in shock. Grace pointed over to an elderly man who was sitting on a crate in a darkened alley. The old man rested his rail thin arms on bony knees and stared straight ahead. He didn't look up at Grace or the big black man standing next to her with his fists clenched. He just stared straight ahead and kept on spitting. The panicked response from the Americans drew a loud laugh from the prostitutes nearby. Rita also giggled.

"Please don't take offense," she tried to explain. "It is not personal. Old men spit all the time in China, old women do also."

Rosary looked down at the old man, who acted like nothing had happened. Heath grabbed Grace's hand and continued walking. Moments later, the trio stopped at a narrow doorway, which was covered by a thick wool blanket. Rita pulled back the blanket and motioned the couple inside.

They entered a small room, which looked like it had been built by a drunken carpenter. It reminded Heath of the tree forts he and his friends put together as kids. Wooden boards of various sizes were nailed together in a haphazard way leaving small holes between each plank. The holes were plugged by rolled up newspaper and other scraps. The crude filler did little to block the cold air from blowing inside. Heath's eyes moved from the makeshift walls to the dusty floor where two brown leaves appeared to be dancing on the wind gusts. Grace stomped her feet and rubbed her shoulders to keep warm. The tiny room was ten square meters around and was furnished with an old chair and a thin mattress on the floor.

"Well, as you can see, she's not here," Rita told them.

"Are you sure this is the right place?" Rosary asked again.

"I'm sure of address, but a woman like that could have just abandoned this shack for another."

The trio was about to leave when suddenly the fortune teller returned home. She entered her spartan quarters carrying a small suitcase of some kind. The old woman shuffled passed her uninvited guests and gently sat down on her mattress with legs folded. Rosary waited for the woman to start yelling something in Chinese about the intrusion, but she only smiled.

"I've been waiting for you," she said in her native tongue.

Her words startled Grace, who paused before translating the words for Heath.

The fortune teller continued smiling as she asked her guests to sit with her. Her attitude was very different from Western culture. She didn't fret about her room or complain about the deplorable conditions. This was where she lived. It was a simple fact of life. Rita was the first to kneel down on the dirt floor and Heath and Grace followed suit. Their actions drew another wide smile from their host.

"I've been waiting for you," the old woman repeated. "You seek fiery white woman."

"Yes," Rita replied. Even she was stunned by the old woman's words.

The fortune teller pointed her bony index finger to Heath and Grace. "You have come a great distance to find her, yes?"

"We have come from America," Grace responded. "We are looking for our friend. She disappeared after you read her palms. Do you remember?"

The woman shook her head yes.

"Do you have any idea where she is?" Grace asked.

The woman shook her head no.

Grace lowered her head in frustration. *Another dead end,* she thought.

"She's still alive," the fortune teller announced.

Rosary was *lost in translation, again.* "What's going on? What's she saying?" he asked anyone who would answer.

"She says that Ms. Miller is still alive," Rita replied.

"How do you know that she's still alive?" Grace asked calmly.

"I have seen her many times," the old woman said, pointing to her temple. "She is alive, but she is in great danger."

"What's happened to her?" Grace asked. This time she voiced her question with a tinge of desperation.

"I see her in my mind's eye," the fortune teller replied. "She is running, running for her life."

Grace stood up, her voice was trembling. "What? What is she running from?"

The old woman closed her eyes. "I see a great dragon lying in a den of flames. He comes for her in the pre dawn hours when the Yang is in the ascendancy. It is when night becomes true day and the dragon is the master over this time. But the dragon is *not* the master over the white woman with hair of fire. She has wounded him. The dragon is angry. She has broken free but now, but the tiger has picked up her scent. The tiger is a nocturnal creature and its ferocity comes from the growing power of the Yang. The tiger will come for her at night. You don't have much time."

*   *   *   *

It was early evening by the time they left the fortune teller in the Dashilan district. The nervousness they had felt when they entered the village hours earlier was heightened now by the darkness. Heath kept the women close as they made their way back to the chain link fence that surrounded the neighborhood. Rosary instinctively grabbed at the small of his back for the cold comfort of a gun that was not there. Fortunately, they made it back to the street without incident. Rita stepped through the fence followed by Grace. Rosary guarded the rear. The cat calls began once the women were out in the street and away from what they thought was a dangerous situation. Rita and Grace were met by a gang of Beijing street toughs decked out in regalia of their favorite Western rap artists.

"Check out the bitches," one skinny teen said to his friends. The Chinese youth wore his baseball cap to the side and was covered with faux gold jewelry.

"You bitches hungry for this?" the skinny teen's fat friend shouted out while grabbing his crotch.

The teens moved closer to the women as Rosary stepped through the chain link fence. His appearance made the young toughs stop dead in their tracks. They had never seen a black man before, at least not in person. Their idea of black America came from pirated DVD's of Jay-Z and Snoop Dogg concerts. Rosary looked at the teens and then to the women. A scowl formed on his face and his intense brown eyes grew wide. The fierce look petrified the young thugs. Rosary stepped toward them and they stepped back. He could see the fear in their eyes. He raised his arms menacingly in the air and growled at the top of his lungs like a bear. The Chinese gangstas' tripped over one another as they back pedaled. They turned on the heals of their Nike sneakers and ran off into the night.

Heath looked back at Grace and Rita. "Are you two okay?"

They both nodded their heads.

Rosary then broke out into a thunderous laugh.

"What's so funny?" Grace asked a little annoyed.

"And here they thought rap music was going to be the death of Western civilization. I bet the critics never counted for *Eastern* civilization. Did you see the get ups they were wearing? I bet they'd never seen a black man before. They either thought I was God or the Devil." Rosary broke out into his Ali shuffle and began shadow boxing, his punches cutting through the crisp evening air. "I'm a baad man."

Grace cut him off before he could finish. "Don't even start, *Cassius*," she said rolling her eyes. "I apologize for my friend here," she told Rita, who stood by quietly not knowing what to make of it. "He's my knight in shining armor, but he's got a knack for putting his iron foot in his mouth."

Rosary saw the puzzled look on Rita's face. "Translation; I'm a nice guy, but can I can also be a real asshole."

Rita nodded her head and laughed. "Ah, asshole," she repeated.

The trio hailed a cab back to the hotel and parted ways. Rita had to check on the other couples, while Heath and Grace sought something to eat.

"Do you want to try a real Chinese meal?" she asked as they walked along the sidewalk in front of the Jiangou Hotel.

"When in Rome, doesn't apply here I'm afraid. I can't work this case from the toilet," he told her. "I did spot a Pizza Hut on the corner."

"You truly are the ugly American," she laughed.

"Damn straight."

They entered the Pizza Hut and were treated as if they were dining at a five star restaurant back in the states. An impeccably dressed maitre d' met them near the door and led them through the restaurant, which was fashioned in art deco. There was even a piano player tickling the ivories near the bar.

"Are we really in a Pizza Hut?" Grace asked Heath.

The maitre d' overheard the question.

"Yes, Pizza Hut," he replied with an enthusiastic thumbs up.

The host placed a pair of menus down on a spotless table and pulled back a chair for Grace.

"Xiexie ni," she responded.

"That means *thank you*," she told Heath.

"Yes, I know that one," he said with his face in the menu. "What's the Chinese word for American beer?"

They were approached by a thin, attractive waitress wearing a sparkling blue dress. "Chinese word for American beer is *Budweiser,*" she said proudly.

"Enough talk about the emperor, bring me the king!," Rosary bellowed.

"You really are a dork," Grace said laughing.

"We'll have two Budweisers and a large cheese pizza," she told the waitress.

The woman bowed her head and disappeared back into the crowded restaurant.

Rosary took off his leather coat and looked around. The Pizza Hut was packed with patrons who were decked out in their finest clothes.

"I bet the Chinese have to save up for a long time just to eat here," he observed feeling a little guilty.

"I wouldn't be surprised," Grace replied. "Do you want to eat first, or should we talk about the fortune teller now?"

"Let's talk now," Rosary replied while reaching across the table for her hand.

"Do you believe her?" Grace asked.

"Well, from what you told me, she only spoke in broad terms. I've never worked with a psychic, but I know people who have. I'm not sure if I buy any of it, but the guys that do believe it say it's easy to point out the frauds because they never offer any specific information."

The conversation was interrupted by the waitress who brought over the beers and two clean glasses. Grace poured hers while Rosary drank straight from the bottle.

He took a long pull, closed his eyes and savored the taste.

"Is it better than sex?" Grace asked quizzically.

"No. It's close, but you win out over beer every time," he laughed.

The pizza arrived next and both dug in. It tasted a little different than it did back home. *Must be the cheese,* Rosary thought. Still, he knew he'd have no trouble keeping this meal down. As he had learned from past cases, one thinks more clearly on a full stomach.

"As I was saying," he continued with a mouthful of pizza. "The fortune teller didn't give us any real information. She talked about a dragon and a tiger. And what was all that 'yang in the ascendancy' stuff?"

"She was talking about the balance of life," Grace pointed out. "The good and the bad, the right and the wrong, the day and night."

"That doesn't help much in an investigation like this one."

Rosary looked into her eyes. She looked tired, but determined. "You believe the old woman, don't you?"

Grace nodded. "I do believe her Heath, and I know that we don't have much time."

CHAPTER 26

▼

HONG KONG

Mister Wong parked his Mercedes at the dock alongside Aberdeen Bay on the south side of Hong Kong Island. He cut a path through the busy open air street market and continued past the Jumbo Floating Restaurant, which glistened under neon lights. In fact, the entire bay sparkled in the moonlight. It was a scene that rivaled the French Riviera, but unlike that glamorous port of call, the luxury liners here were forced to share space with thousands of boat people who called this floating city home.

Aberdeen Bay had served as a notorious pirate's den 200 years ago and was then transformed into a fishing village. Of course, the make-over did not stop illegal activities from thriving on these crowded waters. The area was home to 60,000 people and many boat dwellers had already been forced away from the bay and into housing developments on shore. One junk owner who had refused to leave, had a son who held a powerful position in the Hong Kong Police Department. The father died years ago, but the son kept the junk for situations like this one.

Wong rented a small sampan and navigated his way through the maze of house boats until he came across the one he was looking for. He was still con-flicted about what to do next. He was sick of playing pimp for an impetuous boss. His career was not going as planned. He had enjoyed the work of pilfering paintings and other priceless works of art because it posed a great challenge and no one got hurt. But now, the kidnappings and murders were beginning to play on his conscience. *I have a conscience, how about that?* He mused. Wong wished that the American had actually escaped; he truly admired her fighting spirit. But she had not, and he had given his word that he would see this ugly incident to its proper end.

Wong flashed his pen light three times in the darkness as he steered the sampan closer to the junk. The signal was returned by two flickers from a flashlight. Wong pulled his small vessel up to the larger boat and was helped on board by a set of strong hands. Those hands belonged to Zhou Dan, veteran shift commander for the Hong Kong police.

"I telephoned you as soon as I heard," the cop told Wong.

"Who found her?" Wong asked.

"Fortunately, it was two of my men. They thought she was just some drug addict. She was speaking incoherently about being held captive somewhere by a man in a mask. It wasn't until they mentioned the beizi (cup) that I thought of you."

Wong had often used Zhou Dan's influence at Hong Kong's port authority to secure safe passage for his stolen antiquities. It was influence that Zhou Dan was paid handsomely for.

"Where is she now?"

Zhou Dan pointed back to the cabin of the junk. "My men are taking good care of her inside."

Wong looked at him curiously as the cop led him down a small set of steps and into the cabin, which was dark except for two dimly lit lanterns. Upon entering, he saw two of Zhou Dan's men laughing as they struggled to put their uniforms back on. The cabin smelled of booze and he could hear the American woman's soft whimpers coming from behind the brutes. Wong swallowed his rage. There were questions that needed to be answered before actions were to be taken.

"How many others know about the woman?" he asked calmly.

"No one but us," Zhou Dan replied emphatically. "These boys have been working for me for years. They have my trust, and they expect to be paid well for their work."

"Of course," Wong replied. He turned his attention to the two young rapists.

"Did she bring you pleasure?" he asked with a smile.

The officers laughed and pointed to their boss. "Seniority has its privileges," one young cop said. "The boss got to have her first."

"Is that true Zhou Dan?"

The veteran cop only shrugged.

Wong pulled his pistol from his leather jacket and fired a shot through Zhou Dan's forehead. He turned the gun on the two terrified younger officers who were still struggling with their pants. They screamed in unison as Wong fired two shots dropping them both. Now he only heard one scream. Wong moved forward to get a closer look at the American. Her red dress, the one he'd kidnapped her in was now in shreds across her bruised body. Her once beautiful red hair was now matted down with sweat. Her arms and legs were tied to the iron posts of a ratty old bed. Wong saw that she had struggled mightily. Her face was badly beaten and trickles of blood were dripping down the rope knots on her wrists. *What have I done?* He asked himself. The American was still alive, but just barely. Her hazel eyes were glazed over and she was moaning. Wong could not make out the words. She gazed over at him as he slowly approached the bed. A look of recognition flashed in her sad eyes. Wong wanted to look away, but knew that he had one more thing he must do. He said a prayer for Jessi Miller and squeezed the trigger.

CHAPTER 27

▼

BEIJING

They arrived back at the hotel and Rosary checked the front desk for any messages. There were none. He was growing even more frustrated now. Grace's father had promised the help of his two nephews, men who were supposed to know the city inside out. The nephews had yet to show up. Heath felt helpless, like he couldn't even cross the street without someone leading the way. Of course the language was different, but there were other obstacles to overcome. He was used to blending into the crowd and investigating his cases quietly, but effectively. Rosary knew that he couldn't do that here. He would also feel much safer if he was armed. He no longer worried much about the local firearms laws. He needed his gun. They returned to their hotel room, changed into their pajamas and climbed into bed. They had forgotten to kiss each other good night. Both were exhausted and fell asleep within minutes.

The alarm went off at 5 a.m. the next morning. Without opening his eyes or taking his head off the pillow, Heath reached his arm over to the small table beside the bed. His fingers searched frantically for the alarm clock, but it was not there. During this time, Grace rolled off her side of the bed and walked over to a small writing desk and switched off the alarm clock that was plugged into the wall.

"Wake up, Sam Spade," she groaned. "You're in China, remember?"

Rosary opened his eyes and sat up in bed. He rolled his neck around and could hear several cracks.

"What time is it?"

"It's just after five. You wanted to get up early remember?"

"Why was that again?"

"You wanted to do a little Tai-Chi in the park in back of the hotel."

Rosary rolled over and placed the covers over his head. Grace walked back to the bed; grabbed her pillow and threw it playfully at him. "You are impossible, you know that?"

He responded with a sudden burst of energy. Rosary jumped out of bed and hit the floor. He did 100 pushups followed by 100 sit-ups. After the exercise, he grabbed a hotel towel and headed for the shower.

"Thanks for the pep talk coach," he said pecking Grace on the cheek.

"No problem babe," she responded with a giggle. "Remember; don't open your mouth in the shower. That joke you made about working this case from the toilet, one drink of water here and it won't be very funny anymore."

He thanked her for the reminder and stepped into the shower. Rosary liked his showers hot and this one didn't disappoint. As the water beaded down his face, he tried to envision the day ahead. Grace was to travel with the adoptive group to the Great Wall. She at least had to keep up appearances that she was there to write a book about Chinese adoption. Meanwhile, he would poke around the American Embassy. He hoped his friend; Nikki Tavano would be able to help him cut through the red tape with the embassy liaison officer. The American government didn't welcome help from outside investigators and getting access to Jessi Miller's missing persons file would be tough. Not impossible, just tough.

Showered and shaved, Rosary dressed in a pair of tan slacks, white dress shirt and a blue blazer. He doubted that he would be able to talk his way into the embassy wearing jeans and a sweater.

"Did you save any hot water for me?" Grace asked wrapping her arms around her man.

Rosary was tempted to throw her on the bed and ravish her. Some of their best love making sessions had occurred in the morning. He thought better of it, at least for now. He needed a clear head for the day that would follow.

"Why don't you go down to the lobby and stretch your legs a bit," she told him. "I'll take a shower, get dressed and then walk down to breakfast with Rita. Don't worry; I won't leave the room unless I'm with her."

"If for some reason, you and Rita can't hook up, page me in the lobby. I'll come up and get you."

"Aye, aye Agent Rosary." Grace gave him a mock salute and went into the bathroom. Rosary could hear the water running as he left the room. He checked the floor for any strange faces before taking the elevator to the lobby. Most of the hotel guests were still asleep and the lobby was relatively quiet. A few clerks were busy getting ready for their day behind the reception desk. It was the quiet before their phones would begin to ring almost nonstop throughout the day. The doors to the hotel restaurant were still closed, so Rosary took a seat in the lobby. He was alone, except for a rotund Chinese man who had his face stuck in a copy of USA Today.

"Mind if I take a look at that after you?" Rosary asked assuming the man spoke English.

"Which section would you like first, Mister Rosary?"

The words startled Heath, but he tried not to show it.

"Who are you?"

"My name is Jin-Sheng, but my American friends call me Benny. I'm here on my uncle's behalf," the man replied lowering the newspaper.

"I expected to see you last night," Rosary whispered with his head down. "Tommy Chen told me that you and your brother were to be of valuable assistance to us."

"My uncle is a great man. If he has put his faith in us, you should also."

"So assist me," Rosary said growing more agitated by the second.

"I understand that your group is going to walk the Great Wall today."

"Grace is going on the trip," Heath told him. "I'm gonna stay here and poke around a bit."

Benny shook his head showing his disapproval. "You must be on that bus. My brother is to meet you at the wall." He looked down at the brown nylon backpack that sat on the floor between his legs. "You will carry this with you. I will seek answers here at the hotel. I have a few paid informants on the staff. It is time that they make good on their promises. I have already discovered something quite interesting."

The hefty Chinese man stood up from the chair and left the newspaper folded on the seat. He put on his rain coat, grabbed his umbrella and headed for the door.

Rosary waited a few seconds before grabbing the newspaper and placing it under his arm. He picked up the backpack and walked into the men's room where he found a stall and locked himself inside. He sat down on the toilet and carefully unfolded the newspaper. Tucked between the *Sports* and *Money* sections of the paper was a photo copy of a young man's work permit. It looked like a driver's license and the words were written in Chinese. Under the man's picture was a note written in English. *His name is Pang Lingyi. He is clerk/bartender here at hotel. He was supposed to return to work yesterday after four days off. Did not return. He is considered very reliable worker. Phone calls to flat have gone unanswered.*

Rosary stared at the young man's picture. He had long bangs covering much of his forehead and he wore a thin mustache. Other than that, he looked like just about every Chinese man that Rosary had seen so far in this country. *It's almost impossible to stand out in a crowd,* Heath thought to himself. He carefully folded the photo copy and slid it into the breast pocket of his coat. Hopefully the next answer to this riddle would come at the Great Wall.

He left the men's room and saw that the doors had opened to the hotel restaurant. Tired guests were already flocking to the breakfast buffet. Rosary entered the restaurant and spotted Grace sitting down with another couple. He took his place in the buffet line and placed two blueberry muffins on his plate. He avoided the bacon and sausage, but opted for the scrambled eggs. He piled the eggs high on his plate and walked over to Grace's table.

Grace made the introductions. "Heath, you remember Frank Capolino from the airport. This is his wife Nancy."

Heath shook their hands and sat down at the table.

"Grace tells me that you're not going with us to see the Great Wall," Frank said through a mouthful of sausage. "Why are you gonna sit this play out?"

Rosary hated guys who talked in football terms.

"Change of plans Frank," he announced. "I'm feeling a little better and can't wait to see that wall."

Grace looked at him curiously. Heath nodded his head as if to say, *I'll tell you later.*

CHAPTER 28

▼

The bus ride to the restored section of the Great Wall in Badaling took about 45 minutes. The trip took them away from the traffic choked streets of Beijing and out along the sparse national highway. Once they had left Beijing proper, there was little else to see, the landscape was pretty barren. There were also no housing developments and very few cars were out on the road. Grace had offered Heath the window seat this time. He watched rugged hill after rugged hill roll by as the rain fell softly against the window of the bus.

"Sorry about weather," Rita said standing at the front of the bus. "Hopefully, rain will not dampen your experience. Here are interesting facts about Great Wall. The wall took over 2,000 years to construct and spans 3,700 hundred miles. It is one of eight wonders of the world, but despite the rumor, it can not be seen from space. First section of the wall was built in 500 BC and extended for 300 miles. When China was finally united in 221 BC, existing walls were linked together to protect our country from invaders from the north. At that time, wall was garrisoned by up to a million soldiers. It is our greatest pride. We urge you to take many pictures so you can teach your babies about our culture when they are older."

Rosary was only half listening to Rita's speech; he was too busy thinking about the hotel worker who had not returned to work. Was it merely a coincidence? The worker could just be sick and not well enough to pick up the phone. But he also could have played a role in Jessi's disappearance. Rosary knew that he wasn't going to find the answer sitting on this bus. The answers he was looking for were back at the hotel.

Still, he had to thank Grace's cousins for providing him with what could be the only real lead in this case. It was only last night that he'd been told by a fortune teller to look for mystical dragons and tigers.

Rosary's train of thought was broken by a tower that appeared over a hill in the distance. He soon realized that it was not part of the Great Wall, but it was something just as fascinating, at least to him. Here in the middle of nowhere stood an exact replica of Disneyland complete with Sleeping Beauty's castle. It was an eerie site because unlike the real Disneyland, the park had no visitors. It was completely deserted.

"Rita, what's the story with this amusement park?" he shouted from his seat.

"Like much of China, great plans are sometimes never fulfilled," she told him.

"The government officials who built this park, ran out of money before it was completed. It has been empty for last ten years. What is the American word for it?" she asked before coming up with the answer on her own. "Oh yes, it is ghost town. But China finally has a real Disneyland of its own in Hong Kong. It has already surpassed the Great Wall as the most visited place in China."

The buses arrived in Badaling ten minutes later. The sight of the Great Wall drew applause from the couples on the bus. It was a stunning vision. The massive wall straddled jagged mountain peaks from as far as the eye could see. What really amazed Rosary were the twists and turns in the wall itself. On this mountain ridge, the wall moved side to side like a serpent as it disappeared and then re-emerged from the cloud cover. The sight left Rosary speechless, which Grace knew was no ordinary feat.

They stepped off the bus and watched as Rita and her colleague Claudia got in line to pay for the tickets. Historical sites like this one were included in the adoption agency's travel package. The guides handed out tickets a few minutes later, and Heath and Grace slowly tried to separate themselves from the group without anyone noticing. However, Frank Capolino, the salesman from Stoughton, Massachusetts, noticed everything. He was not about to give up his new best friend without a fight.

"Why don't we conquer this thing together," Frank said. "You can take pictures of us and we'll take pictures of you. We'll be up to the top of that mountain in no time."

Rosary doubted that. Climbing this steep wall would pose a challenge, especially at this altitude. It looked as if Capolino hadn't had a serious work out in years.

"Sorry guys, but Grace here suffers from Vertigo," Rosary lied. "The height of the wall maybe too much for her. We're gonna have to go at our own pace."

Frank and his wife awkwardly apologized to Grace about her condition and then wandered off on their merry way.

"Vertigo?" Grace asked with irritation in her voice.

"Hey, thank Alfred Hitchcock for that one," Rosary tried to explain. "Otherwise, we'd be stuck with them."

The couple held hands and began their climb. Both were athletes, but the steepness of the climb and the size of the large stone steps began taking their toll on their calf muscles before they had even approached the first watch tower.

"Imagine walking this whole thing?" Heath said in amazement.

"Imagine building it," Grace replied as she tried to catch her breath.

Rosary carried the brown backpack prominently over his shoulder as they continued on to the next guard tower. Halfway up, they passed the Capolinos, who looked like they were going to pass out.

"There'll be no end zone dance for us," Frank shouted. "We're going back to the bus."

Rosary nodded to the man and kept on climbing.

"You two are getting to be good buddies," Grace teased him. "I won't be surprised if you invite him over to do a little grilling when we get back."

Rosary was not amused. "You know where I keep my gun. If I ever get the urge to pal around with Frank, do me a favor and just shoot me."

They reached the second tower and stopped to stretch their legs. The area was a narrow, damp space with ancient lancet windows that looked out across the mountain below. Just now they realized how high they had actually climbed.

A tall, thin Chinese man entered the guard tower from the north. He was carrying a brown backpack identical to the one Rosary had.

"Can I take your picture?" the man asked.

Grace turned around and broke into a smile. "Cousin," she shouted with arms wide.

Jin-Xui embraced her and kissed her gently on the cheek. Grace's cousin placed his backpack at Rosary's feet and took the other one as his own.

"Please, do not open it here," he said in perfect English.

"I wouldn't think of it," Heath replied.

"Good. The bag contains a 9mm semiautomatic and a speed loader which will give you more bullets," he explained in hushed tones. "There are three cartridges in the backpack. If you need more ammo, you're in trouble. There are also two satellite phones for use if and when the two of you split up. These are very secure phones that cannot be traced or bugged. Please use these and not a hotel phone or a cell phone that you can buy out on the street. In China, you never know who is listening."

"You could say the same about our country," Grace piped in.

"Spoken like a true democrat," Heath countered with a roll of the eyes.

The stab at humor was lost on the cousin, who was all business.

"There has been an interesting development," he said, immediately getting their attention.

"What's happened?" asked Rosary.

"The hotel worker is now accounted for."

This announcement drew a loud sigh from both Heath and Grace.

"His body was pulled out of a dumpster today along Embassy Row."

*   *   *   *

Grace returned to the mini-bus alone. As she climbed on, she got a curious look from Rita, who had been talking to the bus driver. Grace said nothing as she walked down the small aisle and found a seat near the back of the bus. She closed her eyes as if she were going to sleep. The other couples piled in soon after with an assortment of trinkets they had purchased at the wall. Frank Capolino and his wife Nancy walked onto the bus with new sweatshirts and pendants. Frank was also wearing a fur hat that was part of the standard uniform worn by the Chinese military. There was even a small red star on the front.

"Wait til they get a load of this back home," he told his wife, who laughed.

The mini-bus started pulling out of the parking lot when Frank shouted to the driver.

"Stop," he said. "We're missing someone. Grace, where's Heath?"

If Heath ever invites you over, I'll shoot you myself, she thought.

"Heath won't be coming with us to the Forbidden City," she told everyone. "My cousin lives not far from here and he's been teaching local kids about American football. He asked Heath to give the kids a few pointers."

Grace even surprised herself at how quickly she was able to come up with that lie.

"Chinese kids playing American football," Frank said in amazement. "What I wouldn't give to see that."

*   *   *   *

The scene was cold by the time Rosary and the cousin arrived. The body had been discovered by a sanitation worker in an alley adjacent to the British Embassy early that morning. The trash collector was long gone and so were the police. Rosary was surprised to see that there wasn't even crime scene tape put up around the dumpster. It was as if nothing had happened. Then he remembered the summit that was set to begin the following day. The parties, including the former U.S. President were to arrive that evening. The last thing the Chinese government wanted anyone to know was that a murder had been committed on Embassy Row.

Rosary pulled a pair of leather gloves out from the pocket of his coat and slid them over his hands. He also had with him a small brown bag that he had found in the back of Jin-Xui's car. He carried the bag in hopes of finding any physical evidence that may have been overlooked by the Beijing police, evidence that would hopefully lead them back to Jessi. A forensic scientist friend from his days with the Secret Service had once told him that a simple brown paper bag was the best receptacle for collecting trace evidence. The scientist preferred paper over plastic because the condensation build up in a plastic baggie could contaminate the evidence. Rosary asked Jin-Xui to wait inside the car; he didn't want another set of foot prints scuffing up the crime scene. The distance between the hotel and the British Embassy was just over two city blocks and whoever killed the clerk would have had to drive the body over here to the dumpster. Rosary assumed the clerk was not murdered here in the alleyway. If that were the case, then someone would have heard something. *But not if the killer used a silencer,* Rosary told himself. He inspected the pavement near the alleyway for any tire marks, but found none. *The killer was in no rush to flee the scene.* He then walked carefully toward the dumpster and noticed at least six different sets of foot prints around the large metal container. It looked as if investigators trampled through the crime scene. *Damn, don't they get CSI here in China?* Rosary asked himself. He lifted the heavy dumpster lid and looked inside. It was dark, so he pulled a small flashlight from his coat pocket and shined it into the belly of the container. The dumpster was nearly full with trash. Rosary couldn't make out any signs of blood or anything else for that matter on the garbage bags piled high inside. He needed to get a closer look, so he took off his leather coat and laid it down flat on a hedge next to the container. He then placed both hands on the rim of the dumpster and hoisted himself inside. Rosary was no stranger to dumpster diving, He had solved more than a few cases by sifting through other people's trash. He was paying the price now though, the smell was awful. He began poking around with his flashlight as he moved the trash bags around. He heard a high pitched squeak under the shifting bags and realized he was not alone. He felt something move by his leg and he jumped out of the dumpster. In his eagerness to find any evidence in the case, he had overlooked his biggest fear—Rats. An uncontrollable chill ran up his spine. *Keep it together tough guy. Would Sam Spade be scared off by a few large mice?* After a few moments, he regained his composure and decided to climb back into the container. He had one leg up on the dumpster when he heard footsteps coming from behind him.

"It looks like security is doing a sweep of the area right now," Jin-Xui said. "I've been ordered to move my car. You should come now. It may be hard to explain yourself."

Rosary hated to give up the promise that something important could be buried in that dumpster. But he also did not want to spend the rest of this trip sitting in a Chinese jail. He followed Grace's cousin back to the car.

"I've been meaning to ask you," Rosary said as he settled into the passenger seat. "You speak English as well as I do, have you spent much time in the States?"

Jin-Xui laughed. "I'm as American as you are. I was born here, but grew up in Northern California."

"San Francisco?"

"Thanks for the stereotype," Jin-Xui replied with more than a hint of sarcasm. "Just because I'm Chinese doesn't mean that I grew up in Chinatown. My brother and I actually grew up across the Bay. Our father heads up the classical Chinese literature program at Berkeley College. Jin-Xui is a little hard to pronounce, so my friends back home just call me Joe."

"Why Joe?"

Grace's cousin laughed. "I was raised in Raider country, but I rooted for the 49ers. I was a huge Montana fan growing up."

"Okay, Joe. Why did you come back here?"

"Just look around you Heath. Beijing is undergoing a building boom. The economy here is growing by leaps and bounds. It's like the old gold rush in reverse. People are coming back to China to make their fortunes."

"So what is it that you two do for a living?"

Joe smiled. "We do a little importing, a little exporting and we help foreigners like you find their way around."

The next stop was the Beijing City Changping Mortuary. Joe parked his silver Volvo outside the service entrance, where a man in a white lab coat was waiting for them. The man ushered them inside and down a long dark corridor to an autopsy room bathed in fluorescent light. Rosary squinted as his eyes adjusted to the brightness. Upon entering the room, he counted five bodies lying on slabs.

"It's been a busy day so far," the medical examiner told Joe in Chinese.

"I believe the person you are looking for his over here."

The pathologist led them to a table in the middle of the room. The examiner looked at both men.

"Are you ready?" he asked this time in English.

They nodded their heads and the examiner pulled back the white cotton sheet from the dead man's face. Rosary pulled the photo copy of Pang Lingyi's work permit from his coat. The only difference between the picture and the body lying on the slab was the small bullet hole in the dead man's forehead.

"That's the hotel worker alright," Rosary told Joe. He could hear the zyther music playing in his head as he thought of that classic line from one of his favorite Orson Welles films, *The Third Man.* "You were born to be murdered," he mumbled to himself as he stared down at the bartender's body. Heath turned his attention to the medical examiner. "I suppose Hong Kong police have already run a ballistics test on the bullet. Anything else we could squeeze out of them would be most helpful."

"Or not," came a voice from the other side of the room. Rosary turned and saw two men standing in the doorway. One was Chinese, the other was white.

"Check the toe tag," the Chinese man urged.

Rosary looked at it but couldn't make it out. He handed it to Joe, who read it aloud.

"It says *death by suicide.*"

All focus turned to the medical examiner, who simply shrugged his shoulders and he lit a cigarette. "That tag was printed before body even brought here," he said, while blowing a plume of smoke toward the ceiling. "It is not unusual. We do best that we can here. Just last week, the body of Li Shunfeng was brought here, also called a suicide. Police say she jumped off building. I knew this was lie because woman did not have any broken bones, no bruises. In reality, she froze to death. She was sprayed with high powered hoses and dragged outside in her wet clothes. They kept her out there overnight. Her clothes were in icy clumps stuck to her body when they brought her here."

"Why'd they kill her?" Rosary asked.

"She was Falun Gong," Joe answered. "The group is outlawed here in China."

"What is Falun Gong?"

"It's a religion that melds Buddhist and Taoist principles," he explained. "It has 70 million members here in China and that's more than the number of people in the communist party. That's why the government is so frightened of them."

"Was Pang Lingyi a member of this Falun Gong?" Rosary questioned.

"No, he was just an innocent hotel worker caught in the wrong place at the wrong time," replied the Chinese man standing in the doorway.

"I don't get it, who are you?" Rosary asked as his frustration continued to build.

"Oh I apologize," the Chinese man said stepping forward. "My name is Pu-Yan, I am with the Central Committee."

Pu-Yan shot a knowing glance to the medical examiner, who raised his hands and turned away. A trail of cigarette smoke followed him as he left the room.

Rosary looked curiously at Grace's cousin.

"Do not be alarmed," Pu-Yan said in heavily accented English. "I know all about you Mr. Rosary and what you are doing here."

"What's this, some kind of set up?" Rosary asked Joe.

"No Heath, Pu-Yan may have the answers you seek."

"Answers and photographs," Pu-Yan announced.

The men gathered around the autopsy table and paid little attention to the body that was lying on the slab.

"The kidnapping of your friend was captured by two hotel surveillance cameras," Pu-Yan informed Rosary. "One camera was in the hotel bar, the other in the kitchen. However, the kidnapper was very smart. He was able to hack into the computer that ran the robotic cameras and delete the images from the computer's memory bank. What the kidnapper did not know, was that the images had already been stored in real time in a video data base at the outside firm that handles security for the hotel. I managed to retrieve the tapes before Beijing Police could get their hands on them."

Pu-Yan handed Rosary a manila envelope. "These are still images of the kidnapping. As you'll see the resolution is quite good."

Heath opened the envelope and pulled out the photographs. The first showed Jessi Miller sitting at the hotel bar with a neatly dressed stranger. The second picture showed the stranger dragging Jessi into the hotel kitchen. She appeared to be unconscious. Heath recognized the red dress she was wearing and knew that it was her favorite. He felt a lump in his throat as the rage built up inside of him. The third photograph was taken in the kitchen. This picture provided the best image of the kidnapper. Rosary quickly tried to put the puzzle pieces together in his mind. "Why would the police try to cover up for the kidnapper?"

"They are not trying to cover up for the kidnapper, but they are trying to cover up for his employer," Pu-Yan answered. "The kidnapper made another mistake during his hasty retreat. He managed to erase any record of his stay at the hotel with his computer. His hotel room was also wiped clean of finger prints. However, he did leave a small, crumpled up piece of paper on the floor by the telephone. On the paper was a phone number, which we called. The number led to a British soldier who was apparently waiting for a rendezvous with the kidnapper when our man had other plans. We interrogated the soldier and he admitted that he had planned to sell some ancient Iraqi artifacts to our man."

"Did the Brit give up a name?"

Pu-Yan nodded his head.

"Lemme guess, the name was bogus. Right?" Rosary asked.

This time, the white man chimed in. "Yes, the name is just an alias, but we believe we do know who the kidnapper is."

"Start by telling me who you are," Rosary demanded.

"Excuse me," the white man said with a thick Parisian accent. "My name is Henri Bouchard, I'm a detective with Interpol." Bouchard flashed his identification badge.

Rosary shook the Frenchman's hand. "So who is our mystery man?" he asked.

"He's gone by many names. I know him as Phra Nang, the man who kidnapped Sophie Doucet," Bouchard explained and then pulled out another folder of photos to show Rosary.

"Take a look at these women. Do you see any similarities?" Bouchard asked.

Rosary studied each photograph. Any one of these women could have been mistaken for Jessi Miller.

"I can see the kidnapper's got a profile going," Rosary acknowledged. "He's after white, red haired, beautiful women."

"He's after them, and so is his boss," Pu-Yan explained. "We know that his employer collects stolen art treasures. It appears that he is now collecting something else."

"So why don't you arrest him?" Rosary asked.

Pu-Yan laughed. "He's the wealthiest businessman in China and very politically connected. He's got committee members on his payroll, as well as the military. He's also the main reason for the nuclear summit that is expected to begin here tomorrow. He happens to be close personal friends with the leader of North Korea. He actually persuaded the leader to take part in the talks."

"So where does that leave me?" Rosary asked through clenched teeth. "I've got a friend who may be still alive."

"I think our best bet is the kidnapper himself," Bouchard answered. He looked closely at the kidnapper's image caught by the surveillance camera. "His eyes are a bit wider, and his jaw line is different. It appears that he's had plastic surgery. But, I am convinced the kidnapper is Phra Nang."

"What name does he go by now?" Rosary asked.

"He's called Hu Wong," Pu-Yan answered.

"*Hu*, now where have I heard that word before?" Rosary asked himself.

"Hu, is the Chinese word for tiger," Pu-Yan explained.

Rosary immediately thought back to the fortune teller. "*Tiger*," he repeated. "Holy shit."

CHAPTER 29

▼

HONG KONG

The dragon checked himself in the mirror, but did not recognize the image staring back at him. The hair above his right ear was shaved to the scalp exposing the stitched up wound that ran like a centipede along the side of his head. The injury looked grotesque and it was causing him severe headaches. Ju-Long Lew treated the pain with aspirin, but nothing stronger than that. His mind had to be clear for the coming days. He also promised himself that he would end his love affair with opium. The drug had nearly killed him. Had he been in his right mind, he would have had the strength to snap that woman's neck the moment she fought back. Ju-Long Lew was happy to find out that Mister Wong had tracked the cunt down and killed her himself. Wong had assured him that hers was a long and painful death. Lew's prized chalice was now back in his private gallery and all appeared to be well, except for the scar. Lew would tell everyone in Beijing the same story he told his doctors; that he had simply fallen down a flight of stairs. Only his friend from North Korea would be told the truth. He would be the only one that would understand. The two might even share a perverse laugh over the story.

Lew placed a white fedora hat on his head strategically covering his scar. He then left his master bedroom and walked down to the foyer where his driver and Bao were waiting for him. The daughter's eyes lit up when she saw him.

"Baba, you look so handsome," she said clapping her hands.

"You are being too kind to your father," he replied as he leaned over and took her into his arms.

"How long will you be gone?" she asked with concern in her voice.

"Just a few days," he replied with a smile. "Now promise me you won't spend all your time at Disneyland while I'm gone."

She looked up at him with sad eyes.

"I'm only kidding petal. I've already told my friends at the park to be awaiting your arrival."

Bao smiled and hugged her father once more. She kissed him on the cheek and watched him walk out the door.

"Say goodbye to your mother for me," he shouted, as he climbed in the back of his Mercedes limousine.

The chaffeur pulled slowly down the driveway and waited for the iron gates to open. He looked in the rear view mirror and saw that his boss already had his nose in a stack of papers. The driver turned right as he exited the Lew estate and continued down the winding road that led to the bottom of Victoria's Peak. Ten minutes later, they would arrive at a private air strip where a Lear jet awaited them.

Lixian watched her husband's limousine pull out of the estate from a security monitor set up in his private den. She then walked over to the double oak doors leading to the room and locked them with a dead bolt. She was inside his private office, an office that she believed held more than just his business secrets. She started with the large book case that stood behind his desk. Her fingers rifled through a vast collection of rare books she knew he had never read. She didn't know exactly what she was looking for, but she was hoping to find some evidence that would explain her husband's injury. Lixian did not believe for a second that he had fallen down the stairs. The doctor also did not believe it and shared his concerns with her while her husband was heavily sedated. A fall down the stairs could not explain the scratch marks on his face and back. *Where did the scratches come from?* She asked herself, afraid that she already knew the answer. He was cheating on her, that Lixian was sure of. It was not like she could blame him. Despite her efforts to pleasure him orally, she knew that he wanted more. Lixian was willing to look the other way as long as her husband used discretion. His injury showed a complete lack of discretion and a lack of respect toward her. Lixian could live with that only for her daughter's sake. She idolized her father and as Bao's mother, she knew their girl's fragile life would fall apart if he was not there. What Lixian could not live with was the frightening thought of what he may have done to sustain his injuries. She knew there was a woman out there somewhere who fared far worse than her husband.

Lixian was getting no where with the book shelf, so she turned toward her husband's glass top desk and sat down in front of his computer terminal. She was much more computer savvy than he was. In the early days of the company, it was Lixian who had taken care of all the paperwork and book keeping while he was out drumming up new business. The trick now was accessing his files. She knew that he would keep his computer password simple because he was not a very good typist. First, she entered her daughter's name *Bao-Ling*. When that did not work, she typed in her own name, but was not surprised when it came back as an incorrect password. *What would he use? What would he use?* She looked around the den and saw the large jade Buddha standing against the wall. She typed in *Buddha*, but again had no luck. Her eyes shifted from the walls of the office back to her husband's desk. Sitting by the mouse pad was another sculpture made of jade. It was a tiny, yet intricately carved figure of a dragon. *Could it be that simple?* She typed in the word and saw the computer screen light up.

BEIJING

Steve Trevane was listening to *Joker* by *The Steve Miller Band* on his I-Pod. They had been sitting on the tarmac now for twenty minutes while their Chinese hosts scrambled to set up the proper welcome. Trevane was seated near the back of the plane next to members of the press corps. It was the ultimate insult. It was like entering a fine restaurant only to be seated by the men's room. Officially, Trevane was there to represent the State Department, since the Secretary of State was being shut out of the talks. The Madame Secretary was currently on a tour of India, a trip the president said was just as important as the summit. Everyone knew this was a lie. In reality, the President had wanted to dump her after his first term, but was counseled against it for two major reasons. The Secretary of State was a woman and she was Hispanic. There was a major push within the GOP to attract more minorities and the President's advisors convinced him that such a move would send the wrong message about the Republican Party.

Trevane was supposed to be sending word back to the State Department, but everyone knew he was really there to be the eyes and ears for Buzz Baxter and the Vice President. It was as if he had a sign reading *Neo-Con* taped to the back of his suit coat. Trevane had gone over the policy papers on the marathon flight over and knew the daunting challenge that lay ahead. The U.S. and North Korea had been on a collision course since 2002 when the government in Pyongyang admitted violating a 1994 deal by embarking on a secret uranium enrichment program. In mid-2003, North Korea announced it had completed the reprocessing of spent nuclear fuel rods (to extract weapons grade plutonium) and was developing what it called, a "nuclear deterrent". North Korea's first nuclear test three years later had thrown a curve ball to the world. The stance of the administration was simple. North Korea would have to dismantle its nuclear program or invite an armed response from the U.S. The North had already promised to give up nuclear development in exchange for aid and a security guarantee. The two sworn enemies were never closer together, yet never further apart. The North was still demanding a nuclear reactor for power generation before dismantling its atomic projects. *We've gone down this road with them before and we've been bitten in the ass,* Trevane thought. He knew that if the North did not take this demand off the table, the summit would be over before it began. It was a frightening possibility. Trevane could envision the President ordering an invasion of North Korea under the pretense of protecting our ally to the south. It was now his responsibility to make sure this did not happen.

Special Agent Nikki Tavano stood behind the former President as he greeted the Chinese President on the airport tarmac. The President's father was tall and lean and had to bend down to shake the smaller man's hand. A steady rain had begun to fall and a junior agent covered the protectee with a large umbrella. Tavano welcomed the bad weather because it would cut down on the meet and greet time out here in the wide open space of the Beijing International Airport. Once greetings were exchanged and photographs taken, Tavano ushered *Shepherd* into a waiting limousine. The former President still used the Secret Service code name given to him by the signal corps when he was the Republican nominee for president nearly twenty years before. The codename concept was obsolete now, but the Secret Service adhered to tradition. Code names were originally used when Secret Service communications were not scrambled, but now all their transmissions were encrypted so there really was no need to designate codenames to their protectees.

Tavano had no time to question the logic as she sat next to the former President and coordinated the motorcade with her satellite phone. The motorcade had twenty-six cars with motorcycle outriders. Behind Tavano's limousine was another carrying shift agents and the former President's staff members. There was also a CAT car filled with members of the Secret Service's Counter Assault Team. Those agents wore battle gear and carried automatic weapons. There had already been one "attack on the principal" (AOP) during a trip to Geneva in the first days of the Iraq war. A suicide bomber leaped at the Former President after he finished giving a speech to Swiss business leaders. The principal was unharmed, but the bomber and two field agents were killed in the blast. The agents' deaths were mourned and then studied to make sure it did not happen again. Tavano had little fear of a bomber targeting the motorcade this time around. The limousines had been shipped over from the U.S. and had been armored at Hess and Eisenhart in Cincinnati. The vehicle looked sleek, but in fact was as durable as a tank.

Tavano looked over at *Shepherd* who was staring out the window at the city he once called home.

"Does it feel good to be back sir?" she asked.

"In a way it does," he reflected still gazing out the window. "Much has changed since I was last here. But my fear is that much is still the same."

CHAPTER 30

▼

Grace brushed the hair off her face and hugged herself against the cold. The rain had dissipated, but had been replaced by a brisk wind that was now whipping through the vast open spaces inside the Forbidden City. She stood on the stone steps leading up to the Hall of Supreme Harmony, which was just one of a mind boggling 9,999 rooms inside the walls of the palace. Grace was surrounded by a heavy stream of tourists, yet she felt isolated and totally alone.

Jessi was gone and so was Heath. Grace wondered whether she would see either of them again. It had been four hours since they had split up at the Great Wall and she was eagerly awaiting his phone call. Grace knew that he was in good hands and had more faith in Heath than any person she had ever known. Still, she could not shake her growing belief that something was truly wrong. It was the same ominous feeling that Grace had experienced when she was a teenager and her mother had confided to her that she was battling cancer. Somehow Grace knew what her mother was going to say before she said it. Her mother died eight months later and Grace knew about it before anyone else, even before her mother's caregivers at the hospital. Was she psychic? Grace did not believe so. Unlike the fortune teller, she could not see into the future. But she did know when something was wrong and her heart was telling her that something was wrong now.

She tried to get her mind off Heath and Jessi and rejoined the walking tour. She caught up with Rita minutes later outside the Gate of Heavenly Purity. The guide was surrounded by members of the adoption group including Frank and Nancy Capolino.

"We are standing at the gateway to the inner court," Rita said pointing to a pair of gilded stone lions standing guard by the large open entryway. "This corridor leads to the Emperor's bedroom, which in many ways was the true seat of power in ancient China."

"Where'd they house the concubines?" Frank asked with a laugh.

"I apologize for my husband. He can be a real pig sometimes," Nancy added quickly.

Grace was surprised, but happy to see his wife chime in.

"Frank has just raised a very good question," Rita told the group. "Concubines held very important positions in imperial life. They were not just the Emperor's lovers, but many were his most trusted confidantes. Some strong concubines even made policy decisions for their weak emperors. The concubines lived along the 12 courtyards that surround the inner palace. The Emperor would pick a woman he wanted to see each night, but some could not be trusted. To make sure a concubine did not smuggle a weapon into the Emperor's chamber, she was escorted by eunuchs and left naked at the foot of the Emperor's bed."

The group continued on to get a first hand look at the Emperor's bedroom inside the Palace of Heavenly Purity. Frank tapped Grace on the shoulder as he walked by.

"This should be great material for your book," he whispered.

"The book?" Grace asked in a daze. "Oh right, the book."

*   *   *   *

The guilt was eating away at him as he watched the city of Beijing disappear under a blanket of fog and clouds. *I should have called Grace before hopping a plane to Hong Kong, but how could I explain to her what I've just learned?* Her best friend had been kidnapped, that he knew for sure now. What was gnawing at him along with the guilt was the fear that Jessi was already dead. Rosary believed Grace would blame herself for whatever had happened to her best friend. He wanted to spare her the agony until he had more answers. *Maybe she's still alive,* he thought to himself. He knew it was wishful thinking, especially after getting briefed on the mysterious Mister Wong. Along with the surveillance pictures from Jessi's abduction, Heath was also shown crime scene photos from the Doucet case. He couldn't shake the image of the beauty queen's mother lying in a pool of her own blood in that storage elevator. Rosary had always tried to remain emotionally detached from his clients because it allowed him to think clearly in a time of crisis. But how could he remain emotionally detached now? After all, Jessi was a part of the family. *Hell, we just spent Thanksgiving together.* The memory made him smile. Because of Jessi's trip, they decided to have an early holiday together. The plan ended in disaster when Heath and his uncle James burned the 20-pound bird in their attempt at Southern deep fried turkey. *Shouldn't have tried to place that bird neck down in the fryer basket.* Jessi and Grace were quick to assist with a fire extinguisher. They all had to order out for Chinese food instead. With a few cartons of beef lo mein and a couple of bottles of Kendall-Jackson Chardonnay, it turned out to be the best Thanksgiving ever. *I just wish that I could turn the clock back to that day.* Rosary promised himself that he would call Grace when he arrived in Hong Kong, although he still had no idea what he'd say to her. He also made a promise to himself about what he would do *if* and *when* he found Mister Wong.

"Are you sleeping?" the Frenchman asked.

Rosary opened his eyes and shook his head. "I'm bright eyed and bushy tailed," he replied with a yawn.

They were flying in a large Airbus 340–600 and Rosary was wedged into a window seat next to Henri Bouchard. The two were talking in hushed tones, their conversation impossible to hear over the roar of the jet's four Rolls Royce engines. The other passengers crammed into coach had earphones on and were watching a popular Chinese romance on a pull down movie screen in the center of the cabin.

"So what else do we know about Hu Wong?" Heath asked.

"We know quite a bit thanks to Pu-Yan," the Frenchman replied. "Our man is a master of disguise and a very accomplished killer. He is skilled with an assortment of weapons and also with his bare hands."

"So how do we find his Achilles heel?" Rosary asked.

"That actually may not be very difficult," Bouchard smiled. "Our friend is also a homosexual and frequents several known gay bars in Hong Kong. Pu-Yan's contacts say he's been quite promiscuous lately. It could be a matter of luring him with the right bait."

Both men looked over to Grace's cousin Joe, who was fast asleep in an aisle seat opposite their row. He was young and quite good looking and unlike Rosary and Bouchard, Grace's cousin could blend in with a crowd. Joe would be the perfect bait for such an operation. It was Bouchard's turn to ask a question and he cut right to the chase. "So what is your end game?" he asked in accented English.

Rosary's mood immediately darkened. "Listen to me Henri. I don't know much about you and don't know that I should even trust you. I also realize that I don't have much of a choice. I know that you want to arrest this scumbag before he does it again. When I catch him, he's gonna have to answer some serious questions."

"And if he doesn't?" Bouchard asked.

Rosary offered a steely eyed reply. "If he doesn't lead me to my friend, I'm gonna put a bullet in his head. This is personal for me."

Bouchard nodded as he leaned back in his passenger seat and closed his eyes. *This is personal for me too,* the Frenchman told himself.

CHAPTER 31

▼

HONG KONG

Lixian wiped the tears away from her mascara smudged cheeks and surveyed the damage. Her husband's office was in shambles. Three giant Ming vases now lay in tiny pieces that were scattered across the floor. The large book case was turned over onto what was left of her husband's glass top desk. The computer terminal had its keyboard torn off and its screen kicked in. She had lost control in a way that she'd never though possible before. Lixian tried to compose herself, but still could not erase the savage images from her mind. Her husband was a killer and she now had proof.

Lixian had stumbled upon the images that were stored in his computer. She was fishing around in his files when she found one that was titled; *Pictures from the trip*. She opened the file thinking it held digital photos of a recent family vacation to Bali, but instead she discovered something else. Three small video windows had popped up on the computer screen. Lixian guided the arrow over to the corner of the screen and right clicked onto the first window. The image was slightly pixilated, but she could see her husband smiling into a video camera. The camera shot pulled out to show him standing naked in front of a large bed. Another naked man entered the video screen seconds later. Lixian recognized him immediately. The second man wore oversized eyeglasses and had his black hair combed into a stiff peak high above his forehead. She was now staring at a nude image of the President of the Democratic People's Republic of Korea. The stubby dictator was one of her husband's biggest clients, but it now appeared that their relationship had gone beyond that. Was her husband gay? That thought was dismissed when two young Korean women joined the men on the bed. At first, the video appeared to be nothing more than a stag film. The girls disrobed for the camera and climbed on top of the men. Soon their bodies were bouncing up and down on top of the men until suddenly and almost in unison, the men changed positions and took the girls from behind. Lixian was about to close the video window when she noticed the North Korean leader pick up two bright yellow sashes from the side of the bed. He handed one sash to her husband who brought it over his girl's head and down around her neck. The dictator did the same. Within seconds, the men were squeezing the sashes tightly while the girls fought desperately to free themselves. Lixian was horrified, but she could not turn away. In fact, she looked closer and noticed that the men appeared to be laughing. Moments later, the men released their grips and the girls' lifeless bodies collapsed on the large bed. Lixian dared not open the other windows.

She then stood up from her husband's desk, the room spinning around her. The next few minutes were a blur as Lixian cried, screamed and knocked over anything and everything she could find in the monster's office. The moment of insanity soon passed. Her heart still pounded and her breathing was heavy, but Lixian tried desperately to regain her composure. As she stood silently contemplating what to do next, she heard the unmistakable sound of her daughter limping down the corridor toward the den. Lixian looked around the room. How was she going to explain this to her daughter? She heard a knock on the door, which fortunately was still locked with a dead bolt.

"Are you alright, Mama?" Bao asked from the corridor.

"Yes dear," Lixian answered as she rushed toward the door.

She opened the door and quickly closed it behind her. Lixian looked up and was startled to see her daughter standing next to Mister Wong.

BEIJING

Agent Tavano was positioned just three feet away from the former President as he marveled at the young acrobats from the Beijing Chaoyang Theater. Members from the renowned troupe were providing the after dinner entertainment for the dignitaries gathered here for the six-party talks. The welcoming banquet was being held at the Court of Virtuous Harmony inside the Summer Palace. Following the lavish and exotic seven course meal; the VIP's were escorted over to the palace theater, the largest in all of China. It was a stunning piece of architecture, but it also posed a major security challenge. The three story building was equipped with trapdoors in the floor and in the ceiling, which were designed for the entrances and exits of the actors playing supernatural characters. The Chinese provided protection for the perimeter of the building, but were allowing security agents from the representative countries to assist them in what was being called a joint operation. Tavano made sure members of her team were positioned by the trap doors, which she felt posed the greatest threat to the safety of the principal. Tavano did not want history to repeat itself. All Secret Service agents were students of history and as part of their training, agents studied and dissected political murders dating back to ancient times. Tavano thought back to her re-examination of the Lincoln assassination and recalled how the President's killer, John Wilkes Booth, had used a trap door under the stage in Ford's Theater to conceal himself before he crept up to the President's box and shot Lincoln through the brain. The mere thought of something like that happening here was enough to make anyone shudder, but Tavano also reminded herself that Abraham Lincoln had *no* security on that fateful April night in 1865. In fact, a bill calling for the creation of the Secret Service was still on Lincoln's desk waiting to be signed by the President when he was killed.

Shepherd was seated next to the Chinese President and both clapped at every flip and gravity defying stunt performed by the young acrobats. Nikki Tavano was also impressed by the feats of these body bending kids. The leader of the troupe could not have been older than fifteen. He and another boy were lying on their backs tossing huge earthen pots back and forth with their feet. All the while, eleven other acrobats forming an inverted pyramid, circled them riding only a single bicycle. Tavano wished that she could just sit down and enjoy the show, but she was on the job. Her mission was getting the former President from the Court of Virtuous Harmony safely back to the American Embassy. *Thank God he's not a night owl like some of the other men I've been assigned to protect,* she thought. *Some of the women were even worse,* she thought again. The plan was to have *Shepherd* back at the embassy by 9 p.m., so he could get in his nightly Bible study and also polish up on his talking points for the summit. Tavano wondered exactly whom the former President would be speaking to since there was still no sign of the North Korean leader.

Following the banquet and acrobatic performance, members of the various delegations migrated over to the Hall of Jade Pillows on the grounds of the Summer Palace facing Kunming Lake, which had yet to freeze over. An orchestra played traditional Chinese music as political operatives mingled and laid the groundwork for back channels that would be vital to the summit's success. Steve Trevane was on his third glass of vodka, which he hoped would kill anything still living in his stomach after dinner. Trevane wished he would have passed on some of the more exotic dishes like *haizhe pi*, which he later found to be jellyfish. He sipped his drink and surveyed the room as the delegates spread out to form their own little cliques. The South Koreans and Japanese huddled in one corner of the large hall. The men all wore simple, yet stylish business suits and could have been mistaken for auto executives from Toyota and Kia. The Chinese were on the opposite side of the room speaking with the Russians, who stood with their backs to the Japanese. *Probably still sore over the Russo-Japanese War of 1902,* Trevane smiled to himself. Five members of the North Korean delegation chatted amongst themselves in the middle of the hall. All wore the mustard colored uniform of the Democratic People's Republic and all appeared to be looking at the other delegations with disdain and distrust. Trevane had been warned not to approach any member of the North Korean group directly. Such an act would send a clear and dangerous signal to his American colleagues, who were already treating him like a skunk at a garden party. Instead, Trevane had been told to seek out an important intermediary, one whom had the ear of the North Korean leader himself.

"Are you enjoying yourself Mister Trevane?" asked a voice from behind.

Trevane spun around slowly and extended his hand.

"You have a beautiful country Mister Lew."

"A smart man can find beauty in most things," Lew replied as he shook the American's hand. "Please forgive my appearance; I am recovering from a terrible accident."

Lew did not explain and Trevane did not ask him to.

"I hope that we didn't travel all this way in vain," Trevane told him. "I was a bit surprised that your friend did not attend tonight's banquet."

"You should not be," Lew replied. "He is only committed to attending the summit, but not any of the pageantry that surrounds it."

Trevane looked around the reception, which could have rivaled anything put on by the Waldorf-Astoria back home. In the middle of the room stood a seven-foot ice sculpture of a swan that was illuminated by pink flood lights. Waiters in traditional silk dress floated around the delegates offering them more Chinese delicacies.

"You're right, this doesn't look like his kind of crowd," Trevane observed. "I'll bet that while we're getting drunk here at the Summer Palace, your friend is on his armored train en-route from Pyongyang in the darkness."

Ju-Long Lew chuckled. "Even I do not know exactly where the leader is right now, but I do know that he will attend tomorrow's talks. I must tell you that he does not expect much to come out of it. He is only coming because your President dared him not to."

"That's why I am here sir," Trevane told him as he took another sip of vodka. "You've already spoken to my boss. He has told you that *his* boss is willing to make certain allowances in an effort to keep the peace."

"Why should we care what his boss has to say?," Lew responded matter of fact. "At last I checked, he is not running things in America."

"No, but he will be a year from now. You've seen the polls. He's a sure bet right now," Trevane countered. "And if all goes well, he'll running things for the eight years after that. That is why no matter what happens over the next couple of days, it is very important that your friend not overreact." Trevane drained his glass. "There's a saying in America that goes back to the Old West. Don't provoke a man with an itchy trigger finger. Look at Afghanistan and Iraq, it's plain to see that our current President has an itchy trigger finger."

Ju-Long Lew looked at the American and smiled. "We too have an old saying; a rat who gnaws at a cat's tail invites destruction."

Lew nodded his head to Trevane and walked away.

CHAPTER 32

▼

The American Embassy-Beijing

"You told him what?" demanded Buzz Baxter over a secure telephone line inside his office, which was directly next to the Vice President's office in the Eisenhower Executive Office Building in Washington, D.C.

"I told him that the President has an itchy trigger finger and they shouldn't provoke him," Trevane replied, wishing now that he had also turned down the third glass of vodka and the fourth for that matter.

"We didn't send you there to threaten the North Koreans," Baxter growled. There was a pause in the conversation. Trevane figured his boss was lighting a cigarette.

The no-smoking rule at the EEOB did not apply to Buzz Baxter.

"If I wanted to threaten those bastards, I would've gone myself," Baxter added.

Trevane knew that arguing would be a futile exercise. "So what do you want me to do now?" he asked.

"Do whatever you need to do to set this thing right. He needs to know that he can trust us. Offer him your first born if you have to," Baxter said only slightly joking.

"I'm sure he'll only accept the offer if it's a boy," Trevane replied.

"Leave that morality bullshit to the former President," Baxter snapped. "I need you to keep your eyes on the prize."

"Which is?"

"Keeping us out of another goddamned war."

The secure line went dead. Buzz Baxter was notorious for slamming the phone down on people. For the first time, Trevane was happy to be in Beijing nearly seven thousand of miles away from his irritable mentor. He'd have to set things right in the morning. He checked his watch, which read 2 a.m. *Fuck, it already is morning.* If he could just get a few hours sleep and sneak in a quick run, he'd be ready to take on Ju-Long Lew, or so Trevane thought. After hanging up the phone, he kicked off his shoes, collapsed on the small twin bed and was out before his head hit the pillow.

Hong Kong

Mister Wong sat in the dark sipping a small glass of rice wine. He did not consider himself to be much of a drinker, but he was being called to the bottle more frequently since the murder of the American woman. He did not want to think about her now; those thoughts would undoubtedly come in his dreams or his nightmares to be exact.

He had just returned home from the Lew mansion where his boss's wife had stumbled onto their dark and deadly secret. He probably should have killed her too, but instead Wong poured out his heart and soul to Lixian Lew. He told her about the kidnappings and the murders that followed. His tearful confession was not met with sympathy or understanding, but with a hard slap across the face. Wong could have easily blocked it, but he chose not to. The pain felt good. The pain cleansed him. Lixian then threatened to call the police, but Wong explained why a move like that would not be wise. "Your husband owns the police," he told her. She then promised to take her daughter and disappear. "This also is not a good idea," he warned. "Your daughter is the only thing in this world that your husband truly loves. If you take her away from him, he will spend his entire fortune hunting you down. He will take Bao back and you will meet with a bad accident, or you will simply disappear like Tang-Lung Wei. Your husband's former second in command didn't just disappear, he was cut up and fed to the fish swimming in Aberdeen Bay". Wong did not tell her that he had performed that gruesome task himself.

His graphic honesty made the wife think twice. Both realized they were stuck in similar situations; they were trapped by the same monster. Lixian reached out for Wong and hugged him desperately. The emotions of the moment had stirred something deep inside her, a feeling she long believed was dead. She reached up and tried to kiss him, but he turned away from the embrace.

"Am I not pretty?" she cried.

"You are very beautiful," he told her. "But I lost my love a long time ago."

A short time later, she packed a few bags and had just enough time to hug and kiss her daughter before Wong drove her to the airport. He did not stay long enough to know where she was going. He did not care. Wong's only hope was that his boss would never find her.

Now he was sitting in the dark, trying to fight off sleep for as long as he could. Since the murder of Jessi Miller, Wong's victims had begun to dominate his dreams. He had visions of cut up body parts reforming and regenerating like some terrifying jigsaw puzzle. In the dreams, Wong was paralyzed by fear and forced to watch as his victims became whole again. The horror continued as the women and men came after him, one by one tearing at his flesh and pulling the limbs off his body. The nightmare ended the same way each night with a panicked Wong searching for his missing body parts in the darkness. "Does this await me in the afterlife?" he asked aloud.

Wong then thought of his boyhood hero, China's first Emperor Qin, who was so fearful that his victims would take their revenge against him from beyond the grave; he ordered that he be buried with stone replicas of eight thousand of his finest soldiers. The stone sentinels stood guard around the Emperor's tomb outside the city of Xi'an for centuries before being unearthed by archeologists in 1974. Now, the terra cotta warriors were one of the biggest attractions in China. Wong knew that a stone army would not stop the spirits of the people he had harmed throughout his life. He was also fully aware that he could not erase the past and start over. Faced with this reality, he decided that he would now live for the present and accept whatever fate the spirits had chosen for him. Mister Wong finished his glass of rice wine; grabbed his coat and headed out the door in the direction of the techno music and flashing lights emanating from the street below.

*   *   *   *

Grace hit the *End* button on her satellite phone and stared out the window of her hotel room. The smog had finally lifted, revealing blue skies without a cloud in sight. She had just spoken with Heath, who told her that he was safe and that he was chasing down a lead on the case in Hong Kong. When she asked him to be more specific, he dodged the question and told her that he had to get off the phone. She knew he wasn't telling her the *whole* truth. It was the first time that he had lied to her, but Grace also realized that he must have had a good reason. *He's trying to shield me from something,* she thought to herself as she walked over to the dresser inside their hotel room. She fastened a chain around her neck that held a laminated picture of little Sasha. Grace gazed at the small photo and smiled. It was the same picture that she had blown up to poster size for Jessi's baby shower. Sasha had on a yellow jumper and several ribbons in her hair. The baby offered a toothless smile for the camera.

"Will I even be able to recognize you?" Grace asked aloud. "I bet you're such a big girl now." She brought the photo up to her lips and kissed it before tucking it into her shirt.

Grace then grabbed an overnight bag and left the room locking it behind her. She walked down the corridor and saw that members of the adoption group were already piling into the elevator. Grace picked up the pace and managed to squeeze into the lift with the others.

"Today's the big day," Frank Capolino exclaimed with a big smile.

Grace could feel the love flowing in the elevator. Frank Capolino was right; today was the big day. In a few hours, the couples would finally be united with their babies. Their smiles warmed Grace's heart, but broke it at the same time. She knew that there was one baby whose mother was not going to be picking her up today.

The elevator reached the lobby where the wives met up with Rita and Claudia, while the husbands were sent into the hotel's small convenience store to pack up on snacks and bottles of water. There was no time for a leisure breakfast in the hotel restaurant; the couples had an eight hour bus ride ahead of them. The mere thought of being trapped in a bus for eight hours with Frank Capolino was too much for Grace to bear. Instead, she would be making the trip with her cousin, Benny, who was also waiting in the lobby. Grace had given him the nickname *Buddha* when they were kids. She wasn't teasing him because of his weight; instead it was a sign of affection. Benny, or Jin-Sheng as she had called him then, was the happiest person she had ever known. He had the ability of making her feel better, no matter what the problem was. Benny wore a big smile for his cousin as he escorted her into his silver Volvo, which was the same make and model of his brother's car.

"Try to sleep cousin and leave the driving to me," he told her. He checked the digital clock on the dashboard. It was just after 7 a.m. "This car drives very fast. We should arrive in Datong by 2 p.m."

"Have you heard from your brother?" Grace asked hoping to gain more information about Heath's activities.

"No, I have not," he replied honestly. "Your boyfriend is in excellent hands though. My brother will help them in whatever he has to do."

"What is it that you two do again?"

"For the right price, we do whatever needs to be done," he replied with a mischievous smile.

Benny was true to his word, they entered the city of Datong just after two o'clock. There were no blue skies here; the gritty coal mining town was a charcoal drawing come to life; devoid of any color. Even the 1,500 year old Buddhist grottoes carved into the mountainside looked dark and foreboding. Grace paid little attention to the massive sculptures; her mind was on other things. She could feel her heart beating faster as they got closer to the orphanage, where little Sasha awaited them. *Get a grip,* she told herself. *Don't be a blubbering fool. You're here to make sure the baby is being treated well and to tell the orphanage director that Jessi will be coming for her sooner or later. I hope.*

They arrived at the orphanage well before the others and pulled into a small parking lot outside the main building. Grace stepped out of the car and looked up at the three story concrete structure, which was painted white, but dulled by a thick coating of coal soot which seemed to hang in the air like a thick fog. Extending out from both sides of the building was a high concrete wall topped with circular strands of barbed wire. "Is this an orphanage or a prison?" Grace asked her cousin who just shook his head in amazement. They entered the orphanage through a pair of heavy metal doors and approached a neatly dressed receptionist who was seated behind a small wooden desk in the foyer. Grace nodded to her cousin who offered an introduction. Benny handed over his business card to the woman, who smiled and quickly left the room only to return a few seconds later accompanied by an older man wearing a dusty business suit and thick eye glasses. The man bowed to the visitors. "Nice to meet you," he said in broken English. "I am director here."

Benny continued the conversation in Chinese. "This is a famous journalist from America," he said pointing to Grace. "She is here to check on the well being of one of your orphans."

The man bowed his head again and waved his hand down the hall. Benny followed his direction, while Grace turned back toward the receptionist.

"Zai jian," Grace said. *Goodbye.*

The receptionist did not respond, instead she looked quickly away.

That's odd, Grace thought to herself. She then caught up with her cousin and the director, who were waiting for her down the hall. The untidy orphanage official pulled out a large key chain from his pants pocket and sifted through several keys before finding the right one to open the next set of metal doors. They entered the first floor of the orphanage and were met by the wail of crying babies echoing through the corridor. Grace was prepared for the cries, but she was not prepared for the cold. The building had no heat and she blew warm air into her cupped hands and then stuffed them into the pockets of her coat.

If I'm cold, how must the babies feel?

The director paid no attention to the gesture as he began his tour.

"Nearly eight thousand babies were adopted from China last year," he told them. "400 children were adopted right from our orphanage."

He led them into a room where a dozen newly arrived infants lay three to a crib. All the babies were crying and Grace felt the urge to adopt them all.

"Why are the babies put up for adoption?" she asked.

"Many are given up by couples bound by China's one child policy," the director replied shaking his head. "Others are left by unmarried mothers or poor families. Of course the majority of babies here are girls."

"Why is that?" Grace asked.

"Well, it is said here that a peasant's pension is having a son who will take care of him in his old age. A daughter does not have the same value. Some peasants call baby girls; *maggots in the rice*. Still, it is better now than it was when parents would simply kill a newborn female instead of bringing her here."

Grace had read about China's ancient practice of infanticide, but the reality still made her wince.

"I'm afraid there is little improvement when these girls grow older," the director went on to say. "In fact, just recently three men were arrested in Shaanxi Province for killing two young women and selling them as ghost brides."

Grace was feeling queasy now. "What are *ghost brides?*" she asked, not really wanting to know the answer.

Benny stepped in to explain. "It's a deplorable ritual that dates back to the Han Dynasty. It hasn't been done for centuries, but it's just begun to make something of a comeback in very rural villages. Men who go to their graves unmarried are given a partner to be their spouse in the after life. Some believe the unmarried dead will haunt the living in their dreams unless their ghosts are wed."

Grace shook her head in disgust. "And where do they find these ghost brides?"

"They may be recently deceased women, or they could just be sacrifices," her cousin replied. "In the most recent case, one victim was a prostitute, the other was a mentally retarded girl who had been sold by her family."

How can a country with so much beauty and culture also be so barbaric? Grace asked herself. She wanted to change the subject and turned her attention back to the director.

"Are there ever any boys brought here?" she asked.

"Rarely," the director replied. "The last boy adopted from this orphanage was missing a toe on his right foot. The parents felt disgraced by the deformity and thought their child impure."

"What happened to the boy?" Grace asked.

"He was adopted by a family from America, doctors I believe."

Grace smiled at the thought. *That missing toe turned out to be a winning lottery ticket for that lucky kid.*

The director ushered them out of the newborn room and led them down the corridor toward the toddler area.

"I could not help noticing the high walls and barbed wire surrounding the orphanage," Grace observed. "What is the reason behind it?"

The director paused before answering. "The government ordered additional security last year after five babies were abducted from our nursery," he told them as he began fidgeting with a pen. "It is a sad reality, but abandoned babies have become big business here in China. Gangs steal the babies and sell them to other orphanages or to couples who do not want to go through the process of adopting a child legally. It is also cheaper to buy a baby on the black market."

They stopped in front of another room while the director once again searched his large chain for the right key. "Here is what you have come all this way for," he said with a crooked smile. He turned the key and opened the door where Grace could see six infants seated in high chairs along the back wall of the room. Two nurses were feeding the children a late lunch of steamed eggs and rice congi. The toddlers paid no attention to the visitors as they gobbled up their food with a messy efficiency. Grace was surprised to see that the one-year-olds had already learned how to use spoons. She pulled the chain out over the collar of her shirt and inspected the laminated photo and then scanned the little faces for a likely match. The task should have been difficult. Sasha was older now and the children all looked similar, especially with their faces covered with eggs and rice, but Grace recognized her God-daughter immediately. The baby's hair was a bit longer now, but there was no mistaking the eyes. Sasha's brown eyes had melted Grace's heart in the photograph and now they were taking her breath away in person. Sasha was seated toward the end of the row and she appeared to be staring directly toward Grace.

"She knows," Grace said clapping her hands.

She approached the high chair slowly, not wanting to scare Sasha. The baby dropped the spoon from her tiny hand and lifted both arms up in the air. Grace looked to the nurse, who nodded her consent. She then lifted Sasha up slowly from the high chair and held her tightly in her arms. Tears streamed down Grace's face as she hugged the baby close to her chest.

"Look, she's not even crying," Benny observed.

"She's not, but I am," Grace laughed as she held the baby up and looked into her eyes. Sasha stared back with a curious fascination. The baby reached out and grabbed a strand of Grace's silky hair and pulled it gently.

"I am a friend of your Mommy's," she said choking back more tears. "I have come from far away to see you. You are beautiful my darling, just beautiful."

The excitement proved too much for Sasha who looked over to her nurse and began to cry. Grace bounced the fussy baby up and down in an attempt to calm her. Sasha wailed again and a teary eyed Grace handed her back to the care giver.

"It takes a little time for the children to get used to a new face," the director said apologetically. "So I understand there has been some misfortune surrounding this child's mother?"

"Something has happened to her here in your own country," Grace responded. "The baby's mother arrived in Beijing a week ago and has since disappeared. We are searching for her now and are confident that we will find her. I am here to make sure the baby is being treated well and to assure you that she will be united with her mother very soon."

The director nodded his head. "We have been told to wait for the adoptive parent for three more months before handing the case over to the government and your State Department to sort out."

"What happens after three months?" Grace asked nervously.

"The child will most likely be placed with another family," he responded without emotion. "I do hope that you find your friend soon, for the sake of the baby."

CHAPTER 33

▼

Grace and her cousin were escorted out of the building the same way they went in. This time, there was another young woman manning the reception desk. She offered a pleasant smile and thanked them for coming. They returned to the parking lot and noticed that the mini-buses had already arrived. Right now, new parents were holding their babies inside the orphanage, while little Sasha was probably being returned to her cramped crib in the common room.

"Dammit Jessi, where are you?" Grace shouted in frustration.

Her cousin draped a beefy arm over her slender shoulder. "Your friend is out there somewhere. Heath and my brother will bring her home," he promised. "You have to have faith."

Benny unlocked the passenger side door and helped her inside the car. The cousin then waddled around the vehicle and squeezed his large frame into the driver's seat. As they drove away, Grace spotted the receptionist who had given her the brush off earlier in the day. The young woman was walking toward the building with her arms folded. The receptionist stared at the car and shook her head as Benny pulled out of the parking lot.

"Stop the car," Grace ordered.

Benny slammed on the brakes and Grace lowered the window.

"What's the matter? What are you afraid of?" she shouted to the young woman in Chinese.

The receptionist looked away from her again and ran back into the building.

Grace wanted to get out of the car and chase after the woman, but her cousin stopped her. "Leave the poor woman alone," he pleaded. "She's just a bit odd, that's all."

Grace settled back in her seat, but was overcome with that sinking feeling again. *Something was wrong.*

*   *   *   *

Benny drove to the nearby Hongan International Hotel where they had already booked rooms for the night. The 4-star hotel was located on Binxi Road, just a short drive from the railway station. The hotel's façade was brightly lit and reminded Grace of something she had seen in Las Vegas. The lobby was right out of the glamour days of Hollywood with its marble columns and winding staircase. *Not bad for an old coal mining town,* she told herself. *Heath would love this place.*

The adoption group was also staying there because the eight hour drive back to Beijing would be too much for their new babies to take on the first day. Grace checked into the hotel; received her key pass and hugged her cousin.

"This has been a gut wrenching day," she told him. "Thank you for coming with me. I couldn't have made it without you."

"Your father told us that you've grown up strong," Benny replied. "He said there's nothing you cannot do." He kissed her on the forehead and the two cousins parted ways. Benny made a break for the hotel restaurant, while Grace went immediately to her room where she opened the door and spotted a small crib near the bed. The hotel concierge must have thought she was adopting a baby also. The sight of the crib made her heart sink as tears formed once again in the corners of her eyes. She pulled off her coat and brought it to her nose searching for any remnants of Sasha's scent. Grace smiled as she smelled a slight whiff of rice and eggs on her jacket. She closed her eyes and pretended she was holding the baby once again, feeling her warm breath on her neck. She couldn't stand the thought of Sasha being stuck in that fortress-like orphanage for three more months or even longer.

"What should I do, Jess?" she asked aloud, hoping her friend would appear with the answer. It was a silly request, this she knew. Grace shook her head and collapsed on the bed. She was fully clothed and did not possess the energy to even take her shoes off. She lay there picturing little Sasha in her mind's eye and moments later she was fast asleep.

Grace awoke three hours later to the sound of her satellite phone ringing from within her overnight bag. She rubbed her eyes and stumbled across the room toward the noise. *It must be Heath,* she thought to herself. *I hope he's alright.* She fished the phone out of her bag and hit *Send* before placing it up to her ear.

"Pack your things and meet me in the lobby," Benny said nervously.

"I thought it was Heath," Grace said still trying to shake off the sleep. "What's going on?"

Her cousin had no time for questions. "I can't say right now. Just pack your things because you are not going back to that room. I'll meet you in the lobby in five minutes."

Grace did not have to pack, because she had never unpacked. She grabbed her bag and her coat and hurried out the door. She met up with her cousin moments later in the hotel lobby. "What the hell is going on?" she asked him showing signs of her fiery Chinese temper.

"Lower your voice cousin," he ordered her. "Follow me out to the garage please."

Grace realized that Benny must have had a good reason for the cloak and dagger routine. She did as she was told and followed him out of the hotel toward his car. A short time later, they were alone in the parking garage, or so it appeared. The garage was dark, but as they approached the Volvo, Grace noticed some movement in the back seat of the car.

"What's going on Benny?" she demanded.

"Just get in the car Grace," the cousin whispered.

She opened the passenger side door and looked directly into the back seat where a familiar face stared back at her. It was the odd receptionist from the orphanage and she was not alone. The receptionist was holding Sasha in her arms. The baby was wrapped in several blankets and appeared to be sound asleep.

"What are you doing here?" Grace whispered as to not wake the baby.

"You seem like nice woman," the receptionist whispered back. "I could not let him do this to you."

"Do what?" Grace asked.

"Take your baby," the young woman replied. "This child is to be sold to another couple, a wealthy couple from England I believe."

The information was coming too fast for Grace to comprehend.

"Please," she urged the girl. "Please start at the beginning."

The woman nodded her head and then looked down at Sasha, who was now stirring in her sleep. "The director told you that gangs were taking babies from the orphanage and selling them?"

"That's right," Grace responded.

"It was an inside job," Benny piped in. "The director is the one stealing the children and selling them for profit. Isn't that right An Wu Feng?"

The woman nodded. "This baby is to be taken tomorrow night. That is why I must stop him. Please take baby with you. She is rightfully yours."

"We will take her," Grace promised. "What about you? Are you in danger for what you have done?"

"No, the director will forgive me," the young woman said confidently.

"Why will he forgive you?"

"Because the director is also my husband," she replied.

The woman handed the sleeping baby over to Grace and exited the car.

"How can I thank you?" Grace whispered to her.

The receptionist smiled. "You can thank me by giving this child a good life in America."

CHAPTER 34

▼

HONG KONG

They watched from a roof deck atop a four story apartment building that sat on a hill in Hong Kong's Lan Kwai Fong district. Rosary looked through a pair of binoculars at the high rise a short distance away. He wished they could have been directly across the street from Mister Wong's flat, but the roof deck on Windham Street was the best that Grace's cousin could come up with in such short notice. Joe *Jin-Xui* had sent the apartment's current occupants for an extended stay at the Ritz-Carlton. Rosary asked Joe where the money was coming from to foot the bill, but Grace's cousin said money was no object. Rosary surmised that Tommy Chen was probably covering the expenses from back in Boston. The location did have its benefits however, their surveillance work was shielded by a line of potted fur trees that stood tall along the perimeter of the deck. The vantage point offered them an unobstructed view of the bay windows into Wong's apartment and the front entrance of his building.

It was just shy of 10 a.m. and Rosary had been staring at the apartment for about an hour. There was no movement inside the flat or out on the street. Henri Bouchard was now asleep in the small bungalow that was adjacent to the deck. Before handing Rosary the set of binoculars to begin his shift, Bouchard briefed the American on Wong's comings and goings from the night before. Mister Wong had left his apartment alone at approximately 11:25 p.m. He had returned shortly after 2 a.m. with another man. Bouchard said the two men were hanging on each other and appeared to be kissing on the front steps of the building. The couple then disappeared inside the building and had not been seen since.

Rosary had his leather coat buttoned at the collar to protect from the cold. The climate here in Hong Kong was much warmer than it had been in Beijing, but it was still mid-morning in mid-November and the air was surprisingly chilly, even for a hearty Bostonian like Rosary.

"God, I could go for a large Dunkin Donuts coffee right now," he growled to no one in particular.

Surveillance work is not the most exciting aspect of the job, but some could argue that it is the most important. Heath Rosary certainly believed so. He fought the boredom by replaying his favorite Alfred Hitchcock movie, *Rear Window* in his mind. He pretended that he was J.J Jeffries stuck in a stifling Greenwich Village apartment peeking in on his unsuspecting neighbors.

"But what's Jimmy Stewart without Grace Kelly," he mumbled to himself.

What he really meant was; what's Heath Rosary without Grace Chen? Oh, how he longed for her now. He was angry with himself for lying to her during that quick phone call from the airport. He also knew that she *knew* he was lying.

"Still, the broken trust is better than the alternative, isn't it?"

Rosary was afraid to answer his own question. Instead, he tried to block it from his mind and get back to his little game. The question now, when would Mister Wong appear in the role of Hitchcock's killer Lars Thorwald? His daydream was interrupted by the smell of hot java. "I thought you might like some of this," Bouchard said, carefully handing him a small cup of coffee.

"Much obliged," Rosary replied as he lifted the cup to his lips. The coffee tasted black and strong as it slid down his throat. It was not Dunkin' Donuts, but Rosary could hardly complain.

"Why do all you Americans speak like you're in a cowboy movie?" Bouchard asked with a hearty laugh.

"I guess we only speak that way around foreigners. Why do all you French like Jerry Lewis movies?"

Bouchard pondered the question and knew that Rosary had him beat on this one.

Heath was surprised to see the Frenchman awake."I thought you were gonna get some shut-eye?"

"I couldn't sleep knowing that he's over there."

They both stared at the building in the distance.

"I don't blame you," Rosary replied. "Part of me wants to say the hell with surveillance, let's just shoot our way in and grab his ass."

"Yes, but your friend could be held hostage inside. If we go in with guns blazing as you say, she could get hurt, or worse."

"I can't argue with that. We have a saying in America that goes; the best offense is a good defense," Rosary told him. "What I mean is, we need to learn more about what we're up against first."

"I know what you are feeling though," Bouchard said as he ran his fingers along his bald scalp. "I too would like to put a bullet in Wong's head."

Rosary raised his eyebrows. "I'm surprised to hear you say that. Most cops stick to the training manual. They talk about bringing the perps to justice and all that crap, but they rarely talk about committing murder, and they do *that* only when they're drunk. You don't appear drunk to me Henri. What's your story?"

Bouchard took a long sip of coffee and told him everything. For Henri Bouchard, this mission had little to do with law enforcement and everything to do with love.

"I take it you never told your superiors about your relationship with Sophie Doucet?"

Bouchard shook his head. "How could I? They would have pulled me off the investigation. And despite my love for Sophie, I also know that I'm the best damn detective for this case."

Rosary patted his new friend on the arm. "So this is personal for both of us. That means we have to be more cautious. We can't let our emotions lead our brains on this one."

He looked up at the Frenchman, who had heavy bags under his eyes. "Get some sleep Henri, even if it's only for a couple of hours. If we're gonna have each other's backs in this thing, both of us will have to be 100 percent."

Bouchard nodded and then walked back inside the flat.

The time now was 11:42 a.m. and so far, nothing much had happened. A few people had left the building, but none of them fit the description of Mister Wong's lover. *Probably just neighbors,* Rosary thought. *Wonder what they'll do when they find out there's a sadistic killer living nearby?* Just then, two men appeared at the front door of the apartment building. One man was wearing some kind of dark bathrobe, the other wore white slacks and had a white coat draped over his narrow shoulder. The men chatted briefly before both leaned in for a goodbye kiss. Rosary scribbled the time down on a small note pad, as Mister Wong waved to his lover and closed the door behind him. Rosary unfolded a small street map, reached for his satellite phone and hit the speed dial.

"He's just left the building and is heading west on D'Aguilar street," Rosary said as he examined the map.

"He's heading my way," Joe replied over the phone. "Wait, I see him now. I must go."

Rosary remained at his post with binoculars in hand waiting to find out what would happen next. The wait did not take long. After about 15 minutes, he got a call on his satellite phone.

"I've got our friend with me right now," Joe told him. "I'll see you back at the flat in about five minutes. Please wake the Frenchman."

Rosary roused Bouchard and both were seated on a small maroon sofa when Grace's cousin arrived. Heath opened the door after hearing the pre-arranged signal. Joe knocked twice then paused, and then knocked three more times. It was Rosary who had come up with the signal. He had seen it in an old movie, although he couldn't remember which one and the brain cramp was killing him.

The man in the white pants and white jacket entered the room first. He had a burlap bag over his head and a pistol stuck in his rib cage. Heavy sobs could be heard from under the sack.

"I've told him that we mean no harm but he doesn't believe me," Joe laughed.

"That's because he knows the gun you're holding doesn't squirt water," Rosary replied.

Joe pulled the bag off the man's head and they all watched as his long bangs fell back over his face.

"Sit down," Joe barked at the man, who immediately did as he was told.

The man kept his head down as tears flowed down his cheeks. Bouchard pulled a pack of cigarettes from the breast pocket of his flannel shirt and offered him one.

The crying man nodded his head and his mouth formed a slight smile. Bouchard placed the cigarette between the man's quivering lips and lit it.

He took the smoke into his lungs, savored it for several seconds and blew it back out toward the floor. Wong's lover was no longer crying and appeared somewhat calmer now.

"We mean you no harm," Joe said again in Chinese. He pointed to Rosary and Bouchard. "These men are police. They have come from America and France to arrest the man you were with last night."

Wong's lover looked confused and Grace's cousin could see that his words were not sinking in.

"The man you slept with last night is wanted for the murders of at least four women," Joe told him. "Was there anyone else inside the apartment with you?"

The lover shook his head no and began quivering again.

"You're sure that no one else was inside the apartment?" Joe asked again.

"Yes, I'm sure," the man responded. "He gave me a tour of the place. It's quite small, if you don't count the living room."

"Ask him how long the two have known each other?" Rosary ordered.

Joe translated the question. Wong's lover put his head down and ran his fingers through his thick black hair. "We met last night at Club 97," he said. "He paid for my drinks and seemed kind of cute. I think I'm going to be sick."

Rosary walked over to the couch and put his arm around the man.

"Just relax. I know this is a lot to take in right now. Did he mention anything to you about his private life, what he did for a living?" Rosary asked and Joe translated.

"He told me that he was an antiques dealer. His place is filled with exotic stuff."

It was Bouchard's turn to ask a question. "Do you remember if he used a key to get inside the apartment?"

Wong's lover answered after hearing the translation. "I was pretty drunk," he said. "But I think he typed in a code on one of those electronic keypads."

Of course he did, thought Rosary. *This man's a professional and breaking into his apartment could be an impossible task. What we need here is a Trojan horse.*

"Please take me inside the apartment. Is there only one way in and out? Take me from room to room," Rosary asked him.

After Joe translated the question, Wong's lover asked for something to write on.

"Remind him that you're the only one who reads Chinese," Rosary told Grace's cousin.

"No Heath, he says he's an art student," Joe replied. "He wants to draw you the rooms."

Bouchard retrieved a pencil and note pad from a kitchen drawer and Wong's lover began to sketch. The art student paid no attention as his abductor and the two other men continued to talk around him. Wong's lover certainly had an artist's patience and concentration. He did not look up from his drawing until it was completely finished. He was done within a matter of minutes and proudly held up the work for inspection.

"The kid can sure draw, I'll give him that," Rosary said in amazement.

Bouchard nodded his head in agreement. They were staring at a detailed layout of Wong's flat that would rival anything done by an interior decorator or architect.

According to the drawing, the front entrance led to a large living room that Wong apparently used as a gym and home office. His lover had carefully drawn several pieces of exercise equipment that he had seen positioned near the bay windows of the living room. Along the back wall, the artist had drawn a large desk and computer set-up. A galley kitchen and bathroom were sketched off the living room to the right and a bedroom was drawn across the living room directly opposite the front door.

"Did he use the computer while you were there?" Rosary asked and Joe translated.

"He checked a few emails this morning," the art student replied.

Rosary and Bouchard looked at each other and thought the same thing. It was possible the answers to the disappearances of Sophie Doucet, Jessi Miller and the others could be found stored somewhere in Wong's computer.

"How do we get access to that computer?" Rosary asked aloud.

"We could send him back there tonight for an encore," Joe said, pointing to the art student. "Do you know your way around a computer?"

The student nodded his head in a lukewarm response.

"I could mic him up, fix a camera to a pair of eyeglasses and we're in business," Joe said convincingly.

The confidence was not winning over Rosary and Bouchard.

"Look at him," Bouchard said, pointing at the student. "He nearly pissed his pants when you brought him here. Sending him back to Wong is like feeding him to the lions."

"Or the *tiger*," Rosary added.

"Do either of you have a better idea?" Joe asked.

"I think you need to go out and buy yourself some dancing shoes," Rosary told him.

"I was hoping that you wouldn't say that," Grace's cousin replied with a shrug.

CHAPTER 35

▼

BEIJING

Steve Trevane sat with his right leg folded crisply over his left knee. He was careful not to ruin the tight crease in his gray Saville Row slacks. He had a black binder open on his lap and to the casual observer it appeared that he was reading. He wasn't though, the latest CIA assessment of North Korea's troop strength made his blue eyes glaze over. Trevane was always leery of the information coming out of the Central Intelligence Agency anyway. He felt that it was in the Agency's best interest to over estimate the strength of the enemy. In Trevane's mind; the greater the threat, the greater the need for intelligence. He knew that meant an increase in the cash flow to the CIA when the Washington bean counters divvied up the annual budget.

Instead of reading, Trevane was thinking of a way to get back into the good graces of Ju-Long Lew. If they were back in Washington, Trevane would ply him with women and alcohol. It was a strategy long supported and implemented by his mentor. "When all else fails, break out the double-L's," Buzz Baxter had told him. "Liquor and ladies."

Trevane was growing more concerned because he had not seen his contact all morning. He was sitting with other second tier diplomats in a large, elegantly decorated lobby inside the Zhongnanhai, the ancient garden palace complex that was the true seat of power in Beijing. The building, adjacent to the Forbidden City was where China's President kept his office and it was now the place where the world's most powerful nations were working to prevent a nuclear nightmare. Right now, the Chinese President was using his office for an informal welcoming session for the various leaders that now included the mysterious dictator from North Korea, who had been whisked into the office amid heavy security just moments ago and a full hour after the other diplomats had arrived. Trevane saw only the top of the leader's pompadour hairdo as it bobbed up and down behind a group of North Korean soldiers before disappearing behind closed doors. The actual summit was scheduled to begin after lunch. *My how the Chinese like to pace themselves,* Trevane thought.

Special Agent Nikki Tavano stood just a few feet away from Trevane and nodded a brief hello. He responded with a quick nod before flashing his bright smile. It was a smile that he had once used to lure Tavano into his bed. The pair had dated just over a year ago after meeting during a morning jog along the Potomac River. The relationship lasted about six months before they both realized it was going nowhere. Tavano was married to her career and she kidded him that he was secretly married to Buzz Baxter. The break-up was a civil one and both had promised to keep in touch. That never happened and this trip was the first time they had seen each other since the split.

You're an idiot Trevane, he thought to himself. *Just look at her. How could you let a beautiful woman like that walk out of your life?* Indeed she was beautiful. She stood about 5'7 and weighed 120 pounds with an athlete's build that did not take away from her feminine curves. She wore her black hair longer than she did a year ago; it now flowed down to her shoulders, but her most striking feature though, were her eyes. Those deep brown pools were intoxicating and could make a man buckle at the knees. Trevane's mind wandered as he recalled the last time he had made love to her. It was the best breakup sex he'd ever had. He stared at her now and thought she looked sexy as hell in her Secret Service outfit. She would smack him if she knew that he referred to her blazer, slacks and holster as an *outfit.* He had even managed to convince her to wear it to bed one night. He pretended to be the perp, while she took him down. She finally gave in to the idea after telling him that she'd shoot him if he ever told his friends about it. He promised not to tell and somehow had managed to keep his word. *Who knows? Maybe when we get back to Washington we can give it another go,* he thought.

Tavano caught his gaze. *I know what you're thinking you dirty boy,* she smiled to herself. At that moment, the double doors to the President's office opened and out walked China's foreign secretary.

"The leaders have decided to forego lunch and begin talks immediately," he announced. "They will walk over to the presidential conference room and will have their meals served there."

For both Tavano and Trevane, it was back to work. She escorted *Shepherd* to the conference room just down the hall from the President's office, while Trevane joined his fellow American delegates in a smaller room with a big screen television that would carry a live feed from the summit. The room was set up like a small theater with rows of seats facing the wide television screen. Trevane sat at the end of the front row and placed a small transmitter in his right ear. The device would carry the voice of the American translator. Seated next to Trevane was a forensic psychologist from Langley, who studied the cause and effect of non-verbal expressions. He would be watching the faces of the leaders in an effort to detect their truthfulness. The expert believed that lies could be found in the eyes and it was his belief that unpleasant feelings such as stress, anxiety and pain tended to increase blink frequency, while pleasant feelings such as contentment tended to decrease blink frequency. Trevane thought the exercise was a waste of time because he knew that everyone taking part in this summit would be forced to lie about something at some point. After getting another round of pleasantries out of the way, the leaders got right down to business. Trevane followed along via the big screen television and began taking notes.

"Our goal here today is to bring peace and stability to North Korea and its Pacific Rim neighbors and to end the isolation of North Korea and to welcome her to the community of nations," the former President announced.

The leaders of Japan and South Korea both clapped, while the North Koreans, Russians and Chinese sat stone faced.

Shepherd then addressed the North Korean dictator directly across the table. "However, before we can begin any meaningful talks, we must address an issue of great importance. Since the 2006 nuclear test on Mount Mantap, you have given us assurances that you are willing to dismantle your nuclear program in exchange for economic and fuel aid. But the much needed aid to your country cannot be secured while you continue to deceive your neighbors about your nuclear intentions."

An aide then handed the former President a series of glossy satellite photos which he then laid down on the table in front of him.

"These images were taken by South Korea's Yonhap agency. They show a mushroom cloud that is 4-kilometers wide in an area close to your Yongjo-ri Missile Base, near the Chinese border. The next photo shows a similar explosion that occurred the very next day. Your government claims the blasts were part of a hydroelectric power plant project along the Huchang River, but our experts have questioned this explanation. They say the Huchang River is too small, and could not possibly generate enough energy for a major hydro power plant. Our WC-135 'Sniffer Plane' also detected radioactive particles in the air around the Huchang River. This tells us that you have conducted a second and third nuclear test. I hope that these talks can yield a positive result, but it must be done through honest communications between all parties."

Going right for the throat right off the bat, this is not good, Trevane thought as he watched the drama unfold.

The diminutive dictator showed no emotion as he listened while his translator relayed the former President's accusations. Trevane noticed that the North Korean did not even seem to blink. *This must be driving the expert from Langley crazy,* he thought. The dictator folded his small hands in front of him, but did not speak. Instead, he allowed his foreign minister to respond to the charges.

"The Americans talk about honesty," the foreign minister said addressing the other parties. "However, it is the Americans who are lying to the rest of you. They have told you that our country recently exported nuclear material to Libya. This material was described as uranium hexafluoride, which can be enriched to weapons-grade uranium. It is true that we exported such material, but it was not sent to Libya, it was sent to Pakistan. It was the Pakistanis who then sent the material to Libya. We had no knowledge of that second transaction. The Americans knew this information, but wanted to protect Pakistan, its ally in the so-called War on Terror. The Americans are the ones dealing in lies."

This news sent shock waves around the conference room and around the satellite rooms where officials from the six-parties were all watching the summit live. In an attempt to diffuse the tension which was palpable at this point, the Chinese President called in the wait staff with lunch. No one spoke as the waiters brought in stacks of silver trays, which were then laid out in front of the diplomats. The waiters knew not to serve the leader of North Korea, whose meals were always prepared right in front of him due to his fear of being poisoned.

While the other leaders enjoyed their lunch, the dictator sat in his chair with his hands folded as he stared straight across the table at the former President.

This is going to be disastrous, thought Trevane. His premonition came true. The rest of the day featured a series of starts and stops, and accusations from both sides. The talks were dominated by the Americans and North Koreans, while the Chinese President asserted himself occasionally to play referee. The former President also accused the North of producing at least $45 million in counterfeit U.S. dollars that were currently in circulation around the world. "You are running a criminal empire much like the Mafia," *Shepherd* told North Korea's leader point blank.

The talks were finally suspended for the day just after 5 p.m. much to the relief of everyone involved. Trevane took out his ear piece and rubbed his tired eyes. He looked around the small room and saw that the other officials were equally drained as they appeared to scrape themselves off their folding chairs. The Americans filed out of the room one after the other while Trevane lagged behind.

"Hey Peter, hang on a sec," he shouted to the last man attempting to leave the room.

Peter Barry turned quickly and could not conceal the frown on his thickly bearded face. Barry was a former classmate from Yale, who now worked as a lawyer for the White House and was considered to be one of the select few people in the President's inner circle. Trevane waited until everyone had cleared the room before speaking to his old friend.

"This has certainly become a pig fuck of the highest proportion," Trevane whispered.

"It's not that bad," Barry replied as he pulled a handkerchief from his pocket and blew his nose. "You have to deal with the North Koreans from a position of strength and I think the old man did well today."

"Were you watching the same thing that I was?" Trevane asked flabbergasted. "There's a difference between being strong and being a bully. The old man was a bully today. He wanted to show everyone that he still had a set of balls and he left the North Koreans with virtually no wiggle room."

"I'm surprised to hear that coming from you," Barry replied. "I know that Buzz Baxter sent you here, and I can't believe he's getting soft on the communists now."

Trevane was growing agitated. "It's just that the United States is a bit over extended right now, or haven't you noticed?"

Barry left the comment alone. He did not want to engage his old friend. "I think the old man got pissed off because the North Korean refused to engage him," he surmised. "The crazy midget just sat there like a statue."

"Well, talk to the old man and tell him to pull back the reigns a little bit," Trevane advised. "And tell him not to bring up the human rights issue tomorrow because it will fall on deaf ears."

"I'll see what I can do, but no promises Steve."

Trevane patted his old friend on the back and both walked out of the room.

CHAPTER 36

▼

HONG KONG

Mister Wong had a drink in one hand, the remote control in the other. He was watching a fair haired reporter from CNN describe the first day of the nuclear summit in Beijing. "Progress is being made, but the two sides are still poles apart," the female correspondent said before tossing to her story. The live shot was replaced by a reporter tracked package describing the day's events on video-tape. Wong looked closely at the large plasma screen as diplomats filed out of the summit and shuffled passed the camera. He caught a brief glimpse of his boss as he walked with two other men to a waiting limousine.

Wong was thankful that he had not made the trip. Ju-Long Lew had ordered his special employee to attend the summit with him, but Wong managed to talk him out of it, saying that he was concerned with the media attention surrounding the event and that he did not want to run the risk of being photographed or vid-eotaped. Despite his medically altered appearance, there was a still a slight chance that someone could recognize him. His boss reluctantly agreed and decided to bring his chauffeur north to Beijing instead. The burly driver was also Lew's per-sonal bodyguard and had his eye on replacing Wong sooner rather than later. The man had a mean streak and ruthless nature that would certainly serve him well, but he lacked the intelligence and sophistication needed for the job. Wong would gladly hand over the responsibilities to the younger man if his boss would allow him to simply walk away. He knew that Ju-Long Lew would never let this happen. Wong was the keeper of secrets and was much too valuable to let go.

Wong had another more personal reason not to attend the summit, he truly despised the North Koreans. He had previously accompanied his boss on a trip to Pyongyang and was appalled by the cult of personality the stubby dictator held over his small nation. They toured the golf course where the leader was said to have hit ten holes in one. They also toured the bowling alley where the leader had allegedly bowled ten perfect games. Both sites were now national museums, and Wong was amazed to see visitors treat each location as if it was a holy shrine. North Korea's ministry of propaganda had indeed propped the leader up to be some kind of God.

Even more appalling than the tours of the museums was their inspection of a North Korean work camp, a massive gulag that made Wong's brief stay at Chuanxi prison seem like a summer retreat. This camp was not a prison at all, but a colony roughly 20 miles long filled with thousands of men, women and children all of whom staggered around with sunken eyes and stomachs swollen by malnourishment. During their tour, the dictator proudly led them through a building where a family was in the process of being gassed in a glass chamber. Wong looked on as a father and mother gasped for breath while trying desperately to give their two young daughters mouth to mouth resuscitation. It took three agonizing minutes for the family to die. In another building, they watched a teenager who was forced to stand waist high in ice cold water. The boy had been standing in the frigid pool for more than an hour and his screams soon faded as his legs gave out and he slid under the water never to resurface. Wong asked officials what the boy had done to receive such a punishment. They told him the teenager had been found guilty of humming a South Korean pop song and teaching it to his friends. The grand finale of the tour came when he and Lew witnessed a female prisoner give birth in the camp's medical ward. The baby's delivery was triggered by several kicks to its mother's stomach by the so-called physician in attendance. The infant's life lasted only seconds before the doctor killed it by stepping on its fragile neck with his heavy boot. The dead infant was still attached to its traumatized mother by its umbilical cord. Wong wondered why he'd been forced to witness such crimes, but after watching the baby's murder, he thought he knew. His eyes shifted from the tiny body lying naked on the cold cement floor to his employer, who watched the brutality with unmasked glee. Their eyes met and the message was delivered. Ju-Long Lew was telling his employee; *I rescued you from a place just like this one. I own you.*

"Oh the horror I have seen," Wong whispered as he wept in the darkness. "Oh the horror I have caused." He thought back to the tiger den and for the first time wished he had not been so fortunate that day. He then downed another glass of rice wine and headed for the door.

Rosary watched Wong as he left his flat. He and Bouchard were sitting in a blue mini-van parked a short distance away from the apartment building. Rosary raised the walkie-talkie to his lips and alerted Joe.

"He's on the move," Rosary told him. "Let's hope that he comes your way."

Grace's cousin barely heard the message over the techno music pumping out of several loud speakers inside Club 97. The noise was so thunderous that Joe noticed the top of the bar shaking under his bottle of beer. He was shaking also. He was nervous and showed it by sucking his Budweiser down quickly and then peeling the label off the bottle. Joe twirled the paper label in his fidgety fingers before tossing it onto the bar. He felt naked sitting there without a gun, waiting, hoping the killer would soon arrive. Joe knew that he had to conquer his fear and put his faith in the skills of Rosary and the Frenchman. Both men were highly capable of protecting him, but he still did not like the fact that he was being used as bait. Joe lowered his head briefly and Rosary spotted the beer wrapper on the bar in front of him.

"Relax now," he told Joe in his ear. "Think about your hero. Let's see some of that Montana coolness. Just remember that Super Bowl winning drive against the Bengals. The Niners were down, but Montana was in complete control. Play it like that. Get rid of that wrapper and get a hold of yourself. Now give us a look at the door."

Joe turned slowly toward the front entrance. He was wearing a pair of eye-glasses equipped with a tiny camera hidden in its frame. The live images were uplinked to a satellite and then downlinked to a laptop computer that Rosary and Bouchard were monitoring in the van. They saw whatever he saw. The men had gambled that Wong would return to Club 97 on this night and they were right.

The killer/kidnapper entered the club alone and as he walked closer to the bar, Rosary could see that his hair was not combed and that his oxford shirt was untucked over his pants. He did not look like the debonair businessman captured by surveillance cameras dragging Jessi Miller out of the hotel back in Beijing.

Wong raised his hand meekly to the bartender who immediately poured him a generous glass of rice wine. He took the drink and stood casually at the corner of the bar. Joe pretended not to notice him and instead focused his attention to the sweaty young men coming and going from the bustling dance floor. Grace's cousin silently prayed that no one would ask him to dance.

"Alright Joe, what's our boy up to?" Rosary asked in his ear piece.

He turned slowly back toward Wong, who had not moved from his spot at the end of the bar. The killer caught Joe glancing over at him and he smiled back. Rosary saw the devil's smile on the computer screen.

"Looks like he's interested," he told Joe. "Now remember, you need to play hard to get, otherwise he may smell a set-up."

You're gonna owe me big time for this, Joe said to himself. He ordered another beer and sipped it slowly. This time he fought the urge to peel the label off the bottle. Two more songs played and he realized that Wong was closing in. A few more minutes passed and Wong had managed to position himself just inches away from the bait.

"You look nice tonight," Wong observed boldly.

Joe detected a slur in Wong's voice.

"You look nice too," he replied. The flirting felt awkward to him and he hoped that he would not have to carry the conversation.

"I come here all the time, but I have not seen you here before," Wong continued.

This marked the first time that Joe had found himself on the receiving end of a pick-up line. *Do we all sound this pathetic?* "This is my first time coming to a place like this and I am quite nervous."

"Did you come here for the dancing?" Wong asked as he finished his glass of wine.

"I am not much of a dancer," Joe replied truthfully.

"Neither am I. Can I buy you a drink?"

"No, but I will buy you one."

The seduction was slow and deliberate and Grace's cousin played his role superbly. He bought his new friend three more drinks, which Wong had no trouble finishing.

The more Wong drank, the bolder he got. Soon, his right arm was draped over Joe's shoulder. Grace's cousin took a step away and spurned the advance. Wong's arm fell clumsily to his side.

"Why did you come to this place if you are not seeking companionship?" Wong asked.

"I do seek companionship," Joe told him. "It's just that I don't want to flirt with you if it's not going to lead anywhere." *Heath, you sonofabitch.*

"My apartment is right up the street," Wong said, his excitement growing.

"Take me there," Joe replied reaching out for the killer's hand.

Rosary watched as Grace's cousin followed Wong out of the bar. "Here we go," he told Bouchard, who was checking his Glock in the back of the van. He tucked his revolver into the back of his jeans and climbed into the driver's seat.

"What's happening?"

"They've just left the club," Rosary responded. "They should be passing us on the other side of the street in about 30 seconds."

Rosary watched as Wong took an unexpected turn and Joe followed.

"Scratch that. They just went into a small store. I think it's the one on the corner. It looks like Wong is buying a pack of rubbers."

"Joe is a brave man," Bouchard said in amazement.

"And he's gonna want to kick my ass after tonight," Rosary replied.

Wong made his purchase and they left the store.

"Alright, they're on the move again. I think this is it this time."

Rosary and Bouchard watched through the van's tinted windows as the two men passed them on the right. Rosary turned his attention back to the laptop as they reached Wong's apartment building. It took Wong several seconds to fish his keys out of the back pocket of his pants.

"This is good, he's drunk. His reaction time is going to be shit," Bouchard predicted.

Rosary was not so sure. "Let's hope so."

They remained in the van while Wong led Joe through a small lobby dominated by a large Art-deco sculpture of a topless woman carved from blood wood and ebony. It reminded Rosary of one of those pretentious art galleries on Newbury Street back in Boston. The pair continued up a winding staircase made from shiny interior steel to Wong's apartment where he punched in his security code on a key pad by the front door. Joe had a perfect view of this, and so did Rosary. "859-62-013," He shouted to Bouchard, who then scribbled the numbers on a small piece of paper.

Wong opened the door and led Joe inside. The lights were dim and Rosary had a difficult time seeing the image that the camera was sending back. From what Rosary could see, the room looked quite similar to the sketch that Wong's lover had drawn on a note pad. The living room was quite large and filled with sprawling plants and exercise equipment. Joe walked toward Wong's computer setup so that Rosary could get a visual. The large flat screen sat on a sleek wooden table, a book case used to store computer files stood next to it.

"What would you like to drink?" Wong asked as he disappeared into the galley kitchen.

"Whatever you are having is fine," Joe replied.

Grace's cousin continued to take in the living room with his hidden camera. He noticed a television monitor over the front door, which had a split screen image of the building's front entrance and the entrance to Wong's apartment.

"Shit, he's got cameras in both locations," Rosary told Bouchard, who was also watching the live feed.

"Joe will need to distract him while we make our move," Bouchard said.

Rosary lifted the walkie-talkie and placed it near his mouth. "Got the visual," he confirmed. "In two minutes, I need you to get him away from the television monitor and keep him occupied while we gain access to the building."

Joe casually looked down at his digital watch and then began the countdown in his head.

"Let's take our drinks into the bedroom," he shouted to Wong who was still in the kitchen. *One minute to go,* he told himself. Wong still had not come out with the drinks. Joe quickly realized that he would not have time enough to get the killer from the kitchen to the bedroom. Sweat began forming in tiny beads on his forehead as the seconds ticked away. Joe knew that his best hope was to head into the kitchen and try to stall him there.

Rosary and Bouchard were already across the street near the entrance to Wong's building. Rosary looked at his watch and whispered to the Frenchman. "Go."

Bouchard pulled a small screwdriver and a safety pin out of his jacket and worked quickly to manipulate the front door lock. Bouchard had cased the building earlier in the day and found that the door was secured with one of the strongest locks on the market, a Sargeant six-pin security tumbler. Using the screwdriver as a tension wrench, Bouchard applied a delicate, but firm touch on the lock. With the aid of a small safety pin, he was able to separate the pins in the cylinder wall from the shell of the lock. The entire episode took only twenty seconds. They were now inside the building and heading for the stairs.

Joe entered the kitchen and saw Wong standing in front of a large wooden cutting block. He was carving thick slices of lime with a long thin knife. He smiled as his date walked in. "You couldn't stand to be without me?" Wong asked with a wide grin.

"No, I guess not," Joe replied nervously.

"Before we take our drinks into the bedroom, I must ask you one question."

"Don't worry," Joe told him. "I am drug—and disease-free."

"No my love, that is not the question I need answered."

Wong sprung forward and grabbed Joe by the neck. The swiftness of the attack caught Grace's cousin by surprise and did not offer him any time to defend himself.

Now, he was caught in the killer's powerful grip. Joe had one hand on Wong's wrist as he tried in vain to pull himself free. The other hand was on Wong's right arm, the arm that held the long thin blade.

"Who do you work for?" Wong demanded. All traces of his slurred speech were just a fading memory now.

Joe choked out an answer. "I don't know what you're talking about."

"Don't lie to me. You are not as smart as you are handsome. I saw you staking out my building this morning. I have survived for many years due to a keen ability that I have. I never forget a face. How brave, but foolish of you to walk willingly into the tiger's den."

Suddenly an alarm sounded. Someone was trying to get inside the apartment. Wong lifted his right hand up and brought it slashing down toward Joe's skull. At the last possible moment, Wong flipped the large blade over and struck Grace's cousin with the thick wooden handle of the knife. It was a powerful blow. Joe's eyes rolled to the back of his head and he crumbled to the floor. Wong did not know why he had not simply killed the imposter. There was no time to question is own actions. There was also no time for the self pity and guilt he felt hours earlier. The tiger was in survival mode now. He took the long blade and ran toward the living room.

Rosary punched in the eight digit security code unlocking the front door and Bouchard went charging in. Confident in their belief that none of the women were being held captive inside the apartment, the strategy now was to *shock and awe* Wong with loud noise and firepower in an effort to take away any time he may have had to take Joe hostage.

"Jingcha, Jingcha," Bouchard yelled as he crossed the threshold of the apartment. *Police, police.*

Wong was about 15 feet away from the door when he threw his knife at the moving target. The long razor sharp blade struck Bouchard in the upper chest. The Frenchman fired off a wild round before falling to the floor. Rosary hurdled over his fallen comrade and ran toward Wong with his gun raised.

"Get down on the floor," he ordered.

Wong stood up straight and did not move.

Rosary pointed his weapon at the killer's left knee and squeezed the trigger. Nothing happened. The gun was jammed. Wong smiled at his good fortune. He leapt toward Rosary with his left foot extended. The kick caught Heath in the chest and knocked him across the room to the floor. Wong turned to retrieve his own gun, which was in his bedroom. Despite a burning sensation in his chest, Rosary still managed to get back to his feet. He gasped for breath as he watched

Wong sprint toward the other room. Heath lined the smaller man up and then ran forward with knees bent and arms wide. For a split second, he felt like he was back on the football field at Boston College. He tackled Wong and drove him into the back wall of the living room. The entire apartment rattled from the force of the collision.

"Where is Jessi Miller?" he screamed.

Wong responded with brute force of his own. He thrust his arms up under Rosary's and broke free from the grip. Wong then spun off the back wall and jumped over a sofa toward the exercise area of the room. Rosary turned and saw Bouchard still lying on the floor with a knife in his chest. His first instinct was to help his fallen comrade, but Bouchard, still conscious waved him off. The Frenchman then slid his revolver across the floor. Rosary bent down to grab it and the lights went out. The front door automatically closed taking with it any ambient light. Rosary now had a gun in his hand, but he couldn't see a thing.

The tiger waited patiently in the darkness. Wong had just cut the power to his apartment and now despite the fact that he was one man against two, he knew that he held the upper hand. They were inside his home and the tiger knew every square inch of this battle field. Rosary also remained silent in the darkness. He took three steps to the right to shift out of his fixed position. He did not move any further out of fear that he would cast a shadow against the wall.

Bouchard's on the floor, so any movement above waist level must certainly be Wong. But where is Joe? Don't get careless, Rosary told himself as he scanned the dark room slowly. The tiger slipped off his loafers and made no noise as he crept forward. He could hear two sets of breathing. One was loud and labored and Wong figured it was the man he had struck with the knife, so he moved stealthily in the direction of the softer sound. Wong bent over in a crouched position as he made his way around the sofa where he saw the other figure standing up with his arms extended in a shooting position. *He must have the other man's weapon,* Wong surmised. The momentary silence was broken by a thunder clap as the tiger launched into a jumping front kick. Rosary felt a stinging sensation in his hands as the revolver was knocked out of his firm grip. Wong followed the kick with a powerful jab to Heath's ribs. Rosary cried out in pain and stumbled back. The tiger continued his attack with a series of rapid fire punches at the bigger man's head. Rosary knocked away most of them, but paid the price with his forearms. Blocking Wong's punches was like fending off a steel pipe. With his arms defending against the oncoming assault, Rosary struck back with another weapon, his head. He lunged forward and caught Wong as he came in. Rosary heard a loud pop and knew instantly that he had timed the head butt perfectly.

This time, it was the tiger who was screaming out in pain as he staggered back against the sofa. Rosary rushed forward with three bruising punches of his own, all hitting their mark on Wong's skull. Rosary then wrapped the smaller man in a powerful headlock. He could feel his bicep growing larger, pressing against Wong's left ear.

"Where is Jessi Miller?" Rosary shouted again.

There was no response, so he squeezed harder.

"Talk, or your dead," he threatened.

"She's gone," Wong replied, as he fought for breath.

"Gone where?"

"I mean she's dead," Wong replied and then began coughing uncontrollably.

In the next moment, the tiger let out a loud cry and collapsed in Rosary's arms. Heath looked over his shoulder and saw Bouchard driving the knife deep into Wong's back.

"What the fuck are you doing?" Rosary hollered at the Frenchman.

"You heard him," Bouchard cried. "She's dead. They're all dead. Your Jessi, my Sophie. This bastard murdered them all."

Bouchard let go of the knife and stumbled back clutching his own bleeding wound.

Rosary lowered Wong to the floor where he began frantically looking for a pulse.

"He's still alive," he shouted. "Get some fucking help."

Bouchard painfully dug his hand into his pocket for his cell phone.

"No help," Wong gurgled. "I do not want any help. Please let me die. Please let me be free."

"Free from what?" Rosary asked in a whisper.

"Free from Ju-Long Lew," Wong slowly replied. "I took those women, and I am about to pay a price for that. But he murdered them, that is, everyone but Jessi Miller."

"Who killed her?" Rosary asked loudly, his temper rising again.

Wong stared back at him with a pained look of remorse. "I did. She suffered greatly. She was a very brave woman. I killed her to put her out of her misery. Now please put me out of mine."

Wong grabbed Rosary's large hand and forced it over his nose and mouth, but Rosary pulled it away.

"I won't kill you."

"I am already dying," Wong replied. His breathing was much slower now, but his mind was racing. "Before I leave this earth, let me begin to repay my debt.

The evidence you seek is all on file. He videotaped each murder for his future enjoyment. I made copies just in case he ever turned on me. They will not help me in this life, but they may help me in the next."

Wong stared up at Rosary and smiled as warm blood began to dribble from his pale lips. Seconds later, he was dead.

CHAPTER 37

▼

Rosary tilted his seat back and closed his eyes. The Airbus 240–600 had just taken off from Hong Kong International airport. He patted his chest where he had five computer disks tucked away safely in the breast pocket of his leather coat. These small disks held enough information to bring down one of the most powerful and most sadistic men in China. Rosary had forced himself to watch the murders replayed on Wong's computer. He had seen plenty of violence in his career, but he knew the images on those disks would haunt him for the rest of his life. He did however take satisfaction knowing that Jessi had turned the tables on Ju-Long Lew in that dungeon of his. She suffered, but so did he. Jessi had proved to be a tough Maine farm girl right to the end. *The end. How am I going to break the news to Grace?* He was glad there was no videotape of Jessi's final moments. *I couldn't bear to see that.*

Rosary gazed over to the seat next to him where Joe was fast asleep. Grace's cousin had survived the ordeal with an ugly bump on the head and a little humiliation, but at least he was alive. So was Henri Bouchard. The Frenchman was listed in fair condition at Hong Kong's Queen Mary Hospital. He had suffered a deep stab wound to his chest, but fortunately the blade missed his vital organs. Bouchard's wounds cut even deeper than merely the physical though, and Rosary wondered whether the Frenchman would ever get over the loss of his love.

After the deadly showdown inside Wong's apartment, Rosary placed a call to Pu-Yan in Beijing and told him everything. Pu-Yan immediately dispatched two men to secure the flat. One of the men had demanded the computer files, but Rosary refused to give them up. He would deliver the evidence to Pu-Yan personally. They were now about ten minutes into the flight. An attendant pulled down the movie screen in the middle of the cabin and the passengers reached for their headphones. *Oh great, another Chinese romance.* Rosary took his headphones off and tried to get some sleep.

∗   ∗   ∗   ∗

Grace woke up to the sound of Sasha's high pitched cries. The baby's eyes were still closed and her arms and legs were flailing about. *Poor little girl, you've been cramped in a crib with another baby all your young life. You're not used to having this much room.* They were laying together in the middle of a king sized bed inside a rented room at the Friendship Hotel, a sprawling old inn that dated back to the Mao era. Benny was a friend of the owner's and knew the man would not ask any awkward questions. Grace's rotund cousin had checked her out of the Jianguo Hotel after they had arrived back in Beijing. There was no way that Grace could have explained the baby to the other adopting couples or even to Rita.

She was all too happy to care for little Sasha. It helped keep her mind off Jessi and Heath. She had no time to worry about them because the baby was always in need of something. Right now, little Sasha was hungry. Grace carried her over to a small desk she had turned into a makeshift kitchen. Benny had gone out and bought twenty jars of baby food and 2 gallons of orange juice. The baby bottles sat unused on the corner of the desk. Little Sasha liked to drink from a glass. Grace poured half a cup of juice into a tall glass and placed it to the infant's quivering lips. The baby had an unquenchable thirst and gulped the juice eagerly, spilling some of it down her chin and onto her yellow shirt. The shirt was part of a cute little outfit that included lime green pants and yellow socks with bunny prints on them. The woman from the orphanage had handed the baby over with just the clothes on her back, so once they had safely returned to Beijing, Grace asked her cousin to go out and buy 20 new outfits. The mission had taken Benny nearly a full day to accomplish. Grace laughed as she pictured her cousin completely out of his element agonizing over which baby outfits to buy. She placed Sasha's orginal outfit, a dirty blue shirt and blue pants in a garbage bag. She had no intention of throwing it away; she planned to bring it home so that Sasha could have this little piece of her personal history when she got older. It was easy to prepare for something that was a few years down the road, but Grace had no idea about her immediate plans.

"How am I going to bring you home?" she whispered before kissing Sasha's soft cheek. The baby looked up at Grace, her tiny almond eyes fixed on the woman's concerned face. The practical thing to do would be to bring Sasha to the American Embassy and explain the bizarre situation. However, Grace would have no guarantee that she'd ever get Sasha back and the mere thought of this was unacceptable.

"I promise not to let you out of my sight until your mommy gets here," she cooed.

If your mommy gets here.

Grace took the glass of orange juice gently away from the baby and placed it on the desk. She then opened a small jar of sweet potato and began mixing it with a spoon. Sasha flashed a toothless grin as she bounced and giggled on Grace's lap.

"You like sweet potato, don't you?"

The baby *loved* sweet potato. However, the fussy little eater did not care for any the other food choices.

"Benny, I think we need to get more sweet potato," she shouted to her cousin, who was trying to take a nap on a chair by the bed.

"Okay, okay, I'll go out right now," he replied with a yawn.

Benny lifted his large body off the chair when suddenly there was a knock on the door. He and Grace shared a surprised look.

"Who could that be?" she whispered.

"I don't know, but take the baby into the bathroom and try to keep her quiet while I answer the door."

Grace carried Sasha into the bathroom and closed the door.

"Hush little baby," she whispered to the giggling infant.

Benny stuck his gun in the pocket of his jacket and walked toward the door.

"Who is it?" he asked through the door.

"It's me, brother," Joe replied.

Benny swung the door open wide and pulled his brother in with a warm hug. Rosary passed the pair and entered the room.

"Grace?" he called out.

She heard his voice and came running out of the bathroom holding Sasha. Rosary walked toward her and wrapped them both in his arms.

"They need some time alone," Joe whispered to his brother. Both men walked quietly out of the room and closed the door behind them.

The couple continued to hug and soon both were crying.

"We need to talk," Grace told him.

Heath looked down at the baby in her arms. "I can see that, but I need to tell you something first."

Grace cut him off. She was trying to delay the inevitable.

"Heath, this is Jessi's baby," she told him.

Rosary ran his fingers gently through Sasha's soft black hair. "She's beautiful."

Grace told him the story of how she had come to care for the child. Heath took it all in and did not interrupt.

"I'm the Godmother of this child," Grace said looking into Sasha's sparkling eyes.

"I made a promise to Jessi that I would care for her if something bad were to ever happen." She looked up from the baby to Heath. "I know Jessi's gone," Grace whispered. "You don't have to say it."

"I've failed you baby," he replied. "I'm so sorry."

"You could never fail me darling," Grace told him as she kissed his tear stained cheek. "You did more for her than anyone could have. I should have come here with her. It's my fault."

Rosary shook his head. "It's not your fault baby. Please don't ever think that. What happened to Jessi would have happened if you were there or not. I could have lost you too."

"I don't want to know what happened, but there's one thing I must know. Did she suffer?"

"No darling," he lied.

"Did you find the person who did this?"

"Yes we did. He's dead now." Rosary didn't provide any details. "But he was following someone else's orders," he told her.

"Where is this person?"

As he explained, he could see her brown eyes begin to blaze.

"I've always believed that my strongest trait was the ability to forgive," she said, her voice trembling. "It's the liberal in me, you know. But I can't forgive this time. Heath I want you to get this guy. I want you to make him pay."

Rosary and Joe left the hotel for their rendezvous with Pu-Yan. Heath was surprised and relieved to see how strong Grace had become during this whole ordeal. She had a baby to take care of now. How they would get Sasha out of the country remained a big problem. Heath suggested that Grace's father send over a private jet that would allow them to bypass customs. But what would happen when they got the baby back to the United States? Tommy Chen would have to call in some big markers for this one. They'd simply have to tackle that problem when it came. Right now, Rosary had to get those computer disks to the one man who would do something about them.

"Where are we meeting him?" Rosary asked.

"He sounded pretty freaked out about something," Joe replied as he drove his Volvo through Beijing's crowded streets. "He wants to meet us in the Underground City."

Rosary arched his eyebrow. "Sounds like a Sci-fi movie to me."

"Oh it's science fiction alright," Joe replied. "My father told me the story when I was a kid. The Underground City is a relic from the Cold War, but Mao didn't fear the Americans as much as he feared the Soviets. In the late sixties, the Russians threatened to take over Zhenbao Island, which is in the middle of the Heilongjiang River in northeast China. The tensions were so high that Mao became convinced the Soviets would launch a nuclear attack. He made the citizens of Beijing dig a bomb shelter under the city that is said to be 30 kilometers long."

Rosary was fascinated by the history lesson. "How would the people get inside?"

"It is said that every residence once had a trap door leading to the tunnels."

"Are the tunnels used for anything now?"

"That's the funny thing," Joe observed. "It's now a large shopping center."

A short time later, Joe turned his car down West Damochang Street and parked in front of a small silk shop. They stepped out of the car and Heath noticed a small sign written in both Chinese and English hanging over the store front.

"This is the Underground City?" Rosary asked more than a little confused.

"The entrance is actually through this shop," Joe clarified. "The shopping center in the Underground City does not advertise. In fact, most people don't even know it exists."

Grace's cousin led the way past two small stone lions guarding the entrance of the shop and continued through the narrow store filled with colorful silk prints and swatches. They passed the elderly shop keeper, who didn't acknowledge their presence, and walked toward the back of the store where they found a set of concrete steps leading down to the subterranean city. The stairs led to a large passageway that was dimly lit by a trail of light bulbs hung crudely from the concrete ceiling. They followed the tunnel for roughly two hundred meters.

"This reminds me of the catacombs beneath Paris," Rosary observed.

"You probably won't find any bones or burial plots down here," Joe replied.

"These tunnels were made to house about 40 percent of Beijing's population. It's rumored that Mao and the other leaders had their own separate tunnel to use if they were forced to evacuate the city."

The noise grew louder and the tunnel got brighter as they approached the shopping mall. As they entered, Rosary could hardly believe how large it was. They strolled through a well lit jewelry shop where a group of tourists inspected and haggled over some elaborately carved jade pieces. They exited the jewelry shop and Rosary spotted a group of teenagers sitting on a wooden bench lacing up their roller skates.

"There's actually a roller skating rink down here?" he observed with astonishment.

"Yep," Joe replied. "All this stuff was built more than thirty years ago. Mao had a feeling that his people would be down here for the long haul."

The teenagers followed one another out to the floor and skated to the tune of a Chinese pop song playing over the loud speakers. Pu-Yan stood at the opposite end of the rink smoking a cigarette as he watched the teens roll by. Both Joe and Rosary approached slowly. No greetings were exchanged. Like Pu-yan, the men stood facing the skaters.

"You were right all along Pu-Yan. I've got everything you need to bring this guy down," Rosary said staring straight ahead.

"Don't show me here," Pu-Yan replied nervously. "In fact, don't show me at all. Our operation has been compromised."

The news made Rosary's head snap around. "What the hell are you talking about?"

"Ju-Long Lew is paying someone inside my department. You Americans would call him a mole."

"So what does this mean?" Rosary asked trying to remain calm.

"It *means* that he knows what happened in Hong Kong and he knows about you."

"Why don't you take these disks and simply arrest the mother fucker."

"Hold onto those disks," Pu-Yan pleaded desperately. "If I go back to my office with them, I'm a dead man and those disks will magically disappear."

"So what the hell should I do with this evidence?"

"Give it to your embassy or turn it over to Interpol. They may be able to apply enough pressure on my government to make an arrest."

Rosary thought for a moment. "You said they know what happened in Hong Kong and they know about me?"

Pu-Yan tried to apologize. "I just learned of the leak two hours ago. I've placed myself in great danger just by meeting with you." The committee member looked nervously around the skating rink. "I suspect someone may be following you. Did you come here directly from the airport?"

"No, I had to break the news to my girlfriend first."

"Oh dear," Pu-Yan said as he lifted the cigarette to his mouth, his hand shaking noticeably. "Go to her. Go to her now!

They ran in a full sprint through the winding tunnel toward the street level exit. Rosary climbed the steps two at a time and bolted out of the silk shop like he had just robbed the place. Joe followed close behind and both men jumped into the Volvo and took off with wheels screeching and tires burning. They made it back to the Friendship Hotel in less than eight minutes and tore through the lobby toward the staircase. They reached the hotel room seconds later and found the door slightly open. Rosary pulled out his 9mm semi-automatic and shoved Joe aside.

He pushed the door open and entered the room in a prone position. Both elbows were locked as he pointed the weapon toward the bathroom. The light was on, but the room was empty. Rosary continued up a small hallway toward the bedroom. He had a lump in his throat and his heart was pounding. He entered the room and his worst fears were realized. The desk was toppled over and jars of baby food lay smashed on the carpet. Rosary looked down at the floor and followed the broken glass across the room where he noticed a foot sticking out from behind the bed.

Rosary walked slowly forward and saw Benny's body lying on the floor. His eyes were wide open and his throat was cut. A pool of blood formed a halo around the back of his head. Rosary looked around the rest of the room. There was no sign of Grace or the baby. They were gone.

CHAPTER 38

▼

Joe lay down cradling his brother's head. He rocked back and forth and soon his quiet sobs grew to a loud and agonizing scream. Rosary gave him his space while he silently searched the hotel room for any evidence the kidnappers may have left behind. The room was a mess and smelled of death. Heath rubbed the handle of his gun across his forehead and felt his stomach twist into a tight knot. *This can't be happening. Oh Grace, where are you?* He was alone again. The fear of abandonment he'd kept buried inside him for all those years came spilling out all at once. His brown eyes welled up with tears and he could feel himself hyperventilating. *Please don't leave me.* Nothing was in his control now. It was the first time that he'd felt this way in his adult life. He could hear the voices of Uncle James, of his football coaches and of the instructors at the Secret Service all yelling in unison in his head. *Focus,* they told him. *Get control of the situation.* Rosary listened to those voices as he placed his hands on his knees and began taking deep breathes. He waited for a few moments for his mind to clear and then made a mental checklist of everything he'd seen so far. First, there was the body of Grace's cousin. The collar of his shirt had ripped, suggesting that he'd struggled with his killer. The mattress on the bed was flipped over and the dresser drawers were all pulled out, their contents strewn all over the floor. *They came here looking for the disks. When they couldn't find them, they took Grace and the baby instead.* This was actually a positive sign. It meant that she was still alive and would remain so until Ju-Long Lew got what he had come here for. As Heath was processing this information, his satellite phone rang. Rosary hit the *send* button and placed the receiver to his right ear. "Who is it?"

"I think you know who it is."

Rosary took another deep breath. "I've got what you want, and you've got what I want. Let's cut the bullshit. The disks are yours. Just release Grace and the baby."

"I am in charge here, not you," Ju-Long Lew warned him. "You are not in any position to make demands. You of all people should know that. You've just witnessed what I am capable of. I must thank you though, for saving me the trouble of killing that treacherous cur Mister Wong. I will call you again in 24 hours. I know it will be an agonizing wait, but I want you to feel what it would be like never to see your woman again. Until then, Grace and the baby will be guests of mine. If you contact the police I will know it. If you go running to your embassy, I will find out. You need think smartly Mr. Rosary; otherwise I will be forced to kill your girlfriend and the baby."

"Let me speak to her," Rosary pleaded.

There was a pause on the other end of the phone and then Lew shouted something in Chinese. Moments later, he heard her voice.

"Heath, I'm so sorry," she said, her voice trembling. "Benny tried to stop them, but they murdered him right in front of me. It's all my fault. This whole thing is all my fault."

"Don't think that way, baby. You try to stay strong and protect little Sasha. I'll make sure that nothing happens to you. I love you."

"I love you too," she replied chocking back the tears.

Ju-Long Lew then ripped the phone out of her hand. Rosary could hear her scream something to him in Chinese. Then he heard what appeared to be a loud slap followed by her cries. Rosary's heart sank and his anger grew.

"Don't you fucking touch her," he shouted into the satellite phone. "I'll skin you alive if you lay a hand on her again."

"Your threats mean nothing to me," Lew replied calmly. "I'll call you in 24 hours with a meeting place. Be smart or they will die."

The line went dead. Rosary stared at the phone. *Get control of the situation.*

They were back inside the basement of the Beijing City Changping Mortuary, where Rosary had first met Pu-Yan. Benny's lay on a steel slab covered with a white sheet in the corner of the room. Joe was lost in prayer as he stood with eyes closed over his dead brother. Rosary and Pu-Yan stood together several feet away.

"He's going to kill them, even if you hand over the disks, you know that don't you?"

"I've seen his work first hand," Rosary replied. "I know what he's capable of. I also know what I'm capable of. He will not get out of this alive."

Pu-Yan paused to light a cigarette. He took a long drag and scratched his head. "You need to harness your anger Mr. Rosary. You can not save Grace and the baby this way."

"You're right Pu-Yan. That's why I'm here asking for your help. This is your country, not mine. You know this guy better than me. What are my options?"

Pu-Yan patted Rosary's arms gently. "There is one way to get them back. He has taken something that you love and now you must do the same."

Heath thought for a moment. "What, like his artwork or something like that?"

"No, no Mr. Rosary," Pu-Yan replied shaking his head. "There's one thing that you do not know about Ju-Long Lew, his most prized possession isn't a painting or sculpture, it's his teenaged daughter."

Rosary had a difficult time comprehending this. "I'm supposed to kidnap his daughter?"

"Yes," Pu-Yan replied matter of factly. "It is the only way to ensure the safety of Grace and the baby."

Joe heard the plan and opened his eyes and unfolded his hands. "I want to help you, Heath."

Rosary shook his head. "I couldn't ask you to do this. Look what it's already cost you. I don't want you joining your brother on that slab."

Joe looked down at the body on the cold table. "My brother loved Grace and gave his life for hers." He paused to wipe a tear from his eye. "I don't care about the consequences. This is about family honor. I owe it to my brother to see this to the end."

Rosary nodded, but said nothing. He didn't have to.

HONG KONG

Bao Lew shuffled her way past the long winding line outside the Hong Kong Disneyland. She approached a separate entrance and waved her Disney Fast Pass proudly in front of the female ticket taker, who responded by stamping her hand with a purple print of Mickey Mouse. The attendant did the same for Bao's muscular companion. Bao then took the bodyguard's hand and pulled him into the bustling theme park.

Rosary and Joe stood in line and watched them go in. "It shouldn't be that hard to find them," whispered Grace's cousin. The pair had easily followed Lew's daughter from the family mansion at Victoria's Peak. Her bodyguard took the most direct route possible to the theme park and Rosary realized that they were not dealing with an experienced professional. Heath and Joe had always kept two or three cars back and both were confident that Bao's bodyguard did not catch the tail.

The line slowly moved along and Rosary became more anxious as his window of opportunity grew smaller by the minute. If someone were to tell him a week ago that he'd be at Disneyland in China trying to kidnap a teenaged girl, he would have said they were crazy. But here he was ready to commit the crime knowing it was the only way to save Grace's life. Ten minutes passed and the pair finally reached the ticket counter.

"How many in your party?" asked a cheerful attendant, who wore a large hat complete with a floppy set of Goofy ears.

"Just the two of us," Grace's cousin replied as he counted out some cash.

"You are very lucky," the attendant told them. "You've got the last two tickets of the morning. The rest of the crowd will have to wait until this afternoon."

"Won't they be angry?" Joe asked.

"No, no," she replied with a smile that looked as if it had been permanently stitched to her face. "This is the hottest attraction in all of China. Some people wait days just to get in."

Joe nodded and paid for the tickets. He handed one to Heath and both stepped forward through a pair of metal detectors. The alarm immediately made a loud beeping noise and Joe stepped back and fished through his coat for his car keys. He smiled sheepishly at the attendant as he placed the keys in a tray before stepping back through. The alarm did not sound this time, but the attendant ran an electronic wand over his body just to make sure. Satisfied that Joe was not a threat, she returned his keys and wished him a good day. Heath walked through next without tripping the alarm.

Rosary grabbed a couple of park maps and they continued through a small tunnel into the Magic Kingdom. This Disneyland was set-up much like the theme parks back in the states. There was *Main Street USA*, which sounded odd, especially here. *Main Street USA* branched off into *Adventure Land, Fantasy Land,* and *Tomorrow Land.* The park was choked with visitors and finding the daughter would be more difficult than they had imagined.

"I was wrong, we're never gonna find her in here," Joe said with a groan. "If you were a teenaged girl, where would you go first?"

Rosary gazed down at his map. "It seems like *Fantasy Land* is the place to go. It's got Cinderella's Carousel and all that shit." He finished studying the map and looked up at Grace's cousin. "How you holding up? You gonna be okay with this?"

"I'm doing alright," Joe replied with a shrug. "My dad is flying over to pick up Benny's body. He'll be buried back in California close to my parents. I told them that I'd fly home in a couple of days. I hope this won't take too long. Like you, the thought of kidnapping a young girl makes me kind of sick, but I know it's the only way."

"We're off to *Fantasy Land* then."

"Yup," Joe replied as they walked straight ahead toward the flag covered spires of Sleeping Beauty's Castle.

"When are Baba and Mama going to come home?" Bao asked her bodyguard while the pair strolled through *Fantasy Garden,* where costumed characters seemed to be popping out from behind every tree.

"I'm telling you for the last time, that I don't know," her companion growled as he brushed past an actor dressed up as *Tigger.*

"You don't like coming here do you?"

"We've been coming here every day for the past week," the bodyguard sighed. "Isn't there anything else you'd like to do?"

Bao started giggling. "Oh no," she replied. "This is the happiest place on earth."

"Well let's get on with it then."

"You're not being nice to me," Bao frowned.

"I'm paid to protect you, not to talk to you," the guard shot back angrily. "I was hired to be a bodyguard, not a playmate for a retarded daughter."

Bao was taken aback. Sure, kids at school had made fun of her, but she'd never been insulted by one of her father's employees before. "I'm going to tell my father you said that," she promised.

"I don't care what you tell him anymore," the bodyguard shrugged.

Rosary spotted the girl and her bodyguard as they left the garden. He watched as she hobbled over to an actor dressed as Merlin at the *Sword and the Stone* exhibit.

"Ah, the young lady has returned," Merlin said stroking his flowing white beard. "Who so pulleth out this sword of this stone and anvil, is right wise king born of England," the actor announced with dramatic flair.

Bao gave the sword a tug, but nothing happened.

"Try it again my dear," Merlin advised.

Bao grabbed the sword once more and pulled with all of her strength. The bejeweled sword rose from the rock and horns began to sound. The girl responded with a wide smile.

"You must never give up until you accomplish what it is you set out to do," Merlin told her sagely while patting her gently on the head.

Bao thanked the magician, then took her bodyguard by the arm and pulled him toward another attraction.

Rosary and Joe followed at a slow pace.

"By the size of him, he looks like he can handle himself," Grace's cousin observed.

"Do you think he's packing?"

"I hope not, because *we're* not," Rosary replied. "We've got the element of surprise on our side and that's a good advantage to have."

They continued to follow the girl for the next thirty minutes though *Tomorrow Land* where she ordered her bodyguard to accompany her on the *Buzz Lightyear Astro Blasters* ride, and then onto *Adventure Land* where she was having a tough time climbing through *Tarzan's Tree House*. Rosary had noticed the girl's disability when she limped toward the theme park entrance earlier in the day. Her affliction certainly did not help his conscience. He thought again of the girl's father. *You son of a bitch! I hate you for what you've done, and now you're making me do this? Soon you'll learn the pain I'm feeling right now.*

As the girl struggled down the rope ladder exiting *Tarzan's Tree House*, Rosary looked over at the bodyguard, who seemed to be taking great pleasure in the problems she was having. The girl got her foot caught in the rope and fell forward dangling upside down from the ladder. Seeing that no one was rushing to help, Rosary ran over and lifted her shoulders, while maneuvering her left foot out of the rope. He placed her gently on the ground and smiled.

"Are you okay?" he asked nodding his head.

She did not understand English, but nodded in return.

The bodyguard walked casually over to the girl, grabbed her arm and led her away without ever acknowledging Rosary. Bao looked back at him and smiled.

"So much for staying in the background," Joe whispered. "I hope your good deed didn't just cost us big time."

"I don't think it did," Rosary replied watching the girl as she limped away.

It was now just after 2 p.m. They had been following her for a few hours when finally she decided it was time for a bathroom break. She hobbled into the girl's room while the bodyguard waited outside. At that moment, he did something that even Rosary could not believe. He left the girl's room door unguarded and walked into the adjacent men's room. The bodyguard had just broken the cardinal rule of protective service and Rosary knew that he wouldn't get a better chance. He whispered the plan to Joe and then headed for the men's room. He opened the door and saw a man washing his hands in the sink. It was not the bodyguard. Rosary looked to his right and saw that the urinals were empty. He waited for the man to dry his hands and leave the bathroom before continuing up the row of stalls. He spotted the bodyguard's black shoes under one of the stalls and couldn't believe his luck; they were now alone in the bathroom. But for how long? Heath had to act quickly and he did. He kicked open the stall door with tremendous force catching the bodyguard off guard. The man was sitting on the toilet with his pants around his ankles. He tried in vain to get up, but Rosary caught him with a sharp elbow across the cheek. The man's head snapped to the side as he fell back on the toilet. Rosary threw a thunderous left hook that struck his temple and the bodyguard fell to the floor. Rosary lifted the unconscious man back on the toilet, took a roll of duct tape out of his coat pocket and went to work.

He left the bathroom two minutes later with the unconscious bodyguard gagged and bound to the toilet. Rosary nodded to Joe, who had an arm draped around Bao Lew's shoulder. She spotted Rosary and smiled.

"I told her that her bodyguard had been called back to the mansion, and that her dad wanted us to take her to see him," Joe explained. "She said that she's excited to go and that she never wants to see that bodyguard again."

"She probably won't," Rosary replied with a smile. "Let's move."

They walked at a brisk pace through the theme park back toward *Main Street U.S.A*, where they entered a crowded café and continued past a fleet of tables into the steam filled kitchen. They were met there by a cook who nodded to Joe and guided them to a metal door in the back of the room.

"Take a left at the bottom of these stairs and follow until you see a sign for garbage depot," the cook said in Chinese. "Turn right at the garbage depot and look for an exit. I had your car re-parked near the trash trucks. Good luck to you."

Grace's cousin led them through the metal door and down the steps.

"Why are we going this way?" Bao asked curiously.

"We're going down the rabbit hole," Joe said trying to keep the mood light. "It's the only part of the park you haven't seen. There's a whole city beneath the Magic Kingdom."

This tunnel was much more sophisticated than the Underground City in Beijing, and much more crowded. Chinese engineers shuttled back and forth sharing the narrow space with low-level Disney employees who were hauling trash and laundry through the passageways. Everyone seemed pre-occupied with their work and no one paid attention to the current visitors.

"This is why the park is so clean," Joe explained to the girl. "All the trash is taken down here. All the rides are run from down here too."

This revelation excited her. "Can we see them?" she asked.

"Not this time I'm afraid. We must bring you to your father. He misses you badly."

As they followed the tunnel, Rosary looked around and noticed the absence of surveillance cameras. "No cameras down here huh?"

"They haven't been installed yet," Joe replied. "I know the firm that holds the security contract. There are cameras elsewhere in the park, but the supply ran out. They're awaiting another shipment of cameras. That's why we're going this way."

"Good thinking," Rosary replied. "Where does the cook come in?"

"He flips burgers during the day and drives a truck for me at night."

"Import and export, right?" Rosary said with a smile.

"Not for much longer," Joe replied in a serious tone. "After we do what we have to do, I'm going back to the states for good."

"That makes two of us."

CHAPTER 39

▼

BEIJING

Rosary watched Bao Lew while she napped on the zebra striped sofa inside the Beijing safe house. *It seems impossible that a monster like Lew could have raised this poor sweet girl,* he observed. *But nothing so far has made sense, including where we are now.* The flat was on the 5th floor of a high priced apartment building located near the Forbidden City. Grace's cousins had purchased the apartment as an investment and currently rented it out to politburo members looking for a discreet place to meet with their mistresses. It was decorated with that in mind. The walls were lined with crushed red velvet and the floor was covered by a white shag carpet.

"All that's missing here is a lava lamp," Rosary observed as he sat on a black leather chair by the window.

"Please don't tell Grace about this place," Joe pleaded earnestly. "She wouldn't understand."

"Don't worry," Rosary replied. "I'm glad you have it, I don't know where else we could have gone. I've got one question though."

"What is it?"

"Who decorated this place?"

"Lenny Kravitz did," Joe laughed. "We brought the tape of his episode on MTV's *Cribs* to a decorator and asked for the exact same thing."

Rosary chuckled as he lifted himself off the chair and walked toward the bathroom. He could hear every joint in his body crack along the way. He reached the bathroom and turned on the overhead light. He looked through bloodshot eyes at his reflection in the mirror. "Who are you old man?" he whispered. He hadn't shaved in days and had not slept in the past twenty hours, even during the plane ride from Hong Kong. Joe had continued to pull rabbits out of his hat by securing them a flight on a private cargo plane. The snatch had been a lot easier than he could have imagined, but the one true thing about luck was that it would change eventually. Rosary took the satellite phone off the clip on his hip and dialed Grace's number. After three rings, someone picked up.

"Well Mr. Rosary you are a very impatient man aren't you?" There was an arrogant tone in Ju-Long Lew's voice. "You have broken our little agreement. I make the rules remember?"

"The rules have changed," Rosary informed him as he left the bathroom and headed back to the living room.

"Well, that is very unfortunate for you," Lew replied. "I warned you that if you did not act smartly, your loved ones would die."

"Speaking of loved ones, someone wants to talk to you."

Rosary shook Bao awake gently and handed her the phone.

"Ni hao?" *Hello?*

Ju-Long Lew heard the voice and his blood ran cold.

"Bao, is that you?"

"Shi de, Baba." *Yes, daddy.*

"Where are you?" he asked desperately.

Rosary grabbed the phone out of her hand before she could answer.

"Take a deep breath," Rosary said calmly. "How does it feel?"

"You bastard!," Lew screamed into the phone. "I'll kill you for this. I'll kill your cunt girlfriend and that baby too."

"You harm them in any way, and you will never see your daughter alive again. You need to act smartly now and think of Bao," Rosary advised him. "There will be a simple exchange. Your daughter for Grace and the baby."

"What about the disks?"

"Do they really matter to you now? What should only matter to you is the life of your daughter."

"You are not that kind of man," Lew responded, trying to call his bluff. "You wouldn't kill an innocent girl."

"You created the rules to our little game remember? I will kill your daughter, just as you would kill Grace and the baby. Then the two of us can fight it out in hell."

Rosary's words were beginning to sink through. "Please do not harm my child," Lew pleaded meekly.

"I'll call you back in two hours to set up a meeting place. You will arrive with Grace and the baby, but no one else. If I see that you have hurt them in any way, you'll never see your daughter alive again. Do you understand?"

"Yes," Lew replied.

Rosary hung up the phone, hurried to the bathroom and threw up.

Ju-Long Lew cocked his arm back and almost threw the satellite phone against the wall before he caught himself. The phone was now the only life line he had to his daughter. He placed it gently on a table and rubbed his hand across the track of stitches running along the side of his head. His entire body was shaking now as he paced the floor of the spacious sitting area in his Presidential Suite at the Peninsula Palace Hotel. "What have I done?" he screamed aloud. "What have I done to my fang-hua?" *My fragrant flower?*

The billionaire began sobbing uncontrollably. His cries startled little Sasha, who began crying also. Lew heard the sound and marched down the marble corridor and opened the door to a locked bedroom.

"Quiet that insolent little welp," he shouted with a finger pointed at Grace. "Or I'll throw her right out the window."

Grace tried to hush the child, but her cries grew louder. "Why don't you let her go," she pleaded holding Sasha close to her bosom. "For Godsake, she's just a baby."

Lew responded by slamming the door and storming back down the hall. "Rosary has taken my daughter, what am I to do?" he asked his chauffeur, who stood sipping a cup of green leaf tea. The driver stared at the porcelain cup and said nothing. Lew reached out his hand and knocked the cup and saucer across the room. "Think, you fool," He shouted at his subordinate. "If you want to take Wong's place, you'd better come up with a plan quickly."

Grace heard the shouting from down the hall. "Heath has his daughter?" she whispered to herself in amazement. "Oh please, Baby. Come find us."

Rosary wiped his mouth with a towel and splashed cold water on his face. After drying himself off, he reached for the satellite phone and dialed another number. It was picked up after the first ring.

"Hello? You've reached Special-Agent Nicole Tavano."

"Ginzo, it's me."

"Smokey?"

As best friends and former colleagues, Rosary and Tavano had always addressed each other with these ethnic and racial slurs. It drove everyone else including Grace crazy, but the two got a real kick out of it, especially since it bothered so many others.

"If you're calling to tell me that the Pats won their division, I already know. We get USA Today here in China. Otherwise, I'm pretty busy. It's 10 a.m. here in Beijing, so what, that's like 10 p.m. back in Boston?"

"I'm not in Boston Ginzo, I'm here in Beijing."

It took a couple of seconds before Tavano could respond. "Don't fuck with me Heath. I've got shit up to my eyeballs right now. The North Koreans have just stormed out of the summit and tensions are extremely high at the moment."

"Listen to me, Nikki. I'm here in China and someone has kidnapped Grace."

Tavano could hear the pain in Heath's voice. "You're not kidding."

"No, Nikki, I'm deadly serious and I'm too fucking scared and tired to play games."

"Tell me the whole story," she urged him. "Tell me what's going on."

He told her and she could hardly believe it.

"Are you sure it's Ju-Long Lew?" she asked. "I just saw him yesterday at the summit."

"Yes, I'm positive."

"Well, I know that he's staying at the Palace Hotel," Tavano informed him. "Let's get some police over there right now."

"No," Rosary replied. "He owns the cops around here. We couldn't ensure Grace's safety."

"So what do you want me to do?"

"I'm working on a plan," he told her. "Just let those Marines at the embassy gate know that they could have some party crashers later today."

CHAPTER 40

▼

Ju-Long Lew sat in an elegant Chareau high backed armchair sipping a glass of scotch and biting his knuckle. The dragon was calling him again. How tempting it would be to escape from the reality of the moment and get lost in an opium fog.

Stay strong for your daughter, he told himself. *The opium is not the answer, but the cause of all my problems.*

He was just inches away from the telephone when it rang. Since it was not the satellite phone, he made no attempt to answer it. The chauffeur walked over from across the room and placed the receiver to his ear. He nodded twice and then addressed his boss.

"It's the American named Trevane. He wants to meet with you. He says it's urgent."

Right now, the summit was the furthest thing from Lew's mind. The billionaire was about to dismiss the American with a wave of the hand, when suddenly he had an idea.

"Tell the American to meet me in the hotel bar in ten minutes," he ordered.

The driver relayed the message and hung up the phone.

It was 10:30 a.m. and the Huang Ting Restaurant was still closed. The hotel concierge did convince the manager to open early for one special customer. Ju-Long Lew sat at a round table with another glass of scotch in front of him. He looked around the empty restaurant, his favorite in Beijing and marveled at the design. It resembled a noble courtyard house from ancient China. The tables were surrounded by gray brick walls taken from original hu-tongs. It also had slate floors and ceiling beams taken from a 200 year old mansion in Suzhou. But what really amazed the billionaire was a collection of antique plates and vases dating back to the Qing Dynasty. *Oh, if I'd only limited my collection to this,* Lew thought in hindsight. *My Bao would not be in danger now.* Ju-Long Lew was truly a desperate man. He had lost his wife and his daughter in a matter of days. He would get over his wife's abrupt exit, but he could not live without his fragrant flower. He vowed to get her back and he would use the American diplomat to do it. A smile returned to his face. The dragon was in control again.

The manager of the Huang Ting unlocked the door and welcomed the Lew's guest into the restaurant. Steve Trevane followed the manager to the table and sat down. Lew nodded to his guest, but did not extend his hand.

"What can I do for you Mister Trevane?"

Travane's blue eyes darted around the room.

"I assure you we are alone," Lew told him.

"I want to know what the North Koreans are going to do next."

Lew laughed. "After how you Americans treated them here? Why would I tell you?"

"I know we both want to avoid a military confrontation," Trevane replied. "I also know you hold great influence over their leader."

"I am but a humble businessman," Lew said modestly. "But I do know this. The prevailing belief in Pyongyang is that the United States will eventually launch an attack against the people of North Korea. Should they sit and wait? No, that would be a foolish strategy. Why not invade South Korea now while the Americans are stretched militarily in Iraq and Afghanistan? That would be a wise move indeed."

Trevane tried to remain calm. "And you would counsel their leader to adopt such a strategy?"

Ju-Long Lew sipped his scotch and said nothing, which said it all.

Trevane was beginning to realize now that he was dealing with no man of peace.

"And by invading the South, the North would have to increase its oil supply to keep those tanks rolling. The North gets all its oil from Lew Petroleum. You get richer while thousands and possibly millions die."

"I don't deal in intellectual theories," Lew told him as he let the last drop of scotch roll down his throat. "As I said, I'm a businessman and speculation is part of my business. I speculate that millions of North Koreans are willing to die for their leader. I also speculate that millions of Americans are not willing to die for theirs."

Trevane threw his hands up in surrender. "It's true. They've got us by the balls. How can I convince *you* to convince *them* it's a bad idea?"

Lew had the American right where he wanted him. "If you really want to help your country, you can begin by taking a thorn out of my side."

*   *   *   *

Tavano escorted *Shepherd* out of the back seat of the limousine and back inside the American Embassy. The former president tugged on his red silk tie the moment he entered the compound. Despite several honest attempts, he could not bring the North Koreans back to the negotiating table.

"I need to speak with the President," he told his top aide as they walked down a corridor to the secure communications room, where he could talk privately to his son.

"*Shepherd's* clear," Tavano told her fellow agents in her wrist mic. "Requesting relief."

Another agent appeared seconds later and nodded to his superior.

"*Shepherd's* speaking with the President right now," she informed him. "The way those two talk, he could be in there all afternoon. I'm going to the cafeteria to grab a bite to eat." She looked down at her digital wrist watch. "I should be back here in twenty, if you need me, just holler."

Tavano left the junior agent standing guard outside the communications room along with two U.S. Marines. As she walked toward the dining room, her thoughts returned to her best friend. She had not heard from Heath since his bizarre phone call earlier that morning. It was now close to noon.

"Hey wait up," a familiar voice called from behind her.

Tavano turned and saw Steve Trevane jogging toward her.

"Care to join me for a bite?" she asked. "But it'll be a quickee, got to be back on the job in twenty minutes."

"I need to talk with you," he said.

"Shouldn't have used the word quickee right?"

"Please Nikki, this can't wait."

Tavano noticed the frantic tone in his voice and led him down a flight of stairs to her makeshift office. Once they were inside, he closed the door behind them.

"Your friend Heath is in trouble right here in Beijing."

Startled by his words, she leaned closer and whispered. "How the hell did you know that?"

"Nikki, I have a lot of contacts here in the city and there's talk about a black former secret service guy named Rosary involved in some kind of kidnapping plot."

"You're right," Tavano replied. "One of the Chinese delegation guys took his girlfriend and a baby."

"I dunno anything about that," Trevane replied. "I've heard that Rosary abducted the guy's daughter and is holding her for some kind of ransom."

"Are you kidding me?" Tavano said in disbelief. "He didn't say anything about that. Heath Rosary's not the kidnapper here."

"So you've spoken with him?"

Fuck, she thought. "What's your involvement in this?"

"I just know that he's not gonna make it out of this city alive." He leaned forward and touched her shoulders. "I still care about you, and I know that he's your best friend. I can help him if you let me."

*   *   *   *

Rosary loaded his 9mm and stuck it in the back of his pants under his leather coat.

"Wake Bao and tell her where we're going," he ordered.

Joe gently pulled a blanket off the sleeping girl and whispered in her ear.

"You're just like Sleeping Beauty," he told her.

She giggled and rubbed her eyes.

"Is it time to see Baba?" she asked.

"It's time. We know how much you like amusement parks. We'd like to show you one a short ride from here."

As Joe was busy getting the daughter ready for the trip, Rosary checked his watch and then picked up the satellite phone and dialed Grace's number.

"How is my daughter?" Lew asked immediately after answering the phone.

"You have my word that she's fine," Rosary replied "How are Grace and the baby?"

"You have my word they are fine," Lew answered.

"Your word don't mean shit to me," Rosary answered coldly. "But I believe you. You wouldn't be stupid enough to hurt them knowing that I will put a bullet in your daughter's brain."

"What do you want me to do?"

"An hour from now, I want you to leave your hotel, get in a car and head north toward the Great Wall. I'll call you with further instructions once you're on the road."

*   *   *   *

Tavano was back at her post when the former president emerged from the communications room. His tie was off now and his white dress shirt was unbuttoned at the collar. He looked over to the special agent and smiled. "It's an odd feeling to get scolded by your own son."

"Would you like to go to your quarters sir?"

"The President feels I was a little too hard on the North Koreans," *Shepherd* told her. "What do you think?"

"I'm not qualified to answer that question sir. My expertise is security, not diplomacy."

"That was a very diplomatic answer, Agent Tavano."

The former president turned and started walking down the hall. Tavano was hoping their awkward conversation had come to an end, but *Shepherd* wouldn't let it go.

"As I sat there across from him at the negotiation table, I felt like Neville Chamberlain coming face to face with Hitler for the first time. Only in this case, I knew the man I was dealing with could not be trusted. I did not want to be another Chamberlain."

"I'm sure you did fine sir."

Shepherd shrugged. "The Gospel according to James says resist the Devil and he will flee from you. I think this old preacher has to remind his son of that."

The former president was referring to the North Korean dictator, but Tavano couldn't help thinking of Ju-Long Lew. *I hope Smokey's okay. I hope Steve can help him.*

*   *   *   *

Heath and Joe led Lew's daughter down five flights of stairs to an underground parking garage. The walk was time consuming because of Bao's leg, but they couldn't chance being seen in the elevator or the lobby. They reached the Volvo and Grace's cousin unlocked the door and helped the daughter into the back seat.

The men climbed into the front and Joe started the engine.

"So what's the plan?"

"The ball's in his court," Rosary replied. "If he hands over Grace and the baby, we'll give him Bao. Then we'll hand over the computer disks to Interpol and they can arrest his ass."

"Heath, he murdered my brother," Joe said shaking his head. "Do you expect me to just let him go?"

Rosary reached over and grabbed his arm. "That's exactly what I expect you to do. I know you're hurting. I lost someone close to me in this thing too. But getting Grace and the baby safely out of there *is* and has to be our only objective."

Joe nodded his head. "You're right. But if Interpol doesn't go after this guy, I will."

Rosary placed his hand over his heart. "And I'll be there with you every step of the way, I promise."

As the Volvo pulled out of the parking space, a figure sprung from the darkness and placed his hands on the hood. Heath had his weapon drawn as the headlights flashed across the man's face.

"Heath stop! It's me, Steve Trevane."

Rosary jumped out of the passenger seat with the Glock in his hand.

"Trevane? What the fuck are you doing here?" he asked angrily. "I almost blew your head off!"

"I'm here with the summit. Nikki told me what happened. I'm here to help."

Dammit Nikki! "I don't need any help, Steve. Now back away from the car."

"Look, I know what's going on," Trevane told him. "Lew will have a whole army out there waiting for you. They'll kill you all."

"So if that's the case, how can you help us?"

Trevane pressed his hands against his chest. "I'm here to run interference. They won't shoot a member of the American delegation. Even Lew isn't important enough to spark that kind of international incident without there being major consequences."

"Who else at the embassy knows about this?"

"Right now, just Nikki and me."

Rosary took a few seconds to weigh his options. It was true; he was just an American tourist. They could pop him and make him disappear like all Lew's other victims. But they'd think twice about murdering a diplomat. Governments tended to investigate those cases much more seriously. "Alright," Rosary told him. "Get in."

"Where are we going?"

"You'll see."

CHAPTER 41

▼

An eerie silence hung over the theme park as they stepped out of the car.

"What is this place?" Bao asked. "It looks like Disneyland, but I know it's not."

"This park is not finished yet," Joe replied. "But we can use our imagination to make it come alive." He took the daughter by the hand as they all walked toward Sleeping Beauty's castle.

"How the hell did you find out about this place?" Trevane asked.

"I first saw it on the drive out to the Great Wall," Rosary replied. "I figured it would be a perfect place for the exchange. The park is empty and the castle here provides us a good view of the highway."

"Does he know he's meeting you here?"

"Not yet."

They entered Sleeping Beauty's castle and began climbing the steep tower. The men waited patiently as Bao navigated the winding stone staircase. Joe did a great job keeping her at ease. "We'll play a game," he told her. "You'll be the captured princess and your father will be the shining prince who comes to save you."

"That sounds like fun," she replied with a giggle.

As they continued to climb, Joe stopped in front of an open lancet window and looked out toward the horizon. "Heath, we'd better hurry up. The sky is getting dark and that means a sandstorm will come whipping over those mountains very soon."

Rosary peered out at the sky, which was now turning the color of a blood orange. He pulled out the satellite phone and hit *redial.*

"Are you on the road?" he asked Lew.

"Yes, we've just left per your instructions."

"What are you driving?"

"We're riding in a black Mercedes limousine."

"Are Grace and the baby with you?"

"Of course they are."

"Put her on the phone," Rosary demanded.

Ju-Long Lew oblidged.

"Hi honey," Grace said weakly.

"Hi Baby doll. Are you two doing okay?"

"Yes," she answered. "But I just want this whole thing to be over."

"It will be over," Rosary promised. "It'll be over very soon."

Lew snatched the phone from Grace's hand.

"Now let me speak to my daughter," he begged.

Rosary handed the phone to Bao.

"Are you alright, my flower?"

She nodded. "Shi de, Baba" *Yes, daddy.* "We're playing a game."

Lew gripped the phone tighter. "Where are you?" he whispered.

Rosary took the phone before she could answer.

"Keep driving toward the Great Wall. I'll call you again in twenty minutes with further instructions."

They remained in the tower as Rosary scanned the highway with a pair of high powered binoculars. As time wore on, it was becoming more difficult to see. The sandstorm had reached the nearby mountain peak and mid-afternoon was quickly turning to dusk. Fortunately, there was not much traffic on this stretch of highway. A vehicle passed by about every three minutes or so, and so far there were no limousines.

Trevane walked over to Rosary and tapped his shoulder.

"I know it's bad timing, but I gotta take a piss."

"They could be here any minute, Steve."

"I know, I know. I'd go right here, but I don't wanna offend the girl."

Rosary looked over at Bao who appeared to be playing some kind of word game with Joe.

"You're right," Rosary said. "It is bad fucking timing, but if you gotta go, you gotta go."

"I'll make it quick," Trevane promised as he ran down the circular staircase.

Why did I bother to bring this guy? Rosary thought to himself.

Grace's cousin spoke up. "So, what's next?"

Heath pondered the question while scratching the whiskers on his chin. "Well, we'll let them continue past the park, so that we can be sure they're not being followed. I'll call him when he gets down the road a piece and tell him to double back."

Trevane stepped out of the tower and immediately placed his hand over his nose and mouth to keep the blowing sand away. He ducked into an abandoned building and dialed Lew's number on his cell phone.

"It's me."

"I was beginning to wonder where you were," Lew replied with a grin. "So where are you?"

"I'm with Rosary," Trevane replied. "Don't worry, your daughter's fine. They're waiting for you at an abandoned amusement park about five kilometers south of Badaling. There is a turn off before you get here with a sign pointing to some grocer's market. That's abandoned too. Bring your car around to the back of the park."

"Where is Rosary?"

"He's watching for you from the tower at Sleeping Beauty's castle. But visibility is shit right now and I don't think he'll spot you if you turn off. I'll do my best to get him out of the tower. We'll wait for you in the ticket office," Trevane advised as he took in his surroundings. "It's right under the tower and has a double glass door and two large windows. I gotta go."

"Mister Trevane, it may not seem like it now but you are doing a great service to your country."

"Fuck you," Trevane replied as he ran back to the tower.

If there were a mirror available, Trevane would be repulsed by his own reflection. He had forged a Devil's deal knowing in his heart that what he'd done was wrong. But then he thought about those young marines who would be cut down while trying to take some nameless hill in North Korea and realized he had no choice. For him, it was an act of betrayal for the better good.

After Lew finished talking to the American, he leaned back and smiled at Grace.

"You've just put your daughter in grave danger," she told him.

The dragon laughed. "It takes a very special man to kill a woman. I do not think he is capable of doing such a thing, and I know you don't think so either."

Grace gazed out the window at the dark sky and did not respond.

"However, I am a very special man," he hissed. "After I get my daughter out of harm's way, I will show you what I mean."

Grace turned her attention back to Lew. "What's your daughter going to think when she finds out what kind of monster you are?"

"Watch your tongue woman," he shouted back.

I've clearly struck a nerve, she thought. "Did it make you feel like a man killing my best friend? Did Jessi give you that hideous scar on your head?

"I told you to shut your mouth."

"I'm not afraid of you," she baited him. "You're a coward who beats up on defenseless women, but I know you won't hurt me, otherwise you'll never get your daughter back."

"You're right," he smiled. "I cannot hurt you. Stop the car!"

The chauffeur pulled the limousine over to the side of the highway.

"What are you doing?" Grace asked nervously.

"Don't be afraid," he smiled again. "I won't hurt you."

He then reached forward and pulled the baby from her arms. Grace screamed as Lew opened the car door and stepped out into the sand storm.

"Stop, please stop!" Grace shouted.

"What if I left this baby in the middle of the road?" he asked as he started walking away from the vehicle. "How long do you think she'd survive?"

Grace got out of the limo, fell to her knees and began to cry. "Please, I'm sorry. I'll do whatever you say, just don't hurt the baby."

Lew let out a loud laugh as he returned to the limousine. Grace climbed back inside and took Sasha out of his arms. She held the baby close to her breast and tried to soothe her as the infant continued to scream.

"I would have been doing the brat a favor," Lew told her. "Now she'll grow up to be a bitch like the rest of you. My Bao is different. Because of her disability, she'll never grow up, not mentally anyway. At first I thought her affliction was a curse, but I look at it now as a blessing."

CHAPTER 42

▼

"That was quick," Rosary said pointing to his watch.

"I keep my promises," Trevane replied. *Now how am I going to get you out of this tower?*

"They should be coming this way any minute now," Rosary predicted, placing the binoculars back over his eyes. They waited another ten minutes and there was still no sign of the limousine.

"She says she's gotta pee now too," Joe said nodding toward the girl.

"What the fuck," Rosary sighed. "Tell her to hold it."

"I did," Joe replied. "But she's got something wrong with her bladder and she says she can't."

Trevane observed the conversation and tried to hide his smile.

"Alright, we're moving," Rosary ordered. "I can't see anything because of the sandstorm anyway."

The four of them descended the winding staircase and walked outside choking on the sand and dust as they scoured the area for new shelter. The visibility was poor and there was already an inch of fresh sand on the ground.

"Follow me in here," Trevane called out as he ran toward the ticket office.

Rosary would have liked more time to assess the situation, but sometimes the conditions dictated the actions, and this was such a time. Trevane led the way, followed by Joe and the girl. Rosary covered the rear. Once safely inside, Rosary rubbed the sand out of his eyes and hair. "Where the hell are they?"

"They probably pulled off to the side of the road and are waiting out the storm," Trevane surmised. "We can't even walk in this shit, imagine driving in it?"

"I hope you're right."

Joe escorted Bao past a row of cubicles as they searched for a bathroom, or at least a place she could go in privacy. Rosary reached for his satellite phone and felt the familiar touch of a gun sticking into the small of his back. "This is no time to play games," Rosary said with a nervous laugh. "What the fuck are you doing Steve?"

"I'm protecting my country," Trevane replied calmly. He reached under Rosary's jacket and pulled out his weapon. He now had two guns pointed at Heath's back.

"You're beginning to piss me off Steve," Rosary said with his arms raised high over his head. "What do you mean you're *protecting your country?*"

"Ju-Long Lew, the man you call a monster, is also the man who can keep us out of another war."

"He's a fucking killer," Rosary told him. "And now he's got my girlfriend and a baby. Are you gonna let him murder them too?"

"If it means sparing the lives of thousands of American soldiers, then I think that it's a price worth paying."

"You'll be an accomplice to murder, you know that don't you?"

Trevane laughed. "Look at our history, Heath. Our leaders have long been accomplices to murder. Do you think FDR didn't know about the gulags when we made a deal with Stalin? What about our cozy relationship with the Shah of Iran? Churchill said it best when he said, "nations do not have allies, they have interests". Right now, you could call Ju-Long Lew a very important interest of the United States."

"Thanks for the history lesson," Rosary replied dryly. "So what happens now?"

"I'll turn you over to Lew and this ugly episode will simply disappear."

"You know what, Steve?"

"What?"

"I'm glad Nikki dumped your ass," Rosary told him.

Trevane slammed the butt of a gun into the back of Heath's skull forcing him to the ground. Trevane's head then turned at the sound of Bao's foot dragging across the carpet. Joe followed close behind and saw Rosary lying wounded on the floor. As Grace's cousin reached for his gun, Trevane turned and fired off a wild shot that penetrated the wall behind Joe's head. At that moment, Rosary returned to his feet and drove his elbow into Trevane's stomach. The man keeled over, but still had both weapons in his hands. Heath grabbed Steve's left wrist and snapped it back, breaking the bone. Trevane screamed as one gun fell to the floor. He raised the other firearm and Rosary quickly pounced on him. Heath thrust a knee into Trevane's chest and then grabbed his right arm with both hands. They wrestled for the gun for several more seconds before Rosary could finally apply enough pressure to divert the direction of the weapon. A panicked Trevane was now on his back staring at the nozzle of his own gun. He yelled out as he tried once more to regain control of the Glock. Trevane turned the gun and squeezed the trigger sending a bullet into the ceiling. Rosary brought the weapon back toward the Trevane's face and now had his own finger on the trigger. Heath pressed down hard and the gun went off. Trevane's head snapped back as the bullet entered his right eye at close range. Bao heard the gunshot and cried out as the blood began to bubble up from the gaping wound on the dead man's face.

∗   ∗   ∗   ∗

Lew's chauffeur pulled the limousine into an empty parking lot in back of the theme park. He had increased the power of the vehicle's windshield wipers, but it was still impossible to see. "I've never seen it this bad. Should I tell the other men to abort?"

"You do that and I'll shoot you myself," Lew yelled. "My daughter's in the middle of that storm somewhere, don't you understand? Radio the men and tell them to approach the building with caution."

The driver relayed the message to a team of eight Beijing police officers riding in two white Land Rovers behind them. The Land Rovers entered the parking lot and parked side by side. The officers, all dressed in black, jumped out of the vehicles carrying Uzi sub-machine guns. Grace looked out the window and saw the dark figures moving about in the sandstorm.

"You're putting your own daughter right in the middle of a war," she shouted to Lew.

"My own private army," he informed her. "The firepower is a gift for your boyfriend. These officers are part of an elite anti-terrorist unit. I have full confidence they will rescue my daughter."

"And if they can't?"

Lew looked at Grace and then the baby. "Then my dear, we will all die."

Joe looked out a back window of the payroll building and counted three vehicles. "Shit, Lew's here and he's brought some company," he yelled to Rosary.

"I was afraid of that," Heath replied as he took both guns in his hands. "Quick, you remember the tunnels at Disneyland. This place was supposed to be a carbon copy. You think they tried to build the same thing here?"

Joe grabbed Bao, who was still sobbing, and pulled her down the hallway looking for a way out. He opened office door after office door, but there seemed to be no other exit in sight. "I found something," he shouted from down the corridor. Rosary ran toward the sound of his voice and found them both standing in front of a heavy metal door. Rosary stepped back and kicked it open. Suddenly they heard the sound of breaking glass in the main office area. "Let's move," Rosary commanded, as he lifted Bao over his shoulder and hurried down a set of stairs into the darkness. They were halfway down the staircase when all three of them were suddenly knocked off their feet by a thunderous explosion. Rosary landed face first on the cement floor of the basement. He lay there for several seconds watching the room spin around him. He heard a humming sound in both ears, which was soon replaced by a voice in his head. *Get up! Get up!* The voice said. He stumbled to his feet, dazed and bleeding from his forehead. He shook off the stun grenade, grabbed Joe and Bao and dragged them further into the basement. Rosary could barely see, but he could hear the sounds of Lew's men moving around the office above.

"Heath, I see something," Joe cried, shaking his own cobwebs away. There was a faint light coming from the far end of the basement. Rosary lifted the girl over his shoulder once again and took off in a full sprint. Grace's cousin followed close behind.

Rosary could hear the loud footsteps coming from behind them. Lew's men had entered the basement and were gaining ground. They finally reached the source of the light, a basement door that had been left ajar. Rosary pushed it open with his shoulder and hurried back out into the sandstorm.

Lew watched the drama unfold from the comfort of his limousine. He saw his daughter being taken out of the building, and at first he thought she'd been saved by his men. But as the figures drew closer, Lew realized that Rosary was still calling the shots. Lew stepped out of the vehicle into a blinding cloud of sand.

"Give me your fucking gun," he ordered his chauffeur, who handed Lew his loaded 357 Magnum. "Get the fuck out of the car," he then ordered Grace.

She moved slowly and he grabbed her by the hair. Grace jerked forward and nearly dropped Sasha, who was wailing uncontrollably once again. Lew spun Grace around and pressed the gun to her temple. Her body was quivering with fear.

"Drop my daughter or I'll blow her brains all over this park," Lew screamed over the howling wind.

Rosary took Bao off his shoulder, let her fall to the ground and continued his advance. "Keep her eyes closed," he shouted back to Joe. "Bao's not gonna want to see this."

Why isn't he stopping? Lew thought to himself as Rosary closed the distance. They were now only about 30 yards apart. "Stop right there or I'll shoot her," He screamed. The sand was pelting Rosary's face like a driving rain as he struggled to make out the images standing in front of the limousine. His heart pounded, but his mind was clear. He thought back to his weapons training at Hogan's Alley. All he had to do now was distinguish the bad guy from the innocent victim and pull the trigger. Only this was no drill, and the innocent victim was no cardboard cut out. It was the love of his life. *Just aim and shoot.*

Rosary's intense focus slowed down everything around him, including the sand. He could almost count every grain before it hit the ground. *Just aim and shoot.* Rosary was still running and now had his gun trained on the dragon and his elbows locked. Lew realized that his adversary wasn't going to back down, not now. The dragon tried squeezing the trigger, but Heath fired first—his bullet striking the billionaire just below the hairline in the center of his forehead. *Bullseye!* Lew fell back against the limousine and dropped to the ground in a heap. At that moment, several more shots rang out as Lew's paid mercenaries rose out of the basement of the payroll building.

"Get them in the limo," Rosary shouted to Joe. Heath fired another round through the driver's side window killing the chauffeur before he had a chance to react. Rosary pulled open the door and shoved the dead man's body across the wide seat. He then turned his head quickly toward the back of the vehicle where he saw Joe push Grace, Bao and the baby safely inside. Rosary put the limousine in gear and stepped on the gas.

The Beijing police officers sprayed the vehicle with bullets as it screeched out of the parking lot. The cops jumped into their Land Rovers and immediately gave chase. Rosary had to rely even more now on the skills he'd learned while in the Secret Service. He thought back to the hundreds of hours he'd spent at evasive driving school. They'd all been preparing him for this moment. He swerved the large vehicle in and out of lanes, never allowing his pursuers a perfect target. But the Beijing cops didn't have to be perfect, they just had to be lucky. One officer leaned out the passenger window of a Land Rover and fired off several more rounds in the approximate direction of the limousine. One bullet struck the back window, shattering it upon impact. Everyone screamed as the broken glass rained down over the back seat.

"Is anyone hit, is anyone hit?" Rosary shouted back.

"No, I think we're okay," Joe responded frantically.

Rosary turned his attention back to the road and noticed one of the Land Rovers picking up speed as it came up on the right side of the limousine.

"Everybody hold on," Rosary ordered as he jerked the steering wheel hard to the right. The vehicle collided with the front end of the Land Rover, sending it off the road and into a deep irrigation ditch where it rolled twice before bursting into flames. Heath quickly regained control of the limousine and pressed further down on the gas pedal. The limo was now moving at a top speed of 120 mph, but they still could not shake the second Land Rover. The mercenaries appeared less interested in shooting at the limousine now and more interested in just staying close. Rosary entered the city limits of Beijing and speed dialed Nikki Tavano.

"Where are you?"

"I'm coming in hot and I'm coming in fast," he shouted. "Get those fucking Marines ready."

Rosary did not slow down as they approached the center of the city. He weaved the long, awkward vehicle in and out of traffic, as Grace's cousin shouted directions from the back seat. The Land Rover was never more than two cars back the entire time. The traffic slowed down at a red light and Rosary stepped on the gas. Horns blared and drivers shouted angrily as the limousine continued roaring though the city streets. The commotion caught the attention of an on-duty Beijing police officer, who then began his own pursuit. Now Rosary had two cars chasing him. He passed the Jianguo Hotel and knew they were close.

"Take a right here, and then your first left," Joe hollared from the back seat.

Rosary did as he was told, jerking the steering wheel toward the direction of Embassy Row. Grace held onto Sasha as they both bounced around in the back-seat. Joe did the same for Bao Lew.

The police sirens were wailing louder now.

"C'mon Nikki, have that fucking gate open," Rosary yelled as he continued to speed down the narrow road. He looked up and spotted the American flag waving high atop the embassy. *Almost there.* They were now just a half block away when suddenly, the Land Rover overtook the police cruiser and rammed into the back of the limousine. The force of the collision caused Rosary to lose control of the steering wheel. It also prevented him from slowing down. The limo was still going about 70 mph when he regained control of the steering wheel and turned it hard to the right. The sharp turn lifted the vehicle up on two wheels as it came crashing through the embassy's front gate like a runaway train. The limo then collided with a large water fountain in the center of the compound. Thick chunks of marble were tossed into the air, only to come crashing down on the hood as it lurched forward. The pipe which fed the fountain also ruptured, triggering a small geyser that showered the vehicle with a torrent of rushing water. The limousine eventually rolled to a stop in front of the embassy.

Nikki Tavano ran out the front door of the building toward the battered vehicle. The ruptured water pipe, combined with the steam pouring from the engine, had created a surreal mist that floated around the limousine. Tavano opened the back door and heard the moans and cries coming from the people inside. "I've got a trauma situation, I need medics out here immediately," she shouted into her radio. Two marines helped Tavano pull Grace and the baby out, while others helped Joe and Bao. All were banged up, but conscious and alert.

"Get them inside quickly," Tavano ordered as she ran around to the front of the vehicle and looked inside. "We've got two men down here!"

Rescuers had to cut the driver's side door in half just to get a closer look at what they were dealing with. Rosary's head was resting on the steering wheel; his left leg appeared to be twisted up in the shaft underneath. His eyes were closed. He didn't appear to be breathing. "Oh, God … c'mon Smokey!" Tavano cried out. A medic reached through the broken window and checked for vital signs. "He's alive," the medic yelled as she grabbed an oxygen mask and placed it over Rosary's nose and mouth. It took rescuers another twenty minutes to get him out of the limo and onto a gurney. Rosary regained consciousness as he was being moved. The first person he saw was Grace.

"Is it over?," he asked her.

"Yes, it's over," she told him. "I love you!" She was sobbing now.

Heath reached his arm up slowly and wiped away a tear from her face. He smiled at her and closed his eyes once again.

CHAPTER 43

▼

Rosary awoke from his nap and looked down at his broken left leg. The cast had been signed by just about everyone in the American Embassy, and it was just one of the souvenirs he would be taking back from his first trip to China. The Boeing 737 was somewhere over Hawaii now. The sounds of goo-goos and ga-gas could be heard from the Secret Service area where the agents were playing with little Sasha. *What a great mother Grace will be for that baby,* he thought. Sasha's adoption papers were stamped in short order back at the embassy thanks to Pu-Yan, the new conquering hero of the Central Committee. The government now had control of Lew Petroluem with a generous annual stipend going to his widow, who had returned to care for her daughter Bao. Rosary hoped the girl would not be too traumatized by the ordeal. He looked over to Grace's cousin, Joe, who was also enjoying this private flight home. He was fast asleep under a warm blanket in a window seat. Rosary thought of Benny and then of Jessi. They would never find her body, as if there was even a body to be found. But they would keep their friend alive through little Sasha. The baby had a new mother now, but still did not have anyone to call *daddy*. Rosary was about to change all that.

He wrote a little note and passed it along to Nikki Tavano, who had been waiting on him hand and foot since the plane had taken off from Beijing. She apologized profusely for Trevane's treachery, but Rosary insisted there was nothing to apologize for. Tavano opened the note and read it curiously. She then lifted an eyebrow and smiled. "I've been waiting a long time for this."

She disappeared down the aisle of the plane toward the former president's quarters. After a few minutes, she returned with *Shepherd,* who had his family Bible tucked under his arm.

"Agent Tavano says that you'd like me to perform a little service."

Rosary nodded.

"Does the bride know?" *Shepherd* asked.

"Not yet, Mister President," Rosary replied.

Shepherd smiled. The old man enjoyed being part of this plot. "Do you even have a ring?"

Rosary pulled the diamond ring from the pocket of his sweat pants. "I've been carrying this thing around longer than I want to remember."

The former President turned to Agent Tavano. "What are you waiting for Nikki? Go get the lucky girl."

Tavano gave a salute and took off down the aisle. A few moments later, she came back with Grace, who was holding Sasha in her arms.

"It's good to see that you're awake, babe," she told him. "Nikki said that you wanted to see me about something."

Grace noticed that the former President was holding a Bible. She looked around and saw the other co-conspirators, who could not hide their smiles. Even her cousin Joe had woken up to witness the occasion.

"What's going on here?" she asked nervously.

Heath showed her the ring. "I wish that I could get down on one knee, but this will have to do. Will you marry me right here, right now?"

Grace looked down at Heath and both had tears in their eyes. She handed Sasha to Nikki and leaned down to embrace her man.

"Of course I will," she told him with a warm kiss on the lips.

The two hugged for what seemed like an eternity, and for at least a moment, all was right with the world.

Author's Note

For most writers, the road to every novel begins with the simple question; What if? The seeds of this tragic adventure were actually sewn during one of the most joyous moments of my life, when my wife and I traveled to China to adopt our second child, a precious jewel named Yi Lin Gau, *Beautiful Grasshopper*, whom we named Mia Florence. It was an experience I strongly recommend for anyone thinking about adopting a child. We were awed by the country's history, but even more so by its people. Our time in China was incredible and incredibly overwhelming. To Americans like us, it was like walking on the face of the moon. The smells, the sounds, and the people were unlike anything we had ever experienced before, but as a novelist, I thought to myself; *what a perfect place for a crime.*

In this book, I tried to show you the beauty of this far off land, while also exposing its often cruel underbelly. Places like the Forbidden City offer a fascinating peek inside this ancient culture, but one cannot turn a blind eye to the way this culture treats its women. Unfortunately, the passages included in the book about *infanticide* and *ghost brides* do not come from my imagination and are indeed true.

China is a nation with a split personality. One hand is curled into an iron fist aimed at punishing dissenters and keeping the communist hierarchy in power. The other hand is stuffed with capitalist cash that comes from being the fastest growing economy on the planet. It will be interesting to see which personality wins out in the end. If history is any indicator, capitalism and not communism will guide China's future.

As for that little tiff between the United States and North Korea, plans of the North's nuclear design are laid out accurately and as up to date as possible in this book. Much of the information about the United States Secret Service comes from former agent Joe Petro's wonderfully detailed book, *Standing Next to History* (St. Martin's Press). Some of his real life exploits were fictionalized in this book. The rest was born in my active imagination and any mistakes are my fault alone.

Casey Sherman, 2008

About the Author

Casey Sherman is the author of the Amazon Best-Seller *Black Irish* and the acclaimed true crime thriller *Search for the Strangler*. Sherman is a contributing writer for *Boston* Magazine & *Boston Common*, and is the former senior writer for WBZ-TV.

Sherman has appeared on dozens of network television programs including the *Today* Show, *Unsolved Mysteries*, The History Channel's *Biography* program, The CBS *Early Show* & The *View*. His work has also been profiled by the New York *Times*, *USA Today*, *Newsweek*, and *People* magazine.

Sherman lives with his wife and two children near Boston, Massachusetts.

Coming Soon

DIRECTOR'S CUT

A Heath Rosary Novel

CHAPTER ONE

Blondes make the best victims. They're like virgin snow that shows up the bloody footprints

—Alfred Hitchcock

Molly Stillwood should have taken the day off. Her head was pounding and her throat was sore. She chewed aggressively on a stick of *Wrigley's Spearmint gum*, but still could not stop the stale taste of cigarettes and tequila from bleeding through. Molly felt like throwing up, again. It had been a rough night from what she could remember of it. There was the male stripper at her sister's place, followed by the raucous limo ride into Boston, where she and her bride's maids hit every bar on Boylston Street and then carried the party over to Faneuil Hall. She remembered doing a shot of *Cuervo* and dancing with an Irish guy at the *Purple Shamrock,* but virtually nothing after that. She'd have to get the full story of her bachelorette party from her sister when she got home. Right now, her girl-friends were probably sipping *Bloody Mary's* while the bride-to-be was leading a group of 6th graders on a Friday morning field trip to the Stone Zoo. *Why didn't I take today off?* She already knew the answer. *Because my kids were really looking forward to this trip, that's why. I just hope the little shits, I mean sweethearts appreciate my suffering.*

She stood in the entrance of the Safari Grill sipping a bottle of *Poland Springs* and making sure that none of her young charges got out of line. But these were kids on a field trip; of course they were going to get out of line. At that very moment, her blue eyes darted to the center table of the small café where a chubby boy aimed his straw like a blow gun and spit a wad of paper at a young girl. "Daniel Callahan, that's enough!" Molly snapped as she marched over to the scene of the crime. The boy had already put the straw back in the carton of milk and was staring at the floor when she approached.

"You do that one more time young man, and I'll be having a nice talk with your mother when we get back to school," she warned with a wave of her delicate finger.

The boy nodded his head and continued staring at the floor. *That's showing him who's boss,* she told herself. As Molly turned and walked away, she could hear the students at the table erupt with laughter. She stopped and then kept walking. "Think about Bermuda, you're in Bermuda," she whispered to herself. She would lay on the pink sand at the Elbow Beach Club soon enough. The wedding was planned for Sunday, and then after that, she and Chuck would spend the next two weeks relaxing in the sun. Molly had been a slave to her pre-wedding diet and she couldn't wait to see the look on Chuck's face when he saw her in that gold bikini. She smiled and wondered if he had survived *his* bachelor party. There was talk about a trip to the Foxwoods casino in Connecticut, but she didn't want to know anything after that. Chuck's friends were even crazier than hers.

Molly waved a strand of her gold hair away from her face and looked down at her watch. "Finish up your lunches," she said rallying her troops. "The Birds of Prey exhibit is supposed to start in ten minutes." The news drew a loud cheer from the children, who had been looking forward to this part of the field trip most of all. The students filed out of the Safari Grill in orderly fashion and followed their science teacher along a winding path past the growls of two young jaguars prowling around their cage in the Treasures of the Sierra Madre exhibit. The wide foot path led to a small open space where the growling sounds were replaced by the high pitched squawks from the birds they had come to see. Molly guided the students to their seats and nodded to the bird handler to begin.

"Where are you kids from?" the female handler asked with a smile.

"Marshfield Middle School," the students replied in unison.

"My name is Janice Howard and I'm a bird handler here at the Stone Zoo."

The handler's introduction was drowned out by the loud noises coming from the large bird cage directly behind her. "As you can see, my friends are certainly happy to see you," Howard told the group. She looked back toward the cage and watched the birds as they flew head on into the iron bars of their individual cages. *That's funny, I've never seen them act like that. Looks like this show will have to be cut short.* Janice Howard was a ball of nerves and the odd behavior coming from the birds was making it difficult for her to keep her composure, for today she was on her own.

The cheery brunette had been working at the zoo for three months under the tutelage of the principle bird handler. She had watched him perform these shows three times a day and had committed every line to memory. Working for a zoo like this one, the recent college graduate not only had to be an expert bird handler, she also had to be an expert performer. *Now, only if I can get my fellow performers to cooperate,* she told herself. Between the incessant flapping of wings, she noticed that the least aggressive of the group was a Peregrine Falcon that sat silently on its perch paying no attention to the loud banging going on around it. Howard opened its cage and gently coaxed the falcon onto her gloved hand. "There now baby, be a good boy," she cooed as she petted the bird's black feathered cap. The handler closed the cage door and walked the falcon into the center of the tiny outdoor amphitheater and cleared her throat. *Showtime.*

"Children, I'd like you to meet my friend here," Howard announced. "This is a Peregrine Falcon that we here at the Stone Zoo call Big Papi."

The students pumped their fists and let out a loud cheer for their favorite Red Sox player's feathered namesake. "Yankees suck! Yankees suck!" Daniel Callahan yelled, mimicking the notorious chant that usually echoed through Fenway Park. Molly Stillwood swallowed another Tylenol and walked over and grabbed the boy by the arm. "Let's have a talk, Daniel," she ordered as she led the boy back out to the footpath. The boy's classmates giggled briefly and then focused their attention back to Big Papi.

"Peregrine Falcons like Big Papi here are found throughout North America and as far away as Australia," Howard informed the group. "Can anyone guess where we found Big Papi?"

The young girl who had been on the receiving end of Daniel Callahan's spit-ball back at the Safari Grill raised her hand. "California?" Clarissa Petro asked.

"That's a good answer, but we actually found him a little closer than that," Howard replied. "This guy comes from the Berkshires in western Massachusetts."

Clarissa kept her hand raised. "How big is he?" she asked.

"That's a great question," the handler replied. "What is your name?"

"Clarissa Petro," the girl answered smiling.

Howard laughed. "Well, Clarissa Petro, Big Papi is about three pounds and has a 40 inch wingspan," she answered stretching the falcon's wings. "Now we call this bird Big Papi, but he really looks like Charlie Chaplin. If you look closer, you'll see that he has a black cap and a black mustache. That's means he's an adult, and like all of the birds you'll meet today, Peregrine Falcons are birds of prey. These guys like to eat small birds, rodents and even snakes."

This drew a collective yuck from the audience. "It may not sound appetizing to you," Howard explained. "But a field mouse or a gopher is like a happy meal for birds like Big Papi here."

Howard placed the falcon onto its perch and pointed to the bright girl with the red ponytail and face full of freckles. "Well, Clarissa, since you've asked the smart questions, how would you like to learn how to tie a falconer's knot?"

The girl clapped her hands and walked slowly toward the center of the circle. Clarissa was overjoyed to be chosen, but as she got closer to the fearsome looking bird, she began to have second thoughts.

"Don't be scared, honey," Howard told her. "Big Papi here is a gentle old bird. He won't hurt you." The handler took the girl's hand and ran it slowly down the falcon's feathered spine. Big Papi responded to the girl's touch with a soft purring sound. Howard smiled. "See, Clarissa, he likes you."

The handler turned the girl toward her classmates and pulled a nylon cord from the left pocket of her tan shorts. "Now a falconer's knot is a one handed maneuver used for tying a bird to its perch. To tie a falconer's knot, any length of rope could be used. Stiff leashes are better than flexible ones." *So far so good,* Howard told herself. *At least they're still paying attention.* "First, run the length of the leash through the anchoring point so that the bird's end is under the anchoring point. Then, run it through the ring of the bird's perch." Howard demonstrated the technique while she talked. She quickly undid the rope and handed it to the girl. "Okay Clarissa, you try."

He's testing you, Molly thought as she watched Daniel Callahan blow a huge pink bubble with his chewing gum. *Maybe it's God's way of getting back at me for last night.* "Daniel, I want you to apologize for your behavior today," she said sternly. The boy ignored her and continued to play with his gum. Molly placed both hands on his shoulders and squeezed much harder than she should have. Daniel winced in pain and the teacher let go of his arms and stepped away. *Keep it together girl.* She ran her fingers through her long blond hair and counted to five before she spoke again. "C'mon Daniel," she coaxed in a chummy tone. "You don't wanna miss all the fun do you?" The chubby student shook his head no. *See that wasn't so hard.* Molly smiled and rubbed the fuzz on top of Daniel's crew cut. "Good, let's put this behind us and get back to the birds," she said.

The two began walking back when they heard a heart stopping scream. Molly took her arm off the boy's shoulder and ran in a full sprint toward the amphitheater. The lone scream was now amplified by the cries of all Molly's students, who watched in horror as the Peregrine Falcon pecked the top of Clarissa Pedro's blood soaked head. As the child was being attacked, the bird's handler tried to shoo it away without success. Molly leapt from the crowd and knocked Clarissa to the ground. "Run, honey, run," Molly told the terrified 6th grader. She then looked to Janice Howard, who was screaming something into her walkie-talkie. As the little girl scampered away, the bird of prey set its sights on the teacher. Big Papi dove at Molly with its fierce eyes and razor sharp beak. The falcon dug into her blond hair and Molly collapsed in the dirt. Big Papi's handler was paralyzed by fear and stood shaking as the bird dive bombed the teacher again and again. At that moment, a man slipped into the back entrance of the bird cage. He wore tan shorts and a light blue polo shirt with the zoo's insignia stitched on the front. Loud static was coming from the walkie-talkie that he had fastened to a clip on his hip. The man had jammed Janice Howard's frequency and no one could hear her cries for help. *That should give me just enough time,* he thought. The birds were in a complete frenzy now. He opened their small cages and then lifted a steel lever opening the larger cage setting them free.

The birds took flight like a squadron of fighter planes taking off from the deck of an air craft carrier. Two Red-Tailed Hawks led the assault followed by a Great Horned Owl and the zoo's majestic American Bald Eagle. The birds buzzed past the screaming children as they ran down the foot path. A Red-Tailed hawk gripped the back of Daniel Callahan's shirt and lifted the chubby boy nearly an inch off the ground before it let go dropping him into a thorny bush. The hawk then turned back to join Big Papi's attack on the teacher. Molly lay on the ground with her face in the gravel and she could feel the blood from a gash on the back of her head trickling down behind her right ear. Her white blouse was covered by dirt and blood and her blue skirt was now torn up the side. Molly kept her eyes closed and screamed for help. As the falcon continued to scratch and nip at the back of her skull, she felt another sharp pain on the back of her legs. Instinctively, she rolled over onto her back pushing a Red-Tailed Hawk under her bare legs. The bird flapped its wings and kicked up a cloud of dust as it fought to free itself. The hawk tore into Molly's buttocks and clawed her thighs. The teacher flailed her arms and kicked her legs as if she was making snow angels in the soil. Suddenly, she felt tiny daggers tearing through her blouse and her bra strap. The Great Horned Owl snapped at her breasts and Molly's eyes fluttered as she slipped in and out of consciousness. Her cries were growing softer now. She opened her glazed blue eyes and looked up toward the sun. A large shadow hovered above her blocking out the bright orange light. She recognized the white feathered cap and brown feathered wings immediately. The last seconds of Molly Stillwood's life were spent watching the bald eagle swoop down with its talons extended toward her bruised and blood stained face.

978-0-595-50384-
0-595-50384-5

CPSIA information can be obtained at www.ICGtesting.com
Printed in the USA
BVOW08s0616050316

439185BV00002B/111/P